Voices Behind Closed Doors
Baghdad

باهر زبلوق

Bob Zablok

THE WORD QUEEN
PUBLISHING

The Word Queen Publishing
Published 2012 by The Word Queen

www.TheWordQueen.com

ISBN 978 84 615 8994 4

Typeset in Garamond.

Voices Behind Closed Doors – Baghdad
is dedicated to Paula Tierney and my son, Lee

ACKNOWLEDGEMENTS

Thank you to the following people for helping me to get this book out there: Professor Phil Duke, Murray Morrison, Donna, Heather and Tina, to all my family, to Keidi Keating, The Word Queen, for being one hell of an editor and publisher, and my best friends Salim and Moussa for putting up with me for 34 years.

INTRODUCTION

IN the not so distant past, whenever the name Baghdad was mentioned, people would take on a dreamy look and be mentally transported from the time of Ali Baba and the forty thieves to tales of the Arabian Nights; scenes of flying carpets, and the legends of Sinbad in this magnificent city.

The city of Baghdad was founded on the west bank of the Tigris on July thirtieth, 762 at the request of the Caliph Al-Mansur. However the city was mentioned in pre-Islamic texts as it dates back to 1800BC and ancient Babylon. It was probably built on the site of this earlier settlement.

The origin of the word Baghdad is under dispute, but is thought to be of Persian origin, meaning 'The gift of God.'

Within a generation of its founding, Baghdad became a hub of learning and commerce. The House of Wisdom (Bayt al-Hikmah) was an establishment dedicated to the translation of Greek, Middle Persian and Syriac works.

Most of the famous Muslim and Christian scholars from the ninth to thirteenth centuries had their educational roots in Baghdad. Here, teachers and students worked together to learn the Greek manuscripts; preserving them for all time.

However, the Abbasid dynasty slowly began to die, and five hundred years of unchallenged progress was at an end. The city was brought to its knees by the Mongols and the rivers Tigris and Euphrates reportedly ran red with the blood of thousands of scholars and black from the ink of millions of books, documents, maps and archives. Once it was the richest city in the world and the second biggest after Constantinople, but it was completely destroyed.

Since then it has been invaded many times. It has seen many wars and suffered perhaps more than many other cities in the world. Yet it still prompts people to daydream and sends shivers down the spine of many writers and poets.

Baghdad 1964. This was a city crippled by two bloody coups in the previous year, within months of each other. In February 1963, after General Qassim, 'The Prime Minister', was brutally killed, the Baath party came to power supported by Arab nationalists who, six months down the line and under the leadership of president Abdul Salam Aruff, turned against the Baath Party in an horrific coup where 12,000 people lost their lives, or simply vanished. The three major parties in Iraq fought a dirty war to gain control of the country. Their massive effort caused a total disintegration and destruction of society, the economy and civil rights of individuals.

The parties thoughts were focused on how to make labourers and farmers an educated force in order that they would build for a brighter and more civilised future. They desperately needed to take control and make the people work for their future as humans, not as animals driven by canes or machine guns. After all those parties were from the people to the people and an election was not required. Guns spoke louder than all the voices in Iraq. Religions were used as swords to justify their actions leaving the people wondering who to believe.

Many people supported it, cheered it and followed it. It was a game of survival. They didn't have to believe in it, trust it or even admire it; a nod of the head meant 'yes' and that was all there was to it.

Many scholars, doctors, engineers and scientists escaped the country in fear of their lives, leaving a huge gap for many others to move to the capital, Baghdad. They came from villages and farms, towns and cities. Some came to support the government, others to take advantage of the new regime, either by joining the party, or just by nodding their heads in agreement. Those were the ideal candidates for a Nobel Prize for Hypocrisy if one had been invented.

There were plans for an agricultural and industrial revolution, but only on pieces of scrap paper gathering dust on their long journey around the offices of the government's beautiful buildings, waiting to be signed by illiterate officials who couldn't read or write in Arabic or any other language; their only duty being decorative.

Despite the hard life there was always time for love, romance, and a smile with tearful eyes.

CHAPTER ONE

AHMAD Al-Kalil walked vigorously into the classroom. The muscles in his face tightened, revealing his pent-up anger. He paced the room quietly, stopping every now and then to examine the horified, puzzled faces. The pupils shivered in their seats, waiting and anticipating.

"Morning class..."

"Good morning Sir." They were hesitant in their reply.

"Somehow... I don't think it'll be that good!" He sneered at the terrified faces and turned round to his table. With a theatrical movement, he took out a bundle of papers from his briefcase and threw the lot in the air. A few fell back on the table, while the rest scattered on the floor. A pupil tried to move to collect them, but a glance from his teacher was enough to nail him to his seat.

"These are your appalling test papers" he said. "Where on earth did you learn this rubbish?" he continued. "You aren't worthy of being in this school. This is the worst class I have ever taught. Not one of you passed; not one of you could write in Arabic." Ahmad threw his arms in the air in disbelief. "We were born to speak the language of the gods, but you lot...cannot even...how did you get into this school? How did you pass your exams?"

Ahmad paced the room again. "I'll give you one more chance and if you fail I will send you back to the schools you came from." He examined the effect of his words on their faces. "Understood?"

They managed a few nods.

"I didn't hear you," he insisted.

"Yes sir." The pupils replied reluctantly.

"Well, after this week, I will know whether I'm wasting my time here or not. I want you to write about a subject of your choice, and I want it next week."

"Yes sir..."

He turned to the blackboard. A wide smile crossed his face as he wrote his instructions. He then turned and faced them again. They tried to hide from him.

"Well? What are you waiting for?"

With a clatter they took their notebooks out and pretended to be occupied. "Quiet," He ordered as he took a book out of his briefcase, sat down and began to read.

Ahmad was a tall, slim-built man with black wavy hair. His eyes seemed to penetrate the very soul. He didn't lack confidence as he'd had two books published, as well as many articles and poems; at the age of twenty-four, that was some achievement. Ten minutes later he lifted his head. His eyes caught those of one pupil staring at him. It was the face of a simple and pathetic creature, but one with a distinct feature: a large nose. A smile filled Ahmad's face as he thought of that nose.

"You...Come here..." he ordered.

Tired young legs carried the boy to the massive table, "Yes sir...!"

"What's your name?"

"Rami, Sir…" He answered confidently, straightening his back and pushing his chest out.

"How old are you, Rami?"

"Twelve, Sir… I know I look much older," he said.

The teacher smiled. "And what's so amusing about my face?"

"I don't know…I was thinking Sir!"

"What were you thinking about?" Ahmad was finding the conversation interesting.

"Something to write about… nothing came to my mind at first. Then, I thought you might make a good subject to write about. I mean…what I think you're really like."

"Am I such an interesting subject?"

"No…not really Sir, but if you really want to know…I don't think you are as hard as you pretend to be. I hope I won't get into trouble over this?"

"No…no you won't. Please continue."

Taking a deep breath as he examined his teacher's face to see if he was being sincere, Rami looked behind him to check that no other pupil was listening. Then he decided to speak out.

"The way I see it, you…you are very clever, and my father said so too. He has read both your books. He said that the first was much better than the second, he honestly said that…not me." He put all the blame – if there was any – on his father, and waited for a reaction. When there was none, he continued, "You are a deep thinker, a good teacher and a happy man. That's what I think. You don't need to work at all, you must've made lots of money from the books, and maybe you're doing this job for fun!"

'What a little brat this boy is!' Ahmad thought, but said aloud, "Please carry on. The opinion you have about me is fascinating."

"Thank you, Sir. But I don't think you are a good subject to write about after all. I'd better find another, don't you think?" Rami paused. "Have you got a subject in mind please Sir?"

Ahmad laughed aloud; he couldn't contain himself any longer. "Let me think…how about a journey to somewhere you've never been before?"

"Yes, good idea, Sir….thank you…good idea" he declared.

"You may go back to your seat now."

Halfway to his seat, he turned around and tiptoed back. "Sorry Sir, sorry to trouble you, but how old are you?"

"Twenty-four…! Why?"

"No reason, you only look a bit older like me." Rami shrugged his shoulders and walked to his seat.

'The little brat…!' Ahmad smiled to himself. 'That'll be some laugh in the teachers' room,' he thought.

- - - - - - - - -

Rami was born to a Catholic family. He grew up in wealthy surroundings, with a younger brother and three older sisters. They lived in one of the most elegant suburbs, where the majority of people were Christians. They lived in harmony, no matter what cult or sect they belonged to.

The young boy understood his society and its classes. People were classified according to their religion, origin and whether they came from villages, farms, or cities. Rami grew up in a society where money meant power, as long as the family honour was kept behind closed doors.

He had been educated in Catholic schools from the age of three. Once he completed his intermediate school, his father's wealth and place in the community helped in enrolling him at the American School (Baghdad College). This was a private school and without doubts the best in the country. It had been established by the American Jesuit priests in 1933.

That particular week, Rami closed his bedroom door to the world, writing his little story over and over again, correcting his mistakes, finding new and better words to add or replace. He liked his Arabic teacher and wanted to please him.

- - - - - - - - -

The week passed quickly. In class, Rami gently pressed the palms of his hands on the pieces of paper in front of him as if he was praying; instead he was hoping that he hadn't forgotten anything in his story. He had his eyes closed; he was thinking and wondering when Ahmad raised his voice,

"Rami...! Are you with us or what?"

There was no reply.

"Rami...!" Ahmad called again. Deciding not to wait any longer, he went to stand next to the boy. The pupils laughed but an angry look from Ahmad did the trick.

At long last Rami opened his eyes with a winning smile on his face, "Sorry Sir. Did I keep you waiting long?"

"What do you think you're up to?" Ahmad sneered as he grabbed the papers, and began reading them on his way back to his chair.

"Where did you copy this from?" he suddenly spat.

Rami froze in his seat. He couldn't believe his ears.

"Did you write this or not?" Ahmad demanded.

"I wrote it myself...I didn't copy the stupid thing from anybody or anywhere...I don't need to," Rami protested.

"In that case, would you like to read it for us? Let your classmates share this experience with you?"

Rami did not reply; he wasn't interested in what his teacher suggested.

"A writer is never a writer without audiences."

Rami gave in. There was softness and sincerity in Ahmad's tone. The teacher turned to the pupils and said, "This is our topic today, so be quiet and listen. Come to the front please, Rami."

The young writer examined every face in the classroom, and began reading, "On a wintry night in my small village, the wind was howling with a frightening sound, like thousands of whistles blowing at the same time...."

5

Ahmad was amazed by the lad's ability. He read beautifully, and delivered his story magnificently. He read with passion and true emotions. The pupils were pinned to their seats by the magic of their fellow pupil.

Rami moaned as if in pain. "I don't want to see that city, I don't want to…why me?" The tears almost streamed down his face. His body shook as he read, and the tone of his voice changed. It was hoarse, sad and yet quiet. "I waved goodbye until I lost sight of my family."

Rami stood motionless, with his head down.

"Please do sit down and thank you," Ahmad said quietly.

Rami's face lit up with a huge smile. The eyes of forty pupils followed him in disbelief as he walked back to his seat.

"Any comments please?"

"I think I will never ever hear anything better than that," a pupil remarked.

"And you won't," the teacher concluded.

- - - - - - - - -

Ahmad had a troubled night. He couldn't make up his mind whether to forget what he had seen and heard that morning in the classroom, or to encourage Rami in bringing that hidden talent out into the open.

He saw the intense imagination, the brave voice and the unquestionable self control. It would be selfish of him not to help. Then again, it was Rami's choice to accept or refuse encouragement.

Ahmad saw the quality of a writer to be, but what good was that in a society ruled by old ideas, meaningless and out of date customs and traditions? Any new ideas, thoughts, or changes were labelled as foreign and unacceptable in this country where its people were afraid to lift their heads high in case they lost their right to survive; and where the majority were sheep led by very few wolves.

Rami was innocent and full of life. What could he promise him? When he knew that the main meal of the day was politics a writer was never free to write his thoughts and enjoy his creation. Maybe a bright future or a garden filled with roses? Money and fame? In fact, it was hardship and pain. With those thoughts, he fell asleep.

CHAPTER TWO

THE challenge began. Ahmad took a few of his favourite books to school for Rami to read. He forgot about himself and his own problems, devoting most of his spare time to Rami, helping him to discover himself, directing him on the right track by making him understand his surroundings and accepting it as part of his making.

Baghdad had one of the most complex societies in the Middle East. The different cultures, traditions and religious sects played a great part in forming it. Even the Arabic dialect differed from one district of Baghdad to the other.

Although it was early days, Rami seemed overwhelmed by the attention he received from his teacher, making him believe increasingly in himself and his ability to create. Ahmad treasured those moments, living the dreams of a twelve year old. He wanted to make a man out of him quickly as if he was in a race against time. Rami responded to his teaching and long lectures. Ahmad was trying to open the boy's eyes to the world outside, teaching him to accept and appreciate the gift that had been given to him from birth, and to start building bridges for the future.

"A man is born, lives and dies in one day, but very few live forever, those who create magic that no one has seen, touched or thought about before." Ahmad said one day as they walked through the fields at school during a lunch break.

"I don't understand...!"

"In this life you are on a mission, and you have to find your path and achieve; your name must stay in minds of the people for generations. That is how you live more than one life."

The two had developed a routine, seeing each other at lunchtime and after school while waiting for the bus to take them home. They discussed and argued many issues, solving many daily and global problems. This created an unbreakable bond between them.

The age difference had no effect on their unique friendship as both tried to meet half way. Rami tried to understand the books he was given, producing his own ideas and theories on life in general. Ahmad willingly gave him the chance to talk while he listened with a smile of admiration on his face. He knew that Rami was trying very hard.

Ahmad thrived during their deep discussions; it was a new experience for him as an accomplished writer, and as a teacher. He wanted someone he could trust; in fact he wanted someone to whom he could present his life's conclusions, and who would appreciate his life experience.

Rami's ability to reason and debate developed. He was hungry for knowledge, hungry to please his friend, hungry to be someone everyone looked up to.

"Many people think they are original and unique, but never admit this to anyone, thinking they might be condemned for being conceited. Originality is in the person himself, and there are many ways of admitting it. Tell people in one way or another, and find your own way. You must tell them, for they can't see at times," Ahmad lectured Rami as they walked together after school. He then looked up to the sky and mumbled to himself. Rami could not make up any of the words; nevertheless he had to question him.

"God…What the hell for…?"

Ahmad laughed, thinking how Rami managed to mention God and hell in five words. "Let's head back; your bus will be here soon."

They walked quietly together towards the front of the school. Suddenly, Rami burst out laughing. He tried to explain to Ahmad but couldn't, and the tears streamed down his face. Ahmad joined in the laughter too.

"Are you going to tell me?"

"Oh God, if you could only see yourself, you are so funny, Ahmad…the way you talk, scratch your right ear, rub your nose…stare at the sky…"

"What's so funny about that?"

"You were laughing too…"

"I was laughing at you," Ahmad explained.

"The life of a writer…! I don't think I'll ever be one, or be like one. You came from a different soil – you were made differently. You are so serious in everything you say and do, and you know how to dramatise life. Sometimes you make things look so stupid, or so great. I could never do that, I just tell it as I see it."

Ahmad had no reply, but the expression on his face was enough to make Rami laugh even more.

"Just get on the bus and give me peace."

"God help the woman who marries you, you'll kill her talking," Rami laughed louder as he climbed onto the bus.

Rami stuck half his body out of the window, "Any other advice, Sir?"

"Shut that window, you cheeky devil, and bring me some of your writings from last week...don't forget," Ahmad ordered.

"Yes Sir…no problem."

"And study hard..."

"Yes Sir."

Ahmad turned round and walked towards the main entrance. He threw his hands in the air in disbelief as he entered the building; he found it amusing how Rami acted at times. A feeling of uncertainty overwhelmed Rami for a few days, and there was a good reason for it. He felt as if he was being drawn away from his fellow pupils; he was missing out on their laughter and their simple games. But, after few hours with them, he dismissed those thoughts realising that his way of thinking had developed and there was no joy in being with them.

Ahmad had a charming personality, and Rami's parents found him delightful, caring, honest and sincere. He was well spoken and enjoyed a good hearty debate, sharing his views on many matters with Rami's father, who was also well-educated and spoke five languages.

Rami's father was born in Mosul in the north of Iraq. He was only four years of age when his own father had died in the desert on his way to Syria. For eight years Rami's grandmother had worked and made dresses to support her four children. Rami's father had left school at the age of twelve in search of work to support the family. Through determination and single mindedness he had managed to support his brother through university and helped to send his two sisters to school, until they were married.

Ahmad took Rami everywhere that he thought would be of benefit to the young lad. He told him that it was time for application, time to see and absorb the small world around him. Life existed at all levels of the society not just the high class surroundings where Rami's family lived.

Ahmad took Rami around the city of his birth, and about which he knew very little. He introduced him to the poor, showing him how five or six families lived under the same roof, how they survived on less than the pocket money Rami had. Rami learnt why the government ignored those poor people and refused to help them in any way.

It was far easier to rule a weak and broken society. In fact, they were labelled to be condemned for the rest of their generations, the rich individuals and the powerful government controlled the poor and the vulnerable, as they had no answer to the demands or orders, they had to accept what little was given to them, and what they had to give back in return. Rami cried, realising what little security they had.

It was a whole new world for Rami to observe from a far distant, and learn about prostitutes, pimps, drunks and druggies. He had heard of them, but had never seen them before. He was in pain, realising how hard they struggled, only to be abused by officials from the governments. He witnessed how they were driven to perform unbelievable acts to justify the ugliness of their very existence. And to make matters worse, the government was the biggest pimp of all.

"They are as human as we are. Give them as much as you want, but make sure that you take more out of them" Ahmad explained, "Use them as they are made to be used, they will allow you to do what the hell you want…for a price, but keep a distance from them. Come…we'll go to the art gallery. I think you will enjoy it more than this."

Rami listened silently, absorbing ideas and rules. "Facts of life hey, Ahmad! Facts of life…!" He accepted the pressure he was being put under.

Ahmad took Rami to Souk Al-Shorga, the old bazaar which consisted of networks of small, narrow alleyways and streets, spread over a large area. They were filled with small shops, selling thousands of different commodities. It seemed that even in the hot weather, the ground somehow was always wet. Some people avoided the pot holes as if jumping over an obstacle course was part of the joy of shopping, while others simply didn't take any notice.

At one side was the beautiful sight of men creating ornaments, kitchenware, and souvenirs by magically hammering their brass or copper products to an amazing tune; they created a unique symphony played again and again every day to a perfection,.The sound was deafening to some, but to the members of the orchestra it was every day tune, no conductor was needed. Somehow they managed to talk to each other through the noise, even to tell a joke or two every now and then, yet they took no notice of their punters until they saw the sight of money. The product was incredibly well made and travelled around the world.

"Rami, these products are what made Iraq popular, and the tourists buy them in thousands, as well as being exported to different corners of the world. This is only a simple example of a story for you and me to write about."

In another little street there were many shops selling silver goods and jewellery, handmade by old men with long white beards as part of their religion. They never said much, they never looked up, avoiding all eye contact; they simply went on with their work.

"They are a hundred and fifty years old," Ahmad smiled. "They have no tongues to speak with, no good eyes to see how brilliant their work is, and no ambitions in life except to satisfy their creators." He smiled at Rami, leaving the boy wondering which part of the story was real. "Mothers take their naughty boys to these men to eat them for breakfast," he added.

"I believe you."

"There is a group of people called Al-Subah, and the word means that they are supposed to convert to any new religion that comes along. The story behind the white beard is amazing. I heard this from the goldsmiths in Baghdad; most of these people actually wear a fake beard, and it has to be white. This is because when they work with silver they file, grind and engrave it. If you have noticed, they work with their beards very close to the silver, which allows the shavings and dust to accumulate on their whiskers. Then, when it is closing time and out of public view, they remove the fake beard and dip it in a large bowl of water. The silver rests at the bottom of the bowl, to be collected and used again. What you have to remember is that the silver they collect has already been paid for by the customer who ordered the jewellery; it's like free silver to the jeweller. The shavings would be very visible on black hair, but not white. I have heard this explanation a number of times from people who worked in the industry."

Rami was amazed by the simplicity of these stories, and also to see young boys transporting goods on their three-wheeled carts from one end of the market to the other, screaming their way through and zigzagging to avoid injuring anyone.

"Is this life in the fast lane?"

"You could be right my boy."

But nothing could match the spice market. The aroma was tantalising, a mixture of hundreds of spices and herbs, some grown locally, others brought in from different parts of the country and also from far Eastern countries such as China and India. Somehow the importers managed to distribute them among the spice merchants without the government's red tape.

"Was it because those officials couldn't eat an un-spiced meal?" Rami wondered.

The high ground on the right side of the Al-Jamhoriya Street seemed like a small mountain in Rami's eyes. He was fascinated and wanted to see it for himself.

"How old are these houses?" he asked.

"Old – very old – I don't know to be exact," Ahmad replied. "Maybe when Baghdad was built…!"

The streets were narrow, wet and humid, and the walls of the houses were decaying, as if no one could be bothered to repair them. The sun was completely shut out and the smell of rotten eggs was everywhere, making it extremely hard to breathe. Some streets were lit by just one sixty-watt bulb, while others had old oil lamps. An employee from the council lit those lamps early afternoon and put them out late morning. It seemed bizarre not to have them burning all day and all night.

"You can lean out of those windows on the first floor and touch the window of the people opposite."

"I was just thinking that," said Rami. "This place gives me the creeps."

"It does me, too."

"Who lives here?"

"Ghosts…! With no noses so they could not smell this awful stink," Ahmad replied, laughing.

"Have you seen the people here?" Rami asked but didn't expect an answer."

They ran out of the area to escape the smell and breathe fresh air.

- - - - - - - - -

The eight and a half months of schooling seemed to end quickly. Rami was sad as he hadn't seen or heard from Ahmad for two weeks, in fact since the end of year examinations. It was confusing, as he hadn't planned his summer holiday at all. It was very important that Rami passed these exams, as it would enable him to progress to the following year. But when he went back to school for his results, Ahmad behaved differently when the two met. Although they were overjoyed to see each other, Rami felt that something was troubling his older friend.

"If you only know how proud I am, Rami, your results were amazing." Ahmad said, "To come first in your class was some achievement, but to be third out of the whole first year— well I'm lost for words."

"Thank you…I am amazed too."

"Shall we go out for a bite to eat? It's my treat," said Ahmad. "Not many of my friends are as clever as you."

They walked silently, heading towards Ahmad's car. Rami examined his friend's watery eyes and waited for an explanation.

"I am just happy for you," Ahmad maintained.

It took them ten minutes to reach the restaurant. It was on the north side of the city, overlooking the river Tigris. The building was a combination of old and modern architecture. They went down the twenty-five steps to the front door. A smart receptionist dressed in traditional Arab costume opened the door for them. She took them to their table.

Rami glanced quickly at the luxurious surroundings, and turned his attention to Ahmad as he began to explain. "I helped you to be a writer, and I don't know why I did! As there is no freedom in this country, there are always strings holding you down, even as a writer." Ahmad poured himself a glass of water, but didn't drink it.

"We can change that," said Rami. "You said once that nothing is impossible. Someone will change this government...everything will change...everything will be..." he broke off.

"No, they won't change. Every government learns from the previous one, it's the only way they can rule a country like ours. Their only interest is to fill their fat pockets, not improve standards."

Rami said nothing; he knew there was more to come. He decided to wait for Ahmad to speak again.

"Once a writer makes his big break, he and his pen will belong to the heaviest hand in the country. The government takes over everything, his pen, his paper, his life, and leaves him with nothing except for few ideas of his own, and a handful of 'musts' he has to insert in everything...do you call that freedom?"

Ahmad looked out of the window. A few fishing boats were sailing on the river, a scene he often admired, loved and treasured, but not that day, he only saw dullness.

"Try and stay away from it all, keep your pen to yourself. Your pen is your only weapon for as long as you live, don't let anyone dictate to you what you should write." Ahmad took out a long shaped small box and handed it to Rami. "Don't open it until you get home."

Lunch was served, but neither of them by then was hungry. "I am leaving the country soon...I can't tell you when or where because I don't know myself," said Ahmad. "I don't know what I will be doing. I just want something different to what I have here."

Rami was motionless. His eyes were focused on the plate of food. He tried hard not to show emotion, but he felt he was being cheated on and stabbed in the back by the only person he had ever trusted.

Ahmad was the one who had opened his eyes to the world, to life and set him free. He made him feel important, useful and alive. At that moment he felt he had been dropped into a violent sea and asked to swim ashore. There was no way out, no way back and no light in the distance. He was numb.

"Rami, say something..." Ahmad pleaded.

Silence.

"Say something, please."

Still silence.

"Why are you crying?" Ahmad persisted. "It's my life I am worried about...my future. Why should I explain to you? Look at me...you have everything; you have the security of a family. You are young...I have nothing."

Rami looked away through the window and into the distance, "The waves of the fast Tigris, the dreams of thousands of people washed away with this lonely river, the mystery beneath the depth of the torrents. The river is ethereal, never ending Ahmad, and I am lost somewhere in it. I love this mighty river, and I could never be away from it. It's water runs in our veins."

"Please say what's on your mind," Ahmad begged.

"I am going to miss you…but your life and safety come first. Promise you will write?" Rami asked.

Ahmad drove him home and two days later left the country.

CHAPTER THREE

RAMI suffered at first for the loss of his friend. He was lonely and needed someone to talk to and laugh with. Someone who would encourage him, inspire him and organise his life. He was lost in a sea of words and expressions that made no impression on his daily life, as if it was an impossible jigsaw puzzle to solve.

He wandered around the house one day, thinking of what to do. Finally, he was in his father's study examining the stacks of neatly arranged books on both sides of the room. He picked one up and sat down reading. That was the start of his father introducing him to new topics, buying him a variety of books and encouraging him to read and read. It was really to keep him away from the streets, and the corruption of mind and body. His father had never had much time to spend with his demanding son. He was a businessman, and all that he wanted to do when he returned home at night was rest and unwind from the day's pressure.

Rami's uncle, on the other hand, was a bachelor, as well as a partner in the family's business. But he appeared not to have as much work and responsibilities as Rami's father.

The uncle inspired confidence in the young man. For that, Rami rewarded him with poems and short stories to admire, applaud and debate the ideas behind them. In doing that Rami gained a valued opinion. His uncle had a simple outlook on life. He never complicated issues, but accepted them as part of progress and development.

Smoking was the most forbidden sin at his age. Nevertheless he found many excuses to venture out to the local shop, where many teenagers of different ages met in the back yard, sitting on empty wooden boxes and relaxing with cigarettes burning between their fingers. He would join in the laughter, butting in when the conversation escalated into a full-blooded argument. The experience was pleasurable, especially after reading an intense book.

He realised it wasn't hard for him to mix and talk with others. His only problem was that he couldn't tell a joke, but his comments, facial expressions and the theatrical way he gave his views made everyone uproarious and joyful. He was welcomed whenever he went to the shop.

Rami walked into the living room one Sunday evening. His parents had invited their new neighbours for a meal. It was customary to introduce the family to the new arrivals in the street. His uncle and grandmother were there too.

"Ah...at last...my son Rami...say hello to Dr. Samir and his wife May," his father ordered.

"Good to meet you, doctor."

"Call me Samir..."

"Call me Rami, please..." he giggled, turning round and shaking May's hand, looking deep into her eyes and smiling.

"Hello Rami..." Her voice was soft and gentle.

He had noticed her the day they moved to the street, and for some strange reason, she aroused his feelings and occupied his mind. It wasn't the first time he had looked at her in that manner, but it was the first time she had made his heart flutter uncontrollably. It was a new feeling he hadn't experienced before as a teenager.

"Do you take after your uncle, Rami? Learning all those languages, and hoping to travel the world one day?" He was surprised that she had taken an interest in him and was actually asking him a question. It was a simple question, but it took him a few seconds to think of an appropriate answer.

"I hope so, but I think he prefers to do things his own way; he's a very single minded person...I'm very proud of him." His uncle did the honours.

He was thankful that his uncle had an answer ready, as he couldn't think of one for himself. He was very pre-occupied by May and Samir. In fact, he was searching for clues to connect the two of them together. Samir was tall, slim, and handsome. He dressed immaculately and moved gracefully. May was tall and heavenly beautiful, with long, dark hair which rested elegantly over her shoulders. She possessed full lips, but most striking were her deep green eyes.

"What do you do in your spare time Rami?" she asked, and this time he was quick enough to answer her.

"I enjoy reading...I love reading...also..."

"He writes too..." his uncle added. "I'm so proud of him."

"What do you write about?" she asked casually, noticing that Rami's smile had disappeared.

"Short stories, poems, articles...anything that comes to his mind. He's very clever indeed," his uncle answered again.

"Writings...! It won't put a piece of bread on the table." His father butted in.

"I write too...whenever Samir isn't looking. I write for comfort." May hoped to save the embarrassing situation.

"I didn't know that...remarkable!" Samir added proudly.

Rami was filled with resentment towards both his father and uncle. They had taken his moment of glory away from him. He sat quietly staring at all the faces..

"Rami...Rami...!"

"Sorry May...I was miles away!" He managed a polite smile.

"Tell me about your writings." She wanted to find out more about him.

"He's a very capable writer...he expresses..." said his uncle.

"I like to express my thoughts in a simple, rhythmic way...I write because I want to help others...I write because I have a destiny in my life. I write because there isn't a better way to be heard, because if I scream people will cover their ears and refuse to hear." Rami was only repeating Ahmad's words.

"He's a genius!" his uncle concluded.

May never took her eyes away from him. She was giving him all her attention. She hoped that she was correct with her judgment, that she knew exactly where he was coming from and where he was planning to go.

"Is that a correct assumption? Or was it exaggerated a bit? Are you a genius?"

Somehow she knew the answer to her question.

"Just a child's imagination…! Nothing more, nothing less," his father butted in again. "It won't do him any good in the future. He should study now for next year."

Rami leapt up; there was no reason for him to stay in the room any longer. His lower lip shivered as he spoke. "Excuse me everyone, it's time for my bed…good night."

"You haven't eaten yet!" his mother protested.

"I'm not hungry mum," he explained and left the room.

He lay back on his bed, smiling. He had won his first encounter. A few minutes later, there was a knock on his door.

"Come in."

It was May. "Hi…I brought you something to eat," she said, "You can't go to bed on an empty stomach."

"Thank you…Please come in. I stopped sobbing!" he said jokingly, "Here, let me take that. Do sit down please," he took the tray of food from May's hands.

"Thank you…you're a gentleman…and also one spoiled little brat," she giggled. "You are something else, my dear young man…I can read you like a book."

"Can you now? Can you tell me why my father isn't proud of me? And why my uncle is the opposite? He's so proud he can't shut up…"

May looked deep into his eyes. It was time to bring him down a level or two, she thought, but instead, he stood up to her challenge. She couldn't believe the strength and power of his eyes; she couldn't turn away from him.

She wished she'd never started this game. She felt insecure as his eyes undressed her slowly. And now, she sat there trying hard to cover her nudity. How dare he make her feel so uncomfortable? She wished he would speak out, say a few words to comfort her or even go back to that dull analysis of his father and uncle. She moved one leg over the other, and his piercing eyes followed them. She felt guilty for allowing him to explore her. She wanted that torture to stop, but she couldn't think of what to say next. She was angry with herself.

"I must go downstairs," she said.

"You've only been here for a few minutes. Would you like to read some of my writings?"

"Y…yes I would."

Rami pulled out a notebook from under his pillow and handed it to her.

"I'll read it tonight in bed…I like reading in bed."

"So do I." he agreed.

"Why don't you come to the house tomorrow…I'll give you my opinion?" she said, and hurried out of the room.

"Good night."

He looked at his watch, calculating how many hours remained until morning. A large smile was printed across his face as he fell asleep.

- - - - - - - - -

May had been born in the north of the country, in Mosul, the third biggest city in Iraq. At the age of nineteen, she had married Samir, and they moved to Baghdad when he opened his clinic. May didn't know many people, except for Rami and a few neighbours with whom she had very little in common. In fact, if it hadn't been for Rami she would have been a very lonely person.

"Good morning Rami...please come in," May greeted him.

He stood in the middle of the living room, bemused by its smart yet simple relaxing furniture.

"Please sit down...make yourself at home."

She wore tight blue shorts, with a creamy colour shirt. He tried hard to cover up his obvious embarrassment, but somehow, his lower jaw felt heavier than ever before.

"Close your mouth, Rami. I can see the back of your throat!" she teased, and burst out laughing.

"Sorry...so what do you think?"

"What about? Oh...you mean your writings? Well, I agree with your father...a total waste of time." She teased him again.

"What?" he screamed.

She giggled, "Just joking! You are amazing, really amazing. I wish I could tell you to forget about studying and concentrate on your writings. I wish everyone around you could be brave enough to let you do that."

"My father will never let me do that, plus I enjoy studying and going to school, I really do."

"I hated school..." she laughed. "I hated all my teachers too."

"Tell me then, did you really like them? I don't know with you, whether you are joking or serious!"

"They are good...really good...I would love to read them again and again. Are you happy now?"

"Is that all?" he teased back.

"Okay...I loved each and every one of them. They have depths, new ideas, feelings and they were amazing. You have the ability to see through people. You are also manipulative; you have the ability to describe pain, hardship, happiness, and even the man in the street can understand what you're saying...you are clever."

"I know all that, so when are you going to ask me for my autograph?"

"Very funny...would you like a drink?"

"Please...I'd love one, anything that is ice cold...I need to cool down a bit."

"You can smoke if you like...I know you do." She looked him straight in the eye and walked out.

'He couldn't be more than sixteen,' she thought. Never before had she felt that aching sensation just by thinking of someone, so why him? She had felt it when she'd read his book the night before. She'd even lifted the book to her nose thinking a drug was hidden between the pages; she was disappointed to find nothing. She'd hugged his book long to her chest, without knowing why she did it. She couldn't accept the fact that he made her feel uncomfortable, that he made her shiver, that he unbalanced her very own existence. She'd held his book closely to her flesh yet again, wanting to feel his warmth. She'd wanted him badly that night, and she wanted him badly then.

"You have a beautiful house, May" he said as she entered the room. "Everything in this room has elegance, and a woman's touch."

"I love it, thank you."

She grinned, "I chose it all…will you please stop looking at me like that? I feel very…" she tailed off.

"Vulnerable?" he interjected. "Sorry…I can't help it. I don't know how else to look! I've never made anyone else feel that way, and I don't know why I'm doing it."

"Well don't do it to me…if you want us to be friends," she pleaded.

"Don't worry about me…I'm harmless," he said, taking a deep breath, he continued, "You make me feel the same too."

After that outburst, they talked for a long time. The conversation was light hearted. It was apparent that the initial attraction had disappeared. She was fortunate not to see life the way he did, nevertheless their friendship grew each day. She enjoyed his company, his arguments and his wit. It was a distraction from her daily routine.

"Are you lonely?" she asked him one day.

"Yes, when I'm not with you," he answered back.

She wasn't convinced. She had known him for almost two months now and knew exactly when he was being serious; he wasn't then.

"Are you lonely, Rami?"

"When I was born…nobody was born with me." He laughed again but in reality, he wanted to tell her the truth, to tell her that it hurt him to think about it. He wanted her not to have to ask, but to feel what was brewing inside him. He wanted her to know that the past few weeks, since they had met, were the best he'd ever had. He wanted to tell her that he could never imagine himself without her, and that he wanted her to give him more of her time and herself. She was the ideal candidate to fill the huge gap in his life that Ahmad left behind. But he couldn't tell her any of that, so instead he looked away. She was sad, knowing her question had hit a sensitive chord inside him. It was too late to make amends.

"I care for you, I care very much, and I'll hate myself if I ever hurt you. May, my friend, you are all I think about, and…."

Her eyes watered because of his sincerity. She moved closer to him, held his hand tightly and stared, searching deep into his eyes. Suddenly, she planted a kiss on his hand and ran out of the room, leaving him puzzled by her behaviour. She came back a few minutes later, and handed him a small notebook. He noticed she had tears in her eyes, and quickly apologised.

"I'm sorry May…I didn't mean…"

"You haven't done anything to hurt me. You can read my writings if you like. You might understand a bit about me." She dried her eyes and continued, "I care about you, much more than you think. At times I feel sorry for you because you are somehow lost in a time zone."

"I am from the future, arrived here on a space ship," he joked.

"How old are you? I never asked you before."

"I'm thirteen...why?" he said quietly.

"Just asking...what?" she screamed, when his answer registered in her mind. "I don't believe you... no, never... you're joking, you are...oh my God." She laughed uncontrollably. "Are you telling me you are half my age, and you made me act so silly, so childish, like a little schoolgirl...no way. I haven't been able to think straight for the past few weeks. I can't sleep properly...I've been going out of my mind. Tell me you are joking; tell me, please."

For no reason Rami joined in the laughter. Soon, he fell to the floor, which made her laugh even more.

"Oh please! I have a stomach ache now," she moaned.

"You are so beautiful."

"Just hush up... will you?" She stopped laughing. "You are a devil! I really enjoy your company, Rami...thank you."

"Thank you," he added politely.

"I shall treasure our friendship."

"I will too." He leaned forward to kiss her, but she turned her face away and the kiss landed on the side of her face.

"Don't...you'll spoil everything," she begged.

- - - - - - - - -

Rami was totally confused about how he felt towards May. It seemed at times that friendship alone wasn't enough for him. He needed and wanted to be the centre of her attention. She was adamant she wouldn't give in, believing that she had to put the barriers higher.

She explained her relationship with her husband, and how much she loved him, but it would have been easier explaining it to a brick wall.

"I envy myself for marrying such a man."

"Hhmmmm…"

"Do you know what I miss? Remember when we used to sit here quietly...you wrote and I read, and then debated the subject, argued it. I miss having intelligent conversations with you. Have you stopped writing? I haven't read anything new for days."

"I can't write. I have things on my mind."

"Yes Rami...I wish I could get inside that thick skull of yours. You are such a confused kid, aren't you?"

"Don't call me kid, and I am not confused. I'm going home."

For some strange reason they never stopped seeing each other. His behaviour changed, though, from being confident and funny to feeling miserable and uninterested in anything around him.

"What's wrong with you today? You are quiet!" May asked one day.

"I don't know. It's one of these days when I am not feeling…."

"Oh my God...! Not again," she interrupted. "Please don't start this nonsense! I so dislike moaners."

19

"Forget it." He didn't want to argue. "It'll pass."

"Sure it will. I mean it, Rami. Stop it. I've had enough ...what's wrong with you?"

"Nothing..." He looked sad, avoiding eye contact.

She saw his reaction as she stood in front of the mirror, and couldn't help but feel sorry for him

"Do you like my hair like this?" She allowed it to fall over her shoulders.

"Yes..." His eyes watered.

"Stop that."

"What else do you want me to say?" He lashed out. "I'm sick of people telling me what to say and do. I can't do anything right anymore."

"What's eating you today?"

"School is starting soon...next week."

"Really? I shall celebrate...peace at last...do you like my new dress?"

"Yes...yes," he answered in frustration, "I was with you when you bought it."

"What about the shoes?"

"I love you...!"

"Look here. We are friends, but you are trapping me, Rami...I don't know what you want of me. I'm suffocating, I can't breathe any more. I never encouraged you in any way, so if you have any romantic feelings about me, just drop them now."

"Rubbish...you love me...I know you do."

"Are you serious? Would you like to repeat it again? What a joker you are. I care for you... that's all there is to it."

"I'd better go home."

She took no notice of this. "What I don't understand is that I can sit and hold a clever, intelligent conversation with you for hours on end. I never looked at you as a thirteen year old. I look at you as a mature man, fully grown, fully developed mentally, very interesting to listen to, very funny, and fun to be with. You have read well and thanks to your teacher, your eyes have been opened to so many subjects. But sometimes you behave like a child – a spoiled little brat. I dislike you at times, and I wish I had never let you through my front door. I do take the blame for it; we could have had a unique friendship."

"I'd better go home," he repeated.

"Yes, you'd better...and don't bother to come back. I don't want to see you again."

His eyes were cold and expressionless as he gazed at her. Slowly, they travelled down to the floor, hoping to find an answer, a message printed on the marble.

"Don't forget to take those poems with you."

A comforting feeling swept over her as she sat down with a cup of coffee and her feet tucked beneath her. She felt secure and proud of the way she had tackled the situation. He had left her no choice but to end their friendship.

Samir walked in hours later. "Hi darling" He kissed her. "On your own...?"

No reply.

"What's wrong? Did you have a disagreement with Rami?"

"Why should there be anything wrong?"

"Sorry I asked. I suppose my dinner is in the oven?"

"I didn't cook anything...I'm sorry." She burst out crying. "I'm sorry, please forgive me."

"Don't worry, we'll go out for a change."

"Sit down...I'll cook you something to eat...it won't take long."

"May!" He grabbed her hand. "Sit down for a minute...we'll talk first."

She hugged him tightly. "I love you...I love you completely. I have no time for anyone else in my life...especially a thirteen year old boy."

"You got too deep into this friendship...never mind, you'll soon sort something out."

His words were meant to be gentle and reassuring, but to her, they fell far short of being meaningful. She needed to hear harsh words, angry words. She wanted him to give her a long lecture on how a wife should behave.

"Don't you care? Do you understand what I'm going through? He's only thirteen, for God's sake!"

"Do you see him as a thirteen year old boy? Because I don't...!"

"I don't know...I'm so confused," May replied.

"Can you imagine what he's going through? He doesn't know whether he is a man or a teenager. He doesn't understand the basics of relationships, yet he is so mature, so intelligent for his age. I told you from the beginning you were seeing too much of him, and now, you don't know where to turn, or what to do."

"I have already said that to him." Silence fell between them. She hoped that he understood her situation, that he would give her advice and solves her problem.

"I like Rami, too," Samir said, and May nodded her head. "He makes me laugh with his antics, and makes me think about things I never ever bothered about before. You see, darling, he changed me too. When I used to come home from work, I would rest for an hour, have my dinner, and head to bed. I knew you were there, but my life was different, unexcited. Now, I find his company stimulating, unwinding, and pleasurable. I'd much rather talk to him than those colleagues at work."

"That's exactly how I feel, Samir, but you don't see my problem – probably there isn't one. He's starting school shortly, and I hope all those feelings will sort themselves out."

"I hope so too, for your sake...come on, darling, let's go out for a meal...I'm hungry...a change of scenery will do you good."

- - - - - - - - -

The following day, Rami went to see May as usual, as if nothing had happened between them.

The housekeeper opened the door. "Good morning Rami, May is still in bed," she said.

"That's fine, I'll just go to the shop, and call back on my way home."

"Who is at the door, Hassina?" May shouted from upstairs.

"Rami, Madam."

"Ask him to come up."

"I heard her." Rami smiled as he walked past the housekeeper. When he reached the first floor, he noticed the bedroom door was open, so he entered. May stood looking at herself in a mirror. She wore a short thin negligee, revealing her nakedness underneath. Her slender height and the perfect curves of her figure suggested that she had taken a great deal of pride in her appearance. Rami looked down at his trembling legs, wondering how on earth they were keeping him upright. He felt awkward; his mind was dead and he couldn't think what to do or say next. He was rooted to the spot.

"I...I...sorry...!" His voice had no defined pitch. He was caught unprepared, his lips parted again, but the words refused to come out, racked by emotions. With great difficulty, he turned round and slowly started back towards the door.

"Don't be silly, just close the door and sit on the bed there, please darling," she said seductively.

He was completely disorientated. He felt like a wrecked ship, sinking to whatever fate awaited it.

"Why are you so quiet? I have never known you to be lost for words! Have I stunned you, honey?" She laughed, but it wasn't a laugh as such, it was more like knives carving away the flesh from his body.

He didn't answer her. Instead, he looked out into the distance beyond the window.

"Don't you think I have a perfect figure?" Another laugh escaped her, she was winning at last.

Tears filled his eyes; he was cornered, and couldn't understand her intentions. He had never been in a trickier situation. Hadn't Ahmad taught him to know the way out before entering into any odd situation? To fight back whenever he found himself in unknown surroundings? Then why wasn't he doing something about it? Why wasn't he escaping? He knew it was a game which had no rules. He was losing; it was definitely a checkmate.

"What do you think now?" She let her negligee slip over her shoulders and fall to the floor. "You wanted to see me naked...here I am!"

He sat still on the bed. He was trapped and humiliated. He heard her shouting "Look at me...look at me, Rami...I'm alive...just the way you always wanted me."

He turned around, but couldn't see much. Tears streamed down his face. She ran towards him, grabbing a housecoat to cover her body.

"Oh God...! What have I done?" She cried as she knelt on the floor in front of him. "Look at me...please look at me, my dear young man...it was only a joke."

He raised his face to meet hers and to his surprise, she kissed him tenderly.

"I'm sorry... I didn't mean to hurt you."

"I love you," he declared.

"Thank God you do after what I did to you. I love you too, as a friend, and I always will. I'm crazy about you. But we are going to hurt one another, because we are giving out confused signals."

He looked at her. "You are my dream, my fantasy. I never thought for one minute that you would be mine, but I often wondered…!"

"I'm a married woman," she interrupted him, "and you have read too many romantic novels, too many books, and now you are confused between reality and fantasy."

"I love you, and you love me just as much. We can't sit across the room looking at each other and doing nothing.... it's absurd. I want to touch you, feel you...is that wrong?"

"You dramatise everything. One day, when you are old enough, I will make love to you, but not today... not now."

He was astonished. He never expected to hear that.

"I'm not ready for this...I can't just sleep with you."

He held her face in his hands, and kissed it softly.

"I won't let you go the whole way...do you understand?" she whispered in his ear, and he nodded.

She gave him everything in her power and wasn't afraid to ask for his love in return. She knew exactly how far she could go, where to draw the line, and how much she would allow him of herself. They laughed, talked, cried, danced, and argued. They screamed with happiness, and played games around the room, as if they were two children. In fact neither of them had enjoyed their childhood as much as those two hours. Nothing in the world mattered. They seemed to be in a world of their own.

"You poor thing!" she said, and burst out laughing.

"What are you laughing about?" he asked, watching her fall backwards, her legs spread out high above her head. That made him explodes with laughter too.

"Oh, please stop..."

"I need the toilet," she cried out.

"Me too..."

"God only knows what Hassina thinks of us."

"She thinks we're writing a masterpiece."

She drew him gently to her, and planted a kiss on his shivering lips, which grew to a full-hearted ritual. They were locked together for quite a while.

"That's all you'll be getting; I don't want you to live without a dream."

Her words weren't convincing, as she wanted him badly. She wanted his dreams, his thoughts, and his young, untouched body of his. She wanted him, but he was her fantasy, and better stayed that way.

"What about Samir?" he asked.

May ran her fingers through his hair, avoiding his eager eyes.

"What about Samir?" he persisted.

"I must explain something to you." She pushed him gently away.

"Okay."

"Shall we go downstairs and I will tell you over a cup of tea?"

When they were sitting at the table in the kitchen, she carried on. "Samir had an accident a year after we were married. We were up north then, and he was drafted into the army for a second time. The field hospital was bombed, and out of all the doctors there, he was the only one to survive. It wasn't the Kurds, but our own planes that bombed the hospital. Our government blamed it on the Kurds, of course. Nobody thought Samir would live. He proved them wrong. During that time, they sent us to England for treatment, but it was more like pushing us out of the way. They paid all our expenses, so we wouldn't talk. Anyway, Samir recovered. He still has a few aches and pains every now and then. He blames it on the weather, can you believe that?"

"You went through hell!"

"Hell isn't the word. He had so many shrapnel wounds; they couldn't take them all out. We came back after four months in England, and they gave us lots of money to keep us quiet. We did well, we bought the house, and Samir opened his clinic, as well as spending a year in England studying."

"I'm sorry, I feel terrible now. How can I do that with you? And he..."

"Don't say that." She raised her hand. "You have nothing to feel guilty about, do you understand? Samir can't have sex and not that we had any, and it's..."

He kissed her quickly, and left the house.

Rami was confused and disturbed by his own action. How could he believe that he could love a woman twice his age, and try to make her love him back? And what pleasure in that when another man had been scalded by their action? Luckily nothing happened, and thanks to May.

He contradicted himself over and over again, wanting to ease his pain, and hoping that any reasonable excuse would give him the right to love her.

- - - - - - - - -

It was eight o'clock the following night when Rami decided to come out of the house. It was also the time when Samir returned home from work. When he saw him, he waved him to stop.

"Rami...hi...what's up?"

"I want to talk to you. Can we go somewhere else please?"

"Sure, jump in. Do you fancy an ice cream?"

They drove towards Abu Nawas Street, named after the famous poet who was portrayed in the Arabian Nights. The street ran parallel to the Tigris. On the banks of the river, there were many clubs, cafes, restaurants and parks and a variety of shops on the other side of the road. Some sold homemade ice cream, and others specialised in fresh fruit juices – especially pomegranate, Rami's favourite drink. Those shops remained open until there were no more customers left.

"Do you love May?" Rami asked, leaning back on the car.

"Yes very much."

In a low voice, Rami told him about the events of the day before. He was relieved to get it out into the open.

"Are you going to kill me now?"

"Would you like another ice cream?"

"Please...are you going to poison me?" He giggled in fear.

They strolled back to the shop, the smell of barbecued meat filling the air. Samir said "May told me about yesterday. We don't keep secrets from each other."

"I don't understand, is she still alive?" he chuckled with a grin, "I didn't go to the house today...aren't you mad at me?"

"I'm angry, but not with either of you."

"I'm sorry to deceive you. I betrayed your trust."

"You've rehearsed those words, haven't you?"

"Yes."

"When I had my accident, which you already know about, May was very brave. She handled the situation perfectly, and helped my recovery...I used her strength when I lost mine. She's a very strong willed woman. She fought hard for us and I owe her my life. I know there isn't a sexual relationship between us, but we are still very much man and wife, and also good friends. We are partners, and we love each other completely. What more can I ask for? I'm a lucky man." He paused. "Then you came along. I was jealous at first, as you grabbed all her attention, you had everything: youth, health, sense of humour, intelligence. But the fact is that May and I became closer to each other, closer than ever before."

They turned round, heading back to the car. "Thank you for speaking out. It was very thoughtful of you, very honourable."

Rami was more shocked than relieved. He couldn't believe what he had just heard.

"May lost our baby when I had my accident," Samir added.

"No! You've had so much suffering; so much pain yet so much understanding and love. And I...I intruded on you...Oh God! I feel like an ass." Rami covered his face with his hands. "I feel like the joker in the middle"

"The most needed card in the pack."

"I don't need compliments, Samir...I don't deserve it."

"Let's go home."

"I have so much growing up to do!"

Samir's understanding didn't help to ease their problems. It actually complicated the relationship. They tried hard to make their odd friendship work, but failed.

"One day, when I have my own woman, I'll treat her in the same way as Samir treats you. Don't worry, I'll come and see you often; I don't want to be without you," Said Rami a few days later as he sat in the garden with May.

"Why don't you shut up? You're so childish; it's beginning to bore me. Why don't you go to a drama school? You will do well there," said May angrily, which was totally out of character.

"What have I done now?"

"I'm sick of you." She frowned. "Sick of the way you talk...sick of the way you carry on. You live on cloud nine, and I'm here on earth. I don't think you'll ever grow up, and I don't want to babysit you for the rest of my life. Why don't you leave us alone? I'm happy with my husband. Just go away, and don't think you could destroy us. You aren't welcome in this house anymore...Do you understand?"

He had nothing to say to her. He stood up, and left the house.

She waited until Samir finished his supper before she told him the latest news.

"We are finished."

"Who?"

"Rami and I." She gathered her strength, and continued "I had to do it. I can't go on like this anymore, it was driving me crazy. Do you think he'll ever forgive me? I did it for his sake too. I am sorry, darling! I was unfair to both of you." She wiped the tears away, "Forgive me."

"Whatever happened had to happen; please don't cry."

"I feel so guilty for what I said to him, and the way I behaved towards you. I'm really sorry."

"Oh sweetheart, you are so beautiful, so innocent. There's nothing to forgive you for, and he's probably forgotten the whole episode by now."

CHAPTER FOUR

AN air of uncertainty overwhelmed Rami during his first few weeks in school. He had no close friends to talk to or to confide in. He needed Ahmad and May, but they had deserted him. He accepted the fact that he was lonely and had to learn to get on with life the best he could. He had the freedom to read, study and explore, and the time to achieve whatever he wished for. For him the world was something to be discovered. He was not looking for a way out, but a way in.

He became involved in various activities at the school. He joined several sport teams as well as the school's Sodality, which was mainly a religious, social and intellectual group. He began to enjoy other pupils' company, and they enjoyed his. He learnt to accept others as they were, without judging them. He was the best in his class academically, and they looked up to him. He was not as quiet as he had been the year before, but now spoke and laughed loudly. He enjoyed making his teachers beg him to stop, but he was never punished, mainly because of his funny remarks and perfect timing. In fact, the teachers enjoyed taking his class. It was harmless fun.

He knew exactly what he needed to achieve, and to him, failure was not acceptable. He calculated every move he made, and won. He needed to be the centre of attention, whether he was playing baseball, basketball, or volleyball; he had to be the best. This hunger for success frightened him at times, but over the following two years he learnt to adapt himself to every occasion.

Letters from Ahmad began to arrive frequently. He had settled at last in Lebanon after spending a few months in Cairo and Amman. And, he never stopped lecturing Rami.

"Your last writings were excellent, now I know I haven't wasted my time on you. My friend it's time to start digging, and digging deep. Solid foundation is needed here, so no one can knock you sideways." Rami laughed as he read this letter, thinking how to reply.

It was amazing how every piece of the jigsaw fitted perfectly in those two years. He got what he wanted from it and more. By the end of the third year he came out with flying colours and a passing average of ninety-seven per cent in all his subjects in the national examination. Due to the political situation rumours that the American School would be nationalised by the government, and that all American priests and teachers would be sent home accused of spying, his father decided to enrol him in a public school for his secondary education before entering university.

One problem remained unsolved and that was 'May'. It had been two years since they spoke to each other. He couldn't walk by her house every day without trying to get a glimpse of her; he could no longer pretend and act as if she didn't mean anything to him. One hot summer day, he decided to visit her.

May opened the door with a smile, "What took you so long to come over?"

They both burst out laughing. Their friendship was restored in seconds.

"I brought you some of my writings from the past two years if you care to read them?"

"I'd love to Rami."

"I am sorry"

"So am I. Come in."

"I thought you would never ask," he said as he walked past her.

"Cheeky bastard...!"

"Are we friends forever?"

"I think so...what do you say?"

She examined him carefully. It had been two years since she was this close to him. He had matured; he had lost his baby features, and developed a stern yet comforting face, hard to take her eyes away from it. His smile was invitinghis voice had sharpened and his eyes seemed to be deeper than ever before.

He appeared to be more confident, secure and much quieter than before. But she had her doubts and no matter how close she could get to him, she would never know him fully.

CHAPTER FIVE

SUPERVISED by different bodies from the Church, The Christian Centre in Baghdad was founded in 1962. The aim was to raise a new society of young people to form a solid educated Christian force with the strength to build and survive. This could accept the challenges to fight off the old ideas and the stubborn resistance of ingrained customs by using the most dangerous weapons of all; understanding, education and a different but stronger belief in God.

This was the foundation of a new generation based on open mindedness, which would progress further, perhaps not achieving every goal, but far enough to achieve safety in a country where more than ninety percent were Muslims. The Muslims were made up of Shiites and Sunni's who lived in harmony avoiding sectarian conflict.

There were many facilities available at the centre, including a sports complex, theatre, cinema, meeting rooms and a very large well kept garden, where many activities were held during the summer. In fact, there was something for everyone. Three sodalities were based at the Centre, as well as a Club for the older generation, mainly composed of university graduates.

Rami was accepted in the Young Christian Sodality, because of his experience from the American school, and the excellent references the American Fathers had given him. But as he was under age he was given a three months trial. Now, he had the summer holiday to prove that he was worthy of being a member.

- - - - - - - - -

In 1967 came the six days war with Israel. It created a massive change in everyone's life. People were glued to their televisions and radios; they waited for news, good news to come. Instead gloom clouded the whole media; the war stopped suddenly, after only six days, it didn't even last the week, what a farce!!!

The people were dazed not knowing what had happened. Those with short wave radios listened to foreign stations for explanations, but instead they were listening to anti Arab propaganda. They wanted to know and understand why the mighty Iraqi Army wasn't involved in the heart of the battle, and why it's mighty air force was blown away on the tarmacs of various airfields in Egypt?

It needed such a drastic event to bring people together. They talked to each other, total strangers; they talked in the streets, in places of work, in cafés, on the buses and wherever they met. They could not absorb and accept the fact that a country of two million people could win against the twenty-one Arab Nations, and two hundred million people. Promises and promises by Arab leaders that never were fulfilled.

When the war was over, a deafening silence hung over the young people of the country; they were ashamed of how they were sold out by their leaders. Maybe because they were more nationalist then those who sat on the high chairs, nevertheless that was the holy war they had been waiting for! Why did they go into a war so unprepared? No answers, no explanations only shame, - will they ever recover? Will they ever hold their heads high again? Why did America and the West stand by Israel? Hundreds of unanswered questions, all they knew was that there were thousands of families in desperate need of help because they had lost their breadwinners in a war that wasn't a war. They were killed without having the chance to fire one shot.

Rami was bewildered by all the happenings. He wrote trying hard to build confidence again, he spoke with everyone he met hoping to understand the different points of view. The six-day war brought changes, including the need to raise money for its victims. The charities were working days and nights helping to bring relief to those affected, especially the hundreds of thousands of Palestinians who escaped the Israeli occupation. The war had cost millions, and the Iraqi treasury was not surprisingly empty as usual. Rami and his friends were helping by collecting donations of money, clothes, food, and beddings.

The committee which governed the Christian Centre decided to hold a literary competition among all the sodalities in Baghdad, which numbered over ninety at that time. This would be the first of many such competitions, attracting the cream of writers, poets and scholars.

Nabil was the chairman of the Young Christian Sodality. He was a charming person, intelligent, full of confidence and excellent at what he did. Normally, he could chair a meeting well, but not on this day. He was explaining the rules of the literary competition, but no matter what he did, he could not attract Rami's attention. The boy was just staring at a painting on the wall facing him. The members began to laugh when Nabil stopped talking; they had become used to Rami's funny antics over the past few weeks. They were all growing fond of him and his humour. Rami glanced at Nabil, who said, "Welcome back!" His eyes widened behind the dark-framed glasses. "Thank you. God bless you my son!" Rami laughed.

"And you too!" Nabil replied.

"Sorry, I was miles away, admiring the brush strokes!" He pointed at the painting. By then everyone was laughing.

"Thank God you didn't take the rest of us with you," said Nabil.

"I wouldn't dream of doing that and leave you here talking to yourself, Mr Chairman."

Nabil waited for the laughter to die down before he spoke again. "Let's get back to the serious business of the competition, and Rami, please, I beg you to stay with us this time."

Rami already knew about the competition, and had decided to put in three entries: a short story, a poem, and a small article. He was hoping that at least one of them would be selected.

The list of successful contenders was hung on the board ten days before the competition day. Rami was already nervous as he read the names, but his heart nearly stopped when he saw the list contained famous writers and authors, poets, novelists, and lecturers of Arabic language at various universities. They were the cream of Baghdad's literary society. Rami's face paled as he looked at Nabil.

"You did it!" Nabil tapped on his shoulder.

"Did what? Did what?" He turned round and read the list again, and couldn't believe his eyes when his name appeared three times. "God! What have I done?"

"You are a beauty!" Nabil screamed again, calling other members of the sodality to tell them the good news.

"I will be the laughing stock of the country in ten days – have you seen those names? You couldn't put together a better bunch!" said Rami.

"You can only do your best."

With the help of a tape recorder and a full-length mirror, Rami locked himself away, reading and rehearsing his entries. May helped in choosing his clothes, and also listened to him and advised him accordingly.On the day of the competition, he arrived almost an hour early. His legs turned to jelly as he walked through the front door of the Centre, but froze altogether when he saw the hundreds of people already gathered in the garden that evening. He couldn't move, his hands felt like ice although it was a warm night. He looked around for someone to rescue him, and to his relief, spotted Nabil walking towards him with others from his sodality.

"Hi!" His voice crackled.

"You look great Rami. I like the suit; how are you feeling?"

"I don't feel anything at the moment," he chuckled, and everyone laughed. "I am so nervous; look at me....I'm shaking. Look at those people; I've never seen so many here before. I think I have made a mistake!"

"Rami, you will be fine, take it on as an experience."

"How many are they expecting?"

"They've sold thirteen hundred tickets, and are expecting to sell a few more at the door."

"Shit!"

"Come on, I'll buy you a cold drink."

"A cup of tea please, I am frozen."It was the first competition of its kind at the Centre, and the atmosphere was electric. A northern breeze cooled the air, making it pleasant despite the number of people.After the usual speeches and introductions the first competitor was already reading his entry. The organisers made a blunder by arranging all the short stories together; some were long and hard for people to follow, which made them restless. A few left their seats and others began to talk among themselves

"Aren't you lucky to be the last one?" Nabil whispered.

"No I am not. This isn't fair at all; by the time I get my turn, there will be no one listening to me."

"Calm down and relax, you'll be fine!" Nabil pleaded.

Rami felt ill, as he knew his turn was about to come. His mouth was dry and his eyes were focused on the jug of iced water on the table next to the lady competitor who was about to introduce him. "Ladies and gentlemen, 'A train to nowhere' is our next story, by the amateur writer, Rami," she said. "I wonder how much they charge for those train tickets, and where do you board from?" She got her expected reaction from the crowd, who sniggered.

Nabil stared in disbelief. "The silly bitch…what a bitch!" he said. "Go and give it to them."

Rami walked slowly towards the stage. The woman examined him from head to foot as he passed her. Rami ignored her, and sat down behind the table. He wasn't nervous any more, but he was filled with immense anger. He poured himself a glass of water, and drank it as he waited for the noise to abate. He fiddled with some flowers in a vase, and pushed it gently to the far side of the table. A smile crossed his face as the voices began to die down, so he adjusted his tie, drank some more water, and greeted the crowd with a "Good evening.". That crowd control took him two or three minutes to perform, which gained many appreciating nods from the audience. At last he pushed his chest out, straightened his back, and looked in the direction of two of the judges who were talking to each other. He smiled at the person next to them, who hushed them politely.

Rami started, *"A train to nowhere…"* His voice was loud, clear and powerful. *'He lay on his wooden bed in a four walled room, following the rings of smoke from his cigarette. He smiled and burst out laughing, "My own face flying away from me…look…my face…why?" He looked at the walls and continued. "Emptiness, nakedness and a damn face: my face."*

Rami looked up, examining the faces in front of him, and continued. No one spoke, no one moved; they were all listening to him. He remembered the day he had stood in front of his classmates when Ahmad had asked him to read his little story. He was winning and wanted to smile, but couldn't as his story was coming to a crucial stage. Instead, he paused and briefly looked up at the audience, taking a deep breath as he prepared for the next stint. Nabil nodded with approval, a priest tightened his grip on his cross. *'He looked behind him on the bed, and there she was, laughing hysterically as she moved her hand over her nakedness. For a moment he thought he knew her, but she was a complete stranger. She grabbed his hand and pressed it against her body. There was a great pain, as his hand was cut by broken glass,'*

Rami went on reading. The tone of his voice changed with every word and sentence. He paused a few times, allowing the people to absorb the story. The anger inside had long gone, and he was filled with confidence. He knew deep down that he had practised enough times to present his work perfectly. The audience's agony lasted fourteen minutes, as he came to the last paragraph. *'Fools…! They don't know; they don't know; they only see what they want to see, not what they meant to see. He turned round and walked towards the city.'*

"Thank you."

Nobody clapped, nobody moved; everyone was silent. He slowly pushed his chair back and stood up. Then the whole place erupted. Everyone was standing up and shouting; it was incredible. Rami waited for a few minutes and introduced the next competitor, before walking off the stage. He headed straight to the cafeteria, followed by Nabil.

"Wait for me," said Nabil, hurrying after him. "You were just great, absolutely outstanding…oh you nailed that one."

Rami turned round with tears running down his face. Nabil quickly took him by the hand to a darkish corner, leaving him there for a minute or two, and came back with cold drinks.

"Sorry, I just feel completely drained and exhausted," said Rami. "Thanks for the drink."

"Your sugar level might have gone low," Nabil laughed. "You were amazing, better than I thought, much better."

"Thanks! Can you do me a favour please?"

"Sure, what is it?"

"I don't want to do the article – I am completely exhausted. But I'll do the poem."

"No problem, I'll have words." Shortly afterwards, shouts erupted once more as his name was announced. He ran to the stage, eager to present his poem. Spotlights shone as darkness fell, and hundreds of coloured lights surrounded the garden, adding a majestic feel to the whole event. He decided to stand up this time, pulling the microphone away from the table. "This is only the second time I've ever adjusted one – hang on a second!" He laughed, and they shared his laughter. He wasn't at all nervous as he searched the faces for someone to read to. He found her: an attractive young lady with dark hair and large tender eyes. She was seated in the seventh row.

He smiled in her direction. "Can I start now?" Shouts of "Yes…yes" echoed in all directions, but she remained aloof and silent. "This poem is called 'Don't Cry.' It's about a soldier sent to battle. He wrote to his mother, and she in turn wrote back." His eyes were glued to hers. His moment of glory had come, as his voice echoed through the loudspeakers, shattering the silence. He laughed with the memory of a child, and cried for the mother losing her only son. His body moved with every line, every word; he was filled with mixed emotions and he made sure everyone there shared them. He carried his audience higher and higher, and then gently landed them back on the ground as he stopped to take a deep breath. They were glad, as they needed those few seconds to rest, but he soon began again. He was formidable but not out of control; he knew exactly where the safety line was. The people cheered and asked him to repeat particular sentences, and he obliged them. He read just for one pair of eyes: her eyes. *'Mother, don't let me die inside.'* Rami stopped and took a deep breath.

"Thank you for listening." He begged the audience to be quiet so he could introduce the next competitor, and left the garden. He returned to sit in a dark corner in the cafeteria. His eyes were shut as he tried to calm down.

"Can I join you, Rami? I brought you a coke!" The young lady with amazing eyes stood there with a smile on her face.

"It's you…oh…ah…God…I was thinking…"

"You're lost for words. My my, who would believe me?" She sat down close to him. Her smile turned to a laugh.

"You were great."

"Just great?" he asked.

"Great is enough." He giggled, although he didn't know why. Maybe it was the tension easing off, or perhaps more tension building up as she moved even closer to him. "I read it just for you."

"I know, but why me?"

"Just your face and your eyes; I felt so calm inside looking at you when our eyes met."

With a smile she asked, "Are you always this forward?"

"Yes."

"I'm sixteen, how old are you?" she asked quickly.

"Fifteen…and a bit." He disliked questions about his age.

"I am Nadia."

"Hello Nadia, do you always approach strangers like that?"

"No…just you." She giggled.

"I feel mentally and physically drained," he said.

"I am not surprised." She smiled softly, and found the courage to put her hand on his. Shaking off his exhaustion, Rami began to tell her how he started writing. All the time he examined her simple yet elegant dress, her delicate hand movements, the way she talked and her beautiful dialect. She obviously came from a well-to-do family; she was smart and intelligent, which made him proud to be in her company.

"I like you Nadia, I like you a lot."

"I like you too, and that's why I came to talk to you."

"Can I see you again?"

"I am not going anywhere." She nudged him.

On the stage, the seven judges assembled. Nadia and Rami were called back to the garden by one of the members of the sodality. A piece of paper was handed to the chairman of the Centre. He read the name of the winner in the article category first, and then said, "And now, this comes as no surprise, the winner of the short story and poetry categories, writer and poet of the year is…"

The audience waited in anticipation, and almost everyone was standing up.

"Please welcome Rami on stage again…"

After a quick kiss from Nadia, he ran to the stage. The audience was in uproar, shouting his name. He was so enthralled he could not contain himself, as he jumped up and punched the air. He was asked to speak, but the people wanted another poem. "Please…please. Thank you. It was one hell of night for me – thank you. Unfortunately I didn't bring any other writings with me."

They were still shouting for more, so he said. "Fine I'll make one up now. I can't promise it'll be any good, though." He took a deep breath, lowered his head and closed his eyes. Everyone was quiet now. He lifted his head up, and his eyes found what he was looking for.

"There my love you stood,
From a distance you thought,
Is he real? Or a dream?"

He continued speaking words, jumbled up in a magical, undefined way to produce a stunning poem. "It isn't my best poem, but I just made it up, and I can't think of any more." He giggled, and hurriedly left the stage. Dozens of people shook his hand to congratulate him. Father Philip, one of the advisors at the Centre, introduced him to the guest of honour, Mr Omar, who was the deputy Minister of Education.

"Good to meet you, Sir," said Rami.

"Well done young man, very impressive," said the guest. "You made me feel that there is still some good blood in us after all. Writers with a talent like yours must be rewarded and encouraged."

"Thank you, Sir."

"I must go now. It was a pleasurable evening, thank you," he said to Father Philip, adding, "Rami, come and see me at ten in the morning in my office, and bring some of those writings with you. Do you know where the ministry of education is?"

Rami was puzzled. "I do, Sir; yes I will." As Omar left, Rami saw Nadia and Nabil standing behind him. Nadia held his hand tightly and a look of amazement was printed on her face.

"Who was that?" Nabil asked.

"Deputy Minister for education, and he wants to see me in his office at ten in the morning!"

"Maybe you will be hung tomorrow, or shot by a firing squad," Nadia giggled.

"What do you think he wants?"

"Don't know, I'll just have to wait until morning." He was slightly worried.

"Can we leave please? It's already past ten."

"Yes… I must go."

"Where do you live?" Rami asked.

"Fifteen minutes walk."

"I'll walk you home," he said.

"See you, Nabil."

Hand in hand, they left the Centre. They were quiet at first; contented by their first impression they had made on each other, and the unbelievable closeness they felt for one another. Rami stopped, turned her gently towards him and kissed her on the lips. "Thank you for being here, and for being you. Winning made me happy, but I'm even happier that I met you."

"Thank you, that is so sweet."

He could see she was crying. "Why the tears…?" He took her face in his hands and gently wiped her tears away.

"I am happy, very happy. I lowered my guard for the first time, against everything I was taught and believe in," she said. "Rami, seeing you there on stage tonight you were simply amazing. You were acting; you were manipulating everyone there by your performance. But you belong to those people; you need them, and they need you. It's something I have to learn to live with, if we will continue to be together!"

"Wow…how long did it take you to think of all that?" he teased, at which she hit him on the shoulder. "You have nothing to fear; it's only my first competition, so maybe there won't be another!"

"I doubt it!"

A light-hearted conversation carried them to her house. He promised to visit her the following day to be introduced to her parents.

CHAPTER SIX

RAMI was shown into the waiting room at the Ministry of Education after the usual body search. He sat thinking of his brief meeting with Omar the night before, when his first impression had been of a man constantly stuffing his huge frame with masses of fatty food, and staining everything that he touched with his greasy hands. As the secretary showed him into his office, a beautiful aroma of pipe tobacco filled the air. Omar stood up from behind his elegant mahogany table, and welcomed the young writer.

"Well son, I was hoping that you wouldn't change your mind about coming," he said, then pointed at the leather sofa. "Please sit here, this isn't a formal meeting."

"Thank you."

As the conversation progressed, Rami discovered that Omar was a doctor in biochemistry, very modest and strong willed and knowing exactly what his powerful position in the government meant. He told Rami that he hoped to convince him to send some of his work to the country's main newspaper, which was the mouthpiece of the government.

"Thank you sir, but no thank you, I feel..."

"Work as good as this belongs to the people, so what are you afraid of?"

Rami felt trapped. "Can I speak freely please?"

"You have the stage again." He smiled.

"I enjoy writing. My pen is my freedom to express my thoughts, and I know I am good at it. If I accept this offer, I will be forced to become involved in your politics; my pen will never belong to me ever again. I have seen it many times." He took a deep breath and continued, "There is also the problem of my father; he will never accept the idea at all. He will just kill me! I know how my father thinks, and involvement with newspapers or magazines means involvement with politics, which isn't acceptable in my family Sir."

Omar laughed. "How old are you, son?"

"Fifteen...and a bit!"

"Good God, I thought you were much older than that. Go and sit in my chair."

Rami did as he was told. Omar asked, "How does it feel?"

"Uncomfortable! Why?"

"I should think so too, you won't be a politician, that is a politician's chair. As for your dad, either I'll visit him and talk him into it, or you use a pen name. What do you say?"

"Will I be paid?" Rami was ready to start bargaining, but Omar burst out laughing.

"Yes, you will get paid."

"I'll do it; I trust you, Sir."

"Now, go to my secretary and give her your choice of a story to be typed, while I make a phone call to the chief editor."

"Thank you."

Ten minutes later, Omar came out of his room. "I spoke to him, and whatever you choose will be published tomorrow. What name will you be using?"

"Rami A. Thank you Sir."

"Not at all, you are more than welcome. I look forward to reading it. Good luck."

As Omar promised, the short story was published the following day. Rami was thrilled, especially as a couple of sketches accompanied the story, which made it more noticeable. His dream was now a reality, and people across the country would be reading it, all except for those for whom he cared the most: his parents. That left a bitter taste in his mouth. Nevertheless, he sent a copy to Ahmad, and went to see Nadia.

"Remember me?" he asked as she opened the door.

"Oh it's you. You were supposed to come yesterday!"

"I couldn't, and I forgot to take your phone number to let you know."

"You'd better come in, but you need to apologise properly!" she teased. "Come to the day room."

"I am glad you were in; I've got something to show you."

The day room was spacious and comfortable, with a homely feeling about it. Elegant paintings hung on the walls, and family photos were on the mantelpiece.

"What's disturbing you, Rami? You look sad!"

He couldn't feel the closeness between them that he had sensed the other night. "Am I intruding on something, or have you changed your mind about me?" he asked.

"Why do you say that? Don't be silly."

"You didn't kiss me when you opened the door, and you are sitting so far away I need to shout for you to hear me." He teased.

"Oh come on then; give me a hug, you silly fool. I am on my own in the house, and for a moment I felt…"

"Vulnerable? That I was going to force myself on you?"

"Maybe. I've never been in this situation before, and I do trust you, but I don't trust myself."

She moved closer and put her hands around him, kissing him gently on his neck. "Now tell me, lover boy. What's bothering you?"

He handed her the newspaper. "Read this, please.'

Her small, rounded nose fascinated him; her mouth was beautifully carved with full lips.

"This is deep, and well written," she mumbled, and carried on reading. This gave him the chance to examine her more thoroughly.

"You're eating me alive! Put your eyes back in their sockets please," she smiled.

"I'd love to eat you alive!"

"I'd love you to."

"You're so beautiful."

She nudged him with her shoulder and moved even closer to him. She managed to fit the slender curves of her body into his, and it felt relaxing.

"Now, let me finish reading."

Suddenly, she jumped up as if stung. "This is fantastic, excellent and brilliant." Then she leapt on top of him, smothering him with kisses. "Now, you devil; you do turn me on, and you will pay for this."

"Please, I am a respectable young man," he protested.

"Oh, are you now?"

"What about your mum and dad?"

"They know, I told them about you," she laughed.

"Nadia…do you think I could come up for a bit of fresh air?" he begged, although he didn't mean it.

"No; you are not allowed."

"Am I really your first one you ever kissed?"

"Yes, because you are different from anyone else," she said as she sat on the floor, with her back against the sofa. "They are all after one thing."

"So am I!" His eyes gave him away.

"You are different."

"Different how?"

"You just are! When you picked me out from all those people the other day, you knew that I would respond to you. I know you were sure that you would be walking out of the centre with me."

"Wow. But I am still after one thing."

"I will be happy to give it to you when I am ready, but please don't force me."

"I wouldn't Nadia. I am a good person."

They went on talking for quite a while. He told her about his family, where they came from, how his granddad had died when his father was only four years old. She told him why she was the only child, and about her parents' history.

"Can I ask you a personal question?" she suddenly said.

"Yes sure; ask away."

"Are you a virgin?"

He was quiet for a while. "If you mean have I had sex, I haven't; I've never gone the whole way and had intercourse."

"Do you still see her?"

"Yes."

"Do you still sleep with her?"

Rami didn't answer.

"I really don't know what to say. Get the hell out of here; I don't want to see you ever again. I warn you that if you see her again, you'd better not come back here." She was raging with anger and jealousy.

"Nadia, I wish I could explain, but I can't; just trust me on that."

"When was the last time you did it?"

"I don't think that is a fair question. I told you the truth – or would you have preferred it if I'd lied?"

"Please leave the house so I can think properly." Tears ran down her face. "I just want to be left alone."

"Nadia, I did this before I met you, and I haven't done anything wrong."

"I know, but you said you are still seeing her."

"You have only known me for two days. I am not taking you for a fool; I really like you."

"Okay…but leave me now, please. I need to be on my own."

He walked out feeling more miserable than when he went to see her. He needed cheering up that night, and decided to go to the Centre. Once he was in the garden, his fellow sodality members stood up and began applauding, simply to embarrass him. They could not succeed, though, as he always had the last word. He enjoyed the small theatrical acting.

He sat in the empty seat next to Nabil looking at each one of them individually, "Cut the crap, behave yourself, and sit," he said, and turned to Nabil, "I hope you're not responsible for this?"

"There are ten of us, and I don't have a chance in hell to control them, Mr Rami A," Nabil replied.

"How on earth did you find out?"

"How many writers with the name Rami are there?"

"You bastards, you'd better keep it to yourself or else. My dad will kill me if he ever finds out!'

The conversation went on, serious one minute and funny the next. The circle began to grow as more members arrived.

"How about writing a play, Rami? We need to boost our image here at the Centre," suggested a member.

"I have never written one before. I have never been to a theatre, or read a play." Rami explained. "It isn't as simple as writing a poem or a story."

"You could always try!"

"I'll give it some thought."

Nabil drew Rami's attention to the entrance, where Nadia stood, searching for him.

"I phoned you at the house and I was told you were here," she said. "Are you busy?"

"No, not at all, come and sit with us."

"Not tonight, please; I need to talk to you – I need to explain."

"Okay. Shall we go for a walk?"

He put his arm around her shoulders, and they walked out. She bent her face to his hand and kissed it. "I am sorry," she said.

"So am I."

"I can't help being jealous. I hardly know you, and you don't know me either. I feel I am so naive, so inexperienced, so…."

"My mum was only fifteen when she married Dad," she continued, "and she didn't know anything about the world. We have many friends, and their parents thought it was best for them to be married to make them see sense, be responsible and not stray."

"What are you trying to tell me?" he burst out laughing.

"I lost the plot, I can't remember." she laughed too.

"I thought you were about to say the most sensible thing in your life," he teased.

"Promise me that you'll never ever use me and throw me away?" she asked.

"I do."

"I'd better introduce you to my parents soon."

"I don't want to get married at fifteen!"

She laughed. "You are funny, I never asked you to!"

CHAPTER SEVEN

TWO major newspapers dominated the market, and the government ran both of them. What the government wanted, the government got: a frontline propaganda machine. Yet the papers were also filled with quality literature, worldwide articles and pleasant everyday subjects.

Rami decided to go to the newspaper to collect the fees for his story. He was stopped and searched by security guards at the gates and then he was shown to the reception. He asked for the accounts department.

"Your name, please…?"

"Rami A, I had a short story published three days ago," he said.

After checking a number of papers, the clerk at the reception replied, "Oh yes, I thought so. I have a message for you from the chief editor. He wants to see you right away."

"Trouble…?"

"God knows. Have you met him before?"

"No never. What's his name?"

"Don't you read the paper? His name is always on the front page," the man said.

"Sorry, but I don't read the small print!" Rami smiled.

"Ha! Small print indeed! Wait until I tell the others that Mr Farruk is small print." He continued laughing until his eyes watered. "That was good. Be strong when you see him; stand your ground – whatever it is."

"Thanks for the advice."

"My name is Hassan…"

Rami followed the receptionist's instructions and went upstairs to the first floor. As he opened the door, the clatter of typewriters generated unbelievable noise. He wondered how people could work under such conditions. He had seen this on films, television and the movies, but this was even worse.

The room was vast; more than thirty people sat behind their typewriters hammering away. The air was filled with smoke, and like a cloud, it filled the top half of the room, although few windows were left open.

"Excuse me, please, where can I find Mr Farruk?" He asked one of the ladies who was busy typing.

The woman's face filled with horror. She didn't speak, but pointed to the end of the large office.

"Thank you."

She nodded. "God help you! He's in one of his funny moods," she added.

Like an obstacle course he reached the far end of the room, avoiding empty chairs, small trash bins, legs stretched out to the full, even what it seemed like a broken typewriter left in the middle of the walkway.

"Good morning, you must be Rami? I am Iman, Mr Farruk's secretary, he will be with you shortly. Please take a seat."

"Thank you."

He glanced quickly around the room; it was very well organised and tidy with filing cabinets covering almost three walls. Iman was in her early forties, with motherly comforting features. She seemed friendly and well-respected hence the few telephone conversations and the three journalists who came asking her for advice.

"Is Mr Farruk in a meeting?"

"Not exactly," she answered. "You will know it's your turn when Farruk starts to shout, and the other person walks out and slams the door behind him."

A few minutes later, Iman raised her head up, looked at Rami and whispered,

"Here we go! This is rubbish."And Farruk's voice from the next room repeated that. Rami giggled, and Iman continued, "What do you think this is? A women's rights leaflet or Superman and Batman comics? This is a newspaper, get this in your skull, get out, and don't ever come back with rubbish like this ever again."

Rami laughed, "Shush…wait for this!" Iman said.

The man walked out, and Farruk shouted, "Don't slam my door." The journalist turned towards Iman to complain no doubt, but another shout from the other room, "Get back to work, Iman has far too much to do than listen to you!"

Sure enough, that was what happened. As soon as the man walked out, she turned to Rami and said, "Do I deserve ten out of ten?" Rami decided then that he liked her; she was funny and pleasant.

"Next!" Farruk shouted from the other room.

"Be forceful," said Iman.

Rami knocked on the door and walked in.

"Yes? What do you want?" Farruk asked from behind his desk, without even raising his head.

Rami decided not to speak until he at least looked up and showed respect.

"Well? Speak!" said Farruk.

"I'll come again when you'll have time to waste. After all it was you who sent for me!"

A shadow of a smile crossed Farruk's face. Rami didn't see it as he turned towards the door to walk out. "What's your name, son?" Farruk asked, examining the boy quickly from behind his thick-framed glasses.

"Rami…"

"Sit down, please." It was more of an order than a request, but Rami sat down as Farruk fired his next question. "What have you got to say about all your success?"

Rami was silent.

"Well?" Farruk demanded an answer.

"Having one short story published doesn't make it a success."

"True very true, open that box there; go on, open it," Farruk said, pointing to one corner of the room. "You might be surprised to know that those are letters from readers about you, Rami. Some were sent by post; most of them were delivered by hand. Some want to hang you, but the majority want more and more of your writings; not forgetting those who sent money."

Rami was puzzled as he opened a handful of letters. "Are they all about me?"

"Yes they are. How old are you?"

"Fifteen."

"Good God! I thought maybe eighteen or nineteen; you look so much older."

Farruk was in his late thirties, yet he looked much older, with his olive complexion, brown hair, and thick-framed glasses.

"How long have you been writing?"

Rami quickly told him about the American school and Ahmad, who, it turned out, was a mutual friend. This made Rami feel more at ease. He handed over the notebook which he carried with him everywhere. Farruk in turn read a few of pages quickly to assess Rami's ability.

"Fantastic. This is quite simply the best I have ever read," Farruk said.

Rami had never expected such a compliment. "Thank you very much."

"You're welcome. Now, if I were to offer you a freelance position here.... I'll pay you well; more than anyone here. Say twelve dinars per story? And eight for everything else? What would you say?"

Rami's brain began calculating sums. "How many can I publish in a week?" he asked.

Farruk laughed. "As many as you want, as long as they're good." He was still laughing as he added, "Your face is a picture! Go and give Iman one of your stories to type and be sent downstairs. Is that all right with you?"

"For starters, yes; thank you."

"Okay. That's done." Farruk stood up and shook Rami's hand; the deal was done.

Rami couldn't believe what had happened: one of the most influential men in the country had just shaken his hand.

"Now get out of my room; I haven't got the whole day to waste," Farruk said loudly, but smiling.

- - - - - - - - -

Rami was pleased with himself and the progress he made over the first four weeks. The newspaper became his second home, and Farruk accepted all his submissions without hesitation, making him a regular daily feature. He also obtained a pass for the reference library at the paper, which helped him with new ideas.

Nadia couldn't cope with his success. She was afraid of losing him; afraid he would be a target for all eligible females, and afraid she wasn't good enough for him. All this created tension between them. She argued over anything, which affected his concentration. She continually questioned him, asking what he was doing, who he talked to, and why was he late, even if it was only a few minutes.

It became unbearable, and he began to find excuses not to go to her house. In the end, he decided to break up with her.

The day he left her house, leaving her crying, he didn't look back. He was free again, but promised himself never to get tangled in that situation again. That day, he sat in his bedroom writing an article for the newspaper.

He wrote, 'Who dares point the finger? Who dares speak the truth? Who dares change and modernise our society, so we can function as a unit with other societies in the world.

Our society hides its beliefs and traditions in a jewellery box, and buries it deep in the ground; afraid someone might discover how false, untrue and unrealistic some of our ideas are. It is a society based on contradictions, lies and fear. It gave its individuals one choice: accept or die.'

Rami smiled as he thought that his article, if it was published, would be like an unexploded mine. He went downstairs feeling pleased with himself.

"Oh. You are here?" his mother commented sarcastically. "Must be your belly?!"

"I love you, mum; you're the best."

"And you are very hungry?"

"And that…" He gave his mother a kiss.

"You treat this place like a hotel. I hardly see you."

"I know. I'm sorry, but soon I will be back at school, and you'll be fed up looking at me."

His article was never published, but after reading it over and over again, he decided that it would have done him more harm than good. However, his ideas and style seemed to strike a chord with everyone. The critics praised him one minute, then hanged him high the next. Letters of support and condemnation from the public poured into the newspaper. In all, Farruk loved the interest that Rami created. No writer in the history of the paper had ever made such an impact.

Rami was loved by all the journalists as he created a new atmosphere, full of laughter and joy. Yet many deep discussions, debates and healthy arguments went on too. He was treated like a newborn baby from the minute he walked into the building until the time Farruk threw him out. In a way, he motivated others to write better articles, and he also interfered with almost every issue or subject. They all valued his opinion and his input.

Farruk used to stand by the office door watching Rami giving instructions and directions to other journalists three or four times his age, and with far more years of experience.

"Oh no…! This is terrible! Be more direct and don't hide the truth! No…no…no…you will have all the women in the country screaming at you. Tell them what you think men have done over the centuries; at least you will have the men screaming. Farruk will be happy with that! Don't show him this and put him in a bad mood, please!"

He talked to everyone on his way to see Farruk and if he noticed him standing at the door his remarks and advice changed.

"For God's sake! What do you call this? This is a newspaper, not an adventure magazine!"

If Farruk wasn't there he went to Iman's office, throwing her a kiss or hugging her. Sometimes he would sit on her lap and hear her complain, "Farruk might see us!"

"He knows we're having an affair."

Then, without knocking, he would go into Farruk's office, collect his mailbox from the corner of the room, carry it to the sofa and, without saying a word, start reading the mail. When Farruk finished his work, he would greet Rami, who handed him his latest writings for approval.

Farruk was satisfied with the changes and thanked his young writer, but not in so many words. The newspaper seemed to have been very quiet in the past – apart from chief editor shouting and screaming – a few reports, very few phone calls or letters, and the government's daily announcements. But now, people were phoning, writing and trying to find this mystery writer. Farruk was fair, and published both types of letters: those that praised Rami and those who decried him.

That day, Rami read several letters and split them into two piles. "I've had enough of this!" he announced. "I am not sure this is what I want to do!"

When Farruk raised his eyes and looked at Rami, he saw he had tears running down his face. He hurriedly left the room, and came back with a glass of water.

"Drink this. You'll feel better. Maybe the heat got to you."

"Farruk, I am not enjoying this attention and fuss. Who cares?"

"I do, because I am your editor, and everyone does because they make the time to write to you or about you."

"I am only fifteen; I want to do what fifteen year old boys do: play in the street, hide in corners waiting for young girls to pass by, then chase them and make nasty remarks. Whistle to get their attention, and if I get the chance, I'll pinch their bottoms. I want to be me…me and not some manufactured copy of someone else. I want to have pocket money, just a little pocket money; enough to buy a packet of cigarettes a week and when they're smoked, I'll be begging everyone to lend me money."

"I really don't know what to say, my young friend."

"Exactly…! Everyone expects me to be different even you; even Iman and those journalists outside. I need someone to mother me, instead of me mothering everyone. Do you see me as a fifteen year old?"

"No. I never did! You have quite a lot of money you haven't drawn out yet, though."

"I know, but what the hell do you expect me to do with it? I don't need it now, what am I going to spend it on?"

Farruk understood what Rami was going through. "You have enormous energy inside you. Even writing at this intensity isn't using all of it. You need to stimulate that thick brain of yours!"

"How?"

"There is a whole world out there. You walk through it every day, but you have forgotten how to focus, observe and absorb. You stopped seeing, and you simply became obsessed by yourself. Rami, you forgot what you were all about."

"What was I all about?"

"I know I am right. You came a long way; you're one of the best in the country, and sometimes it's very hard to stay at the top. Your mind, your way of thinking, is that of a much older person. So, be a mature person."

The phone rang. Farruk answered it. "It's for you, Rami."

"Hi…it's me."

"Hello May, how are you?" He was surprised to hear her voice.

"Your mum phoned me just now, looking for you, and I told her you had gone shopping for me," she explained. That wasn't the first time she had covered up for him. "She gave me an address, and said you should go there." Rami used Farruk's pen to write it down.

"Did she say anything else?"

"No."

"Thanks, May. I'll see you later, bye."

Rami looked at Farruk and said, "That is strange – very strange!"

"Maybe it's just what you wanted…something to occupy your mind."

Rami braved the heat wave and left. Different thoughts crossed his mind as he walked to the mystery address. He rang the bell, and turned round to admire the well-planned garden at the side of the house. He turned towards the door, as it opened.

"Wow!" That was the only word he could manage as he looked at the woman.

"Can I help you?" she asked in a Lebanese accent.

"My mother gave me this address. I am Rami."

"Hi. Come in before you melt in this sun." She could see he looked puzzled, and added, "Don't worry; I won't eat you."

"I wish…"

"I am Elaine. Please, sit down."

He tried to thank her, but lost the power to speak.

"Close your mouth, Rami, before something flies into it," she said

"Huh?"

She was laughing, "I was told you are a good actor, do you fancy a drink?"

"Yes please, anything will do as long as it is wet and ice cold."

As she left the room, he started thinking. Ahmad was in Lebanon, and he might have sent him a gift! He tried hard to guess why he was sent to this house by his mother.

She came back into the room. "It's my first visit to Baghdad," she said. "Have a drink. That will cool you down, I promise."

"You are my first one too – I mean, my first Lebanese." He giggled.

"You are just like Ahmad described you."

"I was just thinking that, but then I thought no, it can't be something to do with Ahmad. He has no taste in anything – especially women; there must be an explanation somewhere. Now I am very disappointed, as he proved me wrong, and he knows someone as beautiful as you," Rami said sarcastically. "No, it can't be the same Ahmad that I knew – no way."

"He also said once you open your mouth, you don't give a chance for anyone to butt in."

"He lied: you managed it."

"You are worse than he described you." She laughed.

"How is he?" Rami was serious now. "He is my best friend. He made me, and taught me everything I know."

"He said you were the one who inspired him to write his last three books."

"Lies! Old habits never change. Where did you meet him?"

"I didn't…my sister did," she said.

"Thank God for that."

"Is she as beautiful as you?"

"She is very pretty, Rami, and that's why he married her."

Rami felt as if an ice cold glass of water had been poured over him. His face changed. Mixed feelings overwhelmed him; he was happy, yet angry because he hadn't been told.

"Are you all right?"

"The bastard. I will never ever forgive him for this. It was a really mean thing to do without telling me. I wasn't even his best man. I'll kill him when…"

"You will kill me when you see me." A voice came from behind him.

Rami leapt up, not knowing whether to laugh or cry. He hugged Ahmad tightly, shouting "You bastard! Why didn't you tell me? God you look so good, I am having a heart attack."

"You haven't changed; still as crazy as ever. I just can't believe how tall you are. God, I missed you too, my friend."

"Rami, this is my wife, Jean." Jean was standing next to her sister laughing at the two friends.

Rami looked long at her face, and then looked at Ahmad. "You are made for one another; you are so beautiful together. Now, Ahmad, close your eyes while I hug your wife."

Jean laughed. "Now I have two men to look after me. What a lucky woman I am!"

"I never thought you had taste, Ahmad! But I have one complaint."

"What's that?" Jean asked.

"I never got a hug or a kiss from your sister."

"I was wondering when you were going to ask for one," Elaine laughed.

"Are you hungry, boys?" Jean asked, but it was also an excuse to leave them on their own.

"I am starving," Rami cried out.

"He's exactly what you said, Ahmad," Jean commented. "Come on sister give me a hand, please."

Rami was almost crying with happiness. "Tell me everything, come on…the whole story."

"We met a few months ago and fell in love. She is a Catholic, and I decided to become one so I could marry her," said Ahmad. "After all, I have no family, while she has — so why upset them. We decided to come back because of the war and the closeness of Israel to Beirut. We were married last month but we didn't have a big celebration, and with the help of my cousin, we bought this house a week ago. Rami, we decided to get everything done quickly so we could spend valuable time catching up. And Elaine, she has been a rock…she never stopped for one minute helping us."

"I could have helped, too. It's good to see you again; you have no idea how much you have helped with your letters."

"How is it going?"

"Okay, I suppose. I have a lot of money, which I haven't used yet, because I don't know what to do with it. Farruk accepted every story, poem or article I gave to him and I've been invited to different sodalities to read my poems and short stories."

Elaine came out of the kitchen. "Ahmad, you have been ordered to the kitchen to put your magic touch on things, while I take Rami and show him the rest of the house."

"Is he really only fifteen?" Jean asked.

"Yes."

"He looks much older, but he is a very loving person and funny. He is so famous too, yet he's so down to earth, so fragile, so insecure and so lonely." Jean said.

"He's changed a lot. It's amazing…he has hardened up so much, and he likes your sister," Ahmad concluded.

Upstairs, Elaine and Rami were touring the house. "I love it all. You have achieved so much in such a short time," said Rami.

"Much of the furniture came from Lebanon. Everything fitted in perfectly," Elaine replied

"I am so glad you're not his wife!" Rami suddenly said.

"I am someone else's wife, though."

"Damn. Are you?"

"Yes…and I am twenty six!"

"I don't believe that! You don't look it."

"I am also the mother of two lovely girls."

"No!"

"Yes," she said. "We had better head back now. I think food is being served."

They made light-hearted conversation as they ate. Jean was happy with her house. She could now make new friends and invite them home. She was also happy in the company of Rami and her sister. Elaine, on the other hand was different, she felt very warm and loving towards Rami. Despite his age he was intelligent, a good listener when he wanted to be, and she was looking forward to being on her own with him. She needed a shoulder to cry on, and his was exactly what she was searching for. But, would she dare tell him her life story.

Ahmad had his concerns, and he was angry with Rami, but it was not the time or place to start lecturing him again.

"I read all your writings; we used to get the newspaper every day, even if a day late," he said.

"I read all your books; they were excellent," said Rami.

"They were rubbish compared to yours. They had no heart; no feeling."

"People bought the books and loved them, Ahmad, you never ever were satisfied with your own writings."

"People bought them, bought my name."

"You're never satisfied! You don't believe in yourself."

"Do you believe in your capabilities? Do you believe in yourself?"

Rami took a deep breath. "I believe in my writings; they are good enough for me."

"What are you two discussing now?" Jean butted in. "Am I going to listen to this for the rest of my life?"

Rami and Ahmad looked at each other and burst out laughing.

"I missed Baghdad; I ached inside to come back. There is a saying that once you drink the sweet water of the Tigris, you always come back for more," said Ahmad

"You were missed, my friend," Rami said.

"Slow down a bit, Rami! Slow down and pace yourself. You aren't in a race here; slow down or you will burn yourself out."

"Yes, whatever you say!"

Ahmad gave Rami a warning look. "The papers are full of you. The media doesn't talk about anything or anyone but you – not just in this country, but abroad as well. But you just sit there as if you haven't got a care in the world."

"What do you want me to do? Yes I am famous like you; I am making lots of money, more than a university graduate. How many writers can say that?"

"You were given a chance. How many pieces have you published so far?"

"More than thirty; I don't know. I made lots of money, and that's in only two months. I started on twelve diners per story and article, and eight for a poem. But I twisted Farruk's arm to accept them, and he pays me more now."

"I wish my husband could earn that!" Jean confessed.

"How can you write so many?" Elaine butted in.

"I never wrote that much in my life!" Ahmad admitted.

"Oh, come on, Ahmad! You write books, which is different," Rami said. "I can just sit here, switch off completely, and write two or three stories, all different ideas. I find it strange myself, as if I am describing a clip from a film. I just write the first line to start with; I don't plan anything, and I don't know what the ending will be."

"What if nothing comes to your mind?"

"I'll read a book, or maybe a newspaper or magazine. Just one word might trigger something in my head. My brain is weird; I could be working on three stories at the same time. I can write walking from the house to the paper, and by the time I get there, Farruk will be reading it."

"I wish I could get a job like this – I need the money," Ahmad said, and this captured everyone's attention. He didn't usually talk about money matters; they were taboo and very private. He even kept them from Jean.

"Can you do me a favour, please, Ahmad?"

"Yes. Sure."

"Could you drive me to the newspaper, please? I will only be there for two minutes."

"When?"

"Now is a good time."

The building was ten minutes away by car. Rami went in, and withdrew all his money out. There was over eight hundred dinars, much more than he had expected. He counted five hundred, and put it in an envelope.

Later, they all sat in the living room talking, with Ahmad and Rami planning where to take Elaine and Jean to show them different places.

"Jean and Ahmad, what would you like for a wedding gift?" Rami said suddenly.

"Being with us is enough, my friend," Ahmad said.

"You are so sweet," Elaine commented.

"I know you have something on your mind, and no matter what we say, you'll win," said Jean. "I love table lamps in every room, and candle holders. You could buy me one of each, if you like."

"I have no idea what your taste is like, plus I haven't got the time to go shopping," said Rami, thinking hard how to say what he wanted, without offending them. "Promise you won't refuse my present?"

"I promise…if it makes you happy," Jean said.

He took out the envelope and handed it to her. "To the most beautiful couple in the world; I love you both very much." His eyes were moist as he watched Jean open it and hand it to Ahmad.

"No, Rami. I will refuse this," said Ahmad. "Sorry, but there is no way in the world…I just can't, Rami…"

A few tears ran down Rami's face as he looked from one person to the other in search of support.

"You can't buy friendship," Ahmad said.

"I don't need to, you're all I have in the world. You are my best friend and Ahmad if it wasn't for you where would I be? Playing in the streets, or ….."

"This is a man's wage for months," Ahmad explained. "It's your hard work, day and night; all your hurt, laughter, pain, disappointments and elation."

"And he is giving it to you both." Elaine came to the rescue. "Why not…? Don't take this happy moment away from him." She held Rami's hand tightly, and said to him, "You are a special person." she added, "And Ahmad, I am sure you would do the same for him."

Rami felt a large lump in his throat. Ahmad and Jean stood up and hugged him tightly.

"Thank you; thank you very much, but on one condition," said Ahmad.

"What condition?" Rami quizzed.

"I'll treat you for a night out."

"Brilliant! I love dancing."

"So do I…" Elaine added.

"Can I choose where to go?" Rami asked.

"No!" they all chorused.

CHAPTER EIGHT

SEPTEMBER 1967. The country was in a state of anarchy, the government could no longer govern and the police could no longer police. The economy was in tatters. Thousands of people were unemployed; especially university graduates. Many people were emigrating. The war against the Kurds in the north of the country took its toll, draining the economy even more. Extra arms and armies were moved into the area whilst the rest of the army was still in Syria and Jordan after the six days war. Rami found it hard to understand the political situation, and its effect on the society. The treasury was empty, due to very bad planning of the economy, and the government's high officials lining their fat pockets and their Swiss bank accounts with taxpayers' money. No one knew who tied the knots and who untied them. Many projects were left unfinished, and many plans and designs were left gathering dust on high shelves in various government offices.

There were no investments in industry or agriculture, and the black-market controlled what was left in the economy. People were waiting for something to happen, something that will change the future.

For the first time Rami thought about his future, passing exams to him was easy, but studying the right subject in university was very tricky.

The government decided to add an extra year to the secondary school to solve the unemployment problem, also as a measure to slow down the number of graduates. This brought more hardship to the ordinary families, as they were eagerly awaiting their sons and daughters to complete their studies and so be available to help with everyday expenses in running a home. New taxation laws were introduced, but as usual the poor got poorer, and the rich were unaffected. The government was running out of ideas to control the economy.

The underground Parties were getting stronger by the day, with support coming from outside the country. More and more people joined those Parties, in an attempt to defeat the government. The two main players were The Baath Party supported by Syria and the West, and the Iraqi Communist Party supported by the Eastern Block Countries especially the Soviet Union. Rami sensed the tension at the newspaper, and understood some of the problems through talking to Ahmad and Farruk. There was un-described fear that many journalists joined different parties, but no one dared confess to it. Rami began to take matters much more personally. His writings became more intense, trying to influence the situation and people's beliefs. He wanted to reach ordinary people, who may not have been able to write, but could listen. He used simpler words and images, and superb story lines.

- - - - - - - - -

Elaine was fascinated by Iraq's rich history and despite being conquered throughout the centuries by one army or the other. There were so many sites to see, Babylon and the hanging gardens, Kussra and the ruins of the Persian

Empire, Samerah and so many others. Elaine and Rami borrowed Ahmad's car to explore beauty spots and monuments, and drove for hours. Rami loved history, and became the perfect tour guide. They barely slept, since as soon as they got back to the house they went out again after a quick shower and change of clothes. Sometimes Jean and Ahmad went with them to some of Baghdad's nightclubs and restaurants.

One day Rami walked into the kitchen holding his head with both hands. Ahmad, Jean, Elaine sat around the coffee table.

"My God…! Oh, my head!" he said.

"If you're looking for sympathy, maybe you could try next door," Jean laughed.

"Thanks. Who needs friends when I have you?"

Elaine handed him a dark coffee. "This will either cure you or kill you," she said.

"How did I get here yesterday?" he asked.

"You were carried in at four in the morning, you drunken useless ass!" said Ahmad.

"You promised my parents you would look after me, not let me get drunk! You failed, Ahmad, and failed badly. I will never trust you again," Rami teased.

"That is rich, coming from you! What happened to the 'thank you' for the good time you're having?"

"Thank you, uncle Ahmad. I'm going for a shower."

"You'd better; you stink of alcohol. Do you fancy going swimming?"

"I never say no to swimming," said Rami, leaving the kitchen.

"Why the long face, Elaine?" Jean asked.

"I wish I didn't have to go back. I'm living a dream at the moment; a dream of happiness. But all good things must come to an end…I suppose. I need to get back in case he dies."

"Yes…but remember whatever you decide to do, Ahmad and I will support you."

"Thanks, I wish I could make plans about Joe. It's only a matter of months; I should've listened to mum and dad before marrying him, and then there are the girls. At least they are getting good education in Syria with their aunt. I do miss them though…I miss them a lot."

The three of them were in deep thought, until Rami walked back into the room and announced he was ready. "God knows where you get your energy from!" said Jean. Soon, everyone was happy again.

Baghdad international-size swimming pool, next to the Presidential Palace, was run as a club, only open to families who were members. Men weren't allowed in unless accompanied by a female member of their family.

Rami and Elaine went off on their own, exploring the vast complex.

"I am going to miss you when I get back to Beirut, Rami," said Elaine. "Thank you for a wonderful holiday."

"I will come and see you."

"Yes…you will be welcome."

She wished at that moment he would do more than just make polite conversation. For the last couple of days, he had shown no warmth towards her. She didn't know what she had done wrong, and wondered whether or not to ask him.

She felt alive in his company; a feeling she had lost many years ago. She wanted to hold his hand, sit him down and tell him how she felt. But she wanted him to make the first move; to hold her tightly to him, and never let go. Sometimes, she felt she could walk next to him, grip his arm and squeeze, but she never had the courage, she was afraid that she wasn't capable of coping with her feelings.

When they left the swimming pool some three hours later a beggar sat by the entrance. This was a familiar sight for Rami, who saw them all over the city, but it was different this time as he stared at the old man. He didn't know what struck him, or came over him examining this particular beggar. He was bare footed, and his clothes were tattered and colourless, with layers of filth. The man's skin was dark brown, burnt almost charcoaled by the summer sun, and wrinkled by the cold winters. He looked at Rami, and his face became one of humility and revulsion with himself. He turned his face away, staring into the distance. He looked like a naughty dog hiding from his master, and seemed about to cry. The white of his eyes turned into yellow filled with long awaiting tears, his eye lids were almost shut together from squinting in the sun. Slowly, he turned his head and faced Rami, who gave him ten dinars.

The man looked at his hand, then turned his eyes and looked at Rami, "You are a king, and you will stay a king for the rest of your life, but be careful of the snakes in your way; they bite very hard," the beggar said. "Kill them and don't be afraid...go now and enjoy yourself, my son, my king. May God be with you all the time. Go now, and never look back."

Ahmad appeared behind Rami and led him away.

"Come on let's go."

As they walked towards the car park, Rami turned and looked back. The man had vanished, leaving behind a wet patch where he had sat.

Rami was quiet all the way back to the house, and the others respected his silence. They understood how deeply he cared about certain people and events, and this was his way of fixing them in his mind. As soon as they reached the house Rami picked up his pen and notebook, sat at the dining room table and began to write. The other three sat in the living room watching him, whispering to each other to avoid distracting him.

"Look at his face, and the intensity of his expressions," said Ahmad. "I've never seen him like that before."

"Simply amazing," Elaine commented.

"He is gifted."

"I love him; I really do love him," Elaine confessed.

"I know...I do as well," Jean whispered. "I just hope he doesn't die before he has had the chance to tell the world everything that's inside that brain of his. I know now why Ahmad protects him all the time. He is so precious, naive, innocent in so many ways, so different to others of his age."

"We always fear for those we love. Nothing will happen to him, or to you or Elaine – or anyone we care for. We can't live our lives fearing that something might happen one day."

"Does he know about Jo?" Jean asked Elaine.

"No!"

"So tell him. What are you waiting for?"

"How can I? What do you want me to say? I love you, but I am eleven years older? I love you, but I have a husband and two kids? I love you, but I live in a different country?"

"I think he knows, Elaine!" Ahmad remarked. "The choice is his, not yours."

"He knows I have a husband and two girls...but that's all."

Elaine went to the kitchen and made sandwiches, took some to Ahmad and Jean, and the rest to Rami.

She sat facing him across the dining table. "I love you," she whispered.

He put his hand over hers, acknowledging her presence, and continued writing. She watched him, as if with fresh eyes. Her heart felt as if it was to stop as she thought that she had less than two weeks left with him, and beyond that, who knew what the future held for her. She closed her mind to the thoughts, and was just about to kiss him when his sudden move brought her back to reality. He tore off the first few pages and passed them to her. "Read this, please."

Soon, Ahmad quietly joined in, followed by Jean.

'I was sitting cross-legged on the pavement, with my open hand stretched out. I managed to tuck my bad arm inside my torn jacket. 'I'm hungry,' I cried time and time again. I repeated it many times, whether to myself or out loud. I no longer cared or felt anything. I lost all my sense of being. I waited and waited, turning my head away. I cried with no tears; those have long since dried out. No one cared anymore, and I cried silently to myself until I fell asleep.

It was dark when I opened my eyes. The only way to kill the hunger in my stomach is to sleep. I looked down at my hand; there was nothing but ash, cigarette ash. I thought someone had stolen my small earnings while I'd been asleep, but what did it matter now? Everyone steals from beggars: even other beggars. I struggled to my feet, and went in search of food, dragging my paralysed leg behind me.

It was very late, and the streets were empty except for the street sweepers and others like me. I searched everywhere for a scrap to eat, but as always, someone had beaten me to it. I yelled with hunger. I tucked my arm properly, dragged my leg in position, I smiled to myself to the routine I developed in crossing the road. Strange sounds were coming from behind a closed door. I turned round and headed towards it, but there was nobody there. Hurriedly I adjusted myself, and prepared myself for action. My good hand didn't move, I wanted to knock on the damn door, but my stupid hand refused. I was tired; I had no energy left. I desperately needed to tell someone there that I was hungry.

Suddenly the door was opened, and a strange man put his head out first, followed by the rest of his body. He examined me for a long time, from the top of my head to my feet. One of his eyes was covered with a black piece of cloth, the poor young man must have lost his eye in an accident, I thought. His hair was twisted to one side, and a coloured piece of cloth covered his forehead. His clothes were weird. I had never ever seen anyone dressed like that in my life. People can wear what they like, and it was no business of mine to ask. He lifted the black patch away, and examined me again. I thought if I was amusing him that much, he could carry on as long I got something to eat.

"I'm hungry; very hungry." I turned my face away and cried.

"Man, you are the best I've ever laid eyes on. Everyone will go crazy when they'll see you," he said happily.

I looked at his face and whispered, "I am hungry; please help me."

"By the look of your clothes and body, you look like you haven't eaten for years. You are really great."

He pulled me in and closed the door behind me. It was dark inside, and I nearly tripped and fell down the stairs as he pulled me along behind him.

"Man, you are the best one here"

I nearly fell again, but I managed to balance myself on my rotten stick. At last we reached a deep hole, and it was dark, too, except for some coloured flickering lights. It took my eyes a while to adjust, and I quickly examined my surroundings. I don't understand for the life of me how people could live in a place like this. There were hoards of people. He pulled me into the middle of them all, so they could all see me. I felt like a prize animal in a ring.

He shouted, "Look here everyone. I think I found the winner. Don't you think he is great? Isn't he simply perfect?"

"He is great!" someone shouted.

"Beautiful!" said another. I had never been called that before.

"So realistic!" It went on and on.

I looked around me; everyone was staring, yet they were smiling, which was a relief. They wore strange clothes that I had never seen before. I thought maybe I had slept for so long that I had travelled in time.

"Come on, man. Tell us who you are?"

"I am a beggar, and I don't mind you looking at me, but I am very hungry."

Everyone laughed at me, and more of them sat on the floor beside me.

"Get him some food. What do you want to eat?"

"I piece of bread will do me, "I replied politely. Although I am a beggar, I do have manners.

"Oh…he is good, he is perfect."

Three or four of them came back with masses of food. There was chicken, meat, vegetables, and more food was placed next to me on the floor.

"Is this all for me?"

"You did say you were hungry, my friend!"

I was afraid to touch anything, but one of the girls handed me a piece of chicken. I didn't want to upset her, so I nibbled on it.

"Amazing…he is just like the real thing."

"Ye," someone agreed. I was quiet; it isn't polite to speak with food in your mouth, or eat with it open.

They were good people; happy people, and enjoyed my company.

"Don't you find it difficult using one hand?"

"The other hand is paralysed, sir."

"This is getting better and better. You should be in the movies. You look and act like a real beggar."

"But I am one, sir," replied.

I didn't care why they found me so amusing. After all, they were the first people who had cared for me and treated me well; like a human being.

They gave me something to drink. It wasn't to my taste as it was sour, so I asked for water. Several of them rushed to bring me some. I couldn't have asked for better treatment in a hundred years.

"You have a lovely place here, Interesting!" I thought it was time to be sociable; I wasn't shy or afraid anymore.

"Would you like more to eat? You said you were hungry, and you didn't eat much!"

"No thanks. I had more than enough, thank you. My stomach has got used to only a little. May God be with you all."

"He is the winner; no doubt about it."

"What are you going to eat tomorrow, beggar?"

"God will provide," I replied.

One of them came back with a paper bag and filled it with different foods.

"That's for tomorrow, my beggar."

"Thank you. You are a king, and you will stay a king all your life. Be careful of the snakes as they bite hard; never be afraid to kill them. Thank you, my king. God will be with you, so go now and enjoy yourself." I smiled in his direction as he disappeared into the crowd.

A young lady came and sat next to me. She asked, "Are you real?"

"Yes, I am real."

She was wearing a necklace, and I couldn't take my eyes away from it, "They are real, too," She said.

"What are they?" I asked.

"Pearls you fool pearls!" She laughed.

"I have never touched real pearls before."

"I shall easily solve that problem." She started to pull at my crippled hand, which had no feeling. "Touch them," she ordered.

I gently touched them with my good hand, but at the same time, she jumped backwards and screamed at the sight of my crippled one.

The pearls were scattered on the floor, and I was left holding two of them. Everyone was staring at me; all with different expressions on their faces. If only she had not persisted in pulling my bad arm. It wasn't my fault for being a cripple. I was crawling on the floor, trying to pick her pearls, but I couldn't see very well so I hauled myself up, and managed to switch the lights on.

Everything around me stopped and froze: the music the people, everything. They stood there like statues. I collected all the scattered pearls, and placed them in her palm.

'People don't move except to the sound of drums, and under flickering lights,' I said loudly.

I struggled up those narrow stairs to the entrance; I nearly fell backwards once or twice. I was just about to leave when I remembered that I had forgotten to switch off the lights, leaving them stranded like statues, but it was a long, long way down those dangerous stairs.'

Rami waited until Jean had finished reading. "Well?" he asked.

"Well what?" Ahmad said. "It's brilliant; simply the best you ever wrote. A couple of mistakes, but brilliant."

"How on earth do you plan your story? I love it," said Jean.

"I don't! I don't even know what my next paragraph will be. I don't dictate the story – it's the other way round."

"That was beautiful, just beautiful."

They read it again, and Ahmad corrected a couple of mistakes. "This is a bomb about to explode; I would love to see Farruk's face when he reads it," he remarked.

"Come with me tomorrow and see for yourself."

CHAPTER NINE

THE short story 'The Pearl Necklace' was published twice. At first, Rami thought it was a mistake and decided to go to the newspaper office and find out. Ahmad went with him; it was time he met Farruk again.

As they walked into the journalists' office, everyone stood up and clapped. Rami was thrilled, and pretended to leave his autograph on every table as he walked through. He also pointed at Ahmad, and said that this was the man who had made him.

Iman and Farruk stood by the door, laughing at Rami's antics. The laughter grew as Farruk shook Ahmad's hand and ignored Rami completely. Rami shrugged his shoulders, put his arm around Iman, and stayed in her room, while the other two went into Farruk's office.

"It must've been three years, Ahmad?" said Farruk.

"Yes indeed. How are you, my friend?"

"Keeping my head down and watching every step. It isn't safe," Farruk declared.

Rumours were spreading about the political underground parties and their activities across the country. It felt like something about to happen any minute.

"No, it's not, but thank you for taking good care of Rami. He is a precious friend."

"No need to thank me; he deserves it all. Incredible talent; amazing," Farruk said. "And what about you…? Any new projects in the pipelines?"

"I have a book I am working on, and I have applied for a teaching position." Ahmad answered.

"Come and work for me, in whatever capacity. Name your price."

"Thank you. I will consider it, and I will let you know."

"You do that, my friend."

Just as Farruk said that, Rami walked in.

"Talking about me, I hope?" he said.

"No, we are not. There are far more important subjects than you to talk about."

"Why was it published twice?" Rami asked.

"People phoned and asked us to print it again as the newspaper sold out," said Farruk.

"Strange!"

"The response was incredible; I wish you'd been here to see it. People were phoning to congratulate us; some wanted to see your photo, others couldn't get a copy. It went on and on, so we had to reprint."

"It's funny how people react," Ahmad commented.

"It's a distraction from their daily life," Farruk replied. "It touched something that they could identify with; I don't understand it either."

Suddenly Iman walked in and, before she could say anything, four men barged in as well. Farruk stood up and said angrily, "Who are you? What do you want?"

"Mr. Farruk?" one of the men said.

"Yes, that's me."

"This is my identification," said the man. The others also presented Farruk with their cards, which showed they were from army intelligence.

"What do you want?" Farruk asked.

"We are looking for Rami A."

Ahmad and Farruk avoided looking in Rami's direction.

"What on earth for?" Farruk asked forcefully.

"To help in our investigation, that's all."

"What investigation?" Farruk asked again

"I only have my orders, sir. I don't know." He turned to Ahmad and Rami. "Your names…?"

"In that case, you should come with us now." The man who seemed to be of higher rank said.

Rami stood up quickly. "You are looking at him! It's me you want."

"What a surprise. You'd better come with us."

Rami looked at Ahmad, then Farruk. "Don't tell dad!" he said.

"We won't," Ahmad replied.

Rami was taken away before he could say another word.

Iman ran into the room, crying. "What's going to happen to him?" she said. "Please…please do something quickly, before they kill him…please, Farruk."

The men were in a state of shock, but recovered quickly. There was a deafening silence in the journalists' office; the typewriters were silent at last. Farruk came out of his room, followed by Iman and Ahmad. He didn't have to gain their attention; they were all ears.

"I think I owe you an explanation," he said. "Rami has been arrested. We don't know the charges, but we have a newspaper to get out tomorrow. Every one of you has your own contacts in the government, police, secret police and army intelligence, so if you finish your work, and you want to help, there is your chance." Farruk's voice was shaky; his eyes were wet. "He is only a child; just fifteen."

Rami was blindfolded in the car, and driven for two hours before they reached their destination. He was kept on his own in a room with no furniture, except for one chair.

The building was extremely quiet. He tried hard to make out any sounds, but there weren't any. It had a distinct smell to it, which he couldn't identify it. He was terrified, wondering what he had done wrong.

- - - - - - - - -

Ahmad gently broke the news to his wife and Elaine.

"Oh my God…!" Elaine shouted.

"What will happen to him?" Jean asked.

"I don't know…I really don't know," said Ahmad.

"Rami is dead, isn't he? Isn't he?" Elaine persisted.

"I don't know...I hope not." Ahmad started to cry. "I feel helpless, I can't...I don't know what to do."

"Darling, pull yourself together. You'd better get back to Farruk once you've had something to eat."

"I'm not hungry, thanks."

Farruk was just finishing a conversation on the telephone when Ahmad walked in.

"Have you heard anything? Any news?" asked Ahmad.

"Nothing...it's very strange. Everyone I phoned said they would phone me back," Farruk replied. "Someone must know something, and they are hiding it from us. I telephoned Mr. Omar and told him what had happened. He promised to get in touch with all the people he knew, and promised he would help."

"What are the charges? What could he be charged with, for heaven's sake?"

"I don't know. I am phoning the president now." Farruk then tried, but the president was in a meeting with some foreign dignitaries, and promised to phone back as soon as he was free.

"I have no other choice, have I? I am after the big chief to solve this problem, and he owes me one or two favours. Ahmad, go home to your family, you look terrible."

"I feel responsible; I want to do something but I feel powerless. I want to scream. What on earth has he done? He is such a loving, gentle person – a really funny boy; helpful, sincere...you probably know him better than me."

"We all love him."

The two men sat silently for a while, and then Iman walked in.

"Any news?" she asked.

"No...nothing! There is no trace of his name anywhere. I tried the Ministry of Defence, and spoke to everyone I know, and nothing. I tried the head of the secret police, and also nothing. I really don't like this; nobody knows anything."

"I hope he..." Ahmad choked. He couldn't say what was on his mind.

The phone rang, and it was Omar, saying he would not give up the search. "He can't just vanish without a trace," said Ahmad.

"A lot of people are vanishing without a trace."

As the day passed, the journalists walked into Farruk's office one by one. No one wanted to go home, and everyone had exhausted all their contacts.

- - - - - - - - -

A table and four chairs were brought into the room, and Rami was ordered to get off the floor and sit on the chair facing the table.

An hour later, four men walked in. They looked the same: big built, with dark features, and heavy moustaches. This brought a smile to Rami's face.

"Wipe that smile off," one of the men shouted as he sat down. "There are two ways of doing this. Either you tell us everything you know, or..."

"What do you want to know?" Rami asked. "He didn't hear the answer, as one of the men punched him to the floor.

"Get up, and sit down."

"Don't interrupt next time," another man ordered. "You might not get a second chance!"

Rami showed no pain, and made no noise. "What's your name?"

"Rami A."

"Full name?"

"Rami A."

Another slap landed on the back of his head. Rami stayed calm, looking round to stare into the eyes of the man who had slapped him. Then, he turned to the man asking the questions.

"Your full name?"

"Rami A."

"You have written the story about beggars, and there are none in this city."

"They are everywhere."

A punch to his stomach made him think, he felt as if his heart stopped for a minute or two, he thought that if this was the treatment he was going to get, then it was time for him to get stronger.

"Who do you work for?"

"The newspaper; I am a freelance writer."

"Listen. I have just about had enough. I will get the truth out of you one way or the other. The story you wrote had endless meanings to it."

"It was only a story about a beggar; just a simple story. I am sure you have ways to find out everything you want about me."

"Don't get smart with me. Wipe that smile off your face, or I'll do it for you." The man shouted, "It's against the government, beggars and those who help are kings and so on."

"It's only a little short story."

The questioner punched Rami, knocking him to the floor. The rest of them repeatedly kicked and punched him.

"Now, who pays you to write this shit?" The man showed him a copy of the newspaper.

"The newspaper," Rami replied, tasting the blood in his mouth. "What am I supposed to have done?"

One of the men kicked him in his side. Rami felt an intense pain, as if his ribs were being torn apart. He wanted to scream with pain, but he didn't want to give them the satisfaction that they were getting the better of him. He doubted he could keep up his performance for much longer.

"Why are you against the government?" The questions began again.

"I am not against anyone. My name is Rami, and I am a freelance writer."

"How old are you?"

"Fifteen…! I was born in 52."

"Are you sure?"

"Yes."

"You are lying!"

"I am not; I am telling the truth."

They all took turns to beat him over and over again. He could not protect himself as the punches and kicks came from all directions.

They ripped his clothes off. His body was heavily marked and severely bruised. One of the men tied a rope round his wrists, and with the help of the other two, hung him from the fan in the ceiling. The man sitting behind the desk laughed out loud. "Now we'll see how tough you are. Does it hurt now?"

Rami's smile had long disappeared. They continued to use him as a punch bag, and he passed out several times, to be awoken by a splash of cold water from a bucket. He knew it was the end. He knew he was slowly dying, but he held his head high. He prayed for the first time in a long time.

He felt cold, even though the temperature was in the mid forties. He shivered violently; then he urinated, which was another excuse for the men to beat him. Now, they were using leather straps and metal chains. Then he heard the door open. "Your kebabs have been delivered," a voice said.

"Thank God for that. I am starving," said one of his tormentors.

They all left the room, laughing and giggling as if it was just a part of their daily routine. Another man walked in, and after switching the fan on, began firing a gun near the hanging body. Rami cried when that man left the room, because none of the bullets had found their target, even though he had tried hard to wriggle his body, hoping to catch one of them. Obviously they didn't want him dead just yet.

- - - - - - - - -

Ahmad and Farruk waited anxiously for any news from their contacts. The telephones rang, but with no results. Then, finally, Omar rang. His voice was full of disappointment.

"I can't get any definite answers," he said. "I have tried everyone; some people got back to me, and some didn't."

"Why? What has this child done?"

"He has done nothing wrong, Farruk, my friend, but it seems an issue of national security is involved."

"What? What does Rami know about national security?" Farruk shouted.

"No one wants to get involved. I really tried, but all the doors are shut."

"Then he will die, because no one can help. I suppose he'll be more famous now…"

"He is charged with high treason, and you know as well as I do what the outcome will be," said Omar. "If you interfere, then your turn will be next. What about your family?"

"He is my fucking family!" Farruk slammed the phone down. He was raging with anger, he felt like murdering someone.

"Iman…Iman," he called.

"Yes, Farruk."

"Get me Abdul Al-Rahman Arif."

"The president…? Right away."

Once connected to the presidential office, Farruk was told the great man was not available; that he was still in a meeting.

"It's seven thirty at the moment. I want the President to phone me back by eight, or I will hang out the government's dirty washing for everyone to see," he told the official. "Unless he phones, the newspaper will go out tomorrow with some spectacular headlines." Without waiting for an answer, Farruk slammed the phone down. He then looked at Ahmad, and burst out laughing from sheer anger and frustration.

"It's going to be a long night, I think."

"He's worth it. God will look after him."

Iman entered the office. "There is food on the table outside," she said. "I ordered for everyone here, so please come and join us."

"Thanks, Iman, but haven't you got a home to go to?" said Farruk.

"My husband said its fine by him," she replied.

Ten minutes later, the phone rang. It was the president. Everyone crowded into Farruk's office.

"Greetings Mr. President," Farruk said. "I meant every word, though; it is a matter of life and death." He recounted the events of the day. "If you want to punish someone, than punish me. He's only fifteen."

Farruk listened intently. "Thank you, Mr. President, he is like a son to me," he said, ending the call. "He is phoning me back. Go home and rest, and thank you."

- - - - - - - - -

Rami was eventually cut loose like a dead animal in a butchers shop, and fell hard to the floor. Another kick to the side of his chest, and he was left there.

"Let us know when you want to speak the truth," he heard someone say. Then another voice, laughing, "You're joking! He'll be dead soon," He heard them all leave the room.

His eyes were swollen, but through narrow slits, he looked around the room. There was nothing there for him to use to help him end it all. Despite the pain in his arm, he brought his wrist up to his lips, and bit as hard as he could. Tasting his own blood, he passed out.

He woke again as another bucket of cold water was poured over him.

"We came to say goodbye," a man said. "You will meet the experts soon; we've done our shift for today…have fun." He didn't realise that the original four were in the room, but as they walked out, another three men walked in.

"What have we got here? Check him out," one said.

Another opened Rami's eye and examined it. "He's finished; not long to go," he said.

Rami could smell meat burning; it took a while for the pain to travel to his brain. One of the men had stubbed a cigarette out on him, and the others had done the same.

"What's your name?"

Rami was silent. The man said, "I didn't hear you."

"Rami A."

"Good! How old are you?"

"Fifteen."

"Who do you work for?"

"Newspaper."

These men were experts in inflicting pain. They slashed his body with shaving razors, burnt him again with their cigarettes, and pulled four of his toenails out.

"He refuses to die," one of the men said, taking out a gun. "I've had enough of this. Shall I shoot him for mercy's sake? I think he's telling the truth."

Just then, the door opened and a man walked in. "Is he dead?" he asked.

"Just about...why?"

"Put him in the next room, and you can have a break. It's almost one in the morning. Go home and rest," the newcomer said.

"Thank you, sir."

They left him on a wooden coach wrapped by a dirty rag. A window was open, which was a god sent, as he took a deep breath. At last he could smell fresh air instead the moulded smell of the place. He passed out, and woken up much later. Rami opened his eyes but could see nothing.

He heard a man whispering to another, "We'd better get him out of here before he's finished." Then he felt a hand on his shoulder, and the man said, "We're taking you home now."

Rami managed to nod his head. He was carried to a car. "Where do you live? Where do you want us to take you?" he heard someone ask.

The man leaned forward, and Rami managed to give him May's address.

After a twenty-minute drive, they arrived and three men carried him through the front gates and along the driveway. They left him by the front door, running back to the car after ringing the bell.

CHAPTER TEN

MAY opened the door, reeling when she saw what looked like a pile of flesh lying there. She didn't recognise Rami at first, and then she screamed.

"Oh God no…no…please God, no…Hassina, come here quick."

She shook violently, and her heart was pounding. She couldn't move. Hassina came running. "Shall we take him inside, madam?"

"Yes, but be careful."

"Is he dead?"

They managed to get him inside, leaving him on the floor. May was afraid of moving him in case she hurt him further. Blood was trickling from many wounds. She felt his pulse, "He is alive…just," she declared. "Get me a mattress from the back room, and clean sheets."

As Hassina ran out, May phoned her husband and told him to drop everything and get to the house.

A bed was made up in the front room, and the two women gently carried him to it. Rami moved his fingers, and May grabbed his hand. He whispered a few words, but she didn't understand them.

"Rami…tell me again, baby," she begged, putting her ear against his mouth. "Phone Farruk," he said, and passed out.

"Hassina, get me some hot water and towels, and throw this dirty blanket away, please."

May looked long at this body that she loved. It was covered in cuts, bruises, cigarette burns, and dried blood. She burst into uncontrollable sobs that racked her body.

"Who could do that to you, baby?" she murmured. Hassina came back and they began cleaning him as gently as they could. "I love him, Hassina," said May.

"I know, madam; everyone does."

"Why would anyone do this?"

"Go and phone Farruk. I'll carry on here," Hassina said.

"Thanks Hassina, you're a god's gift to me."

In no time at all Farruk and Ahmad arrived. May took them to the living room. Hassina was about to cover Rami, but May stopped her. "It's okay; they are friends, and the weight of the sheets might hurt him."

The two men could not believe their eyes. Tears ran down their faces, and Ahmad knelt down by Rami's side. He kissed him on the forehead and, taking a clean cloth from Hassina, gently helped her to clean his body.

"Bastards! …animals! In the name of all the prophets, I will make them pay for this," Farruk said. "Is your husband coming, madam?" he asked May.

"Yes…I phoned him at the hospital," she replied.

"He needs urgent attention," Farruk said, and left the room.

They heard the front door open, and heard him weeping. Five minutes later, he came back into the room, accompanied by Samir.

"Oh Jesus Christ...! In God's name, why?" Samir could not believe his eyes. "This boy needs hospital right away."

"No, you can't," May cried. They all looked at her. "I found this paper in the dirty blanket they had wrapped him in. It said 'No hospital or you will be next.' Please, they will kill him there."

Samir carried on examining him. "He needs x-rays, and oxygen. I think he's got broken ribs; I need to get him to x-ray in case he has internal bleeding."

"Use my car; I have an estate," Farruk said.

"We need to cover him completely so nobody will see him," said Samir

"Thanks, Samir," said Ahmad.

"You don't need to thank me."

Samir made a long telephone call while Hassina and May made a soft bed for Rami in the back of the car. Ahmad and Farruk gently lifted him in. By then, Samir had finished his conversation, and followed them to the hospital in his own car.

Rami, covered by a white sheet so he could not be identified, was rushed in for x-rays, and then to an operating theatre, where a team of doctors and surgeons examined him.

Ahmad, Farruk, and the two women waited in Samir's office. It seemed like an eternity.

"What about his family?" May asked.

"I can't let him down. I'll find some excuse, or a story to tell them," Ahmad replied.

"Strange boy; he's more afraid to tell his father the truth, than he was of being beaten up," said Farruk.

More than an hour and a half later, Samir walked in, and sat down behind his desk. He looked mentally and physically exhausted.

"He's asleep and resting," he said. "We did our best, and the next twenty-four hours are vital. We have found a room in the isolation unit; he is to stay here tonight. At least we can monitor his progress."

"Thanks, Samir. God bless you," Ahmad said.

"I wish we could do more." Farruk added.

"What about that threat?" May asked. "What if they came back for him?" She was worried not for herself, but for Rami.

"I will stay with him." Farruk announced. "I have my gun with me, in case they decide to come."

"I will stay here as well," Ahmad said.

"You don't have to worry. He's been sedated, and won't wake."

- - - - - - - - -

Two days later, Rami was moved back to May's house. It took another two days before he opened his eyes for the first time, but he couldn't focus, and went back to sleep. In the afternoon, he opened his eyes once more and mumbled a few words. Then he slept again.

The following morning, May pulled the curtains wide and opened the windows, letting in some clear September air. Rami was awake. "Good morning, darling; welcome back," she said.

He looked at her in horror, realising what had happened to him. His voice was faint and hesitant as he said, "I won...I won'" He turned his face to the wall, and started crying quietly. He didn't cry because of the pain he was in, but the humiliation he felt. His dignity had been stolen away. His body shook uncontrollably as May sat next to him, wiping his tears away.

"That's enough crying for now, baby," she said, kissing his forehead. "A cup of tea?"

"Yes, please."

When Hassina came with the tea, Rami could not lift the cup to his mouth. He had no strength or energy. They had broken him both physically and mentally.

"May..."

"Hush. I'll help you. But drink this first and talk later; you must rest."

"I am very sorry."

"There is nothing to be sorry for."

"I need to talk."

"But not for long."

"How long have I been out?"

"Five days."

"Ahmad...does he know I'm here?"

"Yes, also Farruk. They have all been here. Ahmad's wife went to your parents and collected clothes for you. They said you were going on holiday with them. Your mum and dad were very happy to see the back of you for a couple of weeks!"

"Thanks."

"Iman came to see you yesterday."

"She is a real lady."

"Now go to sleep, and when you wake up, I'll give you a shower."

"May..."

"Yes darling?"

"You are my rock; thank you for saving my life."

May felt the tears burning her cheeks. She tried to control her emotions, but failed. She tried to speak, and tell him how she had been to hell and back in the last five days, but this was not the time.

"Have I upset you?" he asked.

She shook her head. "No...no, baby, you are just so sweet."

By the evening, Ahmad, Jean, Elaine, and Farruk, had come to see him and the bedroom was filled by his dear friends.

"Come on, sit up straight and eat! Stop showing off, now you're feeling a bit better!" May ordered, and everyone laughed.

"That's why I married her...she wears the trousers in the house," Samir teased.

"I was so hungry," Rami suddenly said, and everyone looked at him. "I could smell cooked meat, and I felt very hungry. But it was my meat they were burning. At first it didn't hurt, but after few minutes…"

"You don't have to tell us," Elaine said.

"No. Let him talk; let him get it all out," Ahmad interrupted.

"I kept saying to myself, this isn't happening; I'll wake up in a minute; it's not hurting really; it's all in the mind," Rami continued.

"I am so sorry," Farruk said. "I should have gone with them myself. I was a coward; everything happened so fast; I am so sorry, Rami."

"Not your fault, my friend, I was there too. We can all blame ourselves, but…" Ahmad remarked.

"I climbed on the table, and I jumped up, hoping to catch the bulb. I wanted to electrify myself. I fell after I knocked the bulb out, and hurt my knee."

They were quiet. They knew from the marks on his wrist that he had tried to commit suicide.

"I bit my wrist after that…I had no energy left by then."

"I am not surprised; you have two broken ribs, and so many hairline fractures. Your kidneys weren't functioning well; you were dehydrated, and we had to give you six pints of water," said Samir.

"The smell of that room was awful," Rami went on. "I realised that the holes in the walls were bullet holes. They fired their guns near me; they must have killed so many people there."

"Please have something to eat, Rami," May begged.

Elaine sat on the bed and decided to feed him herself.

"All they asked who employed me? You're not that popular, Farruk, because every time I said 'newspaper', I got beaten up some more," said Rami. They all burst out laughing.

"You have so much mail, it's unbelievable, and it's still coming in from all over the country," Farruk said.

"The bastard said to me as we left, 'no hard feelings, we were just doing our job,"

"No doubt you had to have the last say!"

"I did: I said, 'If I die, I will haunt you, and if I live, don't ever go to sleep; don't close your eyes for one minute, because I am coming to get you.'"

They all looked at each other. "I am not having talk like that in here, Rami. Put it behind you and try and forget. It might be hard, but try." May said.

"Do you need any stories from me, Farruk?" Rami changed the subject quickly. He did that whenever a conversation took a turn he did not like.

"Yes please."

"I will do my best," said Rami.

"You always did, son," said Farruk. "You always did.'

CHAPTER ELEVEN

TEN days went by and Rami's wounds were healing quickly, thanks to Samir and some old family recipes of herb and wild flower. The real wounds were imbedded deep inside him, and they had affected his behaviour. He was depressed because he felt powerless; he was short-tempered with himself and those around him, for no apparent reason. He understood these changes, but found them very hard to cope with or accept. He fought hard to bury the memories of that horrific day somewhere at the back of his mind, but it was impossible.

"How do I look, May?" he asked one day as she was rubbing his body with gel.

"You look great, thanks to my grandmother's advice," she replied.

"So do you still fancy me?"

"I do! I always did and I always will. Are you happy now?"

"I want to go home. I need to get back to normal," he replied instead.

"I know, but your face; your body...."

"No-one has to see my body, and as for my face, boys of my age do get themselves into mischief."

As soon as he walked through his own kitchen door two days later, his mother and sisters burst out laughing at the sight of his face.

"What have you done?" his mother asked, as she hugged and kissed him.

"You should see the other one," he joked.'

"It's more likely you fell somewhere, while you were just being you," his eldest sister remarked.

"Or ended up face to face with a bull," said another sister.

"You'd better have something to eat and disappear before dad gets home!" his mother said.

"I've done nothing wrong. It was a little accident: I slipped," Rami protested.

"I know, son. Are you hungry?"

"I am starving, and I love Dolmas." He had sneaked a look inside the cooking pot. Vine leaves filled with a mixture of rice and meat, with lots of garlic and lemon juice.

"Did you have a good time?"

"Oh yes! I re-generated my batteries; it's school next week."

"No, two weeks at least; the builders haven't finished yet," said his mother. "We had a letter from the school to tell us that."

"Good!"

"We must invite Ahmad and his wife for a meal. After all, he put up with you for all this time."

Rami had not talked to his family for a long time. He knew he had been treating the house like a hotel for the past few months, as his mother had always said.

"I am sorry, everybody. I haven't been good company recently," he said.

"Huh?" Everyone looked at him, before concentrating on their meal again. His mother smiled and nodded, as if to say, 'Thank God you're home, and safe.'

After lunch, he went up to his bedroom, turned on the air-condition, and sat by the window. He felt tired and weak after putting on such a major performance in front of his family.

Looking through his window at the palm trees in his garden calmed him down. He had missed his bedroom; it was so peaceful, especially when his younger brother wasn't about. He looked around the familiar room, thinking perhaps he might re-arrange it one day soon – but not at that moment. He locked the door, took off his clothes, and stood in front of the full-size mirror.

Panic overwhelmed him, he felt vulnerable and he hurried to his bed, covering himself up. His body shook violently until he fell asleep.

- - - - - - - - -

In the morning, he felt like a new person. He walked all the way to the newspaper, which took almost twenty-five minutes. At the door, the two armed guards hugged him, and one of them planted a kiss on the back of his hand: a sign of respect.

He took a deep breath, and opened the door. All the journalists stood up and applauded him. "Oh, sit down and do some work," he responded.

Iman and Farruk guessed what was going on and came out of their office. Iman walked up to him and hugged him long and hard.

"I promise you there won't be a next time. I'd rather die than…" she said.

"Thanks Iman; thank you."

He waved to everyone to be quiet. "Thanks, you lot. Now get back to work. What do you think this is? A Superman or Batman comic? This is a newspaper! Get to work, or else!"

Farruk laughed. He was lost for words. His Rami was back – and back to his old funny ways.

"Who is that?" Rami asked as he went into the office, noticing a new face. She was sitting typing, and taking no notice of the fuss.

"Our new journalist," said Farruk. "She is very dedicated to her work. But how are you feeling?"

"I am fine," he replied. "Thanks to you…!"

He entered Farruk's office, and threw himself on the sofa. He was tired, exhausted. He sat back, and fell asleep in a matter of seconds.

Farruk tiptoed out of the room, and told Iman to hold all telephone calls until Rami was awake. "He needs to rest," he explained.

"That boy is some man," said Iman.

"Yes. He's brave, too."

Rami woke up half an hour later, and went out to talk to the journalists while Farruk caught up with his work.

He strolled over to the new girl's desk. "Hi. I am Rami, and you are new here?" he said.

"Yes. I'm Farrah," she replied, without raising her head up.

"It is my pleasure to meet you," he said, angry that she seemed to be ignoring him. "No-one told me that you were starting work here," he added.

"Should they?" She looked up at him.

"No. But can I ask what you're working on?" He had taken an instant dislike to her. He only needed one answer out of place from her and he would explode.

"I really need to finish this," she said. "Please leave me alone, and go and chat up someone else; I am not interested."

For the first time ever, he did not know how to react. He turned to walk away, leaving the nearby journalists surprised and stunned.

But, he turned around, and said. "Who do you think you are to talk to me in that manner?"

"I am busy working, so please leave me alone."

"No. I want to know what I have done to upset you," Rami insisted.

She stood up and faced him. "I want to be left alone. Do you understand? I have work to do."

One of the journalists came to the rescue, and pulled Rami away. "Come on, brother; leave the lady alone. Farruk has been howling at her every day since she started here," he said.

"I am sorry," Rami said.

"You should say that to her, not me," the journalist replied.

- - - - - - - - -

As the taxi stopped outside Ahmad's house, Rami struggled with five boxes filled with mail. Elaine opened the door. "Good lord, Rami! Here, I'll help you."

She was thrilled to see him. She had had nightmares ever since she had seen his torn and beaten body. She closed the front door and stood examining him. Her lips trembled, and tried to stifle a cry of happiness. He turned around and took her in his arms, and hugged her.

"I am so glad you are here."

He kissed her face; her eyes. Slowly, their lips met for the first time.

"I love you," she whispered, pulling away to examine his face.

"I love you, too."

They had been fighting against this ever since the first day they had set eyes on each other. Now, their feelings erupted. He held her tightly, and his hand moved slowly towards her breast.

"Please, Rami...no...not yet!" she cried out, but in her heart she wanted more. She felt like a little girl being persuaded to do something for the first time. She tore herself away from him, and ran to the lounge.

Rami followed her. "I am sorry; really sorry, and I won't do it again," he said.

"Don't you understand? It has nothing to do with you; it's me!"

"Tell me..."

73

How could she explain? She had never been good at revealing her feelings. She couldn't tell him how she had cried all the time he had been away, thinking she would never see him again. She had prayed like never before for his safety. She had promised herself that she would tell him the truth; how much she loved him, needed him and wanted him. No matter how old he was, or how far apart they were, she would be his whenever he wanted her. But he had gone to someone else. Another woman had cared for his wounds; touched him, and felt every inch of him. When people had arrived, she had covered his body so no one could see what was hers. May had taken everything. Elaine felt there was nothing left for her.

"Elaine, I do love you."

She was crying.

"Tell me, please."

So, with difficulty, she told him how she felt; how happy she was to be with him; how proud she felt when they were together, and how jealous she had been when May was looking after him.

"Please don't laugh at me, please," she begged.

"May is a friend. She is more than a friend – she is my rock," Rami explained. "She is always there for me whenever I need someone; whenever I need a sympathetic ear, a shoulder to cry on or a slap on the face for misbehaving. She is my protector; my guardian angel. She has never judged me, and never will."

"Oh…and?"

"My love for you is white, blue, red, all the colours put together, and it is timeless and ageless; a mixture of happiness, anger, jealousy and passion. I know my age frightens many people, but I can't help that. I missed on being a fifteen year old, and I will probably regret that for the rest of my life, but I'd rather be who I am now."

"Have you finished now?" Her smile turned to a giggle.

"Ok…I know I get carried away, but it sounds good, doesn't it?"

"And true…! Come on now, let's open those letters." They went into the dining room. "You are funny Rami," she added.

"How?"

"You need to be constantly loved by everyone. You live to love and be loved; your life would be empty without love. If ten women loved you at the same time, you wouldn't say no to any of them!"

"No….but what man would?" he laughed. "I'd be a wreck, though."

They began opening the letters and sorting them into three piles: those who liked him, those who didn't, and those who had sent money. The last pile was growing faster than the other two.

It was always thrilling reading people's comments and opinions. Some had even sent him ideas, or stories that had happened to them. It was an amazing mixture. Shortly afterward, Ahmad and Jean joined them.

"Listen to this," said Ahmad. "Dearest, I sent you three cheques in the past, but you never cashed them, or said thank you. That is very ill-mannered, and also humiliating. I am a widow, and I have no family, so please cash the cheques."

"You should, Rami," said Jean.

"I will," Rami replied. "How much has she sent?"

"One hundred dinars…!"

"That is incredible! A university graduate earns less for two months' work."

"Well here is another for fifty."

"Good. I need it!" he announced to the astonishment of the others. They looked at each in disbelief.

"Why?" Ahmad asked. "You're making plenty from publishing."

Rami didn't answer; instead he pretended not to have heard the question.

"You must have nearly a thousand here, and this is only the second box," said Elaine, who was counting it.

"Money is power." Rami commented as he opened another envelope.

Rami never used to be bothered about money. He came from a wealthy family ,and to him, although money was important, it had not been essential.

"Beggars! Who would have thought that at last, someone had the courage to address the issue?" Jean was reading a letter aloud. "It's time for more input to try and resolve the issue of poverty."

"Very positive. My family and I enjoy your writings very much. Keep it up; we want to read more," Ahmad read.

"This is the opposite," Jean said. "Ugly, ugly and ugly," she read. "Mr. Editor, your writer is a joke. Glory is something a man gains through hard work, not by re-arranging a few words and phrases. Writing is a gift, and Rami isn't gifted; not in a million years. Writing is an art, and he is no artist. He is a joke, and a thief who stole his place in your paper, and also the ideas of others. His writings are meaningless, with no relevance to real life. No truth; no reality." Jean handed the letter to Rami. His hands shook with anger.

"This letter will be published in the paper," he said. "I know who it is from, I recognise the handwriting." His bottom lip tightened. "The bitch…she will pay for this, Nadia's hand writing."

"Whoever it is, she wants your attention," said Elaine.

"More money! You can take us out for a meal." Ahmad laughed hopping to change the subject.

Rami was raging with anger. He stood up and marched around the room.

"I'll kill her. I will kill her," he declared.

"What the hell is the matter with you?" Ahmad said.

"Nothing is the matter…just this stupid cow."

"You're in my house. Have some respect and try and to be thankful. What happened to you was terrible, and we all worried about you. But your behaviour is inexcusable. I want my house to be a happy one, and if you don't like it, you know what to do."

Rami knew Ahmad was right, but he could not face him just then. He opened the patio door and went out into the garden.

"That was cruel, Ahmad; there was no need for it. He is still trying to understand what has happened to him, and come to terms with it." Jean remarked.

"I'll go and talk to him," Elaine said.

"No. Leave him be. He needs to cry; he needs to go through the whole episode in his mind and learn to live with it." Ahmad said.

"Ahmad, he's crying in his heart." Elaine begged.

"Yes…that's anger!" Ahmad explained.

They carried on opening letters, looking out every now and then. Rami sat on the bench at the bottom of the garden.

"Ahmad. Do something for me, please?"

Ahmad did not move or speak. Jean was clearly very upset. "Are all Iraqi's as damn hard-headed as you two?" she asked.

Just then, the patio door opened, and Rami walked back in.

"I am starving," he announced, and everyone burst out laughing.

"You can be such a bastard at times, but no matter what, you are my best friend and I love you," he said to Ahmad.

"Are you buying lunch?" Elaine asked.

"I think I can afford it…I will treat you to masgoof!" Rami replied.

"What is that?" Elaine questioned him, as she never heard of the name before.

"Fish cooked by burning special canes that grow in a small island in the Tigris. The cane gives the fish flavour that is out of this world. You usually eat it with pickled mango and Arab bread."

"It sounds delicious."

"And Ahmad will go and get us one," he teased.

"Just one?" Elaine asked. "You're mean!"

"Ha! Wait till you see the size of this fish!"

- - - - - - - - -

"I need a favour; a big favour, Mr. Editor," said Rami the following day later at the newspaper.

"God help me. What is it now?" Farruk replied.

"I saw an apartment this morning, not far from here, by the Al-Masbah roundabout."

"And…"

"I want it," Rami replied quietly.

"You want what?" shouted Farruk, realising what Rami had said.

"I can't get it because of my age, but you could. And I have six months' rent here with me."

"Why would you want that?"

"Why not…? I need somewhere of my own to study, write, do what I want – and have sex," Rami explained.

"Have I got a choice?"

"Not really! Think of all the writings I can give you." Rami smiled.

"Okay. I will do it tomorrow," Farruk promised.

"No. Now, please! Here is the phone number, and you can sign the contract and get the keys in an hour."

"You had it all worked out!"

"Yes."

"I don't believe I am doing this. If you were my son, I would have killed you. I hope my wife doesn't find out; she'll think I have a mistress!"

"She won't," Rami retorted. "I already phoned her and told her."

Farruk made the call and they left the newspaper office, signed the contracts, and were back within half an hour.

"Thanks Farruk."

"Now, behave yourself."

"Yes, I will."

"Can I ask for another favour, in return for two short stories?"

By then, Farruk was laughing, and tears ran down his face. "Tell me."

"If Farrah has finished her article, can I borrow her for the rest of the day?"

"Why?"

"Research; nothing else, just research."

"Okay. Anything else?"

"No thanks, but I will think of something! Thanks, Farruk. You are more than a friend or editor."

Rami left the room and headed straight for Farrah. "Hi…"

"Hi," she replied.

"I am very sorry about yesterday."

"So am I."

"Are you busy?"

She looked at him and smiled. "Sit down and read this; I am almost finished."

Rami read it quickly, it was about women and a changing society, and within minutes, found two ideas which needed changing slightly; he knew exactly how to please Farruk. Farrah agreed with him and made the alterations, then took it to Farruk. Rami waited by her desk until she came back.

"He said it's good," she remarked happily.

"That means it's excellent."

"He also told me that you need me for research for the day."

"That is true, too."

"Come on…What you waiting for?' she asked. "What research are you thinking about anyway?"

He smiled as he sat in her car. "I need a woman's touch in decorating my apartment. Many shops in the city need help in advertising themselves, so if you write an article about them, I will get a nice discount, and you will be the editor for fashion and interior design. There is no one writing about these subjects in the paper, so it's a chance of a lifetime for you."

"You are weird!"

"Well, most of those places will give you discount on your purchases if you are interviewing them. The service will be spot on – maybe even the same day – and my flat will be furnished in no time. You will be famous overnight!"

"Ha! They told me to stay away from you." She was laughing as she drove to his apartment.

"Okay. If Farruk refuses my writings, you will pay me back somehow," she said.

"Deal…"

- - - - - - - - -

Three days later, while Elaine was driving Ahmad's car, Rami guided her to his apartment.

"Where are you taking me?" Elaine questioned him.

"This is my little castle… my domain!" Rami replied.

"You are crazy!"

"I'm crazy about you."

"Please don't be silly."

Rami handed her the front door key. "Come on, open it, please."

She did, and walked in. He followed with a satisfied smile on his face. He knew she would be impressed.

"This is yours? This is where you have been hiding for the last four days?"

"Yes! What do you think?"

"It's amazing. It's…what can I say? Remarkable!" She stood in the middle of the living room, examining every detail. Three shades of colour dominated the room: dark brown, cream and maroon. They complemented each other; giving a masculine, yet gentle feel to the room. Cream leather furniture added a relaxing, homely effect. "The kitchen is spacious, but I haven't decided what to do with it," said Rami. "Here, come and see my study. I haven't designed it yet, but it will have everything I need; a sofa here to relax on and read, books all around, and a nice table with green leather top."

"You look so happy, Rami."

"I've never had anything of my own before; never."

"Show me the rest." Elaine walked into the bedroom; it was the largest room in the apartment. It was dominated by a circular bed which had midnight blue covers to match the carpet and one of the walls. Elegant, yet simple wardrobes also showed that much thought had gone into designing the room.

"This is beautiful. I'm speechless. You did this in four days?"

"Yes…everything."

"How much did it all cost you? You have good taste, too!"

"It will look fantastic when I have some more money to finish it."

"No doubt you spent all that money?"

"Most of it."

"Why all this, though? Is it because of what Ahmad said the other day?"

"I was dreaming about it when I was at May's, and Ahmad made me realise that I need my independence, when he said I have nowhere else to take my rubbish mail."

"I love you."

"One more surprise. Have a look under the pillow."

She did, and found a small black box. Inside was a diamond ring. "This is too much, Rami!" she exclaimed.

She put the ring on, and it fitted perfectly. "It's beautiful! Oh, tell me I am not dreaming!"

"I want you to remember me when you go back tomorrow."

"Oh God!" She realised that the end of their time together was near. She was due to go home. "Thank you for giving me the most wonderful time of my life," she said. "You have made me laugh, cry, worry and dream, but most of all, you have made me feel alive."

Their lips barely touched at first, then as he got closer to her, he whispered, "I want you."

"I know…but you…" she stammered.

"Love me, please."

"I hope you didn't go to all this trouble just so you can make love to me?" she said.

"I did," he said, and lay back on the bed. "Come and lie next to me, please."

"No," She teased. "Ask me nicely." She began to undress slowly.

"Come to me, please," he begged.

"Ask me again. I want to know that you really want me," she replied.

He took his own clothes off, but his eyes were filled by her as she stood completely naked at the bottom of the bed.

"You are so beautiful."

"You made me beautiful," she whispered, as she got into bed next to him. She wanted him badly as her body gently touched his. Their lips met again, and her hand wandered over his body: feeling, touching, wanting.

His lips gently travelled to her neck and shoulders, and a small cry escaped her. She closed her eyes, waiting for the ritual to begin. She was glad she was lying on the bed, as shivers travelled through her body.

"God…! Don't stop! Please take me now," she implored.

His lips touched and explored every part of her; every curve, and every hidden place. He was worshipping that body, and forgot how to make love.

"Take me now, please," she whispered.

- - - - - - - - -

Reality caught up with them the following day.

At the airport, they stood looking at each other.

"Kiss the sea for me," he said. "I have never been to the sea."

"I will…"

They kissed goodbye, and she left the country. Ahmad and Jean went back to their home, while Rami escaped to his.

He went to the bedroom, sat on the bed, and tears ran down his face. He was tired and lonely. He felt he was in a race against time somehow, and was only just winning, though at that moment nothing really mattered. He was insecure, unhappy, and in desperate need for a change, a major change in his whole life. But, he didn't know where to start, where to begin making changes, and what changes he needed to make. He was confused.

CHAPTER TWELVE

RAMI'S world had turned upside down. With Elaine gone, he was lonely, and instead of going out looking for excitement, for more friends and companions to help ease his grief, he shut himself away. He seemed to be in a daze, which disturbed everyone. No matter what they all tried to do to help him, nothing worked. He was unapproachable. He was not interested in his surroundings or his studies, and did not even attend school regularly. Ahmad, who had accepted an offer to teach Arabic at the same school, was worried, but found excuses for Rami's parents about their son's recent behaviour.

Farruk refused to publish quite a few of Rami's latest works, but avoided any deep conversations, preferring to stay at a comfortable distance.

Rami's first monthly examination came, and he failed in almost all subjects. He had tried to study, but it was a waste of time; he couldn't take it all in and at the end, he had given up trying.

He climbed the stairs to the first floor to his apartment, six weeks after Elaine went back, and found Ahmad waiting for him.

"Hi Ahmad," he said, without even wondering how his friend had found out where he lived. He opened the door, and they went into the living room. Ahmad stared at the clutter and dirty ashtrays. A smell of stale tobacco filled the air, and he opened the windows.

Rami poured two glasses of whisky and handed one to Ahmad, without asking if he wanted one.

"Rami, it's three in the afternoon," Ahmad said.

"Yes. I know."

"What's going on?"

"Nothing is going on."

"Don't you dare bullshit me…!" Ahmad shouted, and went into the kitchen. He saw empty whisky bottles, dirty dishes in the sink, and bottles of curdled milk. The smell from the rubbish bin nearly made him choke.

"You're living like a tramp!" he said.

Rami paid no attention. He lit another cigarette, and re-filled his glass.

"No one can mend a broken glass," he muttered.

"Pardon? What are you on about?"

"I was thinking aloud."

"This is filthy; not fit for animals – let alone humans," Ahmad said.

"I have no-one to clean it up," Rami complained.

"Feeling sorry for yourself? Listen here…"

"I didn't ask you to come." Rami said in defence.

Ahmad began to clear the rubbish, and Rami had no choice but help him.

"We are worried about you. I am running out of excuses to tell your father where you are. Farruk said friend or not, if you keep up this hopeless performance, he won't publish any more of your work. He thinks it's childish, shallow, and very ordinary at the moment. Your schoolwork is appalling. You attend when you feel like it. I spoke to many of your teachers, and they couldn't remember seeing you in their classes."

"I am sorry if I am hurting anyone."

"You are hurting nobody except yourself; your behaviour is that of a nine year old. You are on a mission to destroy everything you have worked hard for. What's your problem?"

"Leave me be…" Rami whined.

"No way!" Ahmad responded.

"It's your fault. You made me an adult when I was just a teenager, enjoying a teenager's life," Rami retorted. He was silent for a moment, before adding, "I am sorry. That was cruel."

"Yes it was," Ahmad agreed. "Wake up, you fool! You have turned into a nobody; you're becoming history. People have begun to forget you. Look at yourself; you are drunk already. I don't care if you are or not, as long as everything is working for you. But nothing is, because you are neglecting every meaningful thing in your life."

Rami went back to the sitting room. Tears filled his eyes, and he looked out of the window.

Ahmad sat down. "It's Elaine, I know. I am not stupid or insensitive. I saw what you felt for each other, but I closed my eyes, hoping that once she was out of sight, she would be out of mind, too. I was wrong." Ahmad confessed, "But it wasn't for me to be judge and jury. I rather have love of any kind, than war."

"I miss her so much."

"You should have told me; talked to me."

"I know."

"She has sent you a letter." Ahmad handed him an envelope.

Rami did not know whether to laugh or cry.

"What do I do?" He looked at Ahmad. "What do I do?"

"She is no longer here; that's the reality, and you have just faced it for the first time."

'Dearest,' Rami read aloud. 'I hope all your plans are going smoothly. I hope you have been busy with your lovely apartment. Send me some photos of the place, with you in them of course, hahaha. Also send me some of your writings, as it is very difficult to find Iraqi newspapers here. I miss you very much, and look after yourself. My next letter will be longer. I love you.'

"The dream has ended. It's time to move on," Ahmad commented.

"I love her very much."

"She loves you, too, but she is there and you are here…what can you do about it? Nothing…!"

"I'd better clean this apartment," said Rami, and finally smiled.

"I'll help you."

"Go and get Jean, and we'll have something to eat here," Rami suggested.

"She has already cooked for us. I promised her not to leave here without you –dead or alive!' Ahmad laughed. "Let's clean up and go."

Rami turned to Farrah again to help him get his life in order. In the short period she had known him, she had grown to admire him, and also his taste in furnishing his apartment.

She admired him because he never said anything to make her feel inadequate. She found freedom within their friendship; she listened to him, and in turn he did the same for her.

She was honest enough to tell him the truth as she saw it, without going round in circles trying to find ways of criticising him without hurting him. They debated many subjects, but never with raised voices. Farrah became a regular visitor to his apartment, and he always had an answer to anything which was troubling her.

In return, she helped him come to terms with his own feelings, and cope with the outside world. They drove in her car in search of his beggar on odd occasions, when they had nothing else to do, but they never found him. Rami needed to see him one more time, but had to accept this would not happen.

It was time to move forward, and get back on track.

- - - - - - - - -

By the second week of November, Rami was well-known to every pupil at the school. He joined both the basketball and the volleyball teams, and proved how they had really missed him in their opening games. He caught up with his schoolwork, and impressed all his teachers. But his fame came from his writings, as he produced new work with new approaches, ideas, and images. He was on top again, which pleased everyone.

CHAPTER THIRTEEN

IN a small cafe on Saadoon Street, only ten minutes walk from Al-Sharkiah school, six people met one day. Two of them were teachers at the school; one taught chemist and the other, English. The other four were students. One of them was called Wissam, who was in the same class as Rami, and seemed to be their leader, as he answered all the questions.

"I did as you instructed me," said Wissam. "All four hundred and fifty names are here. I have already separated the names into different categories."

"Good. Have you made copies for us?" asked Mr. Sabah, the English teacher.

"I did," Wissam answered, handing them round.

"How many members do we have in the Party?" asked Mr. Ali, the other teacher.

"Sixty two, but we are working on many more."

"Excellent! Now check the names, and put different letters next to them to show if they are members, sympathisers, against us, and those you know nothing about; also if they are members of other political parties." Sabah instructed.

"We need to find leaders; young men who have the respect of others, and we need at least one from each class," Ali added. "We need those from the fifth year, so they would lead others, and support our cause."

After two hours, they ended up with twenty-six names. Sabah was pleased with their achievement and the effort they had all put in. "I need to know more about those twenty six, and we'll meet here in three days," he said.

"Yes, sir," Wissam replied.

"Arrange for a meeting with supporters from the fifth year; make it next week."

"You can count on us."

Three days later, the six met again. It was time to hear Wissam's report. "From the twenty six, we had fifteen who joined us without a second thought," he said.

"These are the workers." Ali defined them in four words, "Those will do anything you ask them to do, leaders and workers."

"Three were not interested, and we are working on the rest. One is Naim Jamil; he is seventeen years old, excellent with words, and able to express himself with authority. He is a good all-rounder; he could be a leader, and also established himself as the spokesman for his class. Many teachers seem to respect him."

"Good. What are his weak points?" Sabah asked.

Ali answered, "Money; the boy needs money." He lit a cigarette. "I say get him, but don't give him too much in case he turns out to be a greedy bastard."

"Fine. Who is the next one?" Sabah asked, and Wissam went through the list of names. Wissam had a lot of respect for Sabah, who at one time had been the Ambassador for Iraq in London, until he had changed careers. Ali, however, was feared throughout the Baath Party as being ruthless and short-tempered, with no respect for anyone. Rumour had it that he had killed many opponents; he had also been in charge of a torture house when the Baath Party ran the country in 1963. He always carried a pistol, even to school, and he wouldn't hesitate in using it.

Wissam had done his homework well; more than eighty pupils had joined his organisation, and under his command.

"Is that it? Or have you got more?"

"This one is puzzling me! Rami Aziz: he is a very interesting person."

"Yes; I agree," Sabah said. "His English is brilliant, too."

"Yes Sir. He came from the American school. Early in the year, he was very quiet and detached, and kept himself to himself. He also hardly attended school. Suddenly, everything changed and now he is the best in the class in all subjects."

Wissam looked at Sabah, who nodded as if in approval. He continued, "He joined the basketball and volleyball teams, and since then we have won all our matches." Wissam related the rest of Rami's history at the American school.

"What about now?" asked Ali. "And why have you spent so much time on him?"

"I was coming to that," Wissam replied. "I followed him everywhere he went. It wasn't easy, because he was always surrounded by other people. There are two subjects he won't discuss…"

"Religion and politics?" Sabah interrupted.

"Spot on, Sir! He's a very clever boy, and is only fifteen and a half. He looks much older."

"I'll check his file tomorrow," said Sabah.

"There is more, but I need another drink," said Wissam. They all laughed, and more drinks were ordered.

"Well? We are all ears," said Ali.

"I believe he has his own apartment, not far from here. I have often seen him going into the building, and standing by his window. He's there alone. He won the Writer and Poet award of the year at the Christian Centre. I've also followed him to the Al-Thawra newspaper a couple of times. How many famous writers by the name of Rami A. do you know?" Wissam concluded.

"This meeting is top secret," said Sabah "None of this must get out. From now on, you leave Rami to me; I want to handle this myself."

"Yes, Sir."

- - - - - - - - -

Ahmad was worried. All major underground parties were recruiting members at any cost. The Baath and the Communist were the most aggressive of all. Sabah had been trying to befriend Ahmad recently. He had indirectly questioned him about Rami, and when he got no answers, he had turned his attention to his old friend, Farruk.

85

"Sabah; please leave the boy alone. He isn't what you're looking for," Farruk pleaded. "I would've recruited him myself – we are on the same side after all."

"I tried with Ahmad."

"Ahmad is his best friend; his teacher and guardian."

"Now I understand why he avoided me, and never answered my questions."

"That boy has suffered more than anyone else of his age. He's very fragile, and if you think he's in control, I am telling you, my friend, he isn't."

"The party needs him. We need honest people like him."

"For how long…?" Farruk questioned him.

"What do you mean?"

"Until the day when someone tells him what to do; and he has no choice but to obey. Power my friend, and ranks within the organisation, and once someone is in, he won't be able to leave, and if he does, they will hunt him down."

"That won't happen."

"That will happen. You know it and I surely believe it will happen."

- - - - - - - - -

Ahmad was reading a play which Rami had written for the sodality, but he could not concentrate. "Tell me, Rami, have you been approached to join any political party yet?"

"No…not interested," Rami answered casually, and continued writing.

A few minutes later Ahmad asked, "Are you feeling better now?"

"You are funny, Ahmad. Come on, tell me what's eating you" Rami replied.

"It's Mr. Sabah," said Ahmad.

"You mean the English teacher? Charming man, and a good teacher. What about him?"

"He has been asking me about you. He is very high up in the Baath Party."

"Is he? I am not interested."

"It worries me when they begin asking questions," Ahmad said.

"There is only one answer they will hear from me," Rami replied. "I can't see myself believing in their policies. All those Parties are supposed to be for the good of the people, but really, they are only interested in themselves."

"You're right."

"What do you think of the play so far?" Rami asked, changing the subject.

"Very good," said Ahmad.

"Liar!"

- - - - - - - - -

During the next few days, Wissam became friendly with Rami. Rami found him a good company at times. But, he was on his guard, even though he did not know why.

A few issues about Wissam bothered Rami; other aspects he liked. Wissam had invited him to a birthday party at his house. His parents had been out, and there were around fifteen boys and only a few prostitutes at the party. Rami had left without anyone noticing. Sometimes, he had seen Wissam take people to one side and speak secretly to them, and this made Rami both suspicious and angry. Nevertheless, he also enjoyed good debates with him, and they often sat in his father's civil engineering office, which was close to the school. Sometimes, Wissam would politely ask Rami to leave, explaining that one of his father's clients was about to visit. Rami disliked this behaviour, which he found mysterious.

Rumour had it that Wissam was leading a group of students who were about to go on strike, and also that they had formed – or were about to form – a student union, whether the government allowed it or not.

"Have you got a death wish?" Rami asked Wissam one day.

"What do you mean?"

"Are you planning a strike? A revolt against the government?'

Wissam smiled. "I like the way you ask your questions," he said. "Yes, we are."

"Who are you?" Rami was playing ignorance.

"We are simply objecting about the extra year the government has added, and we in the fourth year are the first bunch to be affected. So instead of going to university after next year, we have to wait two years. That means for all of us, an extra year of not earning money to help with the family. A whole year in our lives are wasted because the idiots on top can't think straight"

"I know that, but do you think they will listen?"

"No, they won't, but it will rattle their cages, unsettle them, and be noticed both inside and outside the country. It will arm our people against this government, it will wake them up I hope."

"God…! You aren't stupid, so why tell me all this? Why do you trust me?"

"We need you to help us."

"Why me?" Rami questioned Wissam, "I have no interest in politics whatsoever."

"Rami. You are intelligent, smart, and respected by others. You are a leader."

"Not interested."

"You can't be a writer without being influenced by politics."

"Bullshit" Having a political interest in any one party would prevent me from being a good people's writer. Anyway, how do you know I am a writer?"

"I followed you."

Rami burst out laughing. "I love your honesty! I won't stand in your way; I will support your strike, but I have a limit."

"Great…would you like to come to a meeting at Dad's office?"

"Maybe…when?"

"Tonight at six," Wissam said.

Rami did not turn up. He was not, and neither did he want to show support to one Party and not another. He believed the Christians in the country would be better to concentrate on their education, and holding important positions in industry, research, economics, finance and business. To him, politics was a dirty game, and he knew he had to stay out of mischief in order to survive the turmoil in the country. He would keep his head high, but his eyes low. It was all about survival.

- - - - - - - - -

Three days later, the strike began and four hundred and fifty students marched through Al-Saadoon Street, heading towards the city centre. It was the first revolt since 1958, and people were amazed at the bravery of those few.

They were surrounded by police carrying hosepipes and canes, and fighting broke out. Many students were injured, and there were two arrests. The whole episode lasted less than an hour, and apparently went as planned.

The following day, all students in Baghdad schools went on strike in support of the two who had been arrested. Fighting broke out in various parts of the city. In some areas, police were involved, and in others, the army was called in. There were more arrests, and news spread that one student had died in custody. This sparked to a general strike in all the schools, and afterwards, in other major cities.

On the fifth day of the strike, police opened fire to disperse the protesters. Many were injured and killed. The hospitals were full of injured protesters, as well as innocent people who had got caught in the middle. It was what the opposition Parties needed; all the universities went on strike, followed by the workers and labourers.

Rami just watched everything from a distance. It was interesting to see how people behaved. Wissam stood beside him, as usual, observing, changing tactics, and ordering a retreat when necessary. It was a military operation carried out to the letter, without the use of weapons.

The following day, Rami was at home early evening, when Moustafa, a student in his class, came to see him.

"Wissam has been beaten up and arrested,"

"We went to his house two hours ago, and we heard his mother sobbing and screaming," the boy continued. "She told us he had been badly beaten, and had gone to hospital. But he was taken away from there and now, nobody knows where he is."

"Damn…I hope he's okay," said Rami.

"Do you know Jabber, the one who is always with Wissam? Tall boy in class C?"

"Yes, I've seen him."

"He's dead; shot by Special Branch."

"Good God! What next?" Rami was concerned about the government's heavy handedness.

"I think we will be calling the strike off."

"Why?" Rami asked. "Have you achieved anything?"

"We won."

"How…? We still have the extra year, and we still have the same government."

"We made people aware."

"Yes, but people are dead. Others have been arrested and possibly tortured, and…"

"It's a small price to pay. It was worth the sacrifice," the boy maintained.

Rami refused to accept that losing a life was a worthy sacrifice. A few days later, everyone was back to school and some kind of normality, but more than two hundred families mourned those they had buried. What could justify the death of so many innocent young men, he thought.

He sensed a change in the people's way of thinking, and also in their actions. They began to whisper amongst themselves; afraid to confide in others. Young men carried guns and other weapons, and no-one trusted anyone.

CHAPTER FOURTEEN

ALTHOUGH the majority of people in Iraq were Muslims, Christmas was celebrated almost as much by them as within the Christian community. Imports from other countries may have been limited by the government, but thousands of unusual goods always found their way to hundreds of well-decorated stores. New Year's Eve was the climax of the celebrations, when people in their thousands took to the streets in fancy dress, dancing and singing to a carnival atmosphere. There were no conflicts between Sunni and Shiites, Catholics, Protestants or Greek Orthodox. They were simply men and women of all ages having a good time, going from one house party to another until sunrise.

May and Samir travelled north to spend the holiday with their family in Mosul, while Jean and Ahmad went to Lebanon. Rami had no choice but to spend Christmas Day at home. It was traditional for the men to visit friends, neighbours and relatives, have a drink and eat chocolate, while the women spent most of the morning in church, before serving food they had previously prepared.

"I cannot see the sense in this," said Rami to his father. "They came to us this morning, and now we are going to their house. You aren't keen on them, and I only know them by sight. Why do we have to have such big family?"

"It's our tradition," his father replied. "They showed us their respect, and we are doing the same. You never know – they might even give you something stronger than orange juice!"

"You're blackmailing me, Dad!"

Rami's dad, Aziz, laughed, as they drove to visit some cousins.

"Please don't talk too much. Remember how many cousins you have!"

"I know!"

"How did my great aunt manage to have eleven?" Rami was laughing

"They had no TV or radio in those days!"

"Damn!" Rami was still laughing, enjoying this personal conversation with his dad. "They had good sex life instead, then?"

"How is school?" His father changed the subject.

"We are behind by more than a month, and the teachers refused to do overtime. I've been studying really hard, and I have caught up now."

"Good!" said his father.

"If I don't learn the basics, the next two years will be a disaster for me."

"Have you decided what college you want to go to?"

"Not really. It all depends on my Baccalaureate results," Rami replied.

"Here we are; number one cousin!" Rami's father laughed. "Only fourteen to go!"

- - - - - - - - -

As Rami was leaving Farruk's office the following day, Farrah walked in.

"Merry Christmas," said Rami. "What are you doing here?"

"Hi! I was bored at home, so I decided to come and finish an article," she replied.

"I'm bored too – all that visiting and being visited; making drinks and serving them. Not my cup of tea!"

"Thanks for my present," she added. "I'm sorry I didn't get you anything!"

"Don't be silly, I wasn't expecting anything," said Rami. "Anyway, I earn much more than you."

"Yes I know; people have told me!"

"Jealous?" He giggled.

"No...not at all, but something to aim for."

"Why are you bored?" Rami changed the subject. "Tell me; you never ever talk about yourself!"

"Nothing to tell..."

"Mystery girl! Let's get on with this article then."

"Yes, and then we can go for something to eat'"

Two hours later, they sat in a small restaurant by the river, on Abu Nawas Street.

"I always come here. I love the Tigris, but the Euphrates does nothing for me. Isn't that strange?" said Rami

"You are strange," she joked.

"Am I? Tell me about Farrah. Why do you never talk about yourself?"

"I had a bad upbringing, and if I start talking..." She paused.

"You will cry?" Rami asked.

"Maybe. I hate talking about myself, so it's better if you ask me questions," she replied, as she ordered her meal.

"Okay. Your mum and dad?"

"My real mum died when I was just over a year old, and my dad re-married some years later. He didn't have children with his second wife."

"I am sorry."

"Dad died four years ago; cancer, like mum. I fell apart; I have no family, apart from some relations somewhere in Europe, but that's all I know."

"What about your stepmother?"

"She...we tolerate each other. I suppose she loved dad, and she looked after him well, especially when he was ill. Sometimes I feel like shaking her up to try and get close to her. I was young when dad married her; she never ever interfered in my upbringing. We live together, and dad left enough money to take care of both of us."

"Boyfriends?"

"I've never had a boyfriend. I have a few male and female friends, and I'm not a loner. I'm in my third year of journalism, and I enjoy every minute of it. I love the little bit of money I get from the paper, but it's not as much as you!" She took a deep breath and continued. "I am nineteen, any more questions?"

"Would you like to come my apartment after this?"

"I'd love to."

"Aren't you afraid to be on your own with me?" Rami asked, fascinated by her attitude.

"No…should I? I don't mix with anyone at college, and that's the honest truth. The boys are only there so they don't have to go into the army, and the girls are there to show off the latest fashions. Many of my lecturers think they are lucky to find one good journalist a year. You are my only friend; that's if you want me to be yours."

"I am honoured."

"So you should be," she laughed.

They ate their meal quietly. Every now and then, Rami glanced at the boats and yachts as they passed by, while Farrah watched every movement he made. He had dozens of questions to ask her, but she was debating whether to ask him the one question that bothered her.

"What are you thinking about?" Rami asked.

"Are you a virgin?" she answered with a question.

"No! Why?"

"I am, but I'm not hung up on staying that way until the day I marry. What would happen if the right man did or didn't come into my life? Or worse, if he did and I didn't notice him at all."

"You are funny. I am sitting here in front of you, my love!" said Rami.

"Rami, you are a lovely butterfly; you will never settle down. I get on really well with you; I trust you, and I feel safe with you. I know you will never hurt me, I know you will never let me down, but…"

"I am three years younger?"

"No…I can't explain it. Anyway, I don't want to be tied to one person. I'm only nineteen, and I still have my life ahead of me."

"Come on. Let's go to the flat; I'll introduce you to my house cleaner."

- - - - - - - - -

When they arrived at the apartment, Um Ali, the house cleaner, was already there. She had been working for Rami for some time, cleaning the apartment twice a week.

"Hello Rami, how are you? Merry Christmas," she said.

"Lovely to see you," Rami replied. "This is Farrah."

"What a beautiful girl! You look so good together; so happy for you.'"

"She doesn't want to marry me, Um Ali. She said I am no good for her!" Rami remarked jokingly.

"Don't listen to him; he is teasing you. We are good friends," said Farrah.

"Still, you never know! My son thinks you are the best writer in the country," said Um Ali. "I think so too; he has read me some of your writings."

"So you know I am a writer?"

"Everyone in the building knows who you are." She paused, then added, "I clean for five of them."

"Good for you, Um Ali," said Farrah.

"I'll put the kettle on," said the cleaner.

"You do that, Um Ali, and then come and sit with us," said Rami.

"She is lovely! Where did you find her?" Farrah asked.

"I didn't; she found me," Rami replied. "She saw me leaving a couple of weeks ago, told me off for living on my own and not cleaning my flat, then that I should pay her five dinars a week to do it! That was it; I didn't have a say in the matter."

They were laughing when Um Ali came back with the tea. "It's good to see you laughing, Rami," said the woman. "But I haven't laughed for weeks now."

"You do look worried. Why?" asked Farrah

"It's my son; my only son. He is in second year at university, but something isn't right with him. All those strikes, and getting beaten up by the police and the army. Every day he goes out and I don't know whether he's coming back or not."

"Oh God! Has he got himself involved in politics?" Rami was concerned.

"I hope not! In two years time, God willing, he will be a lawyer. I even begged them to register him as the bread winner in case he is called for national service."

"That was clever of you," said Farrah. "Maybe they won't take him, or if they do, it could only be for six months at the most.'"

"I want to shout at him, but I am frightened he'll leave me and my twin daughters with no man in the house."

"I'm sure he would never leave you Um Ali. Where is your husband?"

"Killed in the war. It was his wish that Ali went to university. My son promised to teach me to read and write once he graduates."

"I'll teach you, Um Ali. That's no problem." said Rami.

"Allah blesses you! I don't know how to thank you."

Rami took money out of his pocket and gave it to her. "There you are. Um Ali; this is an advance on your wages."

"No! I said after a month, and after a month it must be," Um Ali insisted.

"Take it, please, and I will pay you more, too. The apartment looks lovely and clean," said Rami.

"Son, you can't throw your money around like that!"

"Its okay, Um Ali. Rami's got a lot more, and he is loaded." Farrah laughed. "I want to be his private secretary."

"You two are so well-suited. Ask her, Rami. She might say yes! Now I have to go. Thanks for the wages."

They both laughed after she left, at her remarks.

"She is a darling, and trying to match make us, aren't we the lucky generation?" Farrah commented. "She cleans houses; can't read or write, but managed to push her son to university."

"And the two girls as well, probably."

"Tell me about your family, Rami. You never ever talk about them."

"Dad is an extremely strict man," said Rami. "My mother is lovely; very gentle, cheeky, and loving. She's a brilliant mother. There are five of us; I have three elder sisters, and a horrible younger brother."

"So everything is your fault when things go wrong?"

"I am hardly there. I spend quite a lot of time here: studying, writing, listening to music, but I also make sure I spend time at home as well, otherwise dad would ground me."

"So they don't know about this place?"

"No! I am terrified he will find out; he doesn't even know I am a writer."

"Good God! What would he do if he found out?" She was intrigued.

"Scream his head off, probably. He never ever hit us. He simply doesn't like anyone doing anything outside the family surroundings; writing in newspapers means involvement in politics."

"Show me the rest of flat, please."

"I forgot…I love chatting to you."

"Me too," she agreed, as they walked into his study. "This is just amazing; you have such good taste. Look at those books, and your desk: I love leather. Where do you find all these things?"

"Shops! Come and see my bedroom."

"I love it, I love it," she said, as they went in. She sat on the edge of the bed.

"This is like you see in the movies, when the man is trying to seduce the woman without being obvious.""Is it submission as well?"

"Don't hint at things. If you want to be my friend, just ask straight out."

"Okay, deal. And the same with you?"

"Okay, no secrets," she agreed."

They laughed at each other. "Just like kids," said Rami.

She lay back on the bed. "I'd love to spend a night here," she said.

"Why don't you?"

Rami went to a cupboard, and came back with a key. "These are your keys; the entrance door downstairs, and one for the front door here."

"I can't afford this! I haven't got the money to share this with you," Farrah protested. She tried to sit up, but he pushed her back on the bed.

"It's paid for; everything here is paid for, and you don't have to worry about a thing," he said.

"Can I pay with love then?" She laughed.

"I don't know how to take that remark!"

"Rami, thank you," she said.

"The spare room is empty. Do what you like with it, and if you need money, just ask, okay?"

"Why are you doing this?"

"Lovers come and go, but friends are forever. You are my extra special friend," he said.

"You had better hug and kiss me before I start crying; you have made me the happiest girl in the world today."

"Would you spend New Year's Eve with me please?"

She pulled him towards her, and kissed him hard on the lips.

"Is that a yes?"

She kissed him again, allowing her lips to part and his tongue to venture in. That was the first kiss of her life.

New Year's Eve, Rami had been busy all day preparing for his party with Farrah. He wanted it to be a very special night; the start of a long and special friendship. He looked around the living room. It was lit by candles, the table was set by the window, music echoed softly and the food had been ordered from one of the top restaurants.

At last it was eight o'clock. The last half an hour had seemed to drag and drag. The bell rang and he opened the door.

"Hello beautiful," he said.

"Hello handsome, I thought about using my key, but changed my mind." Farrah replied, "Oh Rami! You did all this just for me?"

"Let me take your coat," he said. She let it slip off her bare shoulder. Rami's heart was racing. "What would you like to drink?" he asked

"I'd love a gin and tonic, please."

She looked around the room, which was filled with flowers and candles.

"Do you need a hand, baby?" she asked.

"I am okay, thanks. It's done," he replied.

"I am starving; I've been rushing round all day, and I haven't eaten a thing."

"Good! I am hungry too. Come on; give me a hand." He was smiling proudly as they lifted a tablecloth off the table.

"This is fantastic, and enough for an army," Farrah exclaimed. "You certainly know how to make someone feel very special. Oh Rami; I feel like crying now. Nobody has ever done this for me before. This food is just amazing; really special!"

"I love food and wine, and I love being different," said Rami.

"You are amazing! The freedom that you created for yourself terrifies me, and the freedom you have given me terrifies me even more."

"Try the smoked salmon, and those butterfly prawns," he urged.

"I'm going to try everything!" Farrah retorted.

"You'll pop!" he laughed. "These are called angels on horseback, by the way."

"What a name for a dish!" she said. "If you were thinking about going on to other parties, I would rather we stayed here. I have a surprise for you later." She looked outside through the patio door and commented, "The streets are getting very busy. It would be impossible to get back after midnight anyway."

"I agree. And I love surprises," he said happily as he ate.

"I want to get drunk, for the first time in my life," she suddenly announced.

He re-filled her glass, and his, and continued eating. He had ordered a variety of European dishes as well as traditional. He loved his aubergine dip (Baba Ghanosh), Humus, kebabs, and local bread.

"Would you like to dance?"

"Yes." She stood up and walked into his open arms. "Thank you, slow dance only will do, I am stuffed."

She wrapped her arms tightly around him, and allowed her head to rest on his shoulder. "You are mine tonight. I can tell you all these things without…"

"Hush…I want to listen to your heart." He said.

She kissed his neck at first, and slowly her lips travelled to his. She pushed herself harder against him as their lips parted. He kissed her neck and bare shoulders. She stretched out her hand and switched off the lights. The room was lit only by candles and the coloured lights of a Christmas tree.

His hand moved to her breast. She did not stop him, but reached behind her and undid the zip of her dress.

"Enjoy!" she whispered, as she let the dress drop to the floor. She was completely naked underneath. "This is your surprise."

He was speechless as he took a step back to examine her body.

"Do you like what you see?" she asked.

"I adore you, simply perfect," he replied.

She began to undress him. "Is that your heart I am hearing?"

"Mmmmmm," said Rami.

"Sit there and watch." She stepped back and looked down at his manhood. "Let's see how hard this will be."

She started dancing; twisting and turning before slowly sinking to the floor. Her eyes never left his, except when they travelled down to his manhood. She felt as if she was floating on air. Her hands moved down to her body, caressing her breast, teasing her nipples, and travelling downwards. Slowly, her legs parted. She touched herself gently, and her body arched as she began to stroke rhythmically.

Rami tried to move. "Not yet!" she managed to say.

He could no longer contain himself, and his hand moved down his body to grip his erection tightly.

"I did that to you," she said, smiling. "Take me now, please take me now."

He knelt next to her on the floor. "You are some woman," he said.

"Not yet," she begged. "Let me touch you; I have never touched a man before; never kissed, never played, never felt like this. Let me love you, just for one night."

He rolled over to lie on his back. She kissed every inch of his body; she kissed his lips again and again, and went back to her own adventure. Her body shivered, and she moved on top of him, positioning herself for him to penetrate her.

"No, Farrah," he protested.

"I want you inside me," she said, kissing his face and lips again and again. "You are so special; so gentle and thoughtful. I am yours tonight. Tomorrow, I might not be able to look you in the eye, so take me, please. Don't make me beg."

She lowered herself, anticipating sharp pain, but there was only love. Every part of her responded to him, and ached for more. His mouth, his gentle fingertips, his body – every part of his body moved and explored. She cried out and moaned, wanting more.

"Don't stop. God, don't stop!" She screamed, as the end was almost there. "Oh Rami…" Her body exploded in waves of feeling.

She was glad it was over. She wanted to lye back and let her breathing to return to normal, but that wasn't to be. He did not allow her to come back down to earth, but instead took her higher and higher.

Finally, it was over. "Happy new year…!" He smiled.

"Is it already? Happy 1968, my extra special friend."

They suddenly heard music and singing in the street. He went to the window, and saw hundreds of people dancing on the roundabout in front of the building.

"Farrah, come here and see what we missed."

"Did we miss something? I don't think so," she replied. "Take me to bed. I am shattered: you are some lover! And bring some drinks and a plate of food."

"I'm going to have a shower," Rami replied.

"I'll come and join you."

Afterwards, they fell asleep, curled up in each other's arms. It was almost four in the morning.

- - - - - - - - -

Rami woke up mid-morning. He stretched his arm out, but Farrah wasn't there. He went to the living room; she was sitting staring at a cup of coffee in her hand.

"Farrah, what's wrong?" He asked as he knelt next to her.

She lifted her head and looked at his face, stroking it gently.

"Is it to do with me?" he asked.

"Yes; everything to do with you," she said. "I just can't believe how perfect everything was; I was hoping I wasn't dreaming."

"You weren't dreaming," he said. "Kiss me, please."

"No! Go away; you haven't cleaned your teeth yet," she teased.

"What are you doing today?"

"I have to study a bit, sort out my room at home, and bring some of my stuff here."

"Good…I might go to a party. Do you fancy coming?" he asked.

"No, you go and enjoy yourself. I'll be okay."

"Farrah…"

"Yes?"

"Thank you."

CHAPTER FIFTEEN

FARRAH became a regular visitor to Rami's house. His mother treated her as one of her own, while Rami's two sisters accepted her as a friend and companion. What amazed the whole family was the attention Rami's father had paid to her. He spent a lot of time showing her his marvellous collection of stamps, which was considered one of the best in the Middle East. They also spent much time walking in the garden, where he showed her his collection of roses and bulbs.

"Mum…I think if Farrah moved into my room, and I move out, you won't feel sorry for losing a son, but happy for gaining a daughter," Rami joked.

"He is jealous," his mother said, "He is totally jealous of you, Farrah."

"He is my best friend," Farrah replied. "I wish I had a family like yours; I am the jealous one."

"But you have, and don't ever forget it. This is your home, and you can come and go as you want, my dear."

"Thank you," said Farrah, winking at Rami as she gave his mother a kiss.

- - - - - - - - -

It was the second week of February. Nabil picked Rami up from his house to go to a birthday party for one of the members. On the way there, he told Rami the bad news that the sodality would finish within a month, unless it was completely re-structured. Rami felt guilty, partly for not having finished writing the play he had promised. Nabil assured him that he wasn't to blame.

"Re-structuring is the answer; a new look, mixed sodality; modern…that's the answer," said Rami.

"That's a possibility, Rami. I'll sleep on it, and come back to you when I've decided," said Nabil.

At the party, Rami was discussing the future of the sodality with some of its members when suddenly, he sensed someone staring at him. He looked round to see Nadia standing close by. "Well…well…well! If it isn't the big modern-day critic," he said

"It seems you are still full of shit," Nadia retorted.

"Oh really? Did you discover that on your own, or did someone help you with it?"

"I actually came to say hi and sorry, but I can see you haven't changed. You are still as arrogant and selfish as you always were!"

"Nadia, you are the one who wanted me hung in the city centre, or have my head chopped off, because all my writings are poison."

"That wasn't me."

"I know your handwriting and your style."

By that time, several people had gathered round them. "I won't stand here to be insulted by you," she said.

"Push off somewhere else, then. You are free to disappear," he retorted.

She was raging with anger, wishing she had a glass or bottle to smash into his face.

"You think you are the best in the world." She spoke with a controlled voice, making sure that everyone would hear her. "Best in the country, best lover, but hasn't got a clue about love. The only love you have is for yourself."

"Teach me then…teach me," he taunted.

A friend had stood quietly beside her until then, but now asked her to leave. Nadia would have none of it. "I am not leaving; I haven't finished with him yet," she said.

"Come, Nadia, time to go," her friend suggested.

"No! I hate him with a passion." said Nadia.

"It's a fine line between hate and love, my dear," said Rami.

"I wish you were…"

"Dead? I am leaving anyway, so you have a nice time." Rami had to have the final say.

- - - - - - - - -

Some days later, Rami was sitting talking to Farrah at the flat. He told her about the episode with Nadia on the night of the party.

"Do you love her?"

"No…I don't hate her either, but I hate what she wrote about me," said Rami. "I know I publish them just to get back at her. I feel there is unfinished business between us. She wrote many letters disliking what I wrote, but they were full of hate, and nastiness."

"Why don't you phone her?"

"I can't…what do you want me to say? Sorry?"

"Yes…for starters. Why not? Ask her to meet you, maybe here."

It took him a few minutes to gather his courage and dial the number.

"Hi Nadia…how are you?"

"What do you want, Rami?"

"I am sorry. That's all I phoned to tell you."

She didn't answer, and he spoke again. "I want to see you and talk to you."

"I don't…we said our goodbyes," she replied.

"Wait. Don't go; I am really sorry," he said.

"I really don't believe what I am hearing! You must be lonely, or sick!" Rami was silent.

"Are you okay? This doesn't sound like you," she said.

"Will you come?"

"I'll think about it."

Rami gave her the address and phone number, and put the phone down.

"Is she coming?" asked Farrah.

"She said she would think about it."

"In that case, she will come."

Over the next few weeks, Rami spent most of his time at the apartment, studying hard and trying to catch up for the time lost during the one-month strike. He told his parents that he was studying at a friend's house, the library, or Farrah's place. When he got top marks in the monthly and mid-year examinations, he escaped his father's eagle eyes.

Farrah joined him most days. She had moved many of her possessions to the spare bedroom, which she had converted to suit her. Rami called it 'the mad room'.

They spent hours talking, studying and sharing interests. Farrah was in her final year, and in less than five months, she would be a fully qualified journalist. However, she was finding the work tough.

Farrah found Rami's company very stimulating, and his input had helped her immensely. Their friendship grew deeper by the day, and Rami refused to let her contribute towards any expenses. His argument was that he was earning a fortune, while she was struggling to keep her car on the road. Many times, he sneaked into her room, and hid twenty or thirty dinars in it. She pretended that she had found money she had forgotten about, so she didn't hurt his feelings.

She appreciated and believed in his freedom, and adopted it herself. They never mentioned New Year's Eve again. They needed each other in so many ways that sex wasn't the number one priority at that time.

They created a daily routine. Thursday night was for going out dancing, or for a meal at a restaurant. Fridays they would spend most of the days at Ahmad's, and on Sunday it would be May's turn, after church in the evening. Rami explained his relationship with May, but Farrah never questioned him about it.

Rami could not imagine his life without Farrah. She brought him so much laughter; so much satisfaction with her antics, such as wandering around the apartment with hardly any clothes on, singing one minute, talking to herself, or even shouting abuse at an author. There was nothing shameful in her actions. Every move she made came across as being natural.

One afternoon at the beginning of March, the bell rang. Rami was studying in the living room, while Farrah was stretched out on the floor in his study.

Rami opened the door. "Nadia! What a lovely surprise. Please do come in."

"I am very sorry about everything, please forgive me. The doorman opened the door for me downstairs," she said, "Oh my God! What a fabulous flat you have!"

"Glad you like it. Please do sit down, and I will show you the rest later."

"This is luxury! I am glad you're spending your money wisely, and not wasting it.'"

"Thank you…we need to talk and clear the air."

"Yes we do. You hurt me badly when you walked out. I know I was treating you badly; I know I was very jealous, but you walked away instead of staying with me."

"I am sorry. Maybe it was my lack of experience with relationships," Rami admitted.

"That is a big statement. I am sorry too," she said.

She leaned forward and planted a small kiss on his lips. "Peace?"

"Yes."

"Why this place, Rami? Why the luxury?"

"To do what I like, when I like, how I like, without being told not to."

"And bring whoever you want here?"

"Yes, if I want to, but there is no one I want to bring here."

Just then, Farrah walked into the room. She was wearing one of Rami's shirts. It was held closed by only one button, showing that she was completely naked underneath.

"Oh, I'm sorry. I didn't know you had company, Rami!" said Farrah.

"Who is this? Your mother?" Nadia jumped to her feet angrily.

"You must be Nadia?" Farrah asked.

"Yes!"

"I am Farrah," she said cheerfully. "I didn't hear the door bell, but there's no problem."

"But…" the other girl stammered.

"Rami, go and make some tea please; proper tea – not those horrible tea bags," said Farrah. "I made some cake, which is in the cupboard, also there are lots of good things in the fridge.

"In other words, keep yourself occupied for a while." The two girls looked at each other and laughed.

Although she laughed, Nadia wondered about Farrah's relationship with Rami.

"That's how you should treat them! Come with me, and I'll show you the rest of the apartment," Farrah said.

Rami set the table quickly, clearly trying not to miss any of what was being said. Soon, they were seated around the dining table, talking and laughing.

"Farrah, I do like you very much, although I don't know where to look when I look at you," said Nadia.

"Oh, Nadia, you have my permission to look wherever you want; I am sure you are similarly equipped!" Farrah laughed.

"You are getting worse," Rami commented.

"Nowhere near as bad as you," said Farrah. She stretched her leg under the table, and pressed hard on his crotch.

He wanted to scream in pain, but instead kept a smile on his face.

- - - - - - - - -

The three of them were happy together. Their friendship grew stronger and deeper by the day. They studied together, ate together, and went out together. They had a simple bond but very powerful, and they worked hard to keep it.

Rami's parents accepted Nadia as their son's girlfriend, thanks to Farrah and her powers of persuasion over his father.

"She has class and breeding, and her dad is rich," said Farrah "Anyway, it's much better than letting him go out with some bad girls."

"Yes you are right, but I thought you were his girlfriend?" his father said.

"No dad, I am your fourth daughter," she teased him.

101

Farrah was happy for them. She liked to see Rami happy, and loved him in her own special way. She had her career ahead of her, and everything else came second. She wasn't ready for a long relationship with him or anyone else. She loved hugging him and kissing him whenever she had the chance, though, and also felt confident enough to ask for more than just a kiss.

The summer arrived at last, and the season of parties began. It seemed that swimming every day, and going out every night was part of a daily routine.

"Where do you find your energy from?" Ahmad asked them one day when he and Jean came visiting.

"Mmmmmm…pass," Farrah replied.

"Drinking milk all the time!" Nadia laughed.

"Being looked after by two beautiful ladies," Rami concluded.

"Please tell me, Rami, which one is your girlfriend?" Jean asked.

"Me," Farrah answered.

"No! It's me," Nadia laughed.

"It's one of them," Rami said.

Life was beautiful for all of them.

CHAPTER SIXTEEN

THE violence and strikes left their marks across the city. Many people were killed, others were jailed, and hundreds were injured and kept hidden in hospitals, out of sight.

On the morning of the 17th of July 1968, the people of Baghdad were awoken by the sound of military aircraft screaming low over the city, and the humming noise of tanks and other military vehicles taking their strategic locations in and around the city. The sky was filled with different coloured flares. The people realised it was a coup once their radios were switched on, and recorded message kept indicating that there would be news announcement shortly.

Not a single shot was fired. The guns stayed silent. Baghdad radio eventually came to life and Marshal Laws were declared. The people were also told that a new government had been formed. After several hours, it became clear that the Arab Socialist Baath Party had taken control. That put the fear in everyone's heart, and the memory of 1963, and the blood bath after Prime Minister Qasim was brutally killed.

Rami and the girls stayed at the apartment, or their houses, afraid to venture out, in case violence broke out, and it did. On the 30th of the same month, another coup took place against the powerful secret police. Saddam Hussein, secretary general of the Baath Party, planned this coup, which gave the Baath Party full control of the country. The secret police 'Al-Amin' was disbanded, and later replaced by members of the Party.

Although no-one was killed in this so-called 'White Revolution,' this was not the case after the second coup. Now, though, the government called on its supporters and party members to come to the capital to protect the revolution. They also tried to make pacts with various tribes and organisations, and if the answer was no, then they were executed, or put in prison without a trial.

Baath Party members were given arms, and were called the revolutionary guard. Many were uneducated, and joined the party to escape poverty or national service; others joined purely for their own ends. Although they were supposed to be protectors, in reality many saw them as a threat to freedom.

The people did not feel safe to venture out late at night. Shops and businesses, which used to stay open, began to shut early. Restaurants, cafés, cinemas, and other public places were struggling to survive. The unsettled political situation brought with it much hardship to many people.

Farruk was angry at the revolutionary command. He felt stifled, as he no longer had much of a say in how the newspaper was run. It had changed to nothing more than a propaganda leaflet, listing government messages, new laws, and endless praises. The only readable and enjoyable pages were Rami's, whose high-quality work made him irreplaceable.

It wasn't all gloom and doom. Farrah passed her examinations with flying colours, and was accepted as a freelance writer in three magazines based in Egypt, Jordan, and Lebanon. They were widely read in the Arab world, which was the best start she could wish for. Farrah resigned from the newspaper, despite Farruk's pleadings. He promised her the door was always open if she ever wished to come back.

Rami also passed his exams. He was first in his class, and that warranted a small party for his sixteenth birthday. Nadia also passed, and even though she wasn't as bright as the other two, her results were far better than usual.

The bad news was that the sodality had to close down, but as a goodwill gesture, Nabil and Rami were asked to be on the committee that ran the Centre.

The two girls were worried about Rami in the current situation. They knew how vulnerable he could be. They shadowed him everywhere like two guardians angels, and spent most of their time in the safety of the Centre or the flat. It was not red wine and roses all the time between them, but although they would argue about insignificant issues, none of their tiffs lasted more than an hour at the most.

- - - - - - - - -

"I am telling you, I am bored, I am bored, I am so bored," said Rami one day

"We heard you the first time, Rami!" replied Farrah.

"He is bored!" said Nadia. "Maybe we could go dancing, but it isn't safe to go out."

"How about a nice meal somewhere?" he asked.

"Are you paying?" Nadia asked.

"He always pays!" Farrah took his side.

"Phone Nabil, and see what he is up to, better to have another man's company," suggested Nadia.

"He's got his cousin Khalid staying with him. I think he moved from Mosul to here to find work," said Rami.

"That is five of us," Nadia said.

"I haven't phoned yet." Rami smiled.

"Farrah will phone, and Nabil never says 'no' to her!"

They laughed. Nadia was persuasive, and after Farrah phoned, Nabil and Khalid were at the doorstep within half an hour.

Khalid was a quiet person; tall, fair haired and well mannered. He had studied science at the University of Mosul after his national service, and had moved to Baghdad seeking work.

If Nadia had one fault, it was timing. If anything was troubling her, she would get it out of her system no matter who was there.

"Are you still seeing May?" she suddenly asked during dinner.

"Yes Nadia," said Rami.

"Do you still have sex with her?" Nadia blurted out.

Everyone stared first at her and then at Rami. Farrah butted in quickly, "Nadia…this isn't the time or the place!"

"Why do you always defend him?" Nadia asked.

There was silence. The others were embarrassed. Nadia turned to Rami. "And?"

"Yes…I still see her," he said.

"Do you enjoy it?"

"Enough, I don't question you or Rami about private matters in other people's company, so just leave him alone." Farrah was getting impatient.

"I am sorry. I only want to know the truth," Nadia persisted.

"Here we go again!" Rami raised his voice.

Nabil spoke at last. "I am sorry, but this conversation is making us feel awkward, so we'd rather leave."

"No, wait." Rami pleaded.

Nabil and Khalid left before anyone had the chance to apologise.

"Ten out of ten for this performance…! You not only ruined our night, but theirs too," said Rami.

"What about Farrah?" Nadia asked. "Did you ever sleep with her? I mean, with a body like hers, even I get turned on by her walking naked in front me."

Rami felt trapped, and so did Farrah. They were uncomfortable, and it showed on their faces. Since New Year's Eve, they had only slept together a handful of times, but it was enough to keep Farrah hoping that one day, he would be hers, to be shared with no-one. Then Nadia had appeared on the scene, and Farrah had accepted the fact that her own future and career took priority. She promised herself that there would never be another man in bed except for Rami. The night she had taken her clothes off and danced for him naked, she had told him it was for his eyes only, and she meant it. And that was how it was going to stay.

"Nadia, give it a rest!" Rami was angry.

"Do you fancy her?" Nadia was relentless.

"Yes! I fancy her all the time," said Rami. "No offence to you, but Farrah is beautiful, sexy, has a perfect body, perfect mind, very clever, can hold a conversation and debate a point. She is an incredible lady, and I love to sleep with her. Satisfied now?"

"What about you, Farrah?"

Farrah laughed. "I fancy him when he has his clothes on, but I don't like dangly bits."

"Do you fancy me?" Nadia asked Farrah.

"I'm not a lesbian or bisexual!" she retorted. "I once wondered what it would feel like to sleep with another woman, but that's all it was; a thought."

"Shall we go?" Rami asked.

"Yes. It's getting late," said Nadia.

Farrah drove Nadia home first, and dropped her off.

"Where to now?" Farrah asked.

"Bed…with you," Rami replied.

"I thought you would never ask!"

"Nadia is insecure and her timing is terrible, but she is your girlfriend and has every right to ask."

"You don't complain!" Rami commented.

"I have no reason to. What you have given me is more than you have given to any other woman, including May and Nadia."

"But I don't give you anything."

"That's what you think, my love."

- - - - - - - - -

At the Centre, a new Sodality called 'The Holy Cross' moved into one of the meeting rooms. Very little was known about its members, as they had kept themselves to themselves over the years, but during the previous two and a half months, they had persuaded the committee to accept them. At first, they seemed a very active bunch of boys and girls; mature, talented, intelligent and well-organised. They made a tremendous impact as soon as they began holding their weekly meetings. Within the first three weeks, they staged a theatre play of exceptional quality. The cast gave superb performances, and it was a sell-out for both days.

A few people, however – including Rami and Nabil – took an immediate dislike to this group. They felt something wasn't right, although they couldn't pinpoint it. They sensed the members were not genuine, as if they were hiding something; and if their conversation was rehearsed. They butted in uninvited to other people's conversations. They came over as if they knew better and more than anyone else.

Rami and Nabil voiced their concerns at a committee meeting about the centre, and their remarks were echoed by others.

The new group also took over the organisation of the annual literary competition, which also upset members of other sodalities.

One evening, Rami, Nadia and Farrah sat in the garden at the Centre, waiting for Nabil and Khalid.

"Here comes Johnny," said Farrah suddenly.

Johnny was the chairman of the new sodality, and seemed to want to recruit them particularly Rami, because of his position on the governing committee, which was an advantage to have on their side, as they were seeking to take control of all the activities that went on at the Centre. What bothered Rami and Nabil was their persistence on having Farrah and Nadia joining them too.

"Hi everyone," said the newcomer.

"Johnny! How good to see you!" Rami said sarcastically, as the girls only just managed to keep a straight face.

"Can I join you?" Johnny asked, as he sat down.

He made small talk until other members of the sodality, including Nabil and Khalid, joined them.

"Rami?" said Johnny

"Yes," Rami replied.

"Was it you who won the literary competition last year?" another sodality member asked.

"I won two out of three categories; why do you ask?"

"We haven't received your entry for this year's competition,"

"But I don't belong to any sodality or the Christian Club!" Rami replied.

"You are on the committee, though."

"Thanks. I will think about it."

"Say yes, Rami," Nadia urged.

"I think you are afraid to defend your title," a boy called Talaat said sarcastically. He was second in command on Johnny's committee, and wrote all their plays.

Rami laughed. "Are you a writer? Sorry, I can't remember your name."

"My name is Talaat, I…"

"Oh yes! You wrote that play," Farrah interrupted. "Not a bad effort," she added.

"Yes…he is excellent writer," Johnny butted in. The circle had grown to more than twenty people, and they were all quiet as Johnny continued, "Talaat is very talented. He is our writer of the year, and I don't think anyone has a chance against him."

"So I am challenging him?" Rami asked. "I love a bit of challenge."

"That will be a brilliant competition, as long as we have independent judges," said Nabil, and added, "We don't want anyone saying the result was fixed!"

"I've never read any of your writings, so I can't judge how good you are," Talaat said.

Rami realised then that these newcomers did not know who he was.

"How long have you been writing?" Farrah asked Talaat.

"Five years," Talaat replied.

"Not long enough to be established, but you are heading in the right direction," Farrah remarked. This made Khalid, Nabil and Nadia laugh.

"And what made you such authority on literature?" Talaat asked angrily.

"I know a good writer when I see one, and you are only just a beginner," she said.

"And who are you to judge?" Talaat retorted.

Johnny tried to calm the situation, but with no success.

"I am Farrah Shakier, the writer and journalist. If you ever bothered to buy publications from Egypt, Jordan or Lebanon, you would have seen my name in all of them. Does that satisfy you? And now I am going for some fresh air." She stood up and left, followed by Nadia and the rest of their friends.

Outside, Nadia complimented her "You were awesome; fantastic; brilliant." she said.

"The little shit!" exclaimed Farrah. What a swine! The minute he came in, he couldn't take his eyes off me."

They all laughed as they left the Centre, and decided to go for a meal. Khalid pointed out it could be their first victory over the enemy.

"I was talking to someone the other day, and he thought they should be investigated by the church for their corrupt ways," he said.

"Khalid, I thought you were quiet, and didn't like any gossip," Nadia said.

"I might be quiet but I have my moments, and I love gossip!" Khalid replied. "This is what I was told. When this person first joined them, he loved it; he said the atmosphere was great. But, when he got in deeper, it was completely different."

"I bet black magic is involved here," Farrah suggested.

"You have some imagination, girl!" Rami spluttered.

"You have to do what Johnny and Talaat tell you," Khalid replied. "They have four more gurus as well; all power seekers. They will all go to any lengths just to win. I can't remember all he told me, there was so much but you had all better watch out; especially you, Rami. You are their number one target."

"I'll send them a very bad short story, and one of my best poems, and see which one will be accepted," said Rami.

"Great idea! And whether they like it or not, the audience will demand to hear you."

The meal arrived, and everyone tucked in.

"I want to talk about a project," Nabil said. "I am not happy with my job at all. I can't afford to go abroad and get my Doctorate, and working for the government will never make me a rich man. It's the same with Khalid, so I suggest we start up our own business."

"What type of business?" asked Nadia.

"I have some ideas, but I don't really know," said Nabil.

"It sounds a great project; when do we start? Count me in." Rami laughed.

"Let the man finish!" Farrah butted in.

"Have you got any ideas, wise man?"

"Yes; I was thinking about it the other day," said Rami "I am not happy with the way the newspaper is going, or my future with it. I know it got me known in all the Arab countries as the paper is exported, but its readership abroad is limited. Also the pressure the government has put on all journalists, and what articles they suppose to write, making the atmosphere extremely electric. I am afraid that they put the pressure on me next. I need to venture out, and do something totally different, how about a record shop? There are only two in Baghdad, and they have no idea at all how to run them. They also lack investment. Anyway, think about it; sleep on it, and we'll talk next week."

They all looked at him in amazement. He had obviously planned it all in his head.

"What about money? And investment?" Nabil asked.

"We'll look at the competition, find a good spot, check the rent, shop fittings and equipment, and if we can't afford to do it, then we'll move into something else." Rami said.

"Okay, Rami. Nabil and I will go and check out the competition tomorrow," said Khalid, "We'll sleep on it. But, I know nothing about music, and maybe it's the same for Nabil."

"You learn it like you did when you went to university."

- - - - - - - - -

Over the next few days, they sat discussing their new venture. Sometimes the girls joined in, and their input was appreciated. They decided to look in an up-

and-coming area called 'Al-Mansour,' where the rich and middle classes had begun to adopt. Doctors, engineers, and high government officials had found the area attractive, and the building industry was booming.

Within days, they found exactly what they were looking for: a brand new shop, still unfinished, in a very busy high-class area, and on a busy main road. They contacted the owner, and visited him in his house. Because of Rami's reputation, and his family's good business reputation, the owner accepted them immediately. They signed the contract there and then with a handshake, to be followed by a lawyer's endorsement. Rami paid the first year's rent in advance, to enable the building work to be finished on time.

Everything began to move fast. Rami went to see Farruk, to see if he could help him borrow some money as he now had the contacts. Farruk lent the money himself: six thousand dinars to be repaid within three years.

Rami literally jumped in the air when he saw Khalid and Nabil waiting for him outside the newspaper's building.

"Tell me you did it?" Khalid asked.

"I did, I got six thousand!" Rami replied.

"Wow…I am selling my car; I can get five thousand for it," said Nabil. "My parents will understand; it was their graduation present,"

"And I can get my hand on two or three," Added Khalid, "Well done Rami."

"We are off to a good start," Nabil concluded.

"Please don't tell my parents," Rami begged.

"Yes, Rami; we know…and we won't."

- - - - - - - - -

That same day, Rami and the girls went to see May and Samir to invite them to come to the writing competition, and then headed for Jean and Ahmad's house, where they were always made to feel welcome.

Ahmad was in his study, adding the final touches to his latest book.

"Hi Ahmad, are you done yet?" asked Rami.

"Just about, thank God you are here, Rami; I could do with some help! Is Farrah with you?"

"Yes, in the kitchen with your Jean."

"Ask her to come in, please; she can help as well."

They all sat reading the final chapter, which had bothered Ahmad for quite a while; even his publishers had become inpatient. He had passed the deadline by a week, but they had agreed to wait a bit longer when he had explained to them that it would be his best book to date.

"So? Can I have your opinion please?" he asked.

"It's good, but it lacks something," Rami said.

"Like what?" Ahmad asked.

"It's too dramatic," Farrah said. "Tone it down! It's brilliant, by far your best, but keep it simple. There's no need for big words or long explanations; let the reader imagine what the characters are doing. Simple words Ahmad."

"Spot on! Now get the hell out and let me finish it so I can send it by tomorrow!" Ahmad exclaimed.

"Good luck," said Farrah.

"Thank you, Farrah – you are brilliant."

"I know," she giggled as they both left the room.

In the living room, Nadia was telling Jean about Rami's trick with his entry for the competition.

"They accepted that terrible story because they thought they could beat it, and refused the poem; just what he thought they would do," she said.

"He is funny; he's got the devil inside him," laughed Jean.

Rami went home very happy that night; it was a successful day after all.

The following day, his mother was peeling potatoes in the kitchen. "Mum...are you coming to the competition?" he asked.

"Yes; I wouldn't miss it for the world," she said. "What's bothering you?"

"Nothing really," he replied. But there was, and he explained about Talaat. "I am frightened," he said.

"Of what? That shrimp? Nobody in the whole country is better than you, Rami."

"Mum?"

"Rami A. You had better get on your recorder, and practise like you did last year."

Rami was astounded. He had always been careful to keep his writings in the newspaper a secret from his parents. He was worried that his father might had known as well, and then what will he do if the father insisted that he stops writing to the newspaper? What about the record shop and the money he promised his friends?

"Mum, how did you know?" he gasped.

"You can never hide from mums!" she said. "Oh, son, I knew from day one! I spent hours reading your work in your bedroom; I know your style."

"What about dad?"

"Dad still lives in the dark ages, but with Farrah around, you never know," she replied.

Rami got up and gave his mother a hug and a kiss. "You're the best mother in the world," he said.

CHAPTER SEVENTEEN

COMPETITION day arrived and tickets were sold in their hundreds. Almost all the journalists from the newspaper, including Farruk and his wife, whom Rami had never met but spoken to her on the phone, turned up to watch Rami. Many members of his old sodality came to support him, too, as well as all the usual faces and unusual visitors such as his mother and sisters.

His confidence disappeared the minute he read the programme. He was the last competitor, and he knew the audience would have lost concentration by then. Being last was also worse for him as he knew his nerves would be shot. The six judges were complete strangers, so no one knew what they would prefer.

The competition began, and the Holy Cross sodality brought in members to read short stories and poems. They were exceptional, but to Rami's mind it was doubtful that the two individuals had written them. He thought they had been written by a group of people with much the same style.

"I have no chance." he whispered to Farrah, and walked out.

Farrah followed him. "Rami, calm down! You are the best and you have your followers. I wish they sold alcoholic drinks here; you could do with one or two," she said as they sat in the cafeteria.

When they heard the name Talaat mentioned, they went back to the garden but stood by the entrance. Ten minutes later, Talaat finished reading, and they went back to their seats in the cafeteria, and Rami spoke first. "He's good; in fact he was excellent."

"Yes, he was." said Farrah.

"I have no chance whatsoever of winning."

"Is winning that important? Participation is the most important thing. Coming second or third wouldn't stop people from reading you."

"That's rubbish; it's all about winning."

Shortly Nabil and Khalid came in, a worried look on their faces. Farrah tried to shut them up, but Nabil remarked, "Another one of their members was excellent. It's impossible to have a sodality with half of its members as excellent writers; simply impossible."

Rami was pale and withdrawn; he felt like pulling out. They all tried to talk to him, but as far as he was concerned, it was a hopeless situation.

"I am going to ask for an investigation into their conduct," Nabil said.

"You do that!" Rami said sarcastically. "Can I have the keys to your car please, Farrah?"

"Sure."

"Thanks darling; I just want to be alone."

She watched him walking away. It was probably the first time he had ever called her 'darling.'

"I've never ever seen him like this before. He's probably gone to have a good cry," Nabil commented.

"I don't think it matters to him if he wins or not, as long as it's done honestly," said Farrah. "I wish I could do something to help him."

"You love him to bits, don't you?" Khalid asked.

"I love him with all my heart," she replied. "Our time together will come, but not just yet."

Rami sat in the car. He had just over an hour before he was on stage. He tried hard to remember all Ahmad's lectures, but only one came to his mind: 'A writer without an audience is never a writer.'

He ran his finger round and round the steering wheel, then pulled out a writing pad and began to write. Almost an hour later, he walked back into the garden with a huge smile on his face. Nadia nudged Farrah, and she in turn nudged Nabil; that carried on to the entire group.

"The Bastard…what has he got up his sleeves?" Farrah commented.

There was no need for Johnny to introduce him; the entire audience seemed to recognise him and they erupted in applause. In no time, he was on stage.

"Thank you, thank you," he said, and waited. "Shut up now and listen," he said finally. The audience laughed. He was very natural, and his nervousness had long disappeared.

"I wrote this only an hour ago, sitting in my best friend's car, and I've only just finished it. It says in the programme my latest story, so this is it."

He looked in Farrah's direction and began to read. "I called it 'For your eyes only' and I hope you enjoy it." He took a sip of water, and continued, *'In a dark, damp, dirty room, after a timeless search, he found a corner to lay his bed.'*

Rami carried on reading. It was the performance of a lifetime. He thrilled everyone in the audience, from start to the end.

"Thank you all for listening; I hope you enjoyed it," he said finally.

Everyone in the audience stood up and was shouting for more. He tried to leave the stage, but the audience wouldn't allow him. He smiled and said. "Haven't you got a home to go to?"

Johnny came up to the stage and tried to speak, but gave up and handed the microphone to Rami, who said, "Okay…I will do a short poem. Shut up will you, so I can start! This poem was refused entry in this competition, and I was told it wasn't up to scratch!"

He waited for a few seconds. "It's called Pass the Time, and is one of my favourite poems," he said. "I dedicate it to my mother, who is here tonight. I love you, mum."

He recited it to the audience. His timing was perfection, his voice was powerful, and when he spoke words of love, he made sure everyone felt it.

"I'd love to stay here forever, but I have to be fair to my fellow competitors," he said at the end. "Thank you, I love you all." He left the stage quickly. His friends were waiting for him.

"You bastard; you nailed it!" Nabil said.

"Shush…listen to this." Rami begged.

Johnny announced that although the poem was not the same one as had been submitted before, the judges should consider it because of public demand.

"Excuse my language, but he is one nasty bastard," Farrah said.

"Worse than that..." Nadia agreed.

The ploy by Johnny and his gang had failed, and despite all the cheating, Rami won the competition. When he left the stage, people gathered around him, applauding him, and shaking his hand; others just wanted to show affection by patting him on the back. But there was one person he wanted to talk to, and when he spotted him, he dashed towards him. "Talaat, don't ever stand in my way again! You aren't honest; you are a cheat. Do it again and I will destroy you; that is both a promise and a threat," he said.

It took Rami almost twenty minutes to get to the cafeteria. His mum was the first to greet him with a huge hug. "Son...you made me so proud and happy, and thank you for the dedication," she said.

"I love you, mum," Rami replied.

"I asked them to come back to the house to celebrate."

"That was very kind of you."

Turning to the others, he joked, "If you need any kisses, hugs or autographs, better save it until we get home!"

"Nadia had to go home because her mother is ill," said Jean. "Ahmad has taken her. She phoned the house, and her dad asked her to get home quickly."

"I hope it's nothing serious," said Rami.

Rami's dad had already opened the guest room, and Farrah and his sisters hurried to lay the table while Nabil and Khalid went to collect kebabs, kubbas and a few other traditional foods.

"Did anyone understand my story?" Rami asked loudly.

"As a matter of fact, no," Ahmad replied. "I suppose people liked it because it was beyond their comprehension."

They went on discussing his short story. It was a new style to him, although he didn't copy anyone.

"Am I correct in describing it?" Samir asked laughingly.

"Yes and no," said Rami.

"Tell us then, for God's sake," Jean pleaded.

"He doesn't know himself. Isn't that right, you freak?" Farrah butted in laughingly.

"Spot on! I wish I know the meaning of half the work I do," Rami responded.

"Why that doesn't surprise me?" Samir said.

"I am lost," Rami's dad broke in.

Everyone gave an opinion, until it was Farrah's turn. She stood in the middle of the room. "I have an announcement to make, and only mum – Rami's mother– knows about it," she said.

"Almost a year ago, through Rami, I met you, May and Samir, Ahmad and Jean. You have become wonderful friends, and I love you very much. Nabil and Khalid, if I ever had brothers, I wish they were like you. You treated me as an equal, and with respect. Mum, dad and sisters, you are my family." Tears trickled down her face. "You took me in, never ever questioned me, and allowed me to make this house into my home."

Everyone was tearful and quiet, and she continued, "And you Rami, the most beautiful person on earth. You are funny, sincere, and a good friend. You have helped me so much, and if it wasn't for you, I wouldn't have achieved so much in such a short time. You taught me to dream big, but most of all, you are my rock, and I love you with all my heart."

"I love you too, my extra special friend," said Rami.

"In two days, I am leaving the country," she announced. "I have to go to Egypt, then Jordan, Lebanon, and other Arab countries. I have this fantastic chance to make something of my future. I didn't say anything before, because of the competition."

"Good luck, girl; go for it. We're all behind you," said Ahmad.

"That's all I need: your support and blessing," she replied.

"How long are you going for?" Ahmad asked.

"Two weeks, maybe two months. I really don't know."

Rami was surprisingly quiet. He was shocked, not that she was leaving, but that she meant so much to him.

He left the living room, and she followed him to the kitchen.

"Rami!" she said.

"Sorry. I was miles away," he responded.

"Are you upset with me?"

"No, never. I was just thinking how much I will miss you. But why the long speech? You are coming back?"

"Yes of course I am…are you coming to the flat this evening?"

"If you want me to," he replied.

"I need you."

- - - - - - - - -

Planning and organising a business would have been much easier if the government hadn't put in place very strict laws regarding imports from other countries. Nabil and Khalid travelled to Kuwait city to buy state-of-the-art equipment for the shop. The price difference between the two countries was incredible; import tax in Iraq was three hundred per cent, while in Kuwait it was no more than four per cent. They needed fast reel-to-reel recorders, record players, and cassette recorders. They wanted to give the impression that they were professionals.

They did not buy too much, because they did not want to overload their car, and also, they had an arrangement with one of Nabil's friends who worked on border control. Time was important too, as they had to renew their passports in order to leave the country again, this time to Lebanon. It was not an easy journey, as they had to travel through the desert, where sand storms could erupt at any time. These made driving impossible, and because there were no restrictions, most vehicles travelled at such high speeds that accidents happened almost every day. They drove from the border control at Al-Rutba to Damascus in Syria. This is an amazing city, with much French influence, set in a valley and surrounded by high mountains. It is the oldest inhabited city in the world. Then it was an incredible journey from Damascus to Beirut, along a narrow road, wide enough for only two cars, but where lorries and other commercial vehicles travelled at terrifying speeds. Looking out of the car down valleys from five hundred to more than a thousand feet deep, they could see dozens of wrecked cars, buses and other vehicles.

Once in Beirut, driving became unbearable because of traffic jams. Their impression of the capital was that it had small streets for big American cars, but the city itself was alive and buzzing with people. The shops were filled with commodities they wouldn't find anywhere in Baghdad; everything from clothes to music. Nabil and Khalid made many good contacts before heading back to Baghdad.

Rami went to see Nadia three days after the competition. She refused to speak to him on the phone, and he wanted to find out why.

Her father opened the door. "Hello son. How are you?" he asked.

"I am fine, uncle, thank you. How is your wife, and the young lady?"

"My wife's doing fine, thanks, and the young lady doesn't want to talk to you, although she's standing behind the door here." He pulled her out from behind the door.

"Dad!" said Nadia angrily.

"Do you want to talk about it?" Rami asked.

"No! Go away," Nadia replied.

"Okay," said Rami.

"Wait! I'll come with you," Nadia said suddenly. She ran into her bedroom, put her shoes on, kissed her mum and dad, and joined him. "Why have you been ignoring me?"

"I phoned you every day but you refused to speak to me," Rami replied.

"You could have come to see me."

"I know, but we have been very busy. Nabil and Khalid are in Kuwait. They're due back either today or tomorrow, and then they will unload the car and head to Lebanon. They are using Farrah's car, because they sold theirs."

"You see more of Farrah more of everyone than me! Do you love me?"

"Yes, I do."

"What about Farrah and May?" Nadia asked.

He held her hand tightly. "You are my girlfriend," he said.

"You expect me to watch you sleep with other women, and give my permission," she said sadly.

"No…I don't expect you to do any of that," Rami replied.

"The first time I saw Farrah almost naked at the flat, I was hurt. I didn't believe there was nothing between you two, but after some time, I believed there was nothing but friendship. Then I came to the flat the day Farrah left. She was gone by then, but her knickers were on the floor in your bedroom, the bed wasn't made up, and clearly it looked like two people had slept in it. Are you going to deny it?"

"You wouldn't believe me, whatever I say," said Rami. "I made love to Farrah a couple of times before you came back to me, and yes, we do still cuddle and maybe kiss, but it's a reassurance thing between us." He felt guilty for lying, which went against the grain, but he didn't feel comfortable with her continuous questioning.

"Tell me what happened?" she asked, as they entered the apartment.

"Well, we sat talking in the living room; I went to bed, and she stayed up reading," said Rami. "I woke up later on, and found her asleep on the floor. I tried to wake her up but I couldn't, so I carried her to her bedroom, but her door was closed. I couldn't open it while I was carrying her, so I took her to mine. I took her clothes off, and went to sleep." He smiled lovingly at her.

"I need a cup of tea. Make me one please," said Nadia, changing the subject.

She followed him to the kitchen and sat on a high stool. "Talk to me," she said.

He laughed. "What do you think I've been doing?"

"How much do you respect me?"

He continued laughing. "Let me think of an answer!" was his reply.

"Clever ass!" said Nadia. She took a sip of her tea, and continued, "When I am with you, I feel safe; secure, and completely fulfilled. But when I'm away from you, I feel completely lost. I wander from one room to another, imagining all kinds of things. You have become a habit which is too hard to break. Sometimes you make me feel as if I'm on cloud nine, but at other times, I feel ignored. You maybe don't mean to, and I know you have a lot going on in your head. I'm so confused! Rami, darling, come here and give me a hug."

Rami did what she wanted. Inside, he agreed with her. He even felt sorry for her, and maybe for himself too. He hated himself for lying to her, but the truth could finish their relationship for good. He loved Nadia, and did not want to lose her. He watched as she opened the balcony door, pulled out a chair and sat watching the world pass by.

"I gave you my body willingly, against my upbringing," she went on. "I don't regret it for one moment, and I would do the same again if I had the chance; you are a fantastic lover." She paused, examined his face and continued, "When we make love, I feel you deep inside me; inside my womb, my heart, my brain. You don't just make love with your penis, but with your heart, your soul and your whole body. I can feel your soul making love to mine. Oh Rami! Why can't you come down to earth sometimes, though, and just give me physical sex? I am yours and yours only. You are so special, and I am only trying to understand you."

"I never thought you could talk so much! You really surprise me," Rami teased.

"Will you take me right now; right here, please? Nobody can see anything."

"So you think I can switch on just like that?"

"Yes, with a bit of help from me!" Nadia giggled.

"Come on, then." Rami challenged.

She knelt in front of him, kissing and touching him until she achieved her aim.

"Go on; do it now," she said, smiling.

CHAPTER EIGHTEEN

CAIRO 1968 – the Jewel of the orient, the city of the thousand Minarets, where ancient and modern Egyptian civilizations met; the city where the past melted gently with the present.

Greater Cairo extended on the banks of the river Nile to the south of its delta. On its east side stands evidence of centuries of Islamic, Christian Coptic, and Jewish cultures. On its west side lays the ancient Egyptian city of Memphis (Giza), the renowned capital of the old Kingdom and the site of the Pyramids, the only one of the Seven Wonders of the World that survives. Indeed, a journey through Cairo is a journey through time, through the history of an immortal civilization.

Despite the old sandy impression Farrah had as she flew over the city, she found an inner beauty to it. But she had a sense of magic mingled with sadness, as she drove through the city and she wondered what had become of the wealth and power of the ancient Egyptians. It felt as it had been neglected and uncared for by the masses.

The Egyptian people were friendly, loving, welcoming, clever and very religious. But, they were still living the effects of the six-day war. Some blamed the government led by Jamal Abid Al-Nasser, some simply accepted the fact that they were not ready. Every effort was made to rebuild the army, the air force and all those shattered lives.

In Egypt Farrah became a celebrity overnight. She was a guest speaker at the women's league and interviewed by various newspapers, magazines and radio stations. She met many leading women from the Egyptian society and her visit of two weeks had to be extended to enable her to fit in all the appointments. She didn't want to miss on such a golden opportunity.

She also fell in love with Amman, the capital of Jordan. The people were gentle, honourable and sincere and they went out of their way to make her feel welcome; a true example of Arab hospitality. The influence of the desert tribes had much influence on this proud race, yet she felt sad listening to the stories of war and the homeless people of Palestine.

Despite feeling very welcomed, she was aching to get back to her home and to see Rami. Nevertheless first she had to go to Lebanon, and Beirut was her next stop.

- - - - - - - - -

The summer came to an end and Rami and Nadia returned to school, while the rest of their friends remained out of the country.

It was essential that they concentrated on their studies and worked hard for the national examination the following year. If they achieved high averages in nine subjects they would be able to choose a college or university. But these plans were disrupted the minute that Khalid and Nabil returned from their shopping trip in Lebanon.

They transformed the flat's living room into a recording studio and all the furniture was moved into Rami's study and the bedrooms. They began transferring music from records, into tapes and making charts for every piece of music. The small business they dreamt of was growing bigger and faster than they had anticipated, even before the premises were ready to move to.

Rami felt agitated and wished that he'd never started this venture. His apartment became like a refuse dump, and even his cleaner began to moan.

Khalid had given up looking for work, so he worked at the apartment non-stop day and night, hoping all the recordings would be in place for the day they opened the shop. Nabil joined him late afternoons, as he still worked for the Ministry of Planning and Development.

One night, Rami and Nadia walked in while Nabil and Khalid were busy working.

"Hi everyone," said Rami.

"Hi, what's with the long face?" Nabil asked.

Rami found a space to sit on the floor and Nadia tucked in beside him.

"Rami…?"

"Nothing really, I'm just feeling fed up with all this," said Rami.

"We know," said Khalid. "But, not long to go now."

"Six weeks…it feels like a long time."

"No," said Nabil, "Two weeks. The landlord phoned Khalid and told him."

"Really...? You're pulling my leg"

"Why aren't you jumping up and down?" Nadia asked, laughing.

"We have so much to do," Khalid said, "And I need to take another trip to Beirut, which I'm not looking forward to. Driving all that way on my own isn't fun."

"Have we got any money left?" Rami asked.

"Yes, nearly three thousand." Nabil answered.

"Don't forget the shop fittings!" Rami said.

"That has been taken care of, don't worry Rami."

"Don't go spending money enjoying yourself." Rami added.

Everyone turned and looked at him. There was no need for such a remark, as Khalid was extremely dedicated in making this venture a great success.

Rami's money problems had surfaced in the last few weeks, as he started paying back the loan. The money from his writings barely covered half of the amount he was supposed to be paying. His savings had all been spent, and he no longer had the ability to write in the same volume as before.

As he explained the situation to them, tears filled his eyes. This problem was bigger than he could handle and he refused to turn to his father for help, nor allow his pride to seek Ahmad or Farruk again.

"I'm sorry Khalid, I didn't mean what I said, but I'm worried sick, especially as the rent for the apartment is due shortly."

"Don't worry, everything will be fine," said Nabil.

"I hope so."

"Cheer up, in three or four weeks we'll open shop.'

"Come on Nadia better walk you home and I'd better head home too. I've got homework to catch up with."

Nadia stayed quiet for a while. "Are you in serious trouble?"

"In four or five weeks I will be," he mumbled.

"Even if you open the shop tomorrow it'll take time to build a business and clients." She remarked.

"I know baby. It's not the money. I could always ask Farrah when she gets back if I have to, or even May or Samir…'

"So that's not what's troubling you? You haven't felt excited at all about the shop. You've showed no emotions, no gratitude…nothing. I can't work you out at times. Nabil and Khalid are doing all the work, and all you do is moan. You offer none of them a word of encouragement."

"I'm sorry…"

"When was the last time you opened up and talked to me? I'm not a stupid girl. I do understand." She complained.

"Remember Wissam at my school, the one I told you about?" Nadia nodded, and he continued. "He left and now he's in Al-Mansour school. He's very high up in the Baath Party, and he's in the national student union too and he wants me to be the president of the student union at our school."

"I hope you thanked him but said no."

"What do you take me for? Of course, I said no. However, those people never understand what the word 'No' means. He's very much connected to the government, plus he is also somehow connected to Mr. Sabah and Mr. Ali. I've seen him in their company many times."

"Who are these men?" She asked.

"They were both teachers. One became Deput Minister for Education and the other is on the Revolution Council and about to become Minister for Oil. I told Wissam that I'm not interested but he said if I was his friend then I must be part of the movement."

"Charming!"

"Exactly! I told him that I have friends who belong to many different parties, religions and sects. He left me alone after that, but with a warning, which I didn't like. He said like it or not you will be one of us, we always get what we want."

"The same thing is happening in my school," said Nadia, "Girls were forced to join the union, like it or not, they were promised so much for themselves and their families. It's total madness."

"Have they approached you too?"

"No, but my turn will come I suppose. I usually keep myself to myself and try not to get involved."

"I can't see you being a good politician," he said, laughingly.

"God! It has been a long time since I've seen a smile on that face of yours."

- - - - - - - - -

The government, which was entirely made up of the influential elite of the Baath party, began to establish their control of the country by recruiting masses of people from different backgrounds. Some were recruited by force, others were gently persuaded, and the rest simply joined the Baath party to take advantage of the new regime.

Many key positions in the Ministries and government offices were given to those related to 'Al-Tikrity tribe', or were given to members of the Baath Party, or its supporters, as opposition parties weren't allowed.

Unions were formed and although elections were held, they weren't democratic , as no one opposed the main stream Ba'athists.

Members of opposition parties, ex-ministers and those who had a personal feud with a Ba'ath party member filled the jails yet again. No one dared to speak out or question the authority.

It was a difficult time, and people kept their heads low and got on with their daily routine.

- - - - - - - - -

The key for the shop was handed to them a week in advance, the same day as Farrah returned home. She saw the excitement around her, but everyone was tired and needed a woman's touch to organise opening the shop quickly, in time for Christmas.

With the help of May, Samir, Jean and Ahmad, the shop was ready to open within six days. Nadia, on the other hand, kept away from it all, as she needed to study.

They all stood in the middle of the shop speechless, excited and proud. There was nothing more they could do. Every piece of equipment was cleaned and polished. Every stack of records and tapes were priced and merchandised.

"This is fantastic," said Rami.

"Don't start crying or else I will join you," said Ahmad.

"I've already started," he said and with tears in his eyes he hugged everyone. "I'm so lucky to have friends like you."

"Thanks for your help everyone," said Nabil.

"I'll second that,' Khalid remarked, feeling as if there was a lump in his throat. He had worked harder than anyone else, and he never thought he'd see the day when the shop would be open to the public. But he wasn't one to show his emotions freely. He walked outside and stood on the pavement composing himself. He simply couldn't handle the situation and felt lost with his emotions.

Rami soon joined him, he tapped on his shoulder, and when Khalid turned round, Rami hugged him closely.

"Thanks for everything my friend. You are one in a million."

The shop opened the following day, a Friday, the only day off in the week, being a Muslim country, except for shops and restaurants. It was an incredible success straight away. Most of their tapes, records and singles were sold so ordering more would keep them busy for the following four weeks. Their friends and the public showed them unbelievable support.

"I think we deserve a night out," Nabil said as he finished serving a customer.

"Indeed. I've been trying to contact Nadia, but something is wrong with their phone. You can drop me there and we'll see if she fancies going out, if not I'll stay with her for a couple of hours then walk home."

"Okay, we'll do that. What about Farrah?"

"She's at the flat as she has a lot of work to catch up with. It's best not to distract her."

An hour later there was that uncomfortable feeling that something wasn't right as Rami rang the bell. Someone peered through the curtains, then the door opened. Rami's smile vanished, as Nadia's face appeared from behind the door. Her eyes were swollen, her hair was untidy and she looked dreadful. Rami's heart sank, his legs started to shake as Nadia threw herself into his arms. He hugged her gently.

"Something's wrong," Khalid said and he left the car, followed by Nabil.

"What's wrong Nadia?"

From behind the door a man in his sixties appeared, who looked very like her father. "Who is it Nadia?"

"It's Rami's uncle and his friends."

"They had better come in!" the uncle said.

As soon as the door shut, Nadia's uncle spoke. "My brother and five more from the factory have been arrested this morning."

"Oh no…! In God's name, why?"

The three boys glanced at the faces around the room. Two women sat on the sofa, while another man stood by the fireplace. He looked like he had been crying too. There was no sign of Nadia's mother. Rami concluded that she must have been resting.

"Tell us what happened," said Rami.

"Five men walked into the factory this morning, showed us their ID cards and told me to bring them the six people on the list to help them with their investigations; five men and one girl were taken away." He lit a cigarette and continued. "I came here to tell my sister-in -law and they've already been here to search the house. Everything was in such a state that we have spent most of the day tidying up. I contacted the other five people's families and it seems their houses were searched too."

"Was anything found?"

"Not so much as a bean. I sent a few blankets with the union representative and he returned saying there was no trace of them anywhere. They cut our phones too, so our neighbours offered us their line with an extension. We don't know anyone so we're just sitting here waiting."

Rami felt ill, as if his stomach had been torn apart; the memories of his ordeal flashed before him.

"Why didn't you phone me? I know you were cut off, but…"

"What could you have done?" said the man in the far corner. "He could be dead now. Sorry son but I can't see a way out of this. We've just got to sit and wait."

"You must be the type of person who cries before feeling the pain," said Rami who took an instant dislike to the man. "Come on boys lets go, and Nadia don't worry. What's the phone number?"

They went to Farruk's house. Rami went in while the other two sat in the car waiting. Rami told Farruk all he knew.

"I'll make few phone calls, but I can't promise anything," said Farruk.

"Thanks, but what do you think about this?"

"Oh Rami, what can I say? Everything has changed so fast in this country over the last few months. Look at our streets; on every corner and every roundabout there are men and women with machine guns to protect the revolution, but what revolution? It's to protect the Ba'ath party. We are a barbaric race, yet we possess hearts of gold."

"I've never seen you talk like that."

"And you won't ever see it again my son," said Farruk placing his hand on the side of Rami's face. "In all my life I've never felt the need to protect a person like I do you. You're the son of this nation, with your thoughts, your passion and your belief. You are different. You love people and they love you back. You need them and they need you. Go home son and sleep. Leave this matter to me. I'll get in touch with Mr. Sabah now, he's in the government and the revolutionary command council."

Rami felt shocked to hear that Mr. Sabah and Farruk were friends, as that had never been mentioned in any conversation in the past, yet, he allowed the remark to pass by for the sake of Nadia's father.

He left Farruk's house and went to see Wissam, his old friend. He always thought he was better connected and much higher up in the Ba'ath party than he led people to believe. Wissam promised he'd get in touch as soon as he heard any news of the whereabouts of the six people. From there he returned to Nadia's house.

Two and a half hours later the bell rang. "Wissam, please come in."

"I'd rather talk outside."

Rami knew that it was something important and that he wouldn't like what he was about to hear.

"I have bad news for you my friend."

"Shit, shit, shit. Is he dead?"

"I don't know. He's with the others at the Al-Nehaia Palace!"

"What's that and where is it?"

"It's one of the King's palaces, which has been turned into a torture chamber, and a prison. No one has come out alive yet. That's why it's called the Al-Nehaia – the end palace."

"So he's dead? Are you trying to break the news gently?"

"I don't know for sure. No one was allowed to interfere and my neck will be on the line if I do so. I'm so sorry Rami, it's out of my hands."

"Is this the white revolution we were promised? Is this your idea of a government to control the country? A government that's eager to control the masses by instilling fear into the hearts of people?"

"No, but it's necessary."

"Necessary? Killing this man and hundreds of other innocent people is necessary?" Rami raised his voice slightly, but he felt afraid that he might be heard inside the house.

"In any struggle for survival, innocent people become the sacrifice. No one enjoys seeing them killed, but rather them than me."

"Rather me than them if I was a party member, because I'd be in the government to serve the people not the other way round."

"You're a good person Rami and I value our friendship."

"I'm sorry. I had no reason to take my anger on you. Thanks for your help, I really appreciate it."

"I have other contacts to try. Go to sleep now and I'll see you tomorrow."

"Thanks a million...Goodnight."

- - - - - - - - -

The hours passed slowly and Rami couldn't sleep, waiting for first sign of light so he could go to the newspaper office.

"Good morning Farruk." Rami greeted him as he entered the office.

"Morning son...please sit down." said Farruk with a low voice. "After a few phone calls, I found out where Nadia's father and the other are."

"I already know! Al-Nehaia prison!"

"Yes, they are accused of fraud, corruption and bribery."

"That's a joke! He is so honest..."

"They had information from someone who worked for them for three months in 1963."

"As a labourer I suppose?"

"I don't know."

"And in three months he found out how corrupt those people were?" Rami raised his voice.

"Stay well out of this one. It's much bigger than you think. He told them everything."

"I suppose he told them that he's a spy too? Just like all those who were hanged in the middle of Baghdad?"

"Yes he confessed that he's a spy."

"And no one made him, no one tortured him, no one beat the hell out of him? Come on Farruk, surely you're not serious. What has happened to you? You were the one who objected to all those tactics before. The revolution came, and now you have become one of them. You're no different to those who beat me up, to those who pushed me hard and made me bite my wrist to end it all."

"How do you know he didn't do it?" Farruk said keeping calm.

"Because I know the man and he couldn't hurt a fly. You have met Nadia; do you think she was brought up by a thug?"

"There is no fire without a spark! They must have evidence."

"What evidence? They went to all the houses and came out empty handed. The only thing they have is a lie; a lie by a man who worked there for three months before he was sacked. He joined your beautiful party to get his revenge. Every day hundreds of people are going missing, vanishing, disappearing, and no one knows why…"

"Rami, I order you to shut up, or get out," Farruk shouted.

"What's next Farruk?" Rami shouted back. "Are you going to take out your gun and shoot me? Well go ahead do it. I dare you."

The typewriters outside Farruk's office went silent, and all the journalists listened to the shouting.

"You ordered me to shut up? I never thought you were a two-faced man, but you have proved me wrong. I'm not afraid of you, them or anyone else, so you can pick up your phone and tell them you have a spy in your office. What is there in this country that's worth spying on? You disappointed me, of all the people in my life, Mr. Chief Editor."

Farruk said nothing, just stared at Rami.

"You know where I live, so send your friends to arrest me,"

"Don't be stupid.' said Farruk, his face now visibly flushed.

"What's the use in talking to you, I don't know you anymore. You are my best friend, but you have changed."

"When you finish your rant, get out and close the door behind you."

Rami's body shook with anger and he burst out crying, unable to hold back his tears. "I didn't cry once when I was tortured. They beat me, burnt me, and pulled me apart, but you did it to me…my best friend. I had so much respect for you, so much admiration. I confided in you. You were closer to me than my own father. I loved you more than him. I'm crying because my dearest friend died the day this so-called white revolution came. I wish that you and your party member's burn in hell and you can go ahead and report me because I don't give a damn. I don't owe you my life like I said before; I owe it to someone else who I grew to trust."

Rami walked out and slammed the door behind him. Iman hurried towards him. She had heard every single word along with everyone else in the office.

"Those were harsh words Rami, come and sit down."

"No thanks I'd better go; I won't be coming here anymore, look after yourself and the rest of them."

The intercom system came on. "Iman, get me the president please," said Farruk's voice.

Rami had toughened up since his ordeal, but it took almost a year to show up in him. He had no fear at all inside him; he knew what to expect if it ever happened again. He survived once, and learnt how maybe to survive it again. But, he knew well that Farruk would never hurt him whatsoever.

He felt he needed to apologise to him, but not yet. He had so much anger, so many unsolved issues which needed to be dealt with. But, all in good time.

- - - - - - - - -

That night Nadia's father was released. He was thrown out of the car in front of the house at about seven o'clock, as if he was a piece of unwanted meat.

He had stayed in his bedroom since being found by the neighbours and brought him in. None of them thought about contacting a doctor. Rami telephoned Samir, and he turned up within minutes.

History had repeated itself. His mind travelled back to the previous year and the hurt he had suffered. With strong will, determination and self-discipline he had done well to put it to the back of his mind.

"What am I going to do? Answer me." Nadia begged for an answer, but Rami's mind was somewhere else. "For the fifth time, Rami, what am I going to do?"

"What about...?"

"I said if dad dies, what am I supposed to do?"

"That won't happen. Samir is examining your dad now, and your mother simply couldn't cope so she has shut herself away. She'll be fine Nadia, I'm sure Samir will have a look at her when he finishes with your dad."

Nadia couldn't sit still for more than a few seconds. A look of worry was printed all over her face. Rami, on the other hand, sat still staring out of the window.

"Why is he taking so long?" Nadia asked.

"Samir is being very cautious because of your father's age, and..."

"Yeah, yeah, he's going to die, isn't he?"

Rami stayed silent

Samir came down a while later saying only that he must take Nadia's father to hospital as soon as he wakes up.

- - - - - - - - -

Nadia's father's recovery was slow; he refused anyone to stay the night with him, although at times they could hear him crying. He also refused to meet relatives and neighbours who came to give him their best wishes. Samir was the only one allowed in.

"Dad wants to see you," said Nadia over the phone.

Rami put the telephone down. He had avoided visiting the house over the last few days because it reminded him of his own ordeal. Instead, he buried himself with books and writing, but, he phoned Nadia every day to ask after her and her parents.

Half an hour later, he sat face to face with Nadia's dad. "How are you feeling now uncle?"

"Alive! Alive!"

Examining his face, Rami didn't know who had received more of a beating, himself or the man in front of him. His eyes were red, as if they were on fire, his arms and legs were partly bandaged and his body was swollen.

"You must be in terrible pain?"

125

"I'm healing thanks to Dr. Samir. He's a good, honourable man, and thanks for asking him, he saved my life."

"Not at all!"

A couple of minutes of silence passed between them, which seemed like hours, before Nadia's father spoke. "When I got out of that horrible place, I wished I was dead. I didn't want to be seen like this, I didn't want to be part of this world. I felt so ashamed and overwhelmed by guilt. I lost my self respect." He took a deep breath and continued. "Dr Samir told me about you and how you were treated. I'm so confused trying to make sense of what happened. You are so young, yet so mature. You won, as you didn't let them get inside you and tear you apart."

"What you see, uncle, is only a front, but with time this will all be pushed to the back of your mind. It takes time and willpower." Rami paused to think of the appropriate words to say. "Sometimes I feel glad about what happened to me. I came out tougher."

Nadia's father continued to tell his story to Rami, crying as he explained how he had been tortured. "I lost all sense of time, as I was blindfolded and I didn't see their faces until the day I came out. They all looked very evil. It was such an awful place. All I could hear were shouts, screams and people crying." He paused to dry his eyes, and then continued. "On the last day they removed the blindfold from my eyes, and took me to meet this person who had told them we were spies. I had no choice in the matter, I was dragged into this room, and I didn't recognise the man, as he was covered with blood and bruises. They put a gun in my hand and asked me to shoot him. They told me I'd feel better and revenge is sweet. God knows where my power came from to say 'no', so they sat me on a wooden box covered with blood. They took their knives out and began to slice his body bit by bit as if he was a dead animal in a butcher's shop. I will remember his screams for the rest of my life. He worked for me for a short period in early 1960's. When they had enough of his screaming, one of the men took his gun out and declared that he'd do it on my behalf. He fired his gun once and the man fell to the ground with blood pouring out of his head." He took a deep breath and continued. "I need to forget. I need to take that picture out of my mind for the sake of my family, but I really don't know how."

"Men can't fight back without weapons," said Rami, thinking aloud.

"I don't need weapons, my son. I just need to live another day. Thank you for listening, you have been through the same experience, and you understand. I had to talk to someone and now I feel much better. Can you ask my wife to come in?"

"Sure uncle."

"Thank you my son, and take care."

Even with that last conversation, Rami thought that the man in need of real help mentally. He didn't sound at all normal.

- - - - - - - - -

The graphics of the past events haunted Rami for days after. He kept his distance from everyone knowing he would not be very good company.

One of the stories Nadia's father told him afterwards had unsettled him even more. They forced prisoners to jump off the roof of the building, three stories high. If they survived, they'd send them back to their family severely injured. If they didn't a bullet in the head would make sure they were dead.

He avoided the shop and he avoided speaking to Nabil and Khalid. He went to school, did his homework, and read many books to keep his mind occupied. He wrote with hunger like in the good old days. His writings took on a major change; they were filled with symbolism, directed more to the changing politics of the country and society. He also avoided contact with Farruk and Iman. He had so much anger to release, but he did not want to use anyone as a punch bag.

People avoided speaking out against the government, although at the beginning there wasn't much to criticise, except that there were many foreigners living in the country, and they were doing jobs that Iraqis were capable of doing. It wasn't a major problem, soon enough the government refused to renew their contracts, or their visas, and they had to get out of the country. Rami found that as a positive move to ensure employment to his fellow countrymen.

After a few weeks he felt like he needed help to get back to normality. He decided to visit May.

She opened the door. "Hello stranger, come in."

"Are you busy?"

"No, not really, you can give me a hand tidying up. My helper hasn't been feeling well, so I gave her few days off to recover."

He took May's hand and walked her to the bedroom upstairs.

"Is that all you want me for Rami?"

"Yes."

He took his clothes off, helped her out of hers and lay next to her.

"You have changed so much my dear young man," she said.

"I wish I had stayed young. I wish I had never grown up. I need to close my eyes and see the colours of the rainbow, instead of nightmares. I need to talk, I need to be mentally free. Right now I'm being tortured by my own mind. I can talk to you, but I'm afraid you might think I'm using you."

"You are using me, but I love you for what you are." Her hand wandered around his body. Not only did it arouse him, but it was very comforting too. She kissed his neck gently, and climbed on top.

"I need this May, don't stop."

She put her finger on his mouth, "Shhhh baby…just enjoy it."

As he sat down later on and watched her cook, he told her what had been disturbing him.

"Rami, you came out fighting to get better, fighting to show Elaine you were a tough boy. Although you suffered mentally, somehow you pushed it aside and carried on. You didn't allow time to get over it."

"No one knows me as well as you. You have never judged me or told me what to do."

"What's the point? You'll always do what you want anyway. Rami, you've been hiding, instead of sharing your problems."

"I'm sorry."

"So you should be. You go from one extreme to another; your maturity and intellectual ability somehow at times get confused with your insecurity and naivety. You might think you have all the answers and think that you know it all, but sweetheart you simply don't. And, when living gets tough for you, accept it, and ask for help, I am here, so is Ahmad, Farruk, and the rest."

- - - - - - - - -

Rami's visits to the shop were less frequent. Although the workload increased by the day, he found it rather boring at times. He wanted to concentrate on his studies and his writings. Nevertheless, he began to spend more time with his family, enjoying the small conversations, the little laughter and the safe surroundings of a loving home.

Nadia spent most of her days with him, enough for her to regain her self-belief.

"What's wrong?" he asked noticing her sad expression.

"Nothing," she replied.

He looked deep into her face knowing she would tell him.

"It's dad."

"Is he ok?"

"Yes, but we're leaving the country soon. I didn't want to tell you until the mid-year exams were over. Although I studied to support you, I didn't take them. Rami, dad is very ill mentally, he needs to get out, and mum is not much better."

"Do you have to go too?"

"What do you think? They need me. They look like they've aged twenty years in the past few weeks."

Rami remained quiet. He could not think straight, he felt completely lost.

"I love you very much and I know I gave you a hard time at the beginning, but you will always be in my heart. When are you leaving?"

"In five days, we've sold the house, the business, the furniture and everything else."

Rami gulped. "Where are you going?"

"I don't know, we have visas to England and Canada, but dad said we'll take each day as it comes and enjoy it."

"Will you write to me?"

"Of course I will," said Nadia.

"I'm going to miss you."

"I hope so," she smiled. "I'm going to miss you too."

Five days later, Nabil put his arm around Rami's shoulders as they watched the airplane disappear. A big chunk of his life had disappeared in the horizon, and unforeseen circumstances had forced a major change in his life.

"What next?"

"Life goes on. I feel empty, but in a way I was expecting it. I do love her a lot, but somehow I wasn't in love with her."

"I understand. Come on I've got lots of work to do at the shop."

"And I've got so many things to write about in my head."

CHAPTER NINETEEN

CHRISTMAS was uneventful, just like any other day. Rami's parents felt his sadness, and out of the whole family, they worried about him the most. His father often left him to his own devices, but his mother was quite the opposite. She showered him with extra affection, hoping it would substitute for Nadia's.

He coped very well with the situation, although he barely smiled, joked or involved himself in long conversations. He had so many ideas to write about, yet for some reason he couldn't get them down on paper.

Ahmad, on the other hand, had finished writing another book, which had gone to the publishers for editing and proof reading. His anguish was diminished when he went to see Rami at the flat. There were no ashtrays filled with cigarette butts, no empty bottles of whisky, no food left out of the refrigerator that was covered with mould. Everything was tidier than ever before. A smile crossed his face, which Rami read perfectly.

"No, it's not another Elaine," said Rami.

"I said nothing," Ahmed laughed.

"No, but your face did. How's your better half? And why hasn't she come?"

"She's fine, she sends her love. She thought you needed my company more than hers."

"How's the book going?"

"Finished, thank God! I've never struggled like this before to finish a book. I hope you like the ending. I think it'll do well."

"Ahmad, you're the best novelist in the country."

"Until you decide to write a book," he said smiling.

"I'm about to write one."

"I'm glad. How are you feeling about Nadia?"

"I wondered when you'd ask me that. I do miss her, she was great; loving, sincere, extremely jealous, beautiful, and spoilt by her parents. We spent many hours together after what happened to her father, and I got to know her better."

"I know but?"

"I wasn't in love with her, if you understand what I mean."

"Yes."

"Do you fancy having dinner with me?"

"No thanks, I've got a candlelight dinner waiting at home."

Rami smiled at the idea, he went to his study, and brought out some books he read recently, "Any of these you haven't read? They're good."

"All of them, god where do you find the time to read, write and study?"

"I don't know…"

"Actually I'd better go. Take care, and if you need anything you know where I am."

"Thanks Ahmad, you're a true friend."

Ten minutes later, Nabil phoned inviting him to a New Year's Eve party. He found an excuse not to go as he wanted to spend it alone.

Rami laid the table with few of his favourite dishes, poured himself a generous helping of whisky, put on a reel to reel tape of the latest music from the chart, dimmed the lights, and let the one man party begin.

Two hours later, the front door opened, and Farrah walked in, not knowing what to expect. She saw Rami dancing alone with a glass half full of whisky. She put down her suitcase, and her shoulder bag, and watched him for almost twenty minutes.

"Farrah!" He screamed.

"Hi baby."

Without another word, she was in his arms.

"I'm sorry I'm so drunk."

"It doesn't matter. I like you this way, you're very easy to seduce."

"I love you though."

"You love anyone with a skirt."

"Farrah baby, am I that bad?"

"Yes!"

After dancing with him for a while, she made herself a drink, filled a plate with food, and sat down.

"You're terrible dancer when you're drunk!" she giggled.

"Do you have to tell me that?"

"Yes," she laughed. "I love you so much at times." She stood up, and began dancing with him again.

"Am I making a fool of myself?"' He chuckled happily.

"You are…! You are harmless baby when you are drunk, and very funny." She ran her fingers to the side of his face, "Come with me, you need a shower to wake you up as I have a surprise for you."

When he returned to the living room, she was stood in the middle holding a few magazines. "A total of twenty-five pages of articles about you, plus one serious interview. I knew the answers so there was no point in asking you face to face."

"Do you get paid for this kind of shit?" He teased.

She eased herself between his arms. "Happy New Year my love, this is the best get to know you gift you could have."

"Happy New Year angel, I'm so happy you are here."

"So am I." She took a deep breath. "I've missed being here; this place is us no matter what. Hold me tight Rami, I need to feel you." He did as she asked. "I hate romantic words, I hate being sentimental, but I'm going to be for once so you'd better listen."

"I love you."

"Rami you made me into a free person, you make me feel like a woman when I am with you. My whole body throbs to your touch, the way you look at me in hunger. You took me out of that mould called society and made me walk with confidence. I am Farrah, the model writer, but when I'm close to you, I'm just your little cat seeking attention and wanting your approval. I'm your woman. I want nothing else than to be a seductive woman, to love you, to arouse you, to laugh and cry with you. These simple things might mean nothing to you, but to me, they're my whole life; all I have to keep me going."

"Wow Farrah, I haven't a clue what I did."

"You made me aware of my beauty, and now I use it to get places. I'm aware of my sexuality, and it's only for you to have, to feel, and to use."

"I love you. Let's go to bed."

"I thought you'd never ask," said Farrah grinning.

- - - - - - - - -

Life went on and it was a happy time for everyone. Ahmad's latest book was an amazing success, and it went into print in several Arab countries. Samir became a partner in one of the private hospitals in Baghdad. The shop almost paid all its debts in a short period. And Farrah was offered many positions in various magazines, but she accepted an assistant editor role in a leading women's journal in Baghdad. Nevertheless, she had to travel to Europe to gain experience, visit fashion shows, and to attend various other functions. Her trips were mainly for a few days at a time. She was building an incredible reputation as hardworking and single-minded.

"Do you think I'm your puppet to play with whenever you want?" she said to Rami one day.

"Yes!"

She laughed, but she could never be angry with him. Whatever he said or did was perfectly acceptable by her.

"What's brewing in your mind?"

"I need to do something. I feel restless."

"But you have your writings, your studies, the shop, and me…what else do you need?"

He sat up on the bed, while her fingers ran up and down his spine. Her eyes filled, as he turned and faced her.

"I love you very much Rami. But, I'm not ready for you yet, not now, not tomorrow, but one day you'll be mine."

"You frighten me."

"I look forward to being with you, but I'm going to make some money first for both of us to enjoy. We can buy a house anywhere in the world, and have lots of little Ramis'. And, we can do nothing apart from eating, drinking, and making love."

"I never thought you were such a dreamer," said Rami. "But what if one of us falls in love with someone else?"

"I don't want to think about that."

"Nor do I."

"Make love to me."

"Again…?"

CHAPTER TWENTY

THE Christians in Iraq learnt to survive throughout the centuries. They made friends with people from other religions and they treaded cautiously but nervously. They were trusted in industry, economy, banking, businesses, medicine, and even in high positions in the government especially as advisers.

Government after government respected the minority in the country, and the latest government was no different.

Rami felt that they needed the young Christian society to be informed better, educated better, and helped along the way to improve their quality of life.

"How about starting a new sodality?" said Rami, "There are two empty meeting rooms on the first floor at the Centre"

"When do we have the time to do anything?" said Nabil. "This shop is going brilliantly, and we're working fourteen hours a day. How can we find time to do other things?"

"So you're not interested?"

"I didn't say that!"

"Don't include me in all this, I'm not here and I don't even have an opinion," Khalid teased.

"Be quiet!" the other two said at the same time.

"But I just wanted you to know that I'm your first member." Khalid added.

The other two didn't know whether he was serious or teasing. So they ignored him and continued with their conversation.

"What about the shop, Rami?"

"We can bring someone in to help us part-time. I don't expect you to work all those hours, week after week without any social life." Rami said.

"Nothing wrong with my social life, I come here to rest." Khalid added laughingly, and continued "Why do you want to do this all of a sudden?"

They stared at Rami as he tried to think of the right answers. Finally he spoke. "I feel as if we are losing our identity and that's all those Sodalities in Baghdad aren't doing enough to us. Look what's happening socially around the city. Look at our customers and you will see."

"See what? They come in, they order, we take their money, we say thank you very much and come again. You've been studying too much!"

"Since this government came to power, thousands and thousands of people have moved into Baghdad, driven by the idea of jobs and money, just by joining the Baath Party. Heaven knows if the party was setup to be like this, but that's how it is now. Christians from poorer backgrounds are arriving every day, as well as Sunnis and Shiites and more. They're leaving their farms, their villages, their way of life, and soon our farms will turn to desert, our villages will disappear, and our way of life will change."

"And having a new Sodality will change that?" Nabil argued back.

"I don't know. It's better than sitting on our hands and doing nothing. We'll have upper class marrying lower class; we'll have mixed religion marriages, imagine how children will behave not knowing their real roots."

"Wow…you are serious, and somehow I agree with you." Khalid laughed.

"What can we do then?"

"We can help by opening their eyes to our new way of life. We need to make people aware of each other, talk and listen to each other. We need to get closer to other sects and religions, even helping them to accept one another."

They were quiet for a while; each engulfed in his own thoughts.

"I'm for it, I'll do it," said Nabil.

"So am I, sign me in please," Khalid added.

"I've written a draft principles and laws. Read them at your leisure and tell me what you think."

"We need a strong tough liberal priest as a supervisor. Someone's got to stand up to our beloved Patriarch; he's backward, old-fashioned, and narrow-minded."

"Tell me about it! He would have been old fashioned two centuries ago," Khalid declared, "The man wears blinkers, and can't see what's going on around him."

Events moved quickly and, they were in a race to meet the deadline set by the Committee for the Centre as the end of May. The bad news was that despite the many objections Nabil and Rami had put in against accepting the Holy Cross Sodality; they were given another six months to prove themselves.

Father Allen accepted his position as a supervisor for the new Sodality to everyone's delight. He was keen on the youth movement in the country and keen on the new ideas presented to him. Although he was French, he mastered the Arabic language with confidence.

It didn't take them long before they submitted their constitution, the names of the thirty-one members; a fine mixture of young individuals with varied backgrounds, and levels of education.

By mid-April they held regular meetings at each other's houses in order to strengthen the bond between them.

Nabil and Rami encouraged heated debates, in which everyone could participate and share their knowledge, ideas and experiences. The atmosphere was electric but stimulating each time they met.

The Sodality was accepted to hold its meetings at the Centre, and use the facilities there. However one obstacle stood in their way; tolerating and dealing with the Holy Cross gang.

Father Allen delivered a delicate speech during their first meeting at the centre. "Life is a war of survival. We were born in a jungle, born to fight our way out of that jungle, even if it was familiar to us. By coming here to the Centre, you must not show weakness, you must always stand proud, stand together as one unit, help and support one another. Our world is filled with jealousy and hatred, but it is also filled with love, and the passion to be successful. Watch each other's back, and keep an eye on where you are going."

As they left the meeting, and went to the garden, they were met by Johnny and Talaat.

"Well done Rami; congratulations on the new Sodality. It's been very hard for us not having a real rival, and we hope you'll be one."

Rami tactfully ignored his remark. "May I introduce our committee to you, Maha, Francis, Huda, and Ikbal. I'm sure you'll soon meet the rest of our members."

"It's my pleasure to meet you all," said Johnny.

"Are you the Chairman then?" Talaat muttered.

"No, I'm not on the committee."

"Unbelievable, you lost the election?"

It was time for Maha to butt in. "As a matter of fact we didn't have or need an election. We had more time on our hands so we took the responsibility of looking after the affairs of our Sodality...do you understand?"

"So the founder didn't have the time to help run it?"

"The founder is working on a huge project that has never been done before, and that requires more time than looking after the affairs of the Sodality," Francis declared.

Johnny and Talaat hurriedly excused themselves and walked away as Rami and his friends burst into laughter.

"What project may I ask?" Rami said.

"I don't know, we'll make one up."

"I hate them, they're so slimy," said Huda at last."They give me the creeps."

"Those types of people are everywhere," Maha concluded.

- - - - - - - - -

The record shop proved to be a gold mine. They paid all their debts, and purchased more equipment. Their record collection grew by the day, as Khalid and Nabil travelled to Lebanon and Jordan on a regular basis to purchase the latest releases. To their surprise they could even afford to withdraw a respectable monthly wage. The government had full control on the imports of all goods coming into the country, especially musical records that weren't produced in an Arab country. The three partners' actions might have been interpreted as illegal elsewhere in the world, however it was quite acceptable in Iraq, as otherwise the people would be starved from the western cultures, and music.

They acquired the premises next to their shop and developed it into a repair unit for electrical appliances. They hired two of the best electrical engineers they could find and offered them the deal of a lifetime. As expected the new shop was a great success from day one; it was just what the area needed.

None of their friends believed the success story. And, Farruk was incredibly surprised when six thousand Dinars were counted on his desk. He was amazed waiting for a reaction from his young friend Rami, who had a proud smile on his face.

"Whatever you touch turns to gold! Please touch my table, the papers, my pen, please for God's sake."

"Very funny, we are doing well, but that's it."

But sadly that wasn't the case with his writings. In fact, he was going through a mental block patch in producing new ideas, so he decided to concentrate on his studies and the end of year examinations.

- - - - - - - - -

It seemed the government was spreading its arms in every direction to strengthen its control over the country to every tribe, every family, every street and every neighbourhood. All had to suffer the brutality of the regime in one way or another. The regime wanted to inflict pain, fear, destroy the core of the society, isolate one community from another, build a rift between the tribes, and increase the gap that separated the Sunnis from the Shiats, and other minorities. They were masters in breaking up communities, building the most complicated network of secret police, army intelligence, Baath Party militia, and spies. Listening and reporting to their commanders within their own party was the art of success and the unwritten rules for dictatorship.

They knew many people wanted revenge and they knew how to defend themselves, they created them therefore they knew no one dared to raise his arm high; it would have been hacked from its roots.

This brutality finally reached Rami's family. His uncle was arrested for twenty-four hours and brutally tortured by a bunch of well trained cowards. He died days later from his injuries; he had a rusty nail imbedded in his spine. It was the most devastating chapter to hit the family yet. Words would never be enough to describe what the government had done. There would never ever be tears shed as hot as those by the family over the loss of their son, uncle and a brother.

Rami's uncle was a genius, who spoke and wrote in fifteen languages. He spent his life travelling the world, meeting people and making friends. He ate healthily, he never drank alcohol, he never smoked, and when he went for his medical examination two weeks before his arrest, the doctor told him he had a stronger heart than some men in their twenties.

When the phone rang his father called from the hospital to break the news gently to the family. Rami ran out of the house without actually thinking where he was heading. He ran all the way to his uncle's house, and stood outside looking at it. It looked dull, strange and lifeless. He had laughed with his uncle only two days ago, yet how could he laugh if he was going to die?

'Should I cry?' he asked himself time and time again.

He examined the windows again for the tenth time, but nothing had changed. His uncle's car was still in the driveway and it had not moved for days.

His grandmother opened the door. "Rami, your uncle isn't here. He has gone to heaven."

"I know nana I'm so sorry." He hugged her.

"Did you come to see me?" she asked.

"Yes grandma. I came to see you and be with you."

"Your dad hasn't been nasty to you? Has he?" She asked, and Rami realised that his grandmother was in a bad state of mind.

"No he hasn't, I just wanted to be with you that's all."

"I just put the chicken in the oven for your uncle. He likes his chicken roasted."

"I'd better clean the house."

The eighty-five-year-old woman was in a state of shock, dusting where she didn't need to. Rami had no choice but to phone the rest of the family and tell them. Within minutes, the house filled with people who wanted to take care of the old lady.

The funeral was two days later. Hundreds of people turned up including a few government ministers to apologise for their wrong doings. Relatives and friends came from across the country; from Mosul, Karkuk, Basra and other cities, to pay their respects. The women sat inside the house, while the men sat in a large circle in the garden. There were no empty seats left, and people stood in the street listening to recorded hymns. Two waiters offered black unsweetened coffee and cigarettes to the mourners. Most stayed for no longer than twenty minutes. No one spoke. Rami stayed at home to keep his brother's company. On the second day he went to the church with his parents, which was filled with mourners. Many people stood in the aisles and outside the church as all the seats were occupied.

After the mass, they all walked behind his father towards the grave. He was buried in the church yard. Rami found a side pillar, leant against it, and cried. His legs couldn't carry him further towards the grave; he had an unexplained fear inside him, accompanied with sharp pain. His cousin put his arm around him and guided him to his car.

At his uncle's house, the cars filled the driveway, then the streets. Tens of people walked in but not Rami. He froze in the car, crying. He tried to stop, but the more he tried the harder it became. The pain inside was uncontrollable and he broke down with a wailing roar. His cousin and a few others failed to comfort him; they washed his face with water and opened the car windows, as June was a very hot month.

May came to the rescue; she took his hand and led him out of the car into hers. In her house, she left him in the living room alone to calm down.

Soon, he fell asleep.

She woke him up two hours later, as it was time for lunch.

"Rami, how are you feeling?"

"Angry with myself because I lost control. I'm angry because they killed my uncle, and angry with the whole rotten world."

"You're not the only one who is angry, everyone is angry about what happened to your uncle. He was a beautiful man, and he loved you, and admired you from a distance. He had more faith in you than your own dad."

"You shouldn't mourn his death, you should celebrate his life. Think of the laughter he brought with him after visiting different countries, think of his stories about other cultures and customs. He was one special man."

"I will miss him terribly. I know I didn't see him much, but I knew he was always there."

"Yes, I feel sorry for your grandma. She looked completely lost yesterday, in fact, they all did. Ahmad and Jean helped so much yesterday."

"They are family, just like you and Samir." He said looking out of the window, "I hate yellow sun, a sad sun!"

"You're staying here tonight." She said as she closed the curtains, "Samir is away on a conference in Paris, and I don't like to stay on my own. I've already asked your mum, and she was glad that I'm taking you away from it all."

"I'm sorry."

"Sorry for what?"

"Everything..! I hurt you badly and I used you."

"You didn't."

The following day Rami insisted on going for a picnic by the river away from the city and the people. Somewhere he could relax, breathe fresh air and write. At night they went dancing. She objected at first, but she finally gave in to his demands. Luckily no one they knew saw them; otherwise it would have been the biggest source of gossip in the city.

After that night he sat in the dining room to attend to more serious business. He put the last touches on his first play, he wrote poems and short stories. He hardly slept for the entire week he spent at May's house. Often she would wake up to see him cursing because of a mental block, or praising himself for another masterpiece. She enjoyed watching him and looking after him, providing anything and everything he wished for. He had a big appetite, and he ate well, which gave her endless satisfaction.

"You are feeding two people Rami, yourself and your brain!"

"Very funny madam...I love your cooking."

"You love food full stop."

She provided him with her body too, and she gave it to him generously, and took just as much from him. To her sadness he only stayed for a week.

- - - - - - - - -

It had been a long time since Rami spend an evening in the company of his family. He needed to be part of it again. They all needed him as much as he needed them.

"Son, I don't want you to wear a black tie anymore." His father said suddenly, while they were playing backgammon.

Rami looked at his dad in amazement; he was a traditional man, and wearing a black tie for at least forty days was part of their custom. He didn't want to enter a long conversation about how and why.

"Ok, I won't wear it anymore."

"Are you alright son? Do you need anything?"

"Thanks for asking dad, but I am fine, it's you I am worried about."

"Thank god for Ahmad and Jean, May and Samir. They helped us so much in the last few days, more than the so-called relatives we have. Ahmad never left my sight, he stood by me all the time, and I will never forget that, and so did Jean looking after your grandmother, and aunts. She is a wonderful lady."

"They are good people."

"God bless them."

"Can I work with you dad? I feel it is time to learn about the family business, and you need some help after what has happened."

"Yes fine by me, you can come in for a few hours every week, but your studies come first."

"It's summer!"

"Oh yes, I wasn't thinking."

"Dad you can always talk to me. I know I might not be able to comprehend everything that happened to our family, but I can always try and listen."

The tears ran down their faces as they hugged each other. Rami hated seeing his father cry, but there was nothing he could do to ease the pain. He doubted whether time would ever heal those wounds.

- - - - - - - - -

Rami was keen to learn how to operate every machine in the factory, along with the ordering system, the work schedules, and the stock control. It wasn't easy as his father and late uncle had devised unique methods of keeping tags on everything that went on. He felt part of the work force though, and refused any special attention they showed him at first. He ate with them, sat with them in their tea breaks, and even visited their workingmen's club. He won his place as one of the gang, although they were all like family, as most of them had worked for his dad since the early fifties. All he wanted to do was to impress his father and ease the burden of running the company alone.

During that time, the staging of his first play was a great success. It was held over three days at the Centre and many people who saw it once also bought tickets for the second and third day.

Farrah was spending less time in Baghdad. She felt homesick, but as soon as she was back, she needed to leave the country hurriedly. Rami devoted all his time to being with her whenever she was home. They talked, argued, laughed, went out dancing and dining, and on occasion, they made love. She taught him how to drive, and he enjoyed it. He persuaded Farruk to obtain a special licence for him, and he bought himself a car. He parked it around the corner at the top of the street, so his father wouldn't find out. To his father, a car in a young man's hand is a lethal weapon for corruption.

- - - - - - - - -

The heat of July was intolerable, but that night in particular it was cool, especially after the caretaker of the Centre had watered the large garden, and generously sprinkled all the trees. The garden was filled with members from different Sodalities socialising and listening to background music. Rami sat with his friends laughing and joking.

His attention was diverted when he glanced towards the entrance. "Wow, take a look at the most gorgeous creature God ever created," he whispered to Nabil, who was sitting next to him.

"Close your mouth, too many flies around." Nabil laughed.

"God has taken his time creating her."

One of the girls who sat in their circle ran towards her, and brought her back. Everyone shuffled around to make space for her. "This is Leila everyone," said the girl, "She's in my class."

Rami turned to Nabil again. "I'm in love…"

Nabil laughed. "Put your eyes back in their sockets and please don't show us up."

"Would I ever do that?"

"Yes, you always do!"

Rami's eyes never left her face and her beautifully carved lips. He could tell even from that distance that she had green eyes. She was tall, her skin was tanned, and her figure would melt a mountain.

"How's the car?" someone said, distracting him.

"Good."

"Are you happy with it?"

"Very happy thank you," he said loudly to extract her attention.

"And the factory…? Are you happy there too?"

"Extremely."

Everyone began to laugh; they noticed that he wasn't interested in anyone else but the beautiful Leila, who sat three chairs away from him, and had ignored him completely since she joined them.

"I need to buy a better car this week."

Leila didn't move an eyelid, and simply ignored him. She had come across those who spoke loudly before, who blew their own trumpet, and had nothing to occupy what little they had between their ears.

"Are you in the literary competition this year?"

"Of course…!" He continued to answer loudly. "As long as, there are writers who need to be humiliated."

"Will you behave please?" Nabil begged.

"Well someone had to teach them a lesson last year; do you really think there's a better writer than me?'

"As a matter of fact there are some brilliant writers around." Leila said. "I don't know who you think you are."

At last he had got her attention. "Name me one, you seem to be very well informed," he said.

"I find you big-headed and ill-mannered," said Leila. "I'm sorry to offend my friend, but I can't take anymore of this."

Everyone was quiet, their eyes travelled between Leila and Rami. She decided to carry on, "It's my first visit here, and I find young people like you with no purpose in life, shallow minded, with no culture or intelligence."

"My dear Leila," he said, changing his tone of voice. "I'm sorry if I acted like a child. I can assure you that I'm very serious person; we all are here. We debate serious issues that affect us daily, but sometimes we act like uncultured idiots, just for fun. When we have been working all day in this hot weather, something triggers that little switch within us, to unwind us and relax us to have some innocent fun. I can't see the harm in that, can you?"

She didn't reply to his question and she was about to leave when Rami continued. "So as a peace offering, what would everyone like to drink?"

She smiled, he was a gentleman after all, and he did look smart, he spoke well, and had a magical hoarseness to his voice.

Two people volunteered to carry the order from the bar to where they sat. Rami moved his chair and squeezed in between Maha and Leila.

"I'm sorry Leila; I was just pulling your leg."

"Apology accepted," she said. "Thanks for the drink."

"You're welcome. Tell me, who is your favourite writer?"

"Well there is Rami A, who I've heard is a member here at the Centre."

"He's rubbish," Rami said to the giggles of others. "He hasn't got a clue what it's all about?"

She displayed annoyance at his remark. "I suppose you'll tell me next that you know him well?"

"I know him better than anyone. He's awful, brain dead, and he'll never beat me in a million years."

"He's the best this country has to offer. What do you write?"

"Poems, articles, short stories…whatever comes to mind."

Suddenly the conversation was interrupted as Rami was called for a telephone call.

"Is his name Rami too?" Leila asked her friends.

"Sorry I was talking to Francis and I wasn't listening to you."

"That ignorant person."

"Do you mean Rami? He is lovely, one of the friendliest funniest people I met. Everyone loves him."

"He is one ignorant boy."

"Are we talking about the same person here?"

"I only had to mention Rami A. and he told me how crap he is, and he is much better…I hate him." Leila insisted.

"Yes! He's Rami A."

"No way..! He made a fool out of me." A smile crossed her face. "I'll get him for that one day."

Rami returned. "Well, I've got to go my friends, have a lovely evening, and behave yourselves." Then he turned to Leila. "It was lovely to meet you, I hope you come again."

"Anything wrong?" Nabil asked.

"Ahmad and Jean are at the house and I haven't seen them for days."

"Ok, goodnight and see you tomorrow."

Rami left, but came back an hour later to find out that everyone else had gone home except for Nabil and Maha.

"She has gone Rami!" Maha teased.

"And you forgot to take her phone number!" Nabil added laughingly, and added. "Well I've got work in the morning so I'm going home to bed," Nabil declared. "Do you need a lift home Maha?"

"Thank you, but I think I'll stay a bit longer if Rami doesn't mind giving me a lift home in his fantastic dream car."

Rami sat in silence after Nabil had left and stared into space.

"Hey you, I'm here!" said Maha.

"Sorry, I was just wondering why I behaved like that with Leila."

"We all do things that are out of character for us at times, and we wonder after why we did it."

Maha was a second year student at the science college, University of Baghdad. She had a bubbly personality, and acted like everyone's big sister; dishing them out advice and helping them with their affairs.

"You did make me angry Rami, you out of all people, I felt awkward myself, and I felt sorry for the poor girl."

"I liked her a lot," said Rami. "She's my type of girl."

"Yeah right, you just want to add her to the list of women you've been out with!"

"People like you can give someone innocent like me a bad name," he said.

"People like you should take people like me for a spin in their car," Came back Maha.

Baghdad at night was the most romantic city in the world. Like magic, the city changed its appearance, from the rush of people, the hustle and bustle of cars, men pushing carts loaded with goods, the noise of vehicle's horns, people shouting, the knocking and hammering of metal, shopkeepers screaming at the top of their voices inviting punters to come, people dashing and running between others, to the delicate peaceful slow existence. Baghdad at night was like a woman preparing for her lover, and a long night of passion and lust, a woman with a provoking exquisite nightdress ready to lure her man to hours of true love before sunrise and the invasion by the masses.

The essence of the city created poets, story tellers, and lovers from across the vast land. Men drank wine from the bodies of their lovers, and sang to the melody of a few simple musical instruments. At night Baghdad danced to slow rhythms, along with tens of yachts and thousands of coloured lights scattered unevenly in all directions. The city of a million dreams, with two rivers running through its heart like veins.

"Where do you fancy going?" Rami asked.

"Anywhere you want," said Maha.

As they drove past Al-Nawas Street the smell of Masgoof wafted into their nostrils; fish from the Tigris cooked around a cane fire. The smell tormented him and he couldn't resist the temptation. "Hungry?"

"Mmmm, I certainly am," said Maha smiling, as she read his mind.

For the first time he felt a freedom he'd never felt before. He had his own car and he didn't have to depend on anyone to drive him home.

"It's like committing a sin, the two of us sitting in a corner, eating fish with our hands, Nan bread and pickle. What more can anyone ask for?"

"A newspaper photographer taking a photo of you and me here eating like this. Front page news huh?" She added.

"Headlines will say they let their guard down, and now they are living and eating like animals."

"No...Wasted youth, no manners, no breeding and......"

"No knives and forks."

After the meal Rami drove Maha home. They sat in the car outside her house talking. She told him how lucky she was having trusting parents and how she wasn't over-protected like other girls, even though she was the only female in the family. He told her about himself as well, but she already knew most of it.

"I like you very much, and thanks for a lovely night," said Maha. "I enjoyed every minute of it and I can't ever remember laughing so much before."

"I enjoyed it too," said Rami. "Thanks for coming."

"Wow! You can be so polite when you want to be, I'm impressed."

"You haven't seen anything yet."

"Oh, is there more?"

He was about to pull her towards him and kiss her, but he stopped.

"Why did you stop?"

"It's not right, sorry please forgive me."

She put her hand on his, "I wouldn't have objected."

"I know, but I don't want to ruin our friendship."

"Nor do I Rami."

She leaned forward and kissed him on his lips, "This is for being a gentleman my dear friend."

- - - - - - - - -

With all the friends Rami had, he often felt lonely. Some of his problems he did talk about to Ahmad, Khalid or Nabil , and other subjects he'd have to wait and discuss with Farrah or May. He seemed so confident, and extremely secure, but in reality he was screaming for attention and he lacked self belief. He realised that maybe it was time to step out of it and have a close look at himself. But how could he do that.

Although he came from a good secure home, and a loving family, he had had a very good education, yet he was frightened and wished at times he knew what was troubling him. He stopped analysing himself, as the more he tried to understand his situation, the worse he felt.

He sat alone in the cafeteria at the Centre. It was nine o'clock which was early for him. The night hadn't started yet, but, he felt extremely lazy and too tired to move, or head home to his bed. The big literary competition was only a week away, and he hadn't even put pen to paper yet. The charity ball was in two days, and he wasn't sure whether to go, or who to take with him.

At last he ordered a coffee, and went back to his corner, watching the many faces coming in and out. They were mechanical, like robots, and all they lacked was robotic movements, which at last brought a smile to his face. When he finally went to bed that night, he fell asleep straight away.

In Baghdad, most people slept on the roof of their houses during the summer because it was much cooler than sleeping indoors. Plus, it was magical to gaze at the black sky, with all the diamonds flickering light. That's when he felt safe, completely peaceful inside.

He slept all the way through until morning, which was unusual for him, and he was awoken by a few drops of water splashed over his face.

"I'll kill you," he shouted before he opened his eyes, thinking it was his brother.

"Will you really?"

"Farrah…! What are you doing here?" He leapt out of bed.

"Your mother said breakfast is ready and if you aren't going to work, then you better phone your cousin and tell him so."

"I don't believe it, it's really you."

As he folded his bedding and carried it to the small room on the roof, Farrah was eager to tell him about her latest adventure.

"I'm only here for four days, and I'll be off again," she said as she followed him to his bedroom.

"Why can't you find a job here?"

"I have a job here. I love my jobs; I'm freelancing for many magazines, and I'm assistant editor for one. I do miss being here, but it's a small price to pay for a big career in the future."

Without thinking she followed him to the bathroom, and kept talking while he showered. "Have you got any plans for today Rami?"

"I was going to the factory, but I need a day off."

"I've already sorted that out with your dad."

"Shall we go swimming?" He suggested.

"Yes why not? I'll pack my swimming stuff."

Al-Alwiyah Club was situated in the Al-Saadoon district; created by British officers in the mid-twenties for the elite of the Baghdad society, and foreign dignitaries. Membership was given to the well-known families in the city. Farrah's parents were members, therefore they were permitted entrance.

"Any gossip?" she asked as she stretched by the swimming pool.

"Not really, although the literary competition is next week, and I haven't written anything, in fact, I'm completely dried up."

"Maybe that's because you aren't reading much. Often one idea, one word or one picture can trigger loads of stories."

"Yes Farrah, I remember someone telling you that not long ago."

"What else is going on?"

"I bought a car."

"A car…? You're still under age!"

"I twisted Farruk's hand for a licence, he knows people in the government. I keep it at the top of the street."

"You're amazing."

"I missed you very much, and you're looking extremely relaxed and happy with yourself, unlike me. I'm bored and frustrated with everything. I need an impossible challenge." He said.

"Travelling Europe and other Arab countries opened my eyes to the problems facing our generation and future generations. We have so few opportunities nowadays compared to fifty or hundred years ago. The world has accelerated at such a speed, so if you don't move at that speed or faster, you'll end up achieving nothing. It'll be even more difficult for our children. You can't just up and leave because you are bored of being successful."

"Sorry…!"

"Let's have lunch and get out of this heat, then we'll go to the flat and I'll show you my latest work."

- - - - - - - - -

An Armenian Band called 'Sherag' played throughout the charity dance at the Centre. Over four-hundred people packed into the garden.

Farrah wore a designer dress in a light flowery colour, which she had bought in Paris. As they walked towards their circle of friends, almost everyone turned and admired her. Rami wore a summery beige coloured suit and a multi-coloured tie.

Once they had greeted everyone, they began to dance, and later joined in a quick game to raise more money. Their wit won many laughs. After more dancing they went to the bar for some drinks.

A tap on his shoulder made the two of them turn. "Hi Rami, how are you?"

"Leila! Good to see you! This is Farrah. Farrah this is Leila"

"This is Essa."

"Hi Essa, what are you drinking?" Rami asked as he shook his hand.

"I'll have a beer, and Leila is drinking orange juice."

Farrah noticed Rami's sudden interest. "Essa come and give me a hand with the drinks please," she said.

"She's extremely beautiful and elegant. You know how to pick them," Leila said as the other two walked away.

"She's my best friend. I've known her for a long time. But I do like your boyfriend."

"He's in fifth year medical college."

"You know how to pick them too," said Rami.

"I had no choice in the matter."

A short silence followed.

"Lovely party isn't it?" Rami said.

"It is, and I see you're certainly enjoying yourself. You've hardly left the dance floor all night."

"Why are you so interested in what I do?"

She replied immediately. "How can anyone not notice Farrah on the dance floor? She's stunning."

Essa and Farrah returned with the drinks. "There you are sweetheart, an ice cold beer."

"Thanks for the drinks Farrah. Come on Essa…It was nice to have met you both." Leila said, staring deep into his eyes.

"You're welcome to join us," Farrah said, but, they had already walked away.

"You are wicked."

"Who was that? She's one very jealous female. Do you like her?"

"I don't know, yes maybe. I do in a way!"

"You do, you were undressing each other with your eyes. I saw the look on your faces."

"Oh Farrah!"

"If I didn't come back when I did, you would've been screwing each other on the floor. Mind you Essa is handsome and he's in medical college."

"I know, she told me."

"And she didn't like me at all when I called you sweetheart," said Farrah laughing.

"You did it on purpose," he complained.

"Of course I did!"

"You just destroyed every chance I had with her."

"Good because tonight you are mine. I'm leaving the day after tomorrow."

"Shall we go back to the flat?"

CHAPTER TWENTY ONE

THE phone rang in the office. Rami was busy reading some reports he found in the filing cabinet in his father's office. He felt like letting it ring and ring, but at the end he decided to answer it, in case it was an important call.

"Hello, Rami here."

"My god, you don't sound that happy, have you got the bug now?"

"How are you Farruk?" Rami tried to tease him.

"I'm very concerned about you," said Farruk. "I haven't heard from you for ages. The last time I saw you, you didn't look happy. What's going on?"

"I'm just so fed up with this place," said Rami. "I start before seven in the morning. I unlock the doors, switch on the power, and have the guardsman making me an Arab coffee. Then the workers arrive and the work starts. I'm here until seven at night, then I have my supper."

"That's crazy. You need to get out and see people. What about your dad?"

"He has lost interest in the business. He wakes up very late, eats his breakfast, and sits in his study sorting out his stamps for hours. I send him papers to sign, and that's all he does."

"It sounds like he is going through a serious depression."

"Anyone who dares to tell him that will have their head bitten off."

"Now you know how I feel."

Rami laughed.

"Make some time and come and see me. Come to my house if you like. We need to talk about your writings." He took a deep breath and continued. "I need some pronto. You've only published four bits in the last three weeks."

"I'm sorry. I have written quite a lot but I haven't had the chance to tidy them up. I'll see what I can do."

By the time he ended the telephone call, there was a knock on the door.

"Come in…"

"Good morning Rami…"

"Jaber…This is a surprise!" He said sarcastically, "I was just thinking why you haven't you called me today."

"My wife is having a baby today, I must go home now."

"Not again please…does she produce a baby every month? How many children have you got now, two dozen?"

"Today is the day. If it's a boy I will call him after you."

"No…your wife will let you know when she has the baby. Now get back to work before I'll call the union man. Is she in labour?"

"No…but she will be when I get there, I know, I can feel it in my blood."

"I've had enough, hasn't she got anyone else with her?"

"Yes…we never leave her alone, it's her first baby."

"What? I thought you already have children!"

"Yes, but this is my third wife. She has my first two wives with her, and her mother, but they need a man with them."

Rami couldn't stop laughing, "I heard it all now, what do you want to do with three wives you greedy man? Get back to work Jaber, I am sure they will phone when she is ready, and I'll get someone to drive you to your house."

He smiled as the worker went out of the room, but the telephone rang again, "These prices are wrong, some are under-priced, others we'll be lucky to sell one, what am I going to do?" A shop manager complained.

He disliked that shop manager, the conversation went on and on, and the argument got out of hand. By now Rami was screaming down the telephone, "If you don't like to be in our company then get out, there are hundreds of people who would love to have your job."

"I am sorry I didn't mean to insult you or your dad."

"I'll get someone to phone you back."

He went to the office door, "Can you check the cost on the last few items we sent to Ayad, he's moaning about the price."

"Yes, I'll do it straight away."

"Thanks…I am going home, I've had enough today."

The five office staff looked at each other in amazement, they thought that Rami was in control and enjoyed what he was doing.

As soon as he got home, he went directly to his dad, who was still in bed reading the daily newspaper. "I've had enough of you, the factory, the damn business, the workers, the shop managers…enough is enough."

"What's wrong?"

"Nothing…what could possibly go wrong?" Rami answered sarcastically. "One machine broke down this morning, no spare parts, so I sent the broken wheel to have one made especially, but all your damn workers on that line stopped working, and sat drinking tea. Another machine is just ticking over, and the parts have been ordered, but they're coming from Italy. Jaber's wife is having a baby. And guess what? This is wife number three, so from now on he takes three leaves every year, because each one of his wives will have one brat a year. And Ayad is moaning about the pricing. I was told he moans all the time, so I told them to recheck the costing, and we are not even half way through the day."

Rami's father laughed and laughed. He had never seen his son speaking so passionately about anything before.

"Dad, why don't you just sell the company and be done with it? I'm going out. I haven't seen daylight for days. I'm tired and I've been working seven days a week."

"You asked me for the job, and you're getting well paid for it, aren't you?"

"Yes dad and thanks a million, but I'm resigning as of now." Rami left the room as his dad continued to laugh from behind the door.

"Silly old dad…!" Rami muttered.

- - - - - - - - -

Khalid was on his own as Rami walked into the shop. "Hello stranger."

"Good lord where did you come from! How are you my friend?"

"Don't ask," said Rami. "I've had it up to my neck at the factory with problem after problem."

"Come and sit down, there's a cold coke in the fridge."

"Thanks. Where's Nabil?"

"He won't be long, he's at the bank."

"I'm sorry. I should spend more time here."

"You're not superman, but I guess you can help now. I've got to finish a couple of things. Here's the chart of all the tapes, and this is the order book, so get started! We're ten days behind, and we might have to work extra hours."

"My God!"

"Even with the extra recorders we bought last week, we simply can't cope with the demands."

Rami looked around him, "I thought there was something different."

"If anything goes wrong leave it until I get back, or Nabil might return by then."

As Rami sat behind the table, he checked every recorder. They were all working perfectly. He changed the tapes, and started recording another. A few minutes later, a customer walked in, and he dealt with his request then sat down again and waited for the next tape to finish. A few more people walked in, and he talked and joked with them. He felt relaxed and happy. An hour passed, and it seemed more like minutes.

He picked up the account book from under the table, and flicked through the neatly written pages. He could not believe the figures, purchases, sales, expenditure, and the rent"

Nabil waked in at last. "Oh, you're still alive then?"

"Cheeky bastard! How are you?"

"Good thanks, and you?"

"Don't even go there." Nevertheless he told him about his dad.

"He'll be okay, you will see."

"You never told me how well we're doing."

"Extremely well. These aren't the true figures. Haven't you counted the money I've been giving you each month?"

"No, I've just been putting the envelopes in the drawer in the flat. I never bothered to open one of them."

"There are thousands in those envelopes."

"I never thought it would be this successful."

"It was your idea! So was the repair shop, which is doing extremely well. We have five people there working around the clock."

"I feel it in my bones that you are up to something. Come on, spill the beans!"

"We haven't put any money from the repair shop in our pockets yet. I've been saving that in the bank."

"But we have taken on the third unit here."

"And you don't know what to do with it, right?"

"Yes right! Where's Khalid?"

"He's sorting out a couple of things in the flat."

"His flat is above here," Nabil said pointing to the top of the building. "I'll go and call him. There's something else I want to discuss too."

When Nabil left, Rami went to examine the store room. He was shocked to see thousands of blank tapes.

When Nabil returned he asked Rami what they should do with the third unit.

"Open a bookshop," he said. "There isn't one in this area."

"I agree."

Khalid returned from his flat and the three of them were quiet for a while as they pressed on with the recordings, and served customers, but there were other issues that needed to be talked about.

"The landlord is having serious money problems, not because of this building, but another he owns." Nabil announced.

"So we offered to take this one off his hands." Khalid added.

"Are you out of your mind?" Rami said.

"I told you Rami wouldn't like it," Khalid complained.

"He might sell and he might not," said Nabil. "He hasn't got the money to finish building it. Also it looks like an eyesore when someone passes by, seeing all those empty shops."

"More shops, more people, more money for everyone," Khalid added.

"How much have you offered?" Rami asked.

"There are eight shops. The biggest two can be split into two. Also there are sixteen apartments."

"How much will he sell for?" Rami asked again.

"We offered around three-hundred thousand." Khalid replied quietly.

"What?" Rami shouted. "We've only been in business for eight months or so."

"Nine actually," Khalid corrected him, smiling.

"I'll think about it."

"We already have people interested in occupying the shops and the flats and they're prepared to put money in advance to secure the deals. There'll be no drop in our wages."

"I'm not worried about the wages. I can live on what I get from my writings." He scratched his head. "I'll think about it. I'm under age. If anything goes wrong it'll be my dad's neck on the deck."

"I never thought of that, but here are the figures. Study them first, and then make up your mind."

They were quiet for a while, everyone deep in thought. Suddenly, Khalid spoke. "I've got an idea, how about kebabs for lunch? I am starving."

"Sounds good…here is a deal, as we are opening the bookshop, we need lots of cash to decorate and stock. Can't we at least wait for six months without putting ourselves under so much pressure?" Rami suggested, and the other two agreed straight away.

"Oh! Before I forget, we've been invited to a birthday party tomorrow night." Khalid said.

"Whose?"

"A customer..! She said to ask the two of you," Khalid said. "I forgot to ask for her name, and she didn't give it to me either."

"I could do with a party. I haven't been away from the damn factory for weeks."

Khalid looked at the piece of paper by the phone. "I took the address, but I didn't take the name. What an idiot! I forgot to ask for her name."

"I haven't got a female to take with me," Rami complained.

"You haven't been with anyone since Nadia?"

"I'm not really looking, although I feel very lonely at times."

"You're breaking my heart," Khalid announced as he left the shop to get lunch.

- - - - - - - - -

The house that hosted the party was more like a mansion and it was located by the river. It was built over a two hundred year period during the Ottoman Empire; a gift to a high-ranking government official.

They were shown to a side entrance, after parking their cars in front of the house. A passage led them to the garden, which spread across six acres of land. It was elegantly landscaped with beds of rare flowers, roses, bulbs and shrubs. Citrus and palm trees added more beauty to the landscape. There was a fountain in the shape of a marbled girl, hand carved and holding a cask, from which water poured out. The patio was large, and a number of couples danced to live music. Many people were invited, and they spread themselves around the vast grounds.

"So this is how the other half lives!" Khalid murmured.

"This is fabulous. Look at that table with all the drinks on," Rami said.

"Look at the food...I am starving."

"You are always starving, what's new Khalid?"

They felt it was rather strange that no one had approached them or welcomed them.

"Come on Khalid lets go and mingle, and leave those two lovers alone," He said looking at Nabil and his girlfriend.

"Yes master. We are in need of women!"

"There are all sorts here, blondes, brunettes, tall, short, ugly and beautiful. Any type in particular you fancy?" Rami asked.

"I haven't seen anyone I fancy. I might have to stick to you all night."

"Good god, no! I'm not into tall dark and handsome men these days. Sorry buddy."

"You don't know what you're missing sweetie!" Khalid replied. They laughed, attracting a few people to look in their direction.

"I've never been anywhere without knowing someone, either from the shop, the centre, or school," Khalid commented.

"I do know somebody," said Rami. "Follow me."

Khalid walked hurriedly, trying hard to catch up.

"Leila! Hi, how are you?"

"Rami, good to see you, how are you?"

"Fantastic!"

"Where's your girlfriend?"

"I brought Khalid instead. He's more beautiful." They all laughed.

"I'm Leila, and this is my friend, Sonia."

"And I'm in love," Khalid confessed.

"Is he always like that?" Sonia laughed.

"Are you alone? Have you got a boyfriend?" he questioned Sonia with a begging look.

"I'm alone, and no, I haven't got a boyfriend."

"Not anymore!" He handed his glass to Rami, took Sonia's and handed it to Leila. "Now let's dance."

"Yes please," Sonia giggled.

"He's lovely," Leila commented as the other two walked away.

"I know. He's our third partner. Most girls come to the shop because of him. He's always jolly no matter what problems he might have."

"I like him."

"She isn't my girlfriend," said Rami suddenly.

"Who?"

"Farrah. She isn't my girlfriend."

"Oh well. No harm is done."

"Where's your boyfriend?"

"Essa? He's in Mosul, training at a hospital there."

She held his hand and they walked around.

"I wonder who this house belongs to!"

"Some middle aged couple," She replied. "Do you like it?"

"I adore it. It must've cost millions. I'd love to know the history of the place."

"Are you rich?" Leila asked.

"I'm comfortable but not rich. I'm working on it though."

"Tell me."

"Can I trust you?"

"Of course you can." She tightened her grip on his hand.

In between greeting people and acknowledging others, he told her about the businesses, and their plan for buying the building. He told her about his father's business, and about his beloved uncle.

"I have my own flat too. I've had it two years."

"What for?"

"Sex, women, and wild all night parties."

"Please tell me that's not you."

He laughed. "I just enjoy being free. Come and visit me with your boyfriend one day."

"Yes I'll visit you some time. Shall we eat now? I'm hungry."

"That's the best thing you've said all night," he teased.

She picked up two plates and helped herself to a delicious variety of food for them both, while Rami went to fill their glasses with punch.

"Do you really think I can eat that much?" Rami asked, with a smile.

Before Leila had the chance to answer they were joined by a friend of hers.

"So this must be the man himself? Rami, it's good to meet you."

"Thank you."

"I'm Aida. I've heard a lot about you."

"All good I hope?"

"Yes, Leila has never spoken ill of you. I better leave you now. I need to mingle and there are lots of people I haven't seen for a while."

Aida walked away.

"God, you're beautiful," said Rami. "Tell me about yourself."

"Well, I'm seventeen, I'm starting my sixth year at secondary school and I fancy being a pharmacist."

"And how many times have you been in love?" he asked.

"I fall in love every day or so," she replied, smiling. "What about you?"

"Only once."

"And what are your dreams for the future?" Leila asked.

"I'd love to be very rich and open a hospital for handicapped children. Plus I'd like to get married and have children." They were quiet for a short while digesting his dream.

"Leila…"

"Yes," She answered, raising her head and staring into his eyes.

"I like you very much."

Her cheeks flushed. "I like you very much too."

"What about Essa?" He quizzed her.

She laughed. "Promise me you won't be upset or angry?"

"Cross my heart."

"Well, he's my brother."

"But you told me he was your boyfriend."

"No, you just presumed he was my boyfriend. I never said anything."

"You made a fool of me. I've been telling everyone I was your escort for the night because your boyfriend is in Mosul. No wonder they all laughed."

"I'm sorry, but you did the same with me. What about Farrah?"

"I told you straight away that she wasn't my girlfriend."

"Ok, if I go on my knees kiss your hand and beg for forgiveness, will you still be angry with me?"

"I'd I rather you kissed my lips."

She stepped forward and kissed his lips. "Is that better?"

He nodded and he felt like the happiest person at the party.

They spent the next hour or so dancing, talking to different people and wandering around the garden. They felt extremely relaxed in each other's company, as if they had known each other for a long time.

Shortly after eleven, the patio door opened, and a big cake lit up with candles was wheeled out by a servant. A middle-aged couple followed as the band played Happy Birthday. All the guests strolled towards the patio.

"To our beautiful daughter, may God give her long life and happiness. Where are you?"

Leila walked towards them and Rami couldn't believe his eyes. He watched her full of smiles. She looked so innocent, yet she had made a fool of him all night. He realised why everyone laughed at him when he asked the question; 'whose party was it?'

He walked away, grabbing a large glass of whisky. He didn't want to be part of the celebration to be associated with any of the guests. He wanted to be on his own and find the right moment to leave. He was invited there to be laughed at. As the party progressed and the fireworks exploded around him, he desperately needed to get away.

Shortly he heard Leila's voice.

"Oh, there you are. I've been looking for you everywhere!"

Rami was sitting on the grass feeling sorry for himself. He raised his eyes and looked incredibly sad.

She sat on the grass by his side and hugged him tightly, but he was lifeless. She touched his face gently and planted a deep kiss on his cheek, but he didn't respond.

"Please forgive me Rami. I was just playing around, just to get back at you when we first met. I didn't mean to hurt, I swear."

"Leila, I'm through with playing games." He stood up and walked away. "Oh and here's your birthday present. I never go empty handed to a party." He handed her a small wrapped box.

She opened it straight away and to her surprise she found a delicate golden necklace. She ran after him.

"Please don't go."

He continued walking.

"Forgive me, I beg you."

He stopped and turned around; she wrapped her arms around him. "I was a bitch wasn't I?"

"You took me so high, and dropped me down."

"Would you please put the necklace around my neck? I love it, it's gorgeous."

"I will do that for you, but I've had enough fun for one night to last me a lifetime."

"Please don't go." She begged.

"Look Leila, I never thought that I could be fooled or laughed at by people like you, probably it's the way the rich play. Well I am not game for a laugh. You did this since the minute we met."

"I want you to stay, I want you with me."

"Why? Have you got some more jokes up your sleeve?"

"No...no more jokes."

"Goodbye Leila, have a happy rest of your life."

"But I love you, I'm crazy about you," she said softly with a desperate look in her eyes. "Come with me and let me show you something."

She led him through the patio doors, into the dining room, then to a corridor leading to an arched staircase and up to the first floor. She opened one of the many doors and walked through.

"This is my living room; I study here, have my friends round listening to music, and do whatever I like. I call it my mad room."

Rami walked in and sat down.

"I won't be a minute," said Leila.

She returned with a key, which she handed to him. "Open this cabinet here, and have a look inside."

He did and pulled out a file.

"Open it and see."

"It's my first published story," he said as he watched her sitting on the sofa with her legs tucked underneath her body.

"Turn the page," she said. "You'll find everything you've written up until now, every article that was written about you, every letter that you or someone else answered. I know how you feel, I know how you think. I know when you're happy and sad, in fact, I know all about you. If you didn't write for a while, I phoned the newspaper, because I missed you. I felt lost if I didn't see your name in the paper. I don't love you for your writing, but for you, and how you feel from day to day. I loved you for your looks, those come-to-bed eyes, your body and everything about you. I acted how I did, so you'd notice me."

"You're obsessed!"

"Is that wrong?"

"No, this is amazing. I don't have most of these writings myself." He moved next to her and kissed her. "I'm sorry too, please don't cry."

"You've done nothing wrong. It's me who hurt you and made a fool of myself.""The first time I saw you I turned to Nabil and told him how I want you badly," confessed Rami.

"You didn't?" She smiled.

"I'm crazy about you, and I can't believe all of this."

"But somehow you frighten me. I don't want to end up in the cabinet as one of your files." he added.

"That won't happen, you're too precious to me," she said placing a hand on his leg.

"I think I'll take a chance on you."

She ran her hand along the side of his face. "No dirty games this time. Come on let's join the party."

"Not until you adjust your make up."

"God…! Do I look horrible?"

"Yes!" he laughed.

"Thank you."

She took him into the living room where her parents were watching television.

"This is my Rami," she announced.

"Rami, at last! How are you?" said her father shaking Rami's hand.

"Very well thank you. It's my pleasure to meet you."

"We've heard so much about you, I thought you would be much older than that."

"My god Rami, aren't you polite?" Leila giggled.

"I knew your uncle, God bless his soul. I was at the funeral. What a loss!"

"Yes it was."

"I bet your father is proud to have a writer and a successful businessman as a son."

"My dad is old-fashioned and extremely protective, but one day maybe."

"I am sure everyone who knows you is proud of you, especially my Leila." The mother commented, "For months and months she never stopped talking about you, reading all the comments...and..."

"Mum don't make me blush." Leila interrupted her mother, "Come on you...let's get back to the party."

The rest of the night went without a hitch. They danced, laughed, kissed and then they sat in the middle in the garden with everyone sitting around, and he read out some of his poems.

By two o'clock he left the house with Khalid, promising to return the following day when the party would continue around the swimming pool.

"I'm in love," Khalid declared in the car.

"Me too," said Rami.

"Sonia is one special girl, fantastic night, oh I am so happy I could kiss you."

"No thanks, I'm not into men yet." Rami laughed, "I feel like going to work."

"I'm so happy I feel like working."

They worked until six in the morning, then Rami went home and slept for a few hours, while Khalid went back to his flat.

CHAPTER TWENTY TWO

AHMAD put his arm around Jean's shoulder. "There's no need to cry my love," he said. "Your tears won't solve her problems."

"But she's my sister. I must go and see her."

"Yes go and see her, but remember there's nothing you can do for her. She never accepted anybody's help. She hasn't even cashed any of the cheques we sent her."

"He's been dying for the last three years, so why don't they just let him go, and give her some peace."

"Would you do that for me, if I was dying with cancer?"

"Ahmad, I love you and I would never give up hope, but that bastard treated Elaine badly."

"He's still a human being though."

"Yes...that's all what we can say, poor Elaine, I wish Mum and Dad were still alive."

The door bell rang. "I'll get it," said Ahmad.

"Hello, you lot," Rami shouted from the door. He had one look at Jean, and went and sat next to her. "What's wrong? You have been crying."

"Nothing sweetheart..."

"Has he been treating you badly? I'll kill him if he did." He asked looking at Ahmad angrily.

"No he is too beautiful a person to do so, and you as well. What can a woman want than two men to protect her?" She smiled and gave him a kiss on the cheek, "I'll make you a cup of coffee."

"Oh...I love your coffee."

"What are you after?" Ahmad laughed.

"Nothing...just missed you both." He exhaled noisily. "I've been working all hours at the factory."

"I know, your father told me yesterday when I saw him at the supermarket," said Ahmad. "He mentioned your resignation speech too."

"I lost my temper," said Rami. "I couldn't handle it anymore."

"You must be more understanding to your dad's feelings. He has been through hell and back."

"I know. I'm going back to the factory next week."

"And, what about your writings?"

"I feel as if I've dried out," said Rami. "I'm lacking something, but I don't know what."

"Maybe you're not reading enough. Sometimes one idea can spark a few lights in the brain."

"Well, funnily enough, I came here today to borrow a few books from you."

"Help yourself, you know where they are."

Rami put his head in his hands and sighed.

"What's puzzling you?" said Ahmed. "Come on, out with it."

"Well it's hard to explain, but there are a hell of a lot of things passing by that I'm not noticing. I also feel as if I want to know the end of things before I get involved in them."

"I understand."

Rami continued. "When you write you know the start, the middle and the end. Whereas I used to start without knowing the rest till I came to it, but that's all changed now."

"I don't know what you're complaining about," said Ahmed. "Your success is based on new ideas, but mine revolves around big books and novels. I only write a couple a year, whereas you write hundreds, so you can't compare the two of us."

"I look up and I see beauty," said Rami. "I feel that I am wanted, so I try to stretch out my hand to experience it all, but something deep inside won't let me. I want to hold everything tight to me and not let go in case I get hurt. I'm so afraid of not knowing what the end might be. I feel that I am so fragile I could break easily. Am I talking a load of rubbish?'

Ahmad laughed and glanced at Jean who hadn't heard the whole conversation. "It sounds to me like the boy is in love. Who is she?"

"How did you know?"

"I know you too well, especially when you come up with excuses proving an issue."

He drank his coffee quickly, picked a couple of books, and decided to leave, "Thanks for the coffee Jean and Ahmad, but I must go now because Leila is waiting for me."

"Wow...I knew it...Leila...where is she from?"

"I think her mother is European, well I only care about her."

"Is she beautiful?"

"The Mother is? Oh yes..."

"Cheeky bastard..."

As he drove away, Rami noticed a white Ford Falcon following him. He turned from one street to the other, but the car was still behind him. He was especially worried, as most of these cars belonged to the Special Branch of the Police. "You won't get me this time," he shouted. His heart beat faster and the sweat ran down his forehead. He felt as if his hands could no longer grip the steering wheel. He drove as fast as possible to the newspaper, climbed the stairs to the first floor and barged into Farruk's office.

"Rami, what the hell is going on?"

He tried to speak but he couldn't, as his heart was racing away, he was terrified.

"Sit down and have a glass of water."

By that time a few people stood by the door watching. "I was being followed by a white car. It's a Ford...you know the one?"

"Right, I'll deal with that," said Farruk.

Farruk called the guard and told him about the car. Since the new government had come to power, they'd placed three police cars around the building, and a further two from the secret police. "We'll soon find out, come with me."

They ran downstairs and into the street. The car was surrounded by at least a dozen policemen with their guns pointing at the two men inside.

"Just like in films…!" Rami commented.

"Keep your mouth shut." Farruk ordered.

"Who are these men?" he called to one of the policemen.

"They said that they're police."

"Search them and the car then bring them to me."

The men were handcuffed as they left the car and were brought to Farruk "Name?"

"I can't give you my name, rank, or number, unless ordered by my immediate superior."

"Arrest them," Farruk ordered.

As they returned to the office Farruk spoke. "Don't worry about it. I'll make a few phone calls later."

"Thank you," said Rami "I don't think I can take a second round."

"Where have you been hiding anyway?"

"Here and there!"

"Something not quite right, what is it?"

"I don't know! What are you doing for lunch?"

For lunch they went to Rami's favourite restaurant 'The Strand'.

"This place is fantastic; I should bring the wife here sometime."

"Yes…She will love it." Rami commented.

"You don't think that a place like this exists in Baghdad, do you?"

"Farruk, what do you think of me?" Rami asked.

"Since when do you bother about what people think of you? Nevertheless you're one hell of a writer, but you lack concentration sometimes, but we're all guilty of that when we have a lot going on in our lives. You're a money lover and you like showing it. With you everything screams money and power. When you stand on stage and read a poem, you're something else and I like what I see."

"What's on the outside never resembles what's on the inside."

"What do you mean?"

"I want to lean on someone for a change," said Rami. "I had to kick myself to get where I am and now I want someone to kick me further."

"Thank God you're still a hungry writer," said Farruk. "I think you need a good rest."

"No…"

"What's the matter?" He asked as he watched Rami looking around the restaurant.

"Beauty is a pain which never found a place or a phase in that which I see, only in that which I wish I could never feel. I see the 'unbeautiful' I see and I am numbed by that who will never see my beauty."

159

"That's hard for me to digest with my meal," said Farruk taking a pen out to write the words down. "I'll think about it. It'll probably be in the paper tomorrow."

On the way back to the newspaper Rami noticed another car following them. He told Farruk, who asked Rami to stop the car. Farruk ran to the suspect car and pointed his gun at them. Rami ran after him."

"Rami phone the paper and tell them."

Within two minutes three police cars arrived.

A high ranked officer ran out from one of the cars, followed by few policemen.

"Arrest these two and search them," ordered Farruk. "Let me know the details later at the newspaper."

"What have you been up to?" he asked Rami as he drove away.

"Nothing at all, honestly"

"They were from special branch, I must find out, and I don't want to stick my neck out over nothing. Anyway thanks for the meal, I really enjoyed it."

They were quiet for a minute before Farruk spoke. "Life was so much easier a few years back." He lit his pipe, and continued. "Relationships, love, feelings, everything changed. In the olden days people knew the time to get married and if you couldn't find a girl then your mother would. Most of the time you knew you could trust her judgement. But these days you know what she's going to be like before asking for her hand; you know how she dances, how she kisses, how she makes love and her entire body measurements. There are no excitements left, so in the end the marriage falls apart."

"Not all of them fall apart."

"Fifty per cent do." Farruk added.

"So if I want to get married I should ask my mother to find me a wife? And on the night, I look at her and shout, my God…! She looks like a camel, how on earth am I going to screw her, she is a camel for God's sake?

"A few months later someone would ask me, how is the wife? Oh she is fine, I answer, she is very good, she cooks and cleans, and looks after me, but the problem is with me, for months I've been trying to learn how to screw a camel, riding is one thing, but screwing my friend is another."

Farruk was in fits of laughter and begging Rami to stop. "Thanks for the meal and get your act together because I need some of your writings and please never ask your mother to find you a wife."

"I'll see you in few days," said Rami.

He drove to Leila's house. She opened the door for him and hugged him. "Where have you been, I've missed you?"

"I went out for lunch with my editor."

"Did you have fun?"

"Yes thank you. Is Khalid here?"

"He's been and gone."

Leila took Rami upstairs to her bedroom and waited outside the door while he changed into his swimming trunks.

As they went down to the pool he noticed about twenty of her friends stayed behind soaking up the sun.

"God it's hot today," said Rami.

"Why don't you jump in the water?"

He took off his T-shirt while Leila examined his muscular body with pride. She felt a new sensation inside; she never thought that a man can have a beautiful body.

"Do you like what you see?" Rami joked.

"Very much," she said as she slipped off her robe to reveal a yellow bikini. Rami examined her beautiful tanned figure.

"Is this all mine?" he whispered.

She nodded with a sensual smile on her face.

"I'll race you to the water."

"Ok, go."

They played in the water for what seemed like hours then they sat down to rest.

"I said something to Farruk earlier on," said Rami.

"What was it?"

"Beauty is a pain which never found a place or a phase in that which I see, only in that which I wish I could never feel. I see the unbeautiful, I see and I am numbed, by that which will never see my beauty."

She paused for a minute or two. "Are you saying that you wish you'd never met me?"

"Yes."

"Then what the hell are you doing here?"

"Because I want you and need you. I'm sure of my feelings towards you, and yours towards me, but I'm afraid of the end."

"Oh well, that's better. I thought that you've gone off me for a minute."

"I don't want to be hurt."

"Me neither. I'll never hurt you darling."

"I think I just started to like you." He said laughingly.

"Cheeky bastard...!" she said as she pushed him into the water.

Leila didn't go inside to get ready for the night time party until seven o'clock. She faced the mirror drying her hair.

"There is a towel for you on the bed."

"Thank you."

At that moment he felt incredibly at home; everything felt familiar and right. He returned with a towel wrapped around him.

"Your hair looks lovely."

"And you look sexy with the towel around you." She teased him, "Come on sit down here, I'll do your hair for you."

Rami wondered whether she was wearing anything under her bath robe, and he asked her.

"No why?"

"Nothing, I just wanted to know." He replied.

"You're such a liar; you're so horny you are dribbling!"

He quickly ran the back of his hand across his mouth which made her laugh loudly.

"You are beautiful." She commented.

She carefully styled his hair as she dried it for him, accidentally rubbing herself against him in the process. He was clearly aroused and didn't know how to hide his erection.

"Stand up and let me see your hair," said Leila.

"No need baby, it's the best hair do that I've ever had."

"Just stand up."

"I can't," he laughed.

"Why not?"

When he looked down at himself, she realised what had happened, and collapsed on her bed in fits of laughter.

"You did this on purpose," he said standing up.

"Did I…? Well it looks beautiful from this angle."

He threw himself next to her on the bed and slowly kissed her face until their lips met. His mouth travelled down to her neck and she closed her eyes. His hand travelled to her breast, but she gently caught it.

"Hey you down there, it's time for you to come up," she said laughing again. Their eyes met and the laughter stopped. She could no longer hold back her feelings for him, so she held his face with her hands and drew him to her neck. She raised his face and their lips met once again. An explosion of moans escaped her, as he gently untied her robe. His hand moved curiously, searching, touching, and feeling on its journey of discovery. At last the journey came to a halt, Leila took a deep breath and unhurriedly he stroked her breast, allowing his thumb to tease her nipple to a full erection.

"God, Rami." Another moan escaped her as their lips parted.

He eased the robe away and his hand softly touched every inch of her body. Her back arched upward and as she closed her eyes, her breathing quickened. She felt warm, alive and ready for love. Shivers ran down her body and a feeling of submission overwhelmed her.

"You're beautiful," he whispered. He stopped what he had already started and looked at her with a smile.

"Do you want me?" she whispered back.

"Yes very much."

"Well then take me."

He kissed her eyes, her little nose and her hungry lips, right the way down to her neck and her breast. He talked to her nipples, sang to them, and told them a poem, abandoning life around him. No one else existed in the world at that moment, except the two of them. With the tip of his finger he teased her stomach in a circular motion.

"Oh baby, don't stop."

He was not there to answer her. Instead he tenderly kissed her feet, telling them that he loved them before moving on. He whispered words of love as his lips travelled upward to her thighs.

Leila had abandoned ship a long time ago. He made her feel safe, secure and wanted. She knew she was extra special for him and she trusted him completely, making every minute more intense emotionally than the previous one. She was floating high in the air.

She felt the thundering shivers overwhelm her from her toes to the top of her head. He gave her pleasure and freedom. She didn't feel shy with him; usually she would have run a hundred miles at the sight of a man. But now she wanted more; more pleasure, more love, more of her man, and how could she ask for more, when he hadn't stopped giving. But she did ask for more and he obliged her.

She felt as if her soul had left her body, as if she had fallen from a steep height and now she lay back resting.

He laid next to her and she opened her eyes and looked at the drops of sweat on his forehead.

She wiped them with the side of her finger.

"My man..!"

Rami's face was full of love and satisfaction.

"Thank you."

"I love you." He had tears in his eyes and as he said the words, he felt deep uncontrollable emotions that he could not express. Her fingers performed endless circles round and round his chest, as she rested her head on his shoulder, listening to his breathing.

Her hand moved down his body and un-wrapped the towel. "Close your eyes baby and enjoy me, like I did you."

She began to kiss him. She talked to each part of his body individually, and every part in him talked back to her, responding to her mouth and her hands. Rami looked and listened, loving how she manipulated his body to become sensitive to her touch. He loved how softly she introduced her body, her rhythm, and her music. Every movement developed into a condensed soft timeless effort.

Rami could not remain on his back any longer, he felt lonely and jealous of his own body. He pulled her towards him and held her tight.

"Do you love me that much?"

There was no need for her to answer; her silence said it all.

"For me it's my first time, for you it's just another story in your fancy book."

"No, you're the only story in my book."

"Why didn't you take me fully Rami? I was more than willing to have you."

"It wasn't the right moment."

A new love and he was afraid of its beauty. He wanted to stand away from it all and watch it happening to someone else. He was afraid of its uncertainty, but it was too late for him to back away now; he was drawn so far inside that love story that it felt unreal yet idiotic to walk away from it.

He came to terms with himself as she lay next to him, her hand feeling him again. All he wanted and needed was Leila; loving her, satisfying her, and being with her. Nothing in the world would separate them from one another.

"Rami, make love to me."

Their rhythm met once again as he lowered himself gently on to her. Their movement penetrated each other to create perfection. Their love grew with their action and they gave each other their heart, soul and body.

"You were so gentle." She whispered.

"You are special."

"Are you going to see me again?" she quizzed him after.

"What do you think?"

"Yes…?"

"Correct! I want you with me."

"I was told that once you make love to them you leave them."

"Wrong, I never was like that, shall we join the party?"

"Yes, they'll be worried about us." She commented.

CHAPTER TWENTY THREE

HE went through the side door in the factory instead of the main entrance; everyone was surprised yet happy to see him back. It had been very dull during the past few days when he had been away. Rami told his father he would only work for two or three hours every day, or when it suited him. Once the summer holidays were over, he would have so much studying to do before entering university. His father agreed, as he wanted his son to achieve high averages in the national examination to give him a greater choice of universities and colleges.

Leila had walked into his life at exactly the right time. She inspired him with her deep thoughts and ideas. He adapted some and used them to generate masterpieces that made Farruk a happy man again. He was back on track, as good as the good old days.

Leila created secure surroundings for him, and he walked in with open eyes. She did not hold him back, but pushed him to the limits. After spending two hours at the factory, he drove to pick her up; together they spent three hours helping at the shop. Then, they would go back to her house for lunch and relaxed by the swimming pool reading, writing, debating new ideas and loving their achievements.

There was no stopping her once she had started. She changed his life completely, and he loved the change. It was amusing for their parents, as they resembled an old married couple.

"Hey, how much do you get paid for this?" She was reading a critique he wrote about a book he read.

"Ten Dinars, maybe twelve..."

"They've been paying you that for the last three years. Come on Rami, you should ask for more. You're only given one chance to make money."

"I don't need the money, plus I make more than anyone there."

"They're making millions out of you. Do you think people are bothered what the president is doing? No. But, they are bothered when it comes to you."

"Leila please, it isn't in my nature to ask for money."

"Well are you going to ask Farruk, or shall I do it?"

"Ok I will, I think you are right again, I hate you."

Leila giggled. "I win again."

He knew she was right, and he felt glad to have this incredible person in his life, who never stopped helping him sort out his affairs.

She told him about her father, who was a cleaner in a small shop so he could send his brother and sister to school as their father had died when they were very young. He went to school at night, and by the age of twenty-three he finished his university degree. After his army service, he had three jobs. He slept two hours every day and the whole day Friday. He saved money obsessively. Three years later he opened a shop selling spare parts for vehicles. Then he bought land and started dealing with second hand cars. He got married, sold the businesses, and went into construction. He invested in small solid companies and businesses in Iraq and abroad and he managed to take his wealth out of the country before the 1958 revolution. By the age of thirty-five he was a millionaire. He had houses in four capitals in Europe and he spoke in four languages.

Her brother, Essa, was in his last year medical college. He was quiet by nature, polite, and well spoken. Essa met Maha at the centre, when he accompanied Rami and Leila, and they began seeing each other regularly. He devoted what little spare time he had to her and they planned on getting engaged once he had finished his studies and graduated.

The cars continued following Rami wherever he went. Farruk complained to authorities and government departments, but it seemed nobody knew who had given the order. They did not harm him, but on the contrary, they helped him in many sticky situations; twice when he left his car to fight with fellow drivers and once after leaving a nightclub when a drunken man tried to attack Leila.

He established a funny relationship with them. He knew their names and he often bought them cold drinks and cigarettes to pass the time. Other times they gave him a lift in their cars when he didn't want to drive. He called them his protectors or guardian angels.

He took the situation to the extent of handing them a piece of paper with his schedule for the day in case they lost sight of him in Baghdad's traffic. But to his surprise, Ahmad also had a car following him everywhere he went.

The schools started. It was a very difficult start, as the Ministry of Education had changed the curriculum of many subjects and introduced new ones that the teachers themselves had no experience in. But for Leila and Rami that wasn't a problem, they were determined from day one to study hard.

He worked fewer hours at the shop and went to the factory only when important work needed his attention. He left the committee at the Centre, but he never missed the weekly meetings with the Sodality. He wanted to prove to Leila that he was thinking of their future together seriously. And, whatever he sacrificed then, it would turn out to be beneficial to them both in days to come.

Both parents were happy for them to be together, and they became very friendly with each other, visiting each other regularly and inviting each other to dinner parties.

Farrah finally returned after the many months that she had spent outside the country. She noticed the difference in Rami and she got on with Leila very well, as if they had known each other for years.

- - - - - - - - -

Leila sat next to him in her living room on the first floor.

"Baby, are you happy with me?"

"Do you think I'd be here if I wasn't?"

"Am I too bossy? I won't know unless you tell me. You never slow down, you are on the go all the time, you're always ready to go."

"You made me that way."

"Rubbish."

"What's on your mind? What's wrong?"

"Nothing is wrong. I just want to know if I'm enough for you?"

"Leila, I love you more than my own life. You're all I want, all I think about, and everything I do is for us."

"Take me out."

"Yes my little sweetheart, where would you like to go?"

"Your flat!" She looked him straight in the eyes because he had told her about it, but had never taken her there. She trusted him, but she wanted and needed to share all of his life with him.

"Okay we'll go there, get in the car please."

They sat in the car, neither of them liking the sudden tension. They had never felt so apart from each other before. They never argued and she wished she had never started this, but it was too late.

"Did I do or say anything wrong Rami?"

"No," he answered coldly.

"Then why have you never taken me to your flat? We have been together for months. Do you take other girls to it, is that it?"

"No reason."

"Tell me please, be truthful."

"When do I get the chance of being on my own baby?" He asked her.

There was an uncomfortable silence between them. She tried hard to find something to talk about but failed. She thought that perhaps she had made a mistake and that she was going to lose him for good.

"I'm hungry, I fancy some kebabs," she said trying to break the tension.

Rami stopped at the nearest Kebab House on Saadoon Street and they sat eating in the car.

"How many times have you been with other girls while you were with me?"

He was trapped. Whatever he said, she would not believe him. "Answer me. For heaven's sake defend yourself Rami; tell me something, please."

He laughed awkwardly at the situation that he was in. "Fifty."

"Take me home. I don't want to see you anymore. Take me home now, I feel so cheap and used."

"Jealousy can kill."

"I'm not jealous, but disillusioned."

"Whatever for? You could have done the same if you wanted to, nobody is holding you back."

"I don't go jumping into bed Rami," she shouted, trying hard to stop herself from crying. She took a deep breath and ordered him softly. "Please start your damn car and take me home."

"If that is what you want," he mumbled.

"Plus where do I find time to be with anyone else but you? You are with me day and night...and..." She didn't finish what she was about to say, as she had answered her own question without even thinking.

"Have you or haven't you?" she insisted.

"I'm not answering you, because whatever I'm going to say, you wouldn't believe me. I'm taking you to the flat first, then as you said, we're finished." Rami opened the door for his flat and let her in.

"Have a good look around. You might see some lipstick in the bathroom or some woman's hair in the bed or yellow marks on the sheets. Don't stand looking at me, have a good sniff around."

"You're terrible," she said as she walked away while he went to the kitchen and made himself a drink.

She came back holding a few pieces of women's underwear. "They certainly don't belong to me you fucking bastard." She sat down crying.

He looked at them; he had forgotten about Farrah and he had never told Leila that she lived in the flat.

"They belong to Farrah." He took her hand and led her to the spare bedroom. "Everything here belongs to Farrah. She stays here whenever she's in the city, because she doesn't get on with her family. Any more questions?"

"Why didn't you tell me?" she tried to defend her action. "I'm sorry Rami." she tried to kiss him, but he turned his face in the other direction, pretending he was angry.

"I've never been with another woman since I met you."

"Please forgive me, I...."

"No never." He was bluffing, but she took him seriously. She turned round to leave, but quietly he said. "I love you Leila, I always did and I always will, would you like to be my fiancée?"

She could not believe what he had just asked and she ran and jumped on top of him, kissing him, laughing and crying at the same time.

"So do you agree?"

"Yes you stupid fool, I love you."

"Then why the hell are you crying?"

"Sorry, I didn't realize I was. Oh Rami, a minute ago I thought I'd lost you forever and now I'm yours for good."

"We'll get engaged tonight, just me and you, then when we finish our exams, we'll make it official and we can get married after university."

Rami went to the study and picked up few envelopes of money, which Nabil had given him.

"Come on, it's time to go."

"Where to? It's half past seven."

"Never mind."

When they left the building the two men were sitting in their car. "These two men never give up."

"This situation is getting beyond a joke," said Leila showing her annoyance and frustration.

"My protectors, you know that I've got used to them, I'd feel strange, probably worried if I couldn't see their car, even sometimes I wait for them in case they will lose me in traffic, it's really funny."

"Be careful, people don't get followed for no reason, it's not a joke darling."

"Even Farruk couldn't find out anything."

"I'll be back in a second," he said opening the car door for her.

He strolled to the other car, "Hi friends, I got engaged today."

"Congratulations Rami, she's certainly is a good lady."

"Thank you, do you know good jewellers open at this time of the night?"

"Yes follow us."

When Leila saw what had happened, she burst out laughing; she never laughed so much for a long time. It was an unbelievable situation.

Leila waited for him in the car, while he disappeared for twenty minutes, then came back with a big smile on his face.

"Rami what have you been up to?"

"Nothing, just close your eyes."

He opened the small box in his hand. "Open them now."

A small cry escaped her and she couldn't believe her eyes.

"Do you like it?"

"Oh Rami, my sweetheart, I love you so much and I love this ring." Tears ran down her face.

He had bought her an exquisite diamond ring; an unusual design, but very much in Leila's taste. The stone itself nested on woven thin strands of gold in a shape of a basket.

Rami could not wait to tell everybody, but Leila told him to wait.

"I always dreamt that you would marry me one day and we would have six children, three of each."

"And I sit next to the coal fire, writing, while you sit on the floor knitting."

"I hate knitting, it drives me mental."

They owned the world at that moment, so nothing could come between them. They wanted the moment to be special, just for themselves. They both looked behind them at the other car, parked a few metres away from them. Rami felt as if something was clutching at his throat. He did not want them to be there.

"Where are you going?"

"To talk to them."

And before she could stop him, he had left the car.

"This is getting beyond a joke, aren't you getting bored yet?"

"Sorry mate, there is nothing we can do."

"It has been months now, you do twelve hours, and the other two do the same."

"We are here to protect, and get you out of trouble." He laughed, "We couldn't stop you getting engaged."

Rami felt sorry for them. "Well tell whoever gave the orders tell them I'd like to meet them. Are you two married?"

"I am for the last six months, but he's not." answered one of the men.

"Why don't you get your women and join us for a meal?"

"Great...!"

He found out that they were Law Graduates. After finishing university, they were put with the army intelligence unit as part of their national service.

"Baby you were gone for a long time, I was getting worried."

"I felt sorry for them, so I stood chatting to them." Rami explained. "I told them that I wanted to meet this person who is in charge, and get it over with."

"Very wise, you want to get yourself in trouble?" she said sarcastically, "Why don't you ask them to join us for a meal as well?"

"Good idea…!"

Rami and Leila had an enjoyable night. At the end, one of the men took the girls home including Leila, and the other one took Rami to his flat, and put him to bed. They knew that he could not go home in the state he was in. He was drunk.

They were humans after all. They were more thrilled to be in the company of their favourite writer, introducing him to their women, and enjoying his laughter and funny comments,

"That's life." One of the men said. They sat in their car watching the flat.

"Yes such is life."

"I wish this will stop one day, I do miss being at home with my wife."

"I miss being at home, period!"

CHAPTER TWENTY FOUR

APRIL came and there were only two months to go until the national examinations. The waiting took its toll on everyone including the parents. Their whole future depending on those exams and there was no time to do anything except study. Rumours spread about how hard the examination papers would be and how tight the entries to different universities would affect everyone. The pressure was on from all corners.

It had been ten days since the cars stopped following Rami, as if they had disappeared into thin air. In a way, it felt extremely strange, although he was finally free to go wherever he wanted, and do whatever he wished.

Rami sat in his flat waiting for the bell to ring. His protector is about to call on him, and introduce himself, it was almost eight months since they had started their nasty game. The bell rang; Rami hurried to the door, and opened it.

"Mr Sabah!" He was shocked.

"Hello Rami, can I come in?"

"Yes, please take a seat."

"I hope you aren't angry with us?"

"Not at all!" Rami said sarcastically. "To be followed day and night for eight months how could I bring myself to be angry?" Rami laughed, as in a way he was relieved to see his ex-teacher in front of him.

"You always had a way with words."

"Thank you Sir, do you fancy a cold beer?"

"Yes please."

They sat opposite each other. "What was it all about?" Rami asked.

"We need you."

"Who needs me and for what?"

"What I'm about to say must not go beyond these walls. Do you understand?"

"Yes…Sure, my neck will be on the deck." Although his remark was sarcastic, he knew the seriousness of the moment.

"Any new government starts with many mistakes; they face new problems and new experiences every day. Some they can handle, others are beyond their reach." He took a gulp of his beer and continued. "Our Government and the Baath Party have no experience in those matters"

Rami tried to interrupt, but Mr. Sabah kept talking.

"We tried to solve certain problems between us, and with the help of others, but there are always other diversions to trap us."

"That's honesty for me. You were always one of my favourite teachers."

"Industry has been hit badly since we took power because of the uncertainty of the political stage; we are fighting a different front to that when we were out of power."

"You lack leadership with experience?"

"Precisely, thousands of people moved to Baghdad in 1958 and 1963. They came in aid of the new party, sheltering under its banner. No matter how hard we tried to control our new membership, it seemed to me, and a few others, that it got out of hand. That's the biggest problem that both the government and the party face today. We want to be good for this country, we were born and raised here, and there is no one better than us to give this country a chance to survive. Are you with me so far?"

"Yes...it seemed interesting coming from a high official."

"A friend..."

"Yes, Mr. Sabah."

"There is high unemployment and the jobs which are available are taken up by party members, even if their qualifications are lower than those who deserve those jobs. Others join the party so they keep their jobs and progress to a higher position."

"Many qualified people left the country too, Mr. Sabah."

"That's true too. Some people join the party because it's the fashion these days to have a political mind. Many joined because they believe in us and wish to help make this country great again."

"So where do I fit in? I hate politics, it isn't for me."

"Some of our members boosted their earnings simply by being Ba'athists. They used the poor and took advantage of our mismanagement. Everyone around them feared them, including their own families. Being a Ba'athists is to serve others and not to be served by the others."

"I know all that Mr. Sabah."

"It's better if you hear it from me. These problems are growing fast. The government can only do so much and we can't keep everything under the blanket as if nothing ever happened. It's not as gloomy as I have put it. We have achieved many goals, but we need people like you."

He took a large file out of his briefcase and handed it to Rami. "This is all about you, including all your telephone calls from wherever you phoned, and the rest. I'm sorry but we had to do it this way. And, we find you as straight as a bone."

Rami laughed. "Some bones can be curved or broken."

"But not yours, you have been approached by so many people to join the party but you refused."

"Parties and politics aren't for me."

"What about in the future?"

"No."

"Money? More than you have ever dreamed of?"

"As you probably know, I'll be rich by the age of twenty if I keep doing what I'm doing."

"Yes we know how much you are worth, but..."

"Frankly, I don't believe in most major issues that the party stands for. How am I going to join a party who believes in Arab unity? I don't want to unite with anyone thank you very much. The Arabs agreed a long time ago not to agree. I believe in socialism in a way, but not fully. And the last thing is freedom, and who is free in this country?"

"You are my boy."

Rami felt superior saying all that in front of someone who was very high in the party.

"No, I am not free."

"Explain yourself."

"As a writer I have no freedom to say and write what I like. I have to be careful otherwise I would be chopped to pieces. You can't force laws on people, but they have to accept them as laws. So the people can't say what they want in public, as the government is afraid that they might spark trouble. After all, the people have got to do what they are told by the government because they are not the ones who hold the cane."

"Wow, that's fantastic; you're a good speaker and a thinker. Thank God you don't belong to another party."

"By not belonging I can speak against all of them if I wish it, but I value my life more and my future with my girl."

"Very good, now let's get down to business. I don't want to take any more of your time. I was approached to speak to you; names don't matter at this stage. We need people like you, people who have no interest in money or politics, to help us find our way. This doesn't come from the government, but another body which is much higher, and not more than five people would know who you are."

"I don't understand."

"You would be given proper training, you would have a great responsibility and you won't belong to any establishment except your unit. You would have the power to report anyone, including the President himself, if you see him doing something wrong. as well as many problems we don't want any of our regular units like the police and so on to deal with. Your authority would be higher than mine!"

"Wow…do you want another beer? I can do with another one."

"So could I…"

You'll be free to do anything, examine whatever you want, and whatever you ask for, and you'll be supported by everyone. There will be around fifty men in the unit with you, if you accept. We want people who have only one motive."

"No thank you," said Rami.

"Sleep on it for few days, and let me know later."

"I can tell you now. No thank you."

"Well, if you ever change your mind, you know where to find me."

Sabah left and Rami sat thinking. Suddenly he felt cold and shivery. He thought of Nadia's father and how he wanted to break the necks of whoever did that to him. He thought about himself and wondered whether those who punished him were still working for the government now. They had probably joined the party and kept their jobs. He thought of his beloved uncle.

The door bell rang again and he went to open it. "Leila, thank God."

"You look terrible."

"How did you get here…?"

"Dad dropped me, did he come? Tell me all about it."

"Yes."

"Is that it?"

"I can't tell you anything, but I said no thank you, so rest your beautiful brain."

"Tell me or I won't love you anymore."

"I can't."

But she kept on at him to tell her and promised she wouldn't tell anyone. At the end he had to tell her, only to shut her up and put her mind at rest.

"Thank you for saying no, I don't trust them. Let's go out," she said, feeling relieved. "I rather sit here and study."

"I don't want to study. Please Rami, it's Thursday, and I have a headache. I need some fresh air."

"You should rest; you've been having too many headaches recently, probably an excuse so you won't make love to me."

"Okay I'll make love to you now, if you promise to take me out tonight."

"Okay we'll go out, I'll make love to you later."

"Dancing?"

That evening was their last night out before their examinations. They gathered twenty of their friends and they danced until the early hours of the morning to the live music of Ilham Al-Madfai and his band.

- - - - - - - - -

With four weeks left to the examinations, the episode with Mr. Sabah was long forgotten.

While Leila made up her mind to study Business and Management at the university, Rami kept changing his mind; he did not know what he wanted. A degree was useful for two things; keeping him away from the army service for few years, and to stuff it in his back pocket for a rainy day.

The pressure and anxiety grew as they broke away from school to prepare themselves properly. They became very short-tempered with each other, with their surroundings and with everyone else.

They were sitting in the garden early one night studying when suddenly Rami threw his book in the air.

"I'm finished," he shouted. "I am done with Chemistry."

"You're pulling my leg."

"Here let me help you instead."

"No, go away."

"Okay, I'm going."

"Where to?"

"I don't know, for a spin in the car, or to the shop, or the Centre."

She looked at the fifty pages or so she hadn't finished reading then looked at him sadly. "I have to finish all this tonight. Darling, do me a favour please."

"What?"

"I fancy a pizza."

"I'll get you one."

"And some headache tablets please."

"You're living on headache tablets. Why don't you go and check your eyes?"

"It's only because of all this reading."

"Ok, I'll be back in less than an hour."

"You forgot something."

He gave her a kiss and drove to his flat to collect his swimming trunks and his mail. He opened his front door to find suit cases in the middle of the living room. He knew then that Farrah was back. He followed the trail of clothes to the bathroom, but she was not there, instead she was fast asleep on his bed, completely naked as usual. A smile crossed his face. He had not seen her for five months, and even then, he did not get the chance of talking to her properly. He left the room and closed the door behind him.

He quickly drove to the pizza house, then the pharmacy and back to Leila's house.

"Hi, how far have you got?"

"Only a couple of pages. I've had enough Rami, come here and give me a hug. Thanks for the pizza."

"Why don't you eat your food, and then straight to bed, and have an early night?"

"I might just do that."

"I'll see you tomorrow, look after yourself."

"Drive carefully, I love you."

"I love you more."

An hour later Rami was back at the flat laying the table in the front room. He put soft music on the record player and took one last look at the table. "Very good, but you forgot the champagne you idiot," he mumbled to himself.

He rang his own doorbell and waited to see if it woke her up. She came out of the bedroom looking exhausted and blinked her eyes between gazing at him and examining the table. She quickly tried to cover herself up with her hands.

"Rami!"

"Hello Farrah." She tried to find something to cover her nudity. "Come here, I prefer you like this."

She jumped into his lap and they hugged each other. It felt very strange to be in each other's arms after such a long time.

"This is just what I needed Rami, thank you, you're still as romantic as ever."

"Welcome home."

"Thanks baby."

"Come on let's eat."

"Wait two minutes"

She returned wearing a short silk robe.

"Champagne Madam?"

"Thank you Sir."

Rami uncovered the food.

"This is enough for an army," said Farrah.

Rami loved watching her eating and nibbling with her fingers, to be so natural, doing what she liked.

"I missed you," she said with her mouth full and a smile on her face. "I missed all this food as well."

He looked at her and how happy she was.

"How is Leila? Are you still together?"

"Yes, we are."

"Does she know you're here?"

"No, I lied to her. I came here earlier and saw you asleep then I went back to her house and made up a story."

"You lied for me?"

"I needed to be here with you."

"How's May?"

"She's alright, but I haven't seen her for weeks either."

"You mean you haven't slept with her since you went out with Leila?"

"Yes, what about you? Have you met anyone yet?"

She smiled back at him. "I have met hundreds of men who asked me out, but I told them that my future husband doesn't allow it."

Rami felt uncomfortable at her remark. How could he tell her that he was engaged to Leila. He was cheating on the both of them.

"How are you doing at work?" he asked.

"I'm working non-stop, from eight in the morning until God knows what time. I have been asked to write a novel by one of the publishing houses, so I started working on that."

"What's it about?"

"Us the people, I'll send you a copy when it's published. The shop looks fantastic. I was there on my way back from the airport. Nabil and Khalid told me about buying the whole building. The landlord must be an idiot, he has no money left and he's asking for so much."

"Well I haven't been to the shop for a while, so I don't know what is going on. I told them not to get in touch until I finish my exams."

"You must be making good money?"

"That shop is a gold mine and so are the other two."

"I must go and wash my hands," said Farrah.

"And your face, you look like you haven't eaten for weeks."

Rami looking at the dancing flame of the candle in front of him, while Farrah washed up. When she came back, she picked up the bottle of champagne and headed to the bedroom. "Follow me."

- - - - - - - - -

She woke up at about two in the morning. It was a cold night, so she put the heating on, as she did not want to disturb Rami by pulling the covers on top of him then she headed to the kitchen and made a large cup of coffee and sat in the dark. She drew the curtains open and the lights from the street lit the room.

176

She looked out of the window; how precious these few hours of fulfilments were to her. She lived from day to day to be in that flat and hopefully one day in Rami's arms. She could never feel able to explain to him how hard it had been living between four countries. A woman on her own chased and followed by all different types of men. How difficult it had been to keep up with the world of glamour on television and cinema, and the many invitations to parties that she could not refuse. Some accepted her, but others described her as being a cold and unaffectionate person.

She met some good people and made friends, but hardly the type that she wanted to be close to. Rami was her whole life, she could not bear life without him, even with being so far apart. She could be anything that she wanted with him. She could laugh, talk, and play her little games. Her fantasies were his, and there was no one on earth who she would rather share it with, but Rami.

She wished he was there at that minute. She wished he would hold her tight and whisper love words to her. She turned her head and he was standing there.

"Why are you crying darling?" he asked.

She could not speak. She felt a lump blocking her throat. She tried but instead she opened her hand for him and he took it. He sat on the floor facing her and slowly lowered her next to him. She cried on his shoulder. It was the first time she had cried in front of him, she cried for the both of them, she cried for missing him so much, she cried because she was too much a coward to tell him how she really felt about him.

She was still crying, wiping her eyes and nose with the back of her hand. Rami put the tissue box next to her. "Thank you, I bet you think that I'm a silly little girl."

"No, I think you're a silly big girl," said Rami, trying to be funny with his remarks. But she cried louder than before.

"What's the matter…tell me…why are you crying?"

"Because I want to cry, because I am….What's the use explaining it to you?"

"Search me?"

"Hold me tight please, don't let me go."

"At this time of the night where could you possibly go?"

She pushed him away and slapped him gently on the face. "Even when I want to cry you don't let me, you bastard."

"If you want to cry at this time of the night, who is going to stop you? Carry on dear."

She did not want to hear him laughing and trying to cheer her up. She kept crying and she did not know why.

Rami hurried to the kitchen and opened another bottle of champagne. "This will make you better."

"Just leave me alone, I'm making a spectacle of myself."

"Well as long as you know that." He laughed.

"Do you think it's funny?" She asked angrily.

"I love you, you know, in my own special way?" Rami said.

"I hate all this. I never showed anyone how insecure, frightened and fearful I am. I don't want to work anymore. I want to be a housewife and have children running about the house. It's a man's world out there and if there is a woman in the middle of it, she's got to keep her legs tight all the time. It's a fucking war."

"I know. You've done fantastic and I'm proud of you."

"No, you don't know. I was afraid to take my clothes off in my own apartment in case someone was hiding there, and when I got a woman to share the place with me so I could feel safe, I was hiding from her then. I nearly had to give in to her demands once, for the sake of peace, but by the morning she was out of there."

"Well give up your job then and stay here."

"But I want to do it."

"That is women's logic," Rami giggled.

"Do you think I am good for one thing and one thing only?"

"You are good at sex among other things."

"Oh shut up! I don't know why I bother talking to you."

"It's because I'm the only one who will listen to you. You're on top and that is a very lonely place to be, but you've got me here. I listen, whenever you are feeling low. Farrah, all women look at you in admiration. You have a huge knowledge of art, fashion, science and other subjects. How many people can stand up and say that they have achieved as much as you?" He took a deep breath and continued. "You never opened up or talked about you."

"I did with you and you laughed at me."

"I only tried to cheer you up in the best way I know, and also you look so sexy when you are crying."

"Why didn't you write to me?"

"I hate writing letters."

"So do I! Anyway shall we go back to bed?"

"What for?"

He smiled. "I need my beauty sleep."

"Yes you do."

"Farrah."

"Yes Rami…"

"Never mind!" He was about to tell her about his engagement to Leila, but he lost the courage to do so.

- - - - - - - - -

Two days later Farrah was back in Egypt, back to her usual routine and daily problems dealing with mail, telephones, reporters and other journalists. She lifted her head from her paperwork for a minute and thought about her last night in the flat. She smiled thinking of how Rami had made her laugh with his funny stories.

He had looked very tired and that was a good enough reason for her not to force him to make love to her.

Rami occupied her mind all that day. She was building for their future and although she didn't know how far she would get, she knew one thing…she knew that she loved him.

- - - - - - - - -

Rami and Leila decided to hold their engagement party straight after the examinations, if their parents would allow it, but they could not think of a reason why they would not.

"What are you dreaming about?" Leila asked.

"I was thinking about Farrah and how marvellous she has done over the last few years. I'm very proud of her."

"Yes, she's a fantastic writer, but after tomorrow you'll be back to writing yourself."

"I can't wait for tomorrow to come. Just one more day and everything will be over.""Are you going to study?" She asked.

"No I've had enough, I am going to close my eyes, and dream about the good time we are going to have this summer."

"I am going to sleep, I have another headache."

They both fell asleep by the swimming pool. They were both tired, and luckily the last examination was Arabic, and both of them were very good at it. Two hours later he woke up, "Are you awake?"

"Yes I just woke up."

"Oh I fancy a swim." He stood facing the water. She ran towards him, and pushed him with his clothes on. She also tripped and fell as well in the water.

"Oh no, I haven't got any dry clothes with me."

"Don't worry, take them off, and I'll dry them for you.' As they both stepped out of the water, suddenly she held his arm, 'Rami …"

"What darling?"

"I feel dizzy."

"Come on sit down, I'll get you a glass of water." Rami went to the house, and told her mother.

"You have been studying very hard. Thank God everything will be over tomorrow. You had better help me get her into bed, son."

"Sure."

"What happened to you? You're all wet,"

"Your charming daughter pushed me into the water, and fell in herself too."

The next day Rami finished his exams quickly and drove to Leila's school to pick her up.

"How did you do?"

"Very good thank you, and you?"

"Alright I suppose, well actually fantastic. Oh I love you, we'll go out tonight and get really drunk, calling the troops." He announced. "I am going to the shop, do you want to come?"

"No I rather go home and sleep until tonight."

Rami went to the shop, both Nabil and Khalid shouted, "Rami ... hey good to see you." They sat on their high chairs behind the counter, talking to three girls. "Come around Rami, our missing partner."

Rami walked around the counter, and the third seat had the word "Reserved" written on it.

He laughed, "You don't miss a trick you two."

"Do you like what you see?" Khalid asked, meaning the shop.

"Stunning!" Rami said admiring the girls. "How can I help you ladies?"

"He is worse than you two, yes you can. We've been standing here for half an hour to be served, and these two want us to pay two and a half Dinars per hour of recording, plus the price of the tape, and on top of that they want us to go out with them tonight. What do you think?"

"I'll charge more if you go out with me."

"You are worse than them, like I said before."

"How about it?" Rami asked her again.

"Okay that will be two Dinars," she answered.

"That's too expensive for me."

Everyone held their stomach laughing.

She insisted, 'Its fair isn't it?' Even the girls with her were laughing now.

"For you my darling, my whole empire, but you are a bit late I'm afraid, as I've already promised it to someone else."

Nabil and Khalid looked at each other in amazement.

"Well?" Khalid questioned.

"I'm getting engaged in two weeks."

"That's the end of you; a responsible man now. There's no going out anymore, children and the lot. Fantastic, congratulations."

"She doesn't know yet about the exact date, as I just booked it on the way here." Rami said.

The girls were growing impatient with the three way conversation. "Come on let's have a price." They paid and left.

"Rami, this is Asaad and Huda. They're working full time here. We've tripled our equipment, and you two there, this is your other boss."

"Hi, we've heard so much about you."

"If it's from these two, don't believe one word of it," said Rami. He looked around him. The shop looked much bigger, then he realized that they had knocked the back wall down.

"I like the way you have pushed the wall back."

"We don't need the storeroom anymore; we're using the one in the bookshop. We have a nice office now."

"I feel like a stranger here."

"Nonsense, don't ever say that. Let's go to the office. We want to talk business with you."

As they sat down Nabil spoke first. "He accepted our offer at last, so we've got the building."

"How much?"

"Three hundred and eighty-five thousand, and the lawyers are dealing with it at the moment."

"Great, how are we going to pay for it all and finish the building?"

"Right, these are the figures of our takings from the three shops." Nabil said as he handed the accounts to Rami. "We've worked it out with the accountant."

Rami sat down to study the calculations. He was more than impressed with the way they had presented the case.

"Our three shops will be taken as security for the loan?"

"Yes…and the whole building too."

"So really we don't own everything?"

"Nothing until we pay for the lot."

"We have enough money to finish the shops," Khalid commented while Rami was still trying to understand the figures in front of him.

"We can pay everything in the next six to eight years," Nabil added.

"We will still take the same wages, and more." Khalid remarked.

Rami listened to them, reading the pile of papers. "It seems alright to me, except that I believe in having a variety of shops, not duplicated ones."

"One of the shops will be a food store, the other a butchers, to bring more people to this side of the road. We're thinking that the other five shops should be fast retail businesses, but we've had many people applying for them, so we can have a look later on." Khalid said.

"And if you have any ideas of what business you can start in the shop we'll discuss it some other time. Why don't you take all those papers with you and study them?" Nabil asked.

"Do you approve then?" Khalid asked.

"Yes I do trust you, as nothing has gone wrong so far. Let's go out tonight to celebrate."

"Yeh…. shake hands." With the shake of hands the deal was sealed.

Rami did not feel entirely sure about the whole project, as there were still a few minor details which he did not understand. He decided to ask Leila's father about them. "I'm going home now for couple of hours sleep. I'll meet you at my flat at nine."

"Okay, see you later."

He drove home and he was greeted as a lost son, who they had not seen properly for weeks.

"Mum, dad, how are you?"

His mother and father looked at each other then back to him, as they knew he was about to ask them for something.

"Do you need money to go out with?"

"No dad, but thanks." He took a deep breath. "Can I talk to you in the other room?" And he looked at his brother and sisters. "I don't need an audience"

They went into the adjacent room. "Sit down please; it's nothing to worry about."

"Good, I thought it was something serious."

"I want to get engaged to Leila."

"What?" His father shouted.

"Get engaged now, and get married when we finish our university."

"And how are you going to support a wife just coming out of university?"

"We will both work."

"I must say she is a beautiful girl and from a very good family. But it's too early...I did not get married until I was twenty-eight," his father said.

"Well, it wasn't my fault you didn't meet mum earlier!" Rami looked at his mother for support. He needed her help at that minute more than any other time.

"Darling, I can't see why not. They love each other and you will help them to establish themselves." His mother came to the rescue.

"Of course I'll help. That's my duty as a father, and he's my son after all. I'm helping his sisters when they get married, aren't I?"

"So what do you say, dad?"

"Yes, it's okay with me if it's okay with your mother. I'll phone her father and we'll visit them tomorrow and ask them for her hand."

"But dad that's old-fashioned, Leila already said yes," Rami complained. However his mother interrupted.

"Listen to your father Rami."

"Yes mother." He gave his parents a hug. "She'll make a good daughter in law."

He left the room, his mother said to the father, "They are happy with each other, and being in University next year will put some stability in their life, and it will help them to concentrate on their studies."

"I suppose you are right, anyway he's got a brain between his ears and had better use it for a good thing. I like the girl and her family, we couldn't ask for better."

Rami drove to see Leila the next morning, as she had changed her mind about going out the night before. He went into the room where they were having breakfast.

"Good morning everybody." Rami gave Leila and her mother a kiss and stood behind her father with his hand over his shoulders.

"You have something to say, Rami?" Her father asked smiling.

"Yes, we bought the building for three hundred and eighty-five thousand."

"That's great."

"I want you to have a look over the details for me please, I feel something is not right."

"No problem son, have you got the papers with you?"

"Yes, I left them in the front room."

"Fine, I'll look at them later."

"Your mum and dad are coming to visit us tonight," said Leila's mother.

Rami and Leila laughed.

"What have you two been up to?" her father asked.

"Well, we decided to get engaged and when I told my dad, he insisted that I ask for Leila's hand properly. He's a bit old fashioned I suppose."

"So am I," Leila said in defence.

"So you just want to make it official son?"

182

"Yes ..."

"It's about time. When a man sees an expensive ring on his daughter's hand, he wonders what it's for. I'm very happy for you both."

"Well it's up to Leila. It's her life after all." Her mother commented.

"I gave my answer a long time ago, and I feel stronger about it now than ever before, I love Rami completely, and I am not ashamed to admit it."

"Rami sit down and stop hovering behind my husband's back."

"Mum don't tell my future husband off." Leila laughed.

"Oh no I've got a mother in law now."

"You cheeky devil, and don't ever call me that; you make me feel too old."

"Well you're not in your twenties any more my dear." Her husband laughed.

"You as well, I can see it's going to be three on one from now on, God help me."

"Essa might give you a hand when he is here." Rami commented.

They all laughed, "Come here you two and give mother in law a kiss, I love you both."

"We're having two engagement parties; one for all the friends and one for the relatives and very close friends. What do you think?"

"Yes Rami, you're the boss!"

For the first time in his life he felt as he was attached to someone, he felt secured and fulfilled. Nothing in the world could match what he felt. A feeling of belonging, he was part of someone else's life.

CHAPTER TWENTY FIVE

THE preparations started from the word go. Rami booked one of his favourite places in Baghdad to hold the party. Thousand Nights was located on the first floor of a large building in the Al-Masbah district. It could comfortably hold up to three-hundred people, it had a large dancing area, plus a stage for the band to perform. He paid the owner in advance for all the food and drinks.

His suit was tailor-made, along with his shirt and bowtie. On the night Rami picked Leila up from her house. When she opened the door they stared at each other, stunned at each other's appearance. Leila wore a long silvery dress. Her shoulders were bare and her make-up simple and her hair thrown to one side with tens of flowers embedded in it. Rami looked like a movie star, with a light blue suit, white silk shirt and a dark blue bow tie to match.

Her mum and dad came to the door. "You both look a picture," said her mum.

"Thank you," Rami said, still looking in amazement at Leila.

Rami took a wrapped box out of his pocket and handed it to Leila. "Happy engagement my love."

She peeled off the paper, and opened it. "Wow!" she said mouth agape. "Look what this one went and did." He had bought her a five diamond necklace.

"This is absolutely exquisite young man. You have taste."

"I know, I'm in love with the most beautiful girl in the world."

"Here let me help you," her mother said with tears of joy in her eyes.

Leila opened her handbag and gave Rami a present. "Darling this is from all of us."

Rami opened the box to find a gold watch. His eyes watered, as he had never felt so overwhelmed as he did at that moment. Leila looked at her parents, "Can I kiss him properly in front of you please?"

"He is your man darling." Her father answered.

Leila held Rami's face in her hands and planted a long kiss on his lips. "I love you Rami."

"I love you more. You make me so happy."

"Welcome aboard son. Come here and give the old man a hug. You two put tears in my eyes," her father said.

Rami drove through the city then toward Abu Nawas Street, which ran parallel to the Tigris. He parked the car by the side of the road.

"Isn't it beautiful?" he said as he watched the sun melting away in the distance. "Everything around us is beautiful and you are the most beautiful diamond in the world."

"Do you remember the first time we met?"

"The minute you walked in I thought, 'That's my woman' and I nudged Nabil to have a look."

"You told me and then you started acting silly."

"I was trying to attract your attention, and I thought that I failed, I came back after an hour, but you were gone."

"You never told me that, I thought at first you weren't interested in me, then I met you at the dance with Farrah, I thought I stood no chance with someone so beautiful as her, but when you said that she was only a friend, I thought you were either lying to me or an idiot for not going out with her. But, I decided to have the party, I was determined to have you, you were mine and that's that."

"Oh my god I was head hunted...!" he laughed and continued, "I love you, and I am so much in love with you. You filled my heart, there is no space for anyone else, you filled my mind, and you are the only one I think about, and filled my eyes, I see no one but you."

"Come let's go, I feel much calmer now."

As they walked into the restaurant all their friends stood and applauded; some shouted and cheered, while others whistled. They headed to the large cake in the middle of the dance floor and they held the knife together to cut the cake. He planted a kiss on her lips, and they were stormed by all their friends. It was a custom to have a cake at an engagement party.

After, they sat around the front table with their closest friends Ahmad and Jean, Nabil and his girlfriend, Khalid and Sonia, Essa and Maha. May was on alone as Samir was on another overseas conference.

The band played a tango to open the dancing at Rami's request. They were followed by more than two hundred of their friends.

After the meal, Rami and Leila visited each table to thank them for coming and for their gifts.

It was a perfect evening and they couldn't have wished for better.

"Come on you gorgeous creature let's dance," said Rami eyeing his fiancée.

"I can't dance with this long dress, not to fast music," said Leila.

"Take it off then."

"Listen to this everybody...he wants me to be a wife and a stripper." Everyone laughed.

"You can't ask for a better understanding husband, right?" Essa said to his sister.

"Okay you stand still in the middle and I'll jump around you like a monkey," said Rami.

"Come on then monkey."

Leila danced in the middle with as little movement as possible while Rami danced around her. She laughed and laughed and she was so happy that tears filled her eyes.

Rami loved seeing her happy. He watched her green eyes fill with tears of laughter, her hair float in the air, and her elegant hand movements like an artist painting a picture. Suddenly her hands moved to hold the two sides of her head, he watched her eyes close with horror and pain, she opened them again for few seconds, she looked at him as if she was begging for help, he watched her body melt and tumble to the floor. He caught her the last second before she hit the ground. The music stopped.

"Leila," he screamed.

Essa rushed to her side in seconds. Rami took off his jacket and put it over her, with her head on his lap. "Call an ambulance, someone, please."

"The hospital is only five minutes away," Essa said trying to stay calm.

"I'll get the car ready," Nabil said and ran outside.

"Where is the telephone?" Essa shouted. "I need to phone the hospital."

Rami looked at Khalid; his face was full of fear. "Give me a hand to the car please, gently."

"Yes Rami."

Within seconds Nabil was driving as fast as he could towards the hospital. Khalid sat next to him, while Rami sat in the back with Leila's head on his lap. He held her tightly. "Please darling in God's name open your eyes."

But she didn't. Trickles of blood oozed out of her nose. "She's bleeding, what does that mean?" he shouted at his friends.

Nabil and Khalid glared at each other and Nabil stopped the car in front of the hospital, where a few nurses and doctors were waiting. They placed an oxygen mask over her face as they wheeled her into the theatre. Doctors rushed in from all angles. Khalid, with tears in his eyes, held Rami's shoulder and guided him into the waiting room. Nabil joined them a few seconds later.

"Where's Essa?"

"He's already in the theatre. I saw him going in. Do you want me to phone her parents?"

Rami nodded his head.

- - - - - - - - -

Ahmad sat in the restaurant completely stunned. "How much has that boy got to take before he is pushed to the ground? Between all the days of the year, it had to happen tonight."

"Ahmad, please pull yourself together. He needs you now." Jean begged.

"I helped them carry her to the car, but he didn't even see me there. He needs to be put to sleep for a year, until everything changes, so when he wakes up...oh God what am I saying...poor girl...poor Leila, she looked beautiful tonight. They were so happy together."

"Ahmad you should get in touch with his parents, he needs everyone now for support."

"I think we had better go and see them now, let me see the owner of this place first."

When Ahmad went to see him, he refused to take any money, but gave him the cheque back for what Rami had paid him earlier. Ahmad refused to take it, as he knew what Rami would've done.

Back at the Hospital, Leila's parents were already there. The street outside the hospital was filled with cars of their friends from the party. They all sat there quietly waiting for any news.

Essa entered the waiting room with a white face. "What's happening son?"

Rami covered his ears with his hands. He did not want to listen nor hear anything.

"They're operating now, she's got a brain haemorrhage," he said then he burst out crying.

"All we can do now is pray," his father said with his two hands over Rami's shoulders.

Rami walked out of the room. He could not take any more of the whispering or people looking at him, asking him if he was alright. He felt like shouting in their faces that he was not the one who was ill, but instead he looked for the chapel and went in.

He knelt praying, "God, I'm sorry for neglecting you for all those years, but please don't take it out on her. Put me in her place. She's young and she's needed on this earth. She'll have beautiful children and she'll be a good mother. Please God, don't take her away, she is all I have, and I'll do anything for you…Can you hear me God? I always believed in you, don't take her away."

He cried and cried. "Please God don't harm her, I never ever asked you for anything before."

"Rami," Leila's father was standing behind him.

Rami stood and faced him. "It's all over son…we lost her." Her father watched with amazement as Rami seemed to be talking to someone while someone spoke back to him. Hot tears ran down his face as he walked out of the chapel and he felt an ache eating into his body. He had pain in his sides, pain in his stomach and even pain in his throat which stopped him from shouting and screaming. Her father had his arm around Rami's shoulder. As they reached the waiting room cries and wails were heard. They all stood up when they saw Rami and he in turn looked at each face individually, begging for explanations and answers, his eyes told the story of the pain he was suffering. He saw Ahmad and hugged him tight and cried silently, then he saw the comforting face of his mother. Her lips shivered as their eyes met. She tried to hide her cries from him and to be stronger for her son. Rami walked towards her and hugged her tightly.

"Mum, I'm lost."

"I know son."

He threw his jacket over his shoulder and walked out. "Don't worry, I'll keep an eye on him," Ahmad said.

Rami walked out of the hospital and stood by the entrance for a few seconds examining the skies, which seemed dull and darker than ever before. He threw his hands in the air for no reason and they fell to his sides.

All his friends were standing outside their cars. They knew what had happened inside the hospital just by looking at him. Everyone shed a tear. Some watched him walk by with his head down, followed by Ahmad, while others sat in their cars disbelieving what had just happened. Rami walked to where he had parked his car in front of the restaurant, crying silently. The restaurant owner came out, took one look at Rami and sat on the steps leading to the entrance door, shaking his head and sobbing.

"Lord in heaven," he cried loudly.

Rami put his hands in his pockets looking for his car keys and felt some objects so took them out; Leila's ring and necklace, and the golden watch that her parents had bought her, as an engagement present. He remembered Essa handing them to him to look after. Rami cried with a wailing sound and raised the jewellery to his nose, hoping it would carry Leila's perfume, but there was nothing except the smell of metal. He looked around and noticing Ahmad, he handed him the car keys.

Ahmad did not ask where Rami wished to go, he just drove. The streets of Baghdad were empty; life in the city had stopped suddenly. 'How can anyone love and hate a city like this at the same time?' Ahmad thought. He did not want to be there, he wished he did not come back to this city. There was too much heartache that he could not cope with anymore. He drove to Abu Nawas Street and Rami stopped him with a hand movement and left the car. He walked towards the river and sat on a bench looking at the fast flowing waters. Ahmad stayed in the car watching him. There was a chill in the air.

At the first signs of daylight Rami returned to the car. Ahmad drove back to his house and Rami sat on the sofa, pulled a cushion to him and hugged it.

Ahmad took Jean out of the room as soon as they arrived. He looked at her and they embraced. "How is he?"

"He hasn't said a word."

"Poor thing. Leila's mum told me at the hospital that she'd gone to the doctors two days ago because she had been having a few headaches lately, but no one thought they were serious, and the results of her tests hadn't come back yet."

"I'd better take him a glass of hot milk and phone his parents, just in case."

When Ahmad got back to the living room, Rami was already asleep, hugging the cushion.

At twelve o'clock Rami woke up, looked around him, and realized that this was no bad dream. He nodded his head at Ahmad to say thank you.

"You'd better have a wash; the funeral is in one hour."

Rami drank the tea which Jean had brought him, but left the food.

It was a custom to have the funeral as quickly as the same day or the following day, due to the hot climate.

As he walked into the church, row after row of people stood up. His eyes were drawn to the box at the front of the church. He walked slowly towards the coffin. He knelt at the bottom of it, placed his two hands on its edge and his head leaned forward until it touched the cold wood. Someone tried to help Rami up, but a raised hand from Leila's father stopped him from even taking another step forward.

The service began, but Rami stayed there motionless. He closed his eyes and could hear nothing. He hoped if she was there maybe she would explain to him what had happened.

At last he stood up as the service finished. Two men approached to fasten the top of the coffin, but Rami stopped them. Her father approached him. "What is it son?"

"Can I see her one last time please?"

"You don't need my permission son. She's yours."

Her father moved to the side of the coffin, lifted the top and stepped backward. Everyone rose, it was not the custom that the top of a coffin would be lifted open, once the body was laid in it.

Rami moved to its side. He looked at Leila laying there, dressed in the same dress she had on the night before, and looked as beautiful as ever. "She is asleep. Tell me Leila is asleep."

Leila's father lowered his head to the floor and wept. He could not find the words to answer him.

"God…are you still there? I spoke to you last night. I told you not to take her away from me and you agreed. Why did you change your mind? She's the most beautiful girl in the world and I loved her. She'll make a good angel…look at her there, she's like the sleeping beauty." Rami laughed. "But I am no prince." His voice echoed throughout the whole church and everyone cried silently. "Leila please sit up, I know you like a joke, but you promised not to play another one on me again."

He dug his hand in his pocket and took the jewellery out. "Darling, you'd better put these on. You'll look more beautiful wearing them when you see God. God, please look after her, I beg you."

Rami placed the ring back on her finger her father and her mother stepped in to help him to put the rest on. Rami leaned forward and planted a long kiss on her lips. He cried again, as her father held him.

"It makes no difference now
Why you had to go
Without me
It makes no difference now
When you stopped our dream in the middle of the night
 It will take me a hundred years to know why
                    To understand
                         My love why?
You had to let go.
Why you never said goodbye?
You crossed the line
You've gone to the other side?
My love why?
I can't get you back
It will take me a thousand years to know why
                    To understand
You made my life worth living for
You made my world a better place
You nearly made our dreams come true
And you should know
But you stopped me dreaming in the middle of the night
What now…?
The music died
The laughter died
And I am dying inside

189

You crossed the line
You went to the other side
Oh God help me now
To understand
Don't let me die inside
Let me live for her
Forever I love her
It makes probably no difference now."

Rami looked at Leila's father. "She looks cold in there," he said. "I suppose it doesn't matter anymore. Goodbye angel." Rami looked at her father again, "Uncle is that it?!"

Rami and Leila's father hugged for a long time. They wept together and everyone else joined them.

The coffin was carried to the church yard, where after a short prayer it was lowered into the ground.

Rami walked away, followed by Ahmad. "Rami, Jean brought your car here. Do you want me to drive you?"

"No thank you. I'll just have the keys."

"Are you going back to her house?"

"No I'm going to the flat. I want to be on my own."

"If you need anything just call, you hear me?"

"Thanks Ahmad."

- - - - - - - - -

Never before had his flat felt so empty. Never before had he felt so empty and so confused. He sat on the sofa with a glass of whisky in his hand. After an hour or so he started walking from one room to the other. He felt as if he was searching for his presence there. He found himself crying at times, trying hard to gather himself together. He was told to celebrate her life instead of mourning her death, but how could he do that? She had hardly had a life. He ended up in the spare bedroom, where Farrah had kept most of her belongings. He went through them one by one. He lifted each article and placed it to his nose; the smell was Farrah's. He could not smell Leila any more. He walked to his study, glanced around and he thought how false everything looked. He sat behind his massive table; where Leila sat numerous times in the past, watching him and reading his writings. She loved his table with the green leather top.

He picked a book off the shelves, and opened the first page. It had been a gift from Leila. She bought him tens of books, but he had never read any of them. "I'm sorry," he said. "Forgive me Leila."

He read the first chapter, followed by another and another. He put the book down and looked at all the books Leila had bought him. He pulled them all down to his table and continued reading. He believed that in the books he would understand the real Leila, who had loved him unselfishly.

For a whole week he buried himself in that room, reading and writing. Nothing in the world existed or mattered. Nothing was special enough or important enough anymore and to make him move away from his desk. He had not slept for a week now. The cleaning lady walked in, took one look at him and knew she was only looking at a mere shadow of the real Rami.

"Do you want a cup of coffee son?"

"Yes please," he answered without lifting his head.

A few minutes later the doorbell rang, and rang again before Rami went to open the door.

"Hello Rami."

"Come in." It was Ahmad and Leila's father.

"Good news Rami, we have some good news." Ahmad said.

The expression on Rami's face did not change, what good news could possibly be good news! They sat down while Ahmad handed Rami a piece of paper. Rami looked at it, and read every line, but could not understand it; both men looked at Rami's unshaven face, the dark blue circles around the eyes, and the yellow features.

"You have passed the exams with 92% average."

"Yes...I can see that now."

"Leila passed as well." Her father said.

"Clever girl, which University is she..." Tears quickly filled his eyes, "Sorry uncle I wasn't thinking."

"How are you keeping, everyone is worried about you?"

"No need for that .... I am here."

"I told your father that I had given you a flat, because you wanted to handle the situation on your own."

"Thanks."

Ahmad stood up and left the other two to talk. He went and had a look at the bedroom, and realized that no one had slept in there for days. Then he walked into the study, books upon books, and papers everywhere. He took some off the floor, and he sat down reading.

"Rami you've got to look after yourself; you got to pull yourself together." Leila's father said. "For your sake, as well as ours."

Rami did not answer, he shook his head. Her father said again, "Leila would've loved that; she would wanted you to live your life again."

"When I am ready…"

"We all love you as much as our own."

"I know that…thank you."

"How long since you had a sleep?"

Rami did not want to be pressurised into matters that he was not capable of handling, "Uncle...Leila knew she was going to go soon, she knew, but I was too busy to notice. She gave me books and books and I should've read them. She was trapped, a death trap, and I didn't see it."

"Don't punish yourself, if it's true we all did not see it, where is Ahmad? We must go now, it's nearly lunch time."

They both walked into the study, to find Ahmad sitting on the sofa reading. He raised his face and looked at the two of them. His eyes were full of tears. Rami sat behind his table again, and like an automatic machine, he picked up his pen and started writing again, nothing around was of any concern to him. Leila's father sat next to Ahmad, and started reading what Ahmad had handed him.

Um Ali walked in after putting the shopping in the kitchen. She was relieved to see the other two men there. She went back to the kitchen and made sandwiches.

Their supposed short visit lasted until midnight. None of them said a word to each other. Ahmad and Leila's father left the flat in a daze.

Two days later Farrah walked in, she looked around and found him writing behind a pile of books and paper. The room smelt terrible, from smoke and body odour. The plates and the cups from two days before were left there.

"Rami I came as soon as I could, Nabil sent me a telegram."

Rami raised his face, and looked at her for a second or two, then went back to his writings. He was extremely thin, lifeless, his face was yellow, and his eyes sank in dark blue circles. He was unshaven, and hadn't changed his clothes from the night of the engagement.

"Have you got a cigarette?"

"Yes, I brought you some duty free."

"Thank you."

She came back with a packet and handed it to him, "How long since you've eaten anything?" He didn't answer her. Instead, he lit a cigarette and continued with his usual routine.

As she inspected the whole flat, everything was clean, and tidy except for the study. She looked in kitchen, and she realized that he had not left that room, as he had many packets of cigarettes left on the table, as well as bottles of whisky, and a refrigerator full of food, and a bundle of money. She realized that Um Ali had done the shopping.

She had a shower, changed her clothes, and cooked a meal. She set the dining table, and went back to him. He was still the same as she left him, she didn't want to disturb him, but this time she had to do it, "Rami the meal is ready."

"I am coming, you go ahead and start."

She sat there on her own eating the meal, and waited for him to come, but he didn't. So she put some food on his plate and took it to him.

"Eat..."

He lifted the spoon to his mouth, but a smile crossed his face, as he turned the page, and continued writing.

"Rami eat." She ordered again, and this time he did.

She left the room and telephoned Ahmad. "Ahmad Hi...its Farrah...I'm at the flat."

"I was just about to come over, how is he?"

"Dreadful..."

"Is he still writing?"

"Yes. Why couldn't you help him? Come over and see for yourself; something is going to happen to him."

"I came two days ago, but he is in a different world."

"He is killing himself."

"Well you are there, he'll listen to you better than anyone else between us."

"Ahmad ..... Rami is dying." And she burst out crying.

"I know...did you read what he had written?"

"No...Do you care about him?"

"Yes I do very much, but when you start reading it, you'll understand and realize that there is nothing any one of us could possibly do."

"He is on the edge of collapsing, when would he stop?"

"You just said it, or when he finishes writing, I think he will do that at the same time, he been at it for nine days now."

"Ahmad what exactly had happened that night?" Ahmad told her all the details.

"I am staying here anyway for another month or so."

"Good... Look after him for me."

"And me, bye now, I'll see you when I see you."

She went back to the study, and she started clearing it. She opened all the windows to change the air around. She picked the pile of papers off the floor and the table and started putting them in sequence, and luckily they were numbered, he had never done that before she thought. Then she organized the table for him. He did not take any notice of her; he kept on reading and writing.

Rami put the pen down, and stood up. He dragged himself towards the toilet, she watched his slow movement, his curved back and legs, and he looked so thin. She hurried after him, as he came out, she urgently asked, "How about a shower darling?"

"Yes..." He replied.

She got hold of his hand before he disappeared into the study again, and helped him take his clothes off. He was thin, his bones showed clearly under his skin, she turned the water on, and pushed him underneath gently. She ran to the bedroom and brought him clean clothes, he was still standing there as she left him; he hadn't moved an inch. She took her clothes off and joined him. He'll probably take notice of her she thought, but nothing, there was no life in that who she loved. She washed him, clothed him, and sent him back to his domain.

She phoned Nabil, she felt as if she had to talk to someone, who would understand, "Nabil...I just came today."

"Hello Farrah.....how is he?"

"Terrible..." She told him about the way she found him.

"I think you had better phone a doctor."

"No...I'll phone May in a minute."

"We are still in shock. Khalid and I can't put our hands to anything, we're just worried sick. Khalid was going to get engaged to Sonia, Leila's best friend, but now he wonders whether he is doing the right thing."

"Rami wants to die, he is killing himself. Nobody can go on like that for nine days without food or sleep. I think he is dying now." Farrah chuckled.

"No...Not Rami. He loves life very much."

"I love him very much, I love him Nabil."

"I know...you always did."

"I must go now before I...I'll phone May now, bye Nabil."

"Bye...Give me a phone call if you need me, I hate coming down and seeing him in that state, but I will if you need me."

Farrah phoned May, and she learnt that Samir was away until the morning, but she would come straight away. She told her that she did not think that there was anything she could do there. Farrah did not want another woman in her place looking after her own man, he was hers from now on, and no one else was going to touch him.

She made a pot of tea and took it to him. She sat watching him for a while, and then she picked the first few pages that he had written, and began to read. A few hours later, she realized that she was in a distorted state of mind. She had to shake herself up. Rami had not moved an inch; he read a few lines and wrote a few others on the paper. She thought to herself how many pages a person could write in a day. She made him a few sandwiches. He raised his head and thanked her.

"Farrah here again, I am sorry....."

"Is there... anything wrong?" Ahmad asked.

"I don't know."

"I'll come straight away."

Within minutes Ahmad was there. "Just go and have a good look at him Ahmad." He did and came back with a puzzled face.

"Did you see the same thing that I saw?"

"Yes ... I think so."

"He is empting his brain, he is feeding it with words from one side, and getting rid on the other side on the paper."

"You are right."

"He is writing about a death trap, he had put himself into that situation. He is fighting death on his own, so no matter what we do to him, it will never change the state of mind that he had put himself under. He never used to number the pages, but he did this time, as if he dies, someone would gather all the papers in sequence."

"How far have you read?"

"About eighty pages, not much."

"What he had written has never ever been done. It's the work of a genius. I think, well I am not sure until I read it all, the book is made up of tens of short stories, everyone is an individual beginning, middle and an end, but somehow they are connected. I believe that the last one will tell us where, or what state of mind he is in."

"That is pure creation if it's true."

Both of them went back to the study, and sat down to read from the start. By three in the morning, Ahmad realized that he forgot to tell his wife, so he decided to go home, and come back straight away.

When he came back, Farrah had made fresh coffee and food.

"Has he moved?" Ahmad whispered.

"Only once to the toilet."

"Thank God he remembers to do it." A funny comment, but none of them even smiled.

They sat reading as fast as they could. They were hoping to catch up with him.

Farrah fell asleep by six in the morning, but she was awakened two hours later by Rami going to the kitchen to get himself a glass of whisky.

"Are you going to allow him to drink that?"

"I don't know, probably he needs it, do you want a coffee?"

"Yes please Farrah."

"What about him…?"

Ahmad sat reading again. Suddenly he heard her crying in the kitchen, she could not help bursting out in that way.

"Hey come on, he will be alright."

"Ahmad, he is dying, I know he is, we've got to do something. This is his tenth day. He can't go on like this, hit him on the head or something, I love him, and I am sitting here watching him die, it's terrible, oh Jesus."

"He is writing his last book, he will live forever, he won't die. Come on let's make him something to eat."

Mid-morning, May and Samir came to see them. They tried to talk to Rami but he didn't even acknowledge them, in fact the look on his face told them that he didn't even recognise them.

"Try not to distract him; he is fighting his own battle." Ahmad whispered, "He is grieving his own way."

"What do you mean?" Samir asked.

"I will let you know when the book is finished, I haven't stopped reading since last night, so has Farrah, we are trying to catch up with him."

"I can't do anything then, just give him as much juices and good food as possible, I must go now."

Farrah and Ahmad sat reading again. None of them moved from their seats, apart from when they had to make something to eat.

At four in the morning she fell asleep, she was completely exhausted. Two hours later Ahmad touched her shoulder to wake her up. She followed him to the living room. "We are reaching the end. I had to prepare you if anything does happen."

"How far are you in the book?"

"The last story I think, unless he decides to write another."

Suddenly they heard a thud from the study, "Rami…" Farrah shouted, and the both of them ran to him. His face was lying on its side on top of the desk.

Farrah was pinned to the floor; she could not move another step, "Is he …?"

"He is asleep, thank heavens."

"Let's get him to the bedroom."

They carried him to the bedroom, took his clothes off, and covered him. Farrah sat watching him, while Ahmad went back and read the last of what Rami had written. After a while he came back to the bedroom with a smile on his face, "I can do with asleep as well, and you too, bye now, I'll see you later."

"Thank you…"

As Ahmad left, she sat crying with relief, "I love you, you bastard and you just don't care."

Ahmad came back with Rami's mother. She stood in the bedroom watching her son. Then she walked to the living room and sat down.

"Is this his flat, or Leila's father's?"

"It's Rami's." Farrah answered.

"I know my son's taste."

"He will be alright, I promise."

"I am sure he will, with people like you around him, helping, loving, and covering up for him." She smiled, and took a deep breath, "He is a fighter, I only wish that his father will try and understand his son a bit more."

Ahmad went to the study room, and came out with a large pile of paper, "That's what he wrote in eleven days, would you believe it?"

"All that...?"

"Yes...nearly nine hundred pages."

"How did he manage to do it?"

"I just don't know."

"My Lord...His fingers must be aching by now!"

"That was his last word, 'My Lord' He opened the last few page and read the last couple of lines.

"The Lord creates women, and the Lord takes them away." Ahmad raised his head and looked at the two women, "Listen to this bit...Women are like seeds; we plant them, water them, and feed them. Than we look after them, and appreciate their existence. We cut them, carve them, and make them into Goddesses for us to worship, pray and dream. My Lord I love your dream."

"This is different."

"He called it death trap. He laughed, screamed, cried, wondered, lost, swore, blasphemed, worshiped, ran, stood idle, every movement, every feeling, every word that he learnt since he was a child...Listen to this..." Ahmad took a deep breath, "Why my Lord did you end your creation by taking us away? Why? Is that part of the creation? Or is this the conclusion? The book is made up of fifty six short stories. Every story is different to the other but it continues the plot to a stage further, so if you miss one you miss the whole plot, it's out of this world. How did he write it? If this gets published he will be a legend. The work is priceless."

"That's my boy, shall we go Ahmad?"

"Yes, I'll take this with me, and I'll get a few girls to type it for him, they'll do it in my house, I won't let this get out of my sight, bye Farrah."

"Yes see you both."

"Farrah look after my boy, my baby, for me, please." Rami's mother hugged Farrah dearly.

Rami woke up late morning the following day. He dragged himself out of the bed, to the bathroom, where he shaved and showered, then went back to bed. He did not have the energy to do anything else. Farrah came in after being out to the shops.

"Farrah ... when did you come back?"

"Four days ago."

Something inside his brain triggered, but he did not remember. "Did you hear?"

"Yes...I am sorry Rami."

"She was more sparkling than ever before that night."

"I know baby. I'll make you something to eat."

It took him two days to gather some of his strength back, but he was still not himself. Nabil and Khalid came to see him, and to get his signature on a few legal documents. He told them to go and see Leila's father, as they had got some of their calculations wrong. They told him that he had already been there himself.

"He is a fantastic businessman Rami."

"I must go and see him, I think he was here, but I can't remember."

"He was...he told us."

That night, Rami took Farrah to Leila's house. He stood by the front door and did not move, It took him a while to find his power. Leila's parents greeted him warmly and hugged Farrah for looking after him.

"Rami, I have something for you son," her father said. He left the room and came back with a key. "This is the key to our front door. You come and go as you wish, and bring all your friends with you."

"But I can't."

"No buts, or excuses, if you would explain to him, mother." The father could not talk anymore; he was choking with feelings and emotions.

"Son, we were going to give you the key that day after the party," said Leila's mother. "You are my daughter's fiancé after all, even if she isn't with us anymore."

"Thank you mother-in-law." Rami's hands shook and he smiled with tears in his eyes. He knelt in front of her and hugged her.

Essa and Maha walked in. "You never treat me like that anymore, mother." Essa teased.

Essa tried to shake Rami's hand, but instead they embraced each other. Farrah kept drying her eyes and she turned to Leila's mother. "Tell them to stop all this, I can't take any more."

They all laughed. "Rami, there is one more thing."

"Yes uncle."

"Sit down please. Everything we own will be shared between you and Essa."

"What?" Rami did not understand.

"Leila's share is yours now. I have changed my will."

"No, I cannot accept that. Everything belongs to Essa. He's the only one entitled to it."

"But he's the one who suggested it. We were happier than he was."

"Even if Leila was here I'd have given it back, I don't need it. I'll be a very rich one day." Rami said.

"Rami, don't make me angry."

"Essa needs the money to open his own clinic. I'll help him to open a hospital, but not take money he needs. Ahhh, what's the use arguing with you? You're as stubborn as an ass." They all laughed.

"Also, if the memory of Leila would stop you coming here, we're prepared to sell this house and get something smaller."

"Don't do that. Her memory is here...in me...in the air that I breathe, everywhere that I go, no...I love you all, but I don't deserve all that. I am lost for words." Rami felt like crying, but instead he laughed and joked as if nothing mattered anymore.

- - - - - - - - -

That night he couldn't sleep. He tried hard, but everything that had happened at Leila's house suddenly came to life. He switched on the small lights in the ceiling and looked across the bed to see Farrah lying there with her eyes wide open.

"Can't you sleep either?"

"No."

"You know, I can't take any more deaths. If anything happens to you, or any other person close to me, I would sooner die. I can't take any more."

She leant on her elbow and gazed his face.

"I'm sorry Farrah for not telling you that I was getting engaged. At times I feel I'm not honest to anyone. You, Leila, May, Nadia...am I sex mad or what? I don't understand myself." He paused. "I love you, don't die before me, I'll kill myself, I wouldn't be able to handle it, to handle life without you."

"You will survive, life is full of tragedies but there are always good things."

"What if I die?"

"I promise you one thing."

"What's that?"

"I wouldn't let you."

"What time is it?"

"Three, you must go and see your mother and father tomorrow. Oh, by the way, Ahmad took your book to have it typed."

"What book?"

"The one you wrote recently. He said you'll be a legend."

"I can't even remember. It seems that whenever I write something good, I'm not there to enjoy it."

"You stupid fool."

Farrah bent down and kissed his forehead. She was aching for his touch, his warm body and his seeds inside her, but she could not find it in her to make him love her. She knew he belonged to someone else at that minute; he was not ready for her yet. She wanted to tell him she was not angry about not being told about the engagement, but Rami read her mind.

"Thank you Farrah."

"For what?"

"Being here."

"I'm still here for another three and a half weeks." She said.

"Will you promise me something? Make love to me every day and never stop until I..."

"Yes," she interrupted.

"Then what are you waiting for?"

"For you to make the first move."

CHAPTER TWENTY SIX

A few days later Rami woke up late in the morning. He made himself a cup of coffee and sat on the sofa in the living room. He looked at the telephone for a long time before he finally picked it up and dialled the number on the card he held in his hand.

"Can I speak to Mr. Sabah please?"

He waited for a few minutes before he heard that strong voice on the other side.

"This is Sabah."

"It's Rami here."

"How are you? I heard the bad news. I am very sorry…my deepest condolences."

"Thank you. I made up my mind, I accept."

There was a pause. "Ok, someone will contact you soon, bye for now."

"Bye." As Rami put the phone down, Farrah was standing behind him. He did not say anything to her, instead he just went back to the kitchen. She followed.

"What was that all about?"

"Nothing."

"Rami I know you, and I know that look on your face. Who is Sabah? Is he your ex-teacher?"

"Yes."

"A government minister, a very high ranking member of the party? Am I right? He is also a member of the revolutionary council?"

"Yes, you are." He answered quietly.

"Well tell me then."

"Nothing to tell…"

"I don't believe you and that's the first time since I've known you, as a matter of fact I don't trust you. Do you understand?"

"Look Farrah, there are things I don't like to discuss with you sometimes. What's wrong with that?"

"Nothing I suppose."

"Everything is back to normal," he commented.

"That's what you think, but I wish I'd never come back. You treat me like a piece of shit Rami. You used me, and I allowed you to because I love you. What a fool I've been! Fuck this type of love. You're hiding something important from me." She walked out of the kitchen in a bad mood. Rami remained still and waited for a while before he walked out of the kitchen. He found her packing her bags in the spare bedroom.

"Farrah I love you."

She screamed back at him. "I wish you knew the meaning of the word." But she realised that was harsh comment. "God forgive me for saying that, I wish…"

"I wish I was dead too." He said quickly.

She looked sadly at his face, and ran into his open arms. "Tell me please, I can feel there's something you're hiding from me."

"Okay sit down, and listen."

"Power is what I need and what I want, since I can remember. Somehow, somewhere I failed, so I got one chance of doing it, one chance left for me to take, by letting someone else do it for me."

"What on earth are you talking about? I'm sure your brain isn't working properly. What power? You have money already…you are number one."

"You don't understand," he interrupted.

"Yes I do understand. Your writings move mountains."

"They did, but once you move a mountain you can't move it anymore. It's part of growing up."

"What are you getting involved with?"

Rami told her the whole story and she promised not to tell anyone. She held him close to her to protect him from himself, to stop him from destroying everything he had worked for and believed in.

"Rami you're mad, don't do it, please, for me, say no. I'll do anything for you, I'll stay here and look after you, I won't travel again, but don't involve yourself in all that. You're a writer not a gunfighter."

"I'm doing it for us."

"For us…? How on earth are you doing it for us?" She shouted at the top of her voice, "You are doing nothing for me you are doing nothing for us. You are doing it for yourself only, and fuck everyone else. Who do you want to revenge? Nothing will bring her back, nothing will change the past."

"It's my life and my choice."

"Yes, but you're playing with fate, gambling with your life. Your last book is called Death Trap…that's the last thing you wrote and maybe the last thing you will ever write if you accept Sabah's offer. You waited until Leila was out of the way for you to accept Sabah's offer."

"If someone harms me wouldn't you die for me and avenge me?"

"Yes I will, but if I say no I will be a fake."

"When I was arrested, and Nadia's father as well, not to forget my uncle, I wanted revenge. The day they drove me back to May's house after being released, I told them not to sleep for one minute, because they wouldn't know when I would come"

"That was years ago and what's it got to do with Nadia's father? It's only an excuse, and God took Leila away, so are you going to go out and kill him?"

"I'm not going to go and kill anybody, please understand."

"No...what do I care?" By now she was crying, she was terrified for him.

"You do care, otherwise ..."

"I wouldn't screw with you."

"No I wasn't going to say that, I was about to say, being here."

"Being here! What if you got killed or something? What about me? Or you don't care about me? You're a selfish bastard."

"Farrah, I don't want to lose you."

"Well, you already have. I don't want to be with someone who doesn't give a damn about me."

"Please."

"I'm going as soon as I can get a flight out of the country." She telephoned the airlines and booked a flight for the following day. Rami stood watching, he could not believe how determined she was.

"So is that it? I won't see you again."

"Yes, that's it Rami. The end of us as friends, and lovers."

"What about all these women whose husbands are in the police and the army?"

"I am not married to you Rami."

"I'll phone him and tell him I've changed my mind."

"Rami who are you trying to lie to? Do you think I'm some sort of an idiot?"

"What then, what else do you want me to do?"

"Choose between us being together, or you and your fantasy."

"Stay with me until I make up my mind."

"I'm going tomorrow, so you have until then."

"I love you."

"You love you."

The following day she packed her bags and left. She took all her belongings out of the flat too as she knew he wouldn't change his mind.

Rami went back to his house. He needed the security of a family. He felt heartbroken for both Leila and Farrah. No one from his family said anything about his disappearance for three weeks, after all they knew that he was still grieving.

A week later he received a phone call from Sabah's connections to be ready to be picked up the following day at 8.30am.

"Rami….."

"Yes."

"Mr. Sabah's connections: would you like to come with us, or would you rather follow us in your car?"

"I'll come with you."

As he got into the car, the man smiled. "I'm Sami, your immediate boss."

He felt so relaxed with the comforting Sami's smile.

They drove to a prestigious suburb of Baghdad, and stopped across the road from an ordinary looking house to pick up someone else.

They were driven to the north of the city. Rami had never been to that part of Baghdad before. As they left the main road, they passed many farms growing a variety of citrus fruits, followed by acres upon acres of palm trees. They were so dense they obscured the sunlight completely.

"The building you'll see next is our headquarters, but not where we operate from because of the distance to the city." Sami said. "Once we leave this car, we have exactly five minutes to get inside, as there are tens of guns pointing at us right now from all directions.

"It's like being in the movies," said Rami, laughing.

Sami gave Rami a questioning look. "You might ask why they are pointing them at us when they know I'm the boss, but they don't know who you are. Hopefully they'll get used to you soon."

"I hope so as well, I am still too young to die, I haven't enjoyed myself properly yet."

The building was an ordinary looking storage compound. As they walked into the building, Sami pointed out the various security systems that were in place. Inside, it was smartly decorated with expensive furniture throughout the rooms. They were taken to a large room, where many men were gathered, and they were handed a bundle of papers to read. A few minutes later another group of men entered. To Rami's shock Ahmad was among them. They looked at each other angrily, and sat apart, not saying anything to each other.

Sami appeared again. "Good morning everyone…I'm Sami, and I'm the only one who will give you orders; no one else has the power, not even the president." He looked at each of them and continued. "You start training tomorrow for three months. Although you will be trained by the elite from the Iraqi army, do not discuss anything with anyone. Keep your mouths shut. You will be trained to fly, drive a tank, and use all the latest weapons. You will not be trained to march left right left right."

Everyone laughed, although many of them didn't find his words funny at all. "You will address me as Sami, not sir, boss or anything else."

Sami continued to explain that they were going to be trained in the art of survival, self defence and many other aspects involved with being an elite crack unit, including crime detecting techniques and investigations.

The training began the following day. For some it proved too complicated, but to the majority it was no more than keeping fit exercises. Their training lasted for five hours every day and they were taken to different army camps, where they received more instructions from officers. They enjoyed their training. The regular units saw them as a bunch of freaks, but soon they found out they were much more capable than the regulars.

The first two months of training were over. Sami called everyone around him and they formed a circle with him in the middle.

"As you know, twenty-eight of you will be based in Baghdad, and the rest in different parts of the country. I have a list here of you and your partners. Every group will be issued with a number. Use your number when you contact us, or vice versa."

Rami ended up, as he expected, with Ahmad. For two months they had hardly spoken to each other. Rami could not find it in him to ask why he had joined when he had a wife to care for.

Sami continued talking. "Your cars are ready. We have been working on them for the past two weeks and you may take them away today. Be careful when you drive them out of here, as the engines are far more powerful than before." He explained how to operate the radio control, the red SOS automatic button, and how the radios ware hidden under the dashboard.

They were given three identification cards each, secret police, army special intelligence, and one from their own unit, The Central Intelligence Command CIC, not to be used unless in an emergency.

- - - - - - - - -

Days flew by and Rami tried his best to find out what was wrong with Ahmad, but he could not.

One day Ahmad and Jean went to visit Rami's parents. His father was not at all happy that Rami was accepted at the science college, as he had good enough grades to go into engineering or medical college, but when Ahmad spoke in Rami's defence, his father agreed reluctantly.

"He did not fancy playing with dead bodies, as he said."

"The truth is that he seems so far away from us these days. Thank God he's got you. He's changed in so many ways since the age of thirteen or fourteen."

"He's changed since Leila passed away," said Ahmad. "He doesn't want to be with anyone, including me. He has become afraid of close relationships with anyone because he doesn't want to be hurt."

Rami walked in. "Hi there, what are you talking about?"

"You, who else?"

"I gathered that. Are you and Jean taking me out?"

"I'll take you out for a quick spin in my new car if you like?"

"Okay, come on. We won't be long dad."

Rami understood that Ahmad had something serious to talk about urgently."What is it Ahmad?"

"Get in the car first."

As the car moved away Ahmad started to speak. "I've got a letter from Farrah."

"A letter?"

"Yes, she gave it to me just before she left the country, but for some reason I didn't give to you."

Ahmad looked into Rami's face to tell him not to ask why, and he did not.

"I wrote to her five or six times, but she didn't answer my letters."

Rami opened the letter and started reading.

'Dearest...

As you know, I have not changed my mind, and I am sure you have not either. I don't wish to see you anymore. Please try not to write to me unless you are sure that you want me as I want you. Do you know that you've got two lives to look after, yours and Ahmad's? He refused at the beginning, but the idiot joined them because of you, to protect you, not from anyone or anything, but from you. Be careful, as it's his life and yours as well. I wish you a long life. I love you forever, Farrah.'

Rami looked long at the paper in his hand, "Did you read it? Did you know what's inside this?"

"Yes I did."

"Why did you keep this letter until months?"

"I don't know."

"So your blood is in my hands. Why did you really join Ahmad?"

"I wanted to. It's a good cause, it's for the future of this country. The government is thinking more about the people than themselves for a change."

"I know all that, but did you join because of me?"

"Partly, I didn't want you having all the fun on your own."

"Well if I get myself into trouble, there'll be nothing for you to do. I'll make sure of that."

"How?"

"You won't walk into the fire with me hand in hand. Ahmad get out of this now, you have Jean to think about. Get out now. They told you that you're free to leave anytime you want."

"And you have Farrah to think about."

"She'll come round later. She loves me and anyway we are more like friends than lovers."

"I think you're right about Jean. I'll stay for few months and see."

"Now Ahmad, get out now."

Suddenly the red light flashed in the car. Rami pressed a button under the steering wheel and the radio flapped down from the dash board. "Car 11, go ahead Control."

"Are both of you in the car?"

"Yes."

"Look for a green and white Dodge taxi, I believe it's the 1963 model. Other cars will arrive in your area shortly. All police cars are alerted, but they aren't allowed to act, do you understand?"

"Yes Central."

"Keep your distance and don't intercept. Check the Wathiq area properly."

For almost an hour all police cars, as well as sixteen cars from the CIC were looking for the taxi, but they did not find it.

"Car 11 to Central."

"How about pulling all police cars out of the area? They will not come out of their hiding place with all these cars around."

"Good thinking. They'll be pulling out in a minute."

Half an hour later the taxi was spotted on 52 street. The radio echoed again. "All cars this is Control; the taxi is on 52 street, heading towards new Baghdad district. Follow but keep your distance."

Ahmad looked at Rami with a sparkle in his eyes. "This is our first job, do you realize that we are professionals now?"

"Come on, put your foot down, there they are. Keep your distance, remember?"

"Do you want to drive?"

"Yes why not? After all, I drive better than you!"

"Swap over."

"Now…?" Ahmad swallowed hard.

"Now."

"You are crazy! Did I ever tell you that?"

"Hundreds of times. Haven't you seen them in the movies?"

"Are you serious?"

"I am…hurry up."

Somehow they managed to change seats.

"Car 11, we are right behind them."

"You are in charge now."

The taxi sped away. "Car 11 to Control, he's speeding away from us."

"Keep up with them, all the other cars are behind you."

"What if we get spotted?"

"Don't worry I'll be joining you shortly."

Ahmad laughed and said, "He must have a plane."

"You never know what that devil gets up to, he probably can fly himself. No need for a plane! Look how fast that taxi is going." They were quiet for a minute, as the speed of the car increased.

"Ahmad I am sorry about all this, I should start thinking about others, not only myself."

"I am enjoying it, I feel ten years younger."

"You sound like an old man! You're only thirty for God's sake."

"I should've given you that letter. But I think we were made to do this job, it's good, useful, and for a good cause. Otherwise they wouldn't have spent all that money over nothing. As well as unlimited wages, they paid me a thousand last month."

As Ahmad looked behind him at the other cars, Rami shouted. "We've been spotted and he's got a gun. Duck your head."

One of the men in the taxi fired at them. "Car 11 to Control, we are under gunfire."

"All cars keep your distance and don't fire back, just follow. Don't fire back, as they have a hostage."

After a long chase the taxi slowed down, stranded behind a lorry with an oncoming lorry on the opposite side.

"Ahmad, shoot the tyres," Rami shouted.

The taxi was forced out of the road, onto a field, where it came to a halt.

"Control we've got him, they've stopped in the middle of a field."

"All cars surround him. Car 11 is in charge."

All the cars did exactly as they had been ordered. They had done that in practice so many times before. All the men left their cars and hid behind them, guns pointing at the taxi.

"This is Control, hold your fire until I get there." Sami ordered.

But as the men in the taxi started firing in all directions, Rami gave the orders to fire in the air above the taxi. He wasn't going to wait, and ran towards the taxi without warning anyone of his action. Another two joined him. He was surprised at their quick thinking, and smiled to them when he bent down underneath the taxi.

"Well done lads." He whispered.

"Are you crazy Rami?"

"No one asked you to get here."

"What next?"

Ahmad was angry. His eyes focused on that crazy friend of his and what he might decide to do next. Ahmad shouted. "You in the taxi, come out with your hands up now."

"We have a girl here," said a voice back. "We'll kill her." They started firing in all directions. Rami signalled to Ahmad to fire at the top of the taxi again. In the same instant, the three of them pointed their guns at whoever was in the car.

"Drop or we'll shoot."

"Don't shoot, don't shoot."

As the men stepped out of the taxi, a helicopter landed with Sami in it. One of the men rushed to him to explain what had gone on.

"Rami come here." Then he turned to the other man. "Take the two men in different cars and bring the girl here. Has she been harmed?"

"No Sami."

"Okay, then let's get out of here and go home."

Rami stood next to him, while Ahmad held the girl close to comfort her.

"Young man, what you did was stupid, yet it seems I missed it all. Good fun was it?"

"No, I was shivering and shaking all over."

"Just like in the movies," Sami commented. "If you say so boss." Rami laughed.

"What you did out there was dangerous. You've watched too many films."

"Oh yes...! And how were you supposed to get the girl out safe?"

"You and the others are more important in here, than the girl, even if she was a Minister's daughter."

"Wow....She wasn't that beautiful, as a matter of fact she was ugly."

"Get out of here. Well done."

"See you soon boss."

"And don't call me boss." he replied, smiling.

As Rami went to the car, Ahmad approached Sami to have a word with him, "Sami...he did all that for me, he thought that if this would carry on any further, somebody might get hurt, and it could be me, so he did what he thought best. We had a disagreement earlier on."

"You better calm him down. Mind you he did fantastic, and he's got real guts."

- - - - - - - - -

The university started a week later. Rami found an old friend, back from the American School, whose name was Maad.

He was from a well-to-do Muslim family and he had the freedom to do exactly what he wished. Maad had light brown hair, with a small beard to support his outstanding looks. He owned a car and was a fashionable dresser. He loved wearing hats and he possessed a fascinating collection.

As Rami walked into the classroom on the first day, he heard someone shouting his name and pointing at a seat next to him. "Maad! Good to see you."

"How are you?"

"Good thank you. And you?"

"I couldn't be better."

They became good friends. They went to college together, taking it in turns to drive. They studied together for two hours every day in the library then they had their basketball or volleyball training.

Rami's life became a daily routine. After college he went to the shops and worked for few hours then he went to his father's factory to do some paperwork, and twice a week he went to the centre. He kept up his visits to the newspaper and he never forgot his friends, Ahmad and May, or Leila's family. His writing became less imaginative, as he wrote articles, or conducted interviews with various known individuals. His book was going to be published in Lebanon and marketed in all Arab countries.

University life was completely different to life on the outside. Rami found there were many activities, societies and clubs to keep him occupied. His reputation as a writer followed him, thanks to Maad; they found themselves surrounded by a large group of students. They kept their distance from having relationships with any of the ladies, which made them more popular, and trusted as friends to talk to, and to laugh with.

The new students at the university had a hunger and thirst about them. They had hunger for knowledge. They came prepared for it to be pumped into them, ready to get rid of their past. Not everyone had the style of Rami and Maad. In fact, some of them had never even been in the company of the opposite sex, apart from their immediate family.

The female students came from a society which kept them under lock and key decade after decade. Now education was essential. The need was to earn more money, which was essential to improve standards and maintain it,.So parents sent their daughters to colleges and universities, and perhaps if they didn't have it in them to obtain any qualifications, then the chances of finding a good husband with good prospects for the future, and hopefully from a good family or a tribe, were much greater.

Female students came with open minds, challenged to face the tough side of the human race. They looked for the driving force men claimed to have over them. They came to show that they were matured and educated, and that they knew how to look after the future generations.

The male students, on the other hand, came to learn how to mix and to talk to the softer half of the society. They hoped to change their lives completely and to have open relationships, which they heard so much about. They wanted to stop spending money in red light houses, or picking prostitutes up from street corners; and having what they called sex with them, in the uncomfortable positions on the back seat of their car or hired taxis. They came looking for love, understanding, fruitful relationships, and long lasting friendships. They came to spread the word, 'That men and women were equal; and no longer women are treated as second class citizens.' But did they really believe in that?

Both sides lost their initial battle to break through the barriers of the other side. They were struck by a huge walls; the silent behaviour of their opposition including traditions, customs and old-fashioned ideas.

Neither side wanted the other to agree on everything that was said, but they looked for a fight or an argument. Instead the two sides agreed by their silence.

The two boys stayed away from all that bickering, and found that their popularity increased. Rami was appointed the head of the entertainment society at the university and for the first few weeks he introduced many activities, from art shows, to science exhibitions and even a play.

Throughout the first few months at university, Rami and Maad spent many hours together, until Maad became seriously involved with a Muslim girl called Fatin.

Rami found he had more time on his hands, which he saw as a welcoming break. He had time now to return to his writings.

CHAPTER TWENTY SEVEN

FARRAH was still in Egypt and although she ached for Rami, she decided to stick to her guns never to see him again. His life became like a rollercoaster, and she felt that he wasn't able to control the changes, as if he was controlled by some unknown force.

As she left the doctor's, she felt down-hearted and sad and the dull weather only added to her low spirit. She took a taxi back to her apartment. It was late afternoon and she wanted to be alone, but her housemate was there.

"What did the doctor say?"

"Exactly what I feared," Farrah announced.

"So what are you going to do?"

"I'm going to have the baby."

"What about the father? You've never talked about him."

"I don't know. I'm afraid...oh God." She burst out crying.

"Why don't you answer his letters?"

"No way!"

"But he loves you Farrah."

"I love him too. I'm so proud to have his baby."

"But you can't keep it a secret."

"Yes I can...until the day he changes his mind."

"What did he do to deserve this treatment?" The housemate asked.

"I can't tell you."

"Did he go out with another woman?"

"No."

"Hit you?"

"No. He has always been kind to me. He's a gentleman."

"Is he from a different religion?"

"No...No use...I can't tell you."

"I think you're being stupid then. Don't tell me you'll never go back to Iraq?"

"I don't know right now, I feel like writing to his friend, but what's the use? His college, his parents, the difference in our age, he can't be completely free until he's twenty-one, but it isn't that."

"Money?"

"You must be joking, he'll be a millionaire in the next four or five years. Oh, I'm so afraid that he might do something stupid. I must write to his friend."

Farrah wrote to Ahmad and explained the whole situation. She also asked him not to tell Rami about the baby, but to help her get him out of the special service.

Ahmad wrote back telling her how good their job was for the country, that even he had started believing in the idea of the CIC and that there was no danger at all. He told her that the number of operations they had to tackle was very small and most of them were very humane. Their job was very important to the progress of the country. He told her that if she wished to stay away, then that was her choice and not Rami's, as he was very happy.

Ahmad hoped Farrah would change her mind, come home, and face the reality that Rami was happy, especially after what he had to go through. He wanted her to come and face Rami and talk face to face. But, she decided not to write back.

Ahmad was going round in circles, as he felt he had interfered in Rami's life in many ways. Jean told him he should have told Rami and let him decide. It was almost a month since he had written to her, but he didn't receive an answer, so he wrote again, telling her that for the sake of the baby, she must come back, so the three of them could talk it over. But his letter came back marked, 'Moved away, forwarding address in England unknown.'

- - - - - - - - -

"Rami, what would you do if your girlfriend got pregnant?" Maad asked him one day.

"Have the baby. I don't believe in killing. I would also marry her, as it's my responsibility as much as hers. It's the least I could do. Our society doesn't forgive unmarried mothers. Why?"

"My father will kill me."

"Then you should have been more careful." He stared at Maad for a while, disapproving of what he did.

"It was just one mistake."

"Oh no...What have you done?"

"Fatin is pregnant."

Rami looked at Maad in anger. "What's stopping you from marrying her?"

"I've been promised since I was a kid to marry my second cousin and there's no way out of it, plus I like my future wife to be."

"But the goalpost has been moved now."

"I know that, but it'll make no difference."

"For God's sake, all that money, power and education, yet you are still living in the dark ages. This car and that stupid hat on your thick head are all for show. It's all hiding the real you."

"It's not my fault."

"Well then whose fault is it? It wasn't you who screwed the poor girl? You've got to leave the house and marry the girl."

"And how will we live? I'll lose everything; my father's money, the company, the houses, everything. How will we live tell me wise man?"

"So her life doesn't mean anything to you? You could work at night, or during the day and go to college at night. I'll help you."

"She does mean something to me, but she's only a passerby."

Rami raged with anger. "So when you decide to fuck an honest girl and all the promises that go with it, it was only to make her open her legs then after that she is nothing, just a piece of meat?"

"It's her fault for believing me. Can you help me Rami?"

"What the hell for? I don't like people like you and I don't want to be in your company anymore."

"Don't be so hard on me, it was a mistake, please try and help me."

"What do you want me to do?"

"We tried all the doctors we can think of, but no one is prepared to give her an abortion. That's what she wants."

"I've heard of some illegal houses."

"Where are they?"

"It'll cost you a lot of money."

"I have money."

"Leave it with me, and I'll find out for you, but I can't promise anything, take me to my car, not to the house."

"Thank you Rami, you're a good friend." Maad was quiet for a while, then he decided to hit back at Rami, "Well, you talk about my father, yet you hide everything from your father all the time."

"Its material things, not people's lives, but my mother knows."

"So does mine."

"I think she should tell your father."

"I think mother did, but he pretended not to know."

"Maad, your father chooses not to know? I don't believe this, and no doubt the money came from him?"

"Probably, my mother gave me the money, and she was ready to give me more."

"I think I've heard enough."

Maad stopped his car next to Rami's, "Will you let me know?"

"Yes I will, but remember that I am only doing it for Fatin, and not for you."

"Thank you."

When Maad left, Rami sat in his car thinking about his friend, he could not understand how anyone could be so cold-hearted.

"Car eleven," he said into his radio. A woman voice answered.

"Is Sami there?"

"Yes," said a woman's voice.

"Tell him I'm coming to see him in a few minutes."

"Will do."

Rami walked into Sami's office and explained the situation. Sami made a few phone calls and handed Rami a piece of paper with an address on it. "Her name is Julia and she's the best, but she's watched day and night by the secret police. It's in the pipeline to close her down; she has been going on for some years now. If you go tonight or tomorrow night you'll be alright, as you might have just heard me, I have just lifted the police watch."

"Can I make a phone call please?"

Rami telephoned Maad to tell him everything was booked for that night. Sami interrupted, "You'll have to take the girl yourself."

"I'll meet you at six where I was parked earlier and I'll take Fatin myself. Bye for now." Rami put the phone dawn. "Thanks Sami."

"We're only trying to help. I just hope that there won't be any complications. When you get there, tell her that Jaber had sent you."

"Fine...I just hope so as well."

"If anything goes wrong, get in touch with me straight away."

"I will. I must go now. I have to eat, change, then meet the poor girl."

"Ahmad was here this morning," said Sami.

"What for? He should have been in school."

"He asked me to look up the address of a girl in London."

"I didn't know he knew anyone there. Never mind, I won't tell his wife." Rami smiled.

- - - - - - - - -

Rami arrived to where he supposed to meet Maad, and saw Fatin waiting for him.

"Where's Maad?"

"He said he couldn't wait as he felt nervous. He gave me this envelope for you."

"The bastard. Who the hell does he think he is? This is it...we are finished as far as I am concerned. Nothing will change my mind.'

"I'm sorry to put you through all this Rami."

"Don't be silly."

Fatin got in the car as Rami opened the door for her. His heart sank for the poor girl. God only knew how small she felt; a strange man, whom she had only met a few times taking her to have her baby aborted. "Are you alright?"

"No, I'm frightened and very ashamed."

Rami put his hand on hers.

"I told my parents that I'm staying the night at a friend's house."

"Good."

"Thank you for everything. Maad told me you are doing this for me and not for him. He also told me what you said to each other."

"I'll break his neck one day." Rami was still angry. Matters like those disturbed him, but felt in control to handle it, only for the sake of the poor girl.

"Do you think I am cheap?" She asked.

"No...I don't, I think he is."

"He gave me an engagement ring."

"When...?"

"The day that it happened, the day he slept with me."

"What happened after that?"

"I hardly saw him."

"I am learning about him, the only one who had me fooled out of all the people that I know."

"Have you got a girlfriend?"

"No, I have many friends, but no girlfriends."

"Why?"

"Oh it's a long story."

"Tell me...It helps to talk about something else, as well as to relax me."

He was quiet for a minute, and then told her briefly what had happened on the night.

"Rami don't say anything If you don't want to, if it hurts."

"I've never spoken about it before...On the day we had a big party, and she just, collapsed, God...I can still see her face.Two hours later at the hospital she passed away. She was beautiful, my Leila."

"Oh Rami forgive me."

"I wanted to talk about it to someone, don't feel sorry for making me talk, I still visit her family, they are fantastic people. What a comforting feeling for me to know that they are there whenever I need them."

"You are a good man Rami."

"You don't know me."

"I know one when I see one, and I don't know how I 'm going to repay you."

"Stop seeing him."

"I've already told him that. I come from a very respectable family, I was brought up well, and I always..." she couldn't continue and burst out crying.

"Here we are! This is the house. I'll park here and I'll come back for you. I know you've been lied to and treated like dirt."

Rami left his car and walked towards the front door. He rang the bell and waited. A young woman opened the door. "Hello, is Julia here?"

"Yes…"

"Jaber sent me."

"Yes, I've been expecting you. Bring the girl."

Rami walked back to the car with a strange feeling about that house.

"I hope they close this house forever, the death house." He repeated in his mind.

He went back with Fatin. The woman was still standing by the door.

"Where is Julia?" Rami asked.

"I am Julia!" A look of pride crossed her face.

"Oh sorry, I thought...never mind."

"You'd better come with me" she said to Fatin, then she turned to Rami and pointed to her left. "And you can wait in that room."

Their eyes met for a flash of a second as Julia turned around, and walked out of the room. Rami was amazed by her simplicity. She was in her late twenties or early thirties, a medium height and build with by far the sexiest legs he had ever seen. She was extremely feminine with rounded hips. The furniture was simple yet adequate in the waiting room. The walls were bare, except for two paintings by some unknown artists. But it was extremely clean. He moved the ashtray next to him and lit a cigarette. A few minutes later another woman entered.

"Tea or coffee?" she asked.

"Coffee if you don't mind."

"Won't be a minute..."

When she left the room, Julia walked in and she sat facing him.

"Can I have one of your cigarettes please? I left mine upstairs."

She quickly examined him, while he was taking the packet out of his pocket. She made her mind up that she liked him. Rami held the packet out for her then lit her cigarette.

"Steady hands." She commented.

"How is she?"

"I haven't started yet. I've just given her a few injections." She shook her head in disapproval. "Men..!"

"She isn't my girlfriend. She went with someone I used to like."

"She said so herself."

The old woman returned with a tray and left it on the table. Rami took the initiative to pour the coffee. "How do you like it?"

"No milk or sugar, I've got to look after my figure."

She was testing every move he made, every reaction to her double meaning words. He was elegant and precise in everything he did. He had confidence, she was amused and interested.

Rami handed her the cup and examined her. It was a game that had no rules, they obviously liked each other, but who would make the first move. He felt at ease in her presence.

She found his looks, his searching eyes too obvious, but they did not bother her. She was sitting with her legs slightly open, an indication of how tired she was.

"I can't see anything wrong with your figure." A shadow of a smile printed on his lips.

"That's the way I like to keep it."

She felt slightly uncomfortable, but on the other hand she was thrilled when his eyes kept staring at her legs, but she didn't make an attempt to close them.

"What's your name?"

"Rami..."

"What are you?" she asked, gazing into his eyes.

"A man!" he replied looking with a smug smile. "Do you want to find out for yourself?"

"I meant Muslim or Christian."

"Christian."

"Me too."

"I know…you wouldn't be called Julia otherwise."

"Do you always look at other women the way you are looking at me?"

Rami smiled. He enjoyed the challenge of direct questions. "Only when they fascinate me and when they have the most perfect legs, like yours."

Her giggle grew into laughter, "The girl said that you are something else, but I didn't think of you in this way."

"What way?" Rami was thrilled that by the time Julia gave Fatin the injections, she had a quick chat concerning him.

"I don't know."

"How long have you been doing this?" Rami asked.

"Eight years."

"Are you married?"

"I was, but now I'm a war widow. My husband died in the north, he was a dentist."

"I'm sorry."

She was surprised at how at ease she felt with Rami, she could talk openly to him, as if she had known him for a long time.

"Don't be. It was eight years ago and I hardly remember what he looked like."

Rami did not think she was telling the whole truth, a part of the story was missing.

"I must go back now. It won't take long."

"Good luck."

"Thank you."

He poured himself another coffee and waited. The minutes passed slowly. He remembered the night he spent at the hospital waiting for someone to tell him news about Leila. He never thought he would be in that situation again, but this time it was different. The panic struck him as he looked at his watch. Nearly a whole hour had passed and he had heard nothing. He wondered what happen if she died. He'd kill Maad for sure. He was licensed to do so and no questions would be asked.

He tried to listen for a noise or movement, but all he could hear was the clock ticking in the adjoining room. He felt like leaving the place and running away.

"God don't do it again." he prayed.

He looked at his watch again and again, but something inside him stopped him from leaving, he looked at the ashtray next to him, and realized that he was chain smoking. He opened the window slightly to let some fresh air in, and let the smoke out. At last Julia appeared. She gave him one tired look, and collapsed in the seat facing him with her legs stretched out and wide open. Rami lit a cigarette and handed it to her, but her eyes were closed.

"Julia," he whispered.

"Thank you," she said, taking it out of his hand. "Thank God that's over. She is resting."

She opened her eyes again and looked into Rami's face as if she were searching for something. Words weren't necessary, as her eyes begged him to make the first move. She wouldn't say no, she begged him to keep looking at her hungrily as it turned her on, made her forget the past eight years.

He in turn stared into her eyes, hoping to find the answers before he made a fool of himself. He searched for a response to his questioning eyes. She searched his tender face, his strong features, and his truthful eyes. But both of them could not find many answers, except a relief inside that the other person was there in the same room waiting, and wanting to be noticed by the other.

Her breathing deepened and her eyes stayed closed, she had drifted into a deep sleep. The old woman came back into the room to ask Rami if he would like more coffee.

"Don't disturb Julia, she's asleep."

"Never …" She said surprisingly.

"I took the cigarette off her hand, and she didn't notice me. She is very asleep." Rami whispered.

"I've been here five years, and I've never seen her sleep, day or night."

"How is the girl?"

"She is asleep, you can see her tomorrow. My God it was hard. If it wasn't for Julia … others would've given up. That's why she is the best, even doctors send for her when they are in trouble."

"I was told that."

"She is a wonderful woman. God give her a long life," The old lady prayed, "I owe her my life."

"What was wrong with the girl?"

"She is young, and everything was pretty small. Ah you don't want to bother your young ears with all that." She smiled to him, "How is the coffee?"

"Perfect."

He moved to the kitchen and chatted to her. It was a good experience for him to talk to someone so ordinary.

"Can I make a phone call?"

"Yes son, but the phone is bugged by the police."

"That's no problem."

Rami telephoned Sami and told him that everything was fine then returned to the living room. Julia was still fast asleep. He watched her pleasing face. She wasn't stunningly beautiful, but very attractive nevertheless. She had long blond hair and her lips were full. His eyes travelled down her body, examining the slightly tight white overalls she wore. He could see clearly the outline of her figure. As she moved, one of the top buttons of her overalls came undone and he clearly saw that her breasts were her best feature by far. She was not concerned about the way she sat before, or even then, the way she had stretched and opened her legs. 'Some woman…!' He repeated many times.

He had not been with another woman since Farrah had left, but at that moment he felt different, it had been a long time since he felt so strong towards anyone.

At last Julia opened her eyes. "Oh dear, I must have slept."

"Yes for two hours," said Rami.

"And you spent all that time sitting here with me," She felt at ease. Even when she looked down at herself, and saw her overalls were half way up her thighs, and her undone button, which showed most of her breast, she did not move, but challenged him with another penetrating look.

"I very much like what I see," he confessed.

"What do you like best?" She surprised herself for talking in that manner. She had never ever talked like that before to any man, including her husband.

"I like you all, your face, baby face, your breasts your legs, all of you."

"Thank you."

"I wish you'd give me the chance to get to know you."

"What time is it?" she asked, dismissing Rami's revelation.

"Ten past eleven."

"I must go and see how the girl is doing."

"She's still asleep, the old woman told me."

"Who are you?"

"Rami...!"

"I know."

"I'm taking you out for a meal tonight."

"Now...?"

"Yes."

"But I never leave this house. The police will follow you everywhere."

"So you want me to stay here with you?"

"No I don't, just go home and come tomorrow for the girl."

"Julia, please close your legs, stand up, and go and get changed. I'm going to take you out whether you like it or not."

"But...!"

"No buts and no excuses."

"You are serious about going out, aren't you?"

"Do I look any other? I always get what I want."

"I am sure of that." She laughed, she liked him from the minute she set her eyes on him, but he was too young for her, he was too honest, and from a good background, and the last thing that she wanted to do, is to get him involved with her affairs with the police.

"Thank you, but no."

His face changed. He looked sad and hurt. His eyes for the first time that night, moved to look in the distance. She felt guilty for causing all that hardship in him, "These beautiful sleepy eyes!" she told herself. She said what she had to say to protect him, better getting hurt now, then later on. But, she wished that he would ask her again, insist again, order her to move, she would say yes this time, she had never said yes to a man since her husband died, but Rami was different. 'Please Rami ask again, don't give up on me now you won me.' She prayed to herself.

Rami wasn't giving up that easily. His voice raised a few pitches higher. "This is your last chance. I'm hungry, I haven't eaten since five, so please go and change or I'll do it for you. I'm taking you out and that's final."

She stood up and smiled. "I hate men who order me around."

"I hate women who refuse to do as they're told."

She laughed softly.

"Does that mean yes?"

"Yes...Yes...Yes."

He was overwhelmed so he stood up, hugged her and planted a small kiss on the side of her face before leaving to go home and get changed. She took a step backward and he realized what he had done.

"Sorry it's just...I am sorry, I am just happy."

"Don't be sorry, I never expected a man to be so happy to be in my company." But what she really wanted to say, was that she never thought that a man could get so near to her.

"Come on...go...go...go." He pleaded.

"Okay... don't rush me."

"I'll go home and change myself. I'll be back in twenty minutes at the most."

"It'll take me more than that."

"Twenty minutes." Rami said as he walked out.

She stood there looking at the door closing behind him. A smile crossed her face, as she touched the very spot where he had kissed her.

He went to his flat and dressed quickly as he walked from one room to the other, checking that everything was clean and tidy.

When he returned the old woman opened the door for him. "My God son, you look special and you made Julia leave her house for the first time in years."

"Is she ready yet?"

"She will be down in a minute; she's had a shower, done her hair and even shouted at me for not having anything proper to wear. She's like a fifteen-year-old again." The old woman laughed. "What did you do to her?"

"I just asked if she'd go out for a meal with me. She deserves a break."

"Yes, but it's nearly midnight?"

"That's no problem."

"They say Baghdad never sleeps at night."

"Like a woman in love." Rami commented.

Julia walked into the room, "What have you two been talking about?"

"Wow... Good lord, you look stunning." Rami complemented.

"You look a picture." The old woman said.

"Will I do Rami?"

"I am honoured to be in your company Madam."

"Smooth talker, come on you lets go before I change my mind."

Rami drove to his usual restaurant, The Strand.

The head waiter rushed over. "Mr. Rami, good to see you Sir."

"Are we too late for the last orders?"

"No, not at all." He smiled. "You're always welcome. Same table as usual?"

"Yes please?"

Rami handed him five Dinars, but he refused to take it. "It's for the kids, I insist." Julia looked around her, "This place is fantastic, I can't believe it, and you have been here before." Julia concluded.

The waiter approached the table. "Mr. Rami, pleased to see you again, what would you like to drink, sir?"

Rami looked at Julia, she quickly said, "Anything that you like is fine by me."

"Champagne please, the lady loves it. And tell the chef that we'll have whatever he fancies cooking for us."

"Yes sir."

Julia looked at his face; she was so amazed by his maturity and his way of handling people. Rami lit a cigarette and handed it to her, before lighting another for himself.

"That's the second time you have done that today. It's beautiful; you did it as if it's a habit between us two."

The waiter returned, and poured the drinks and left.

"Here is to you." Rami raised his glass.

"Who are you?"

"Someone who is trying hard to impress you…!"

"I'm very impressed," said Julia. "Tell me about yourself."

"Ladies first."

"There's nothing much to tell. I did nursing in England, and that's where I met my husband. We moved here after we got married, but he was called to the army and killed. I had to find a way to earn some money."

"Why this job?"

"For the money, I had to find the best way to pay what we owed on the house and being a nurse at the hospital doesn't pay enough. I hate what I do, but at the same time I'm helping many girls."

"What else?"

"I used to make a lot of money, but not anymore, because of the police."

"And…?"

"Nothing else, tell me about you."

"I'm in my first year at university."

"I want to know more, what's with the expensive car outside and your expensive clothes?"

"Well, I'm also a writer."

"Liar!"

Rami took out his newspaper identification card and showed it to her.

"Now do you believe me?"

"Yes, I believe you. Oh my god you are famous" said Julia. "I am sitting with someone famous like you! Fancy that! Life is full of surprises."

"It makes the night more interesting."

"You big headed devil, I thought you would be much older."

"And I thought you would be fat and ugly."

They laughed, "Did you really?"

"Now I've told you my secret, tell me yours."

"Well, I have a deformed child, in a special clinic in England, who I must pay for. I call him my child, but he belonged to a friend of mine. She died when he was born and the father disappeared, he was completely destroyed, God help him, he will never recover, they were so much in love, it's a long story."

"Such is life…!"

"How old are? I've been dying to ask you all night."

"A hundred and one," Rami laughed.

"I'm still a few years older," said Julia.

"To you, old woman," said Rami, raising his glass again and looked her in the eyes.

"You're a very special person," said Julia. "You made me come alive again." She leaned forward and kissed him on the lips.

"Thank you." He was touched with the simple showing of feelings. There was no high drama, Just simplicity.

"Do you fancy dancing?"

"Yes but nobody else is."

"We will." They danced for almost half an hour until their meal was brought to the table.

"I feel out of condition, I am out of breath, I haven't danced for years."

"Stick by me and you'll dance every night."

"Liar…"

"Eat your meal before it gets cold."

The Chef excelled in cooking a variety of dishes. Lamb chunks marinated in garlic, crushed coriander seeds, lemon juice, and cooked over charcoal, presented on a bed of saffron rice, with a faint aroma of rose water. And, okra cooked in a sweet and sour tomato sauce, with more pieces of lamb, accompanied by a variety of salads.

He went on talking, she felt contented, happy and proud to be in his company. She wondered what attracted her to him, his sleepy eyes? Or was it his lips? She was hooked to that honest face, and she could not take her eyes away from it.

"You danced beautifully." He remarked.

"You were leading me."

He watched her eating. Her delicate flawless features and her sensual body sent him to insanity. To him, she was a complete woman.

"I want to see you again," said Rami as he put his knife and fork down and held her hand.

"No Rami, tonight was something I'd like to treasure for the rest of my life, tonight belongs to the two of us, but tomorrow…"

She suddenly fell quiet. Rami quickly changed the subject, as he did not want to pressure her. They had a long conversation and they danced a few more times, until they were ready to leave.

"Thank you."

"Not at all, thank you for coming out with me."

As they sat in the car, Julia held his hand. "Rami, what's going on in your head? What's eating you?"

"Change your job." She looked long in his face she knew that he was clever enough to know the answer.

"I'll find you a new one."

"But you think you have all the answers, I make thousands every month, who is going to pay me that much?"

"What would you do if you could have another job?"

"I'm not sure….perhaps a hairdresser."

They were both quiet for a while until he spoke first. "Will you try and see me again." He begged.

"I'll try. It's very sweet of you to…"

"I want you…" He interrupted her.

"I need you tonight." She whispered.

They pulled up outside Rami's flat and entered. She giggled nervously, she never ever been with another man but her husband. She was happy, and she surprised herself by saying to a man that she needed him. She wanted to see him again, and again, even though there was no future in any relationship with

221

him. Her problems with the police troubled her seriously for the first time, her job, and her reputation. She saw how well he was treated at the restaurant. But tonight is her night.

"This is a magnificent flat, how many women have you brought here?"

"Hundreds, no I am joking."

"Good, I like a man with a bit of experience. Is the bed clean?"

"Yes."

"I don't like to sleep in a dirty bed." But she did not continue. She felt anxious and tried to talk herself out of her state.

"Clean towels and unused tooth brush." Rami smiled.

"How about coming here and holding me tight?"

He held her close to him. "You're trembling," he said.

"I am," she said feeling embarrassed.

She went into the bedroom and closed the door behind her. He followed a few minutes later to find her already in bed.

"You are quick!"

"I like your bed. I've never been in a round bed before."

He switched off the lights and put on the small ceiling lights. She stretched back leaning on her elbows as he sat next to her. "You are a romantic devil."

"For the first time in my life I don't feel any sexual needs. I know we want each other, but being here with you is enough."

"You don't have to do anything, it's not important."

"I can talk to you, I don't have to act, and be someone else."

"Rami take your clothes off and come to bed."

He did as she ordered. She noticed how slowly and carefully he undressed, how he folded his trousers and shirt, and laid them neatly on the chair. How beautiful his body was. He was not shy at all, he had self confidence.

"I like what I see." She commented.

He pulled the covers away and laid on his back looking at the ceiling.

"I never get bored with looking at these lights."

"It's so peaceful in here."

She moved nearer to him and he put his arm under her head and pulled her gently towards him. Like a loving cat, she fitted herself in the curves of his body, as if their bodies were shaped to fit one another. She closed her eyes and listened to his breathing, and heart beats. She felt safe, that was what she had missed all those years, love, and protection.

"I'm sleeping with a woman I haven't even kissed yet." said Rami.

In the darkness of the room, he saw her face light up with a loving smile.

"I'm not stopping you!"

Their heads met halfway and they felt the heat from each other's lips. She was afraid that she was about to lose control, but so be it, she gave up at the end. It was like a dream or a story out of a fantasy world. He felt afraid to touch her body at first, but it felt alive next to his. Their short kisses developed into a passionate ritual. She pulled away from him, breathless, trying to force fresh air into her pounding lungs.

She planted a small kiss on his shoulder. "Oh God, I love your body." she confessed.

"I want you so badly."

She pushed herself towards him, her body was throbbing next to his, she wanted him inside her that second, she wanted him to fill her up, she wanted him abuse her hungry body.

Rami kissed her eyes tenderly. He found her lips were aching for more. She giggled, "I am so happy, I want more."

"Now you know what you have been missing?"

"Enjoy me," said Julia. "It's only for tonight."

Rami did not reply, as he knew this was not a one night sex madness. He knew he was too good for a woman to turn down. But he also knew that she had an incredible sense of self control.

"Stop I want to talk," she said.

But he knew differently; she was only trying to stay in control of herself.

"What Julia? Aren't you in the mood? Or have you developed a headache suddenly?"

She giggled again. "Give me a chance to breathe."

"Take what you like." He sat on his knees and slowly pulled the covers away and threw them to the floor. His eyes travelled down her body. He set the challenge, and she accepted it. She wanted satisfaction, she wanted him, she knew her powers, and knew her weaknesses, but never in her life knew how much she needed a man, needed him, and him alone. Her eyes travelled down his body, and settled where it mattered to her.

"Have you seen a hungrier woman than me?"

"You are beautiful, just perfect."

"I want you Rami, I need you."

He leaned forward and kissed her. She closed her eyes as the tip of his fingers travelled from her shoulders to her breast. She let out a small cry. "I love you," she whispered.

His hands settled between her thighs. She did not move or object. She simply opened her eyes begging him not to stop. His hands moved away from where she wanted him and they barely touched her flesh, sending shivers all over her body. She felt his mouth kissing and loving her feet and she cried again. "I love you, don't ever leave me Rami, oh God how much I want you."

His mouth travelled upward, kissing, tasting every inch of her body. She could not stop him for her to be in control again. She was his to do with her what he liked.

"I love you Rami, promise you won't leave me."

He did not answer, he was enjoying her.

"Oh Rami, I love you, Ah..."

Every part of her responded to the attention he gave it, every stroke, every kiss, and every gentle touch. Suddenly it was concentrated to one spot. An explosion of mixed feelings overwhelmed her as she felt him penetrate her. She was lost in a sea of emotions. She didn't want to be found out, but if she was, she wanted to be lost again, and forever.

Rami felt as if he was making love to his past, his future, and the present, his only woman. He felt it was too late to close the dangerous door he had opened. It wasn't love, surely it was lust; love of a body, love to satisfy, love which is perfection, complete…no it was lust for sure. He shall never have another woman like her ever again. She gave him everything and took him to heights he had never reached before, and brought him down safely, to let him rest, so she could take him and herself even higher, the next round of lust.

"I love you Rami. Once more please, I still need you, tell me that you love me."

He tried to stop her, he tried to tell her that he had enough, but he knew that was not the truth. He still wanted her as much as she wanted him.

She felt as if her whole body did not belong to her anymore. Rami played with it like a child with a new toy. He treated her body like a sacred gem to be worshiped and looked after. He gave her what she longed for. He gave her the security she never had. He took her on a long journey, giving her, his body and his young soul.

The next day Rami woke up first, it was late morning. He looked around the room at the uproar that their love making caused. He smiled as he looked at Julia, still fast asleep. He got out of bed and stood there watching her. He felt like waking her up and starting all over again, but she was sleeping so peacefully that he did not want to disturb her.

Finally she opened her eyes to see him sitting next to her drinking coffee. She pulled a pillow to cover herself up and smiled. "Hi gorgeous, it's very warm in here."

"I've got central heating."

"Where…? Inside you?" She giggled as she looked at him wickedly.

"Do you fancy a coffee baby?"

"Yes please."

When he returned she was in the shower. As she came back into the bedroom she had the towel wrapped around her.

"You look fabulous in yellow."

She looked at herself in the mirror, "Oh yes, it does, yes, okay.! Thank you for pointing that out." She said coldly.

As he watched her getting dressed a strange feeling came over him. She avoided eye contact at the same time as showing him her body, she was very discreet. The sparkle she had possessed the night before had disappeared. Another face, another body, was all she was to him at that moment. He did not like the coldness between them.

"Are you going to get dressed?" she asked.

"Yes, I'll just have a quick shower and a shave."

He was glad to leave the bedroom. Her changeable attitude irritated him, but she followed him silently and stood by the door watching him shave. "I miss watching a man shave," she said.

He did not answer her. Somehow he resented her for being there. What on earth was he doing with someone who didn't value life? What she did for a

224

living was against all his beliefs and principles. Killing an innocent soul to save someone's reputation was not an honourable job.

"I really like your flat." She commented and distracted him.

"Good."

"Do you sleep here all the time?"

"Sometimes..."

"Rami,"

"Yes…"

"Thank you for everything. I shall treasure the memory of last night."

"Any time, it's my pleasure."

"Don't spoil what we had, I beg you."

"But you change your mind from one minute to the other. Last night you told me you loved me and you couldn't live without me. Then earlier you brushed me aside with a dry attitude, as if I'm only a memory, a one night passerby, a one night stand."

"I'm sorry."

"Can I see you again?" He did not know why he asked that question, as he already knew the answer. He turned round and faced her, "When?"

"No more, never again."

"Why? We had a perfect night. We enjoyed each other's company and we made love like we understood each other's needs. Is it because I'm younger?"

"Age doesn't come into it. I enjoyed what we had, enjoyed being with you, and it gives such a thrill that a younger man still wants me after he had me."

"And?"

"Rami wake up and look ahead. I'm different to all the other girls you have around you. I'm not the type that a man would like to be seen with. It's like going out with a whore. If we go out together and somebody looked at me differently, you will go out of your head, wouldn't you? If they whisper or laugh, you'll think they're laughing at us. You're a writer and people respect you wherever you go. You are young and full of life and you have your own friends."

"But ..."

"We had perfect sex, that's all. I like you a lot, but people look up to you; you're an icon, a symbol, the people like to look at you as the perfect man, you shouldn't go out with an abortionist.'

"I don't care what others think, I always do what I choose and I always keep my private life to myself."

"Sweetheart no, let's just leave it at that. We had a wonderful time and that's enough."

He took his house robe off, and got into the shower. She watched him; she wanted to touch his body again, for the last time. She never thought that a man's body could turn her on so much. She never believed herself insisting on saying no, how could she? Why was she afraid for his reputation? Why did she care for him, and was she trying to protect him? Would it be different if he was someone else?

"Do you want me to dry you?"

"Thank you, but I can manage."

"I want to."

He handed the towel to her, he tried to hold her and kiss, but she pulled away. "Your hair needs a trim."

"I know."

"I like a broad shouldered man."

"You are not turning yourself on again?"

"I don't have to." She smiled.

"Then why not?"

"Because..."

"What would you like to do if you weren't a nurse?"

"I don't know, probably a hairdresser."

He took Julia to her house, collected Fatin and drove her home. When he got back to his flat, Sami telephoned to say he was on his way to his flat.

"Well, Rami, how did it go?"

"Okay, the girl is back in her house."

"I meant with Julia."

Rami examined Sami's face, trying to find out exactly what he meant.

"She was here all night, wasn't she?"

Rami shook his head in amazement. "You had me followed?"

"Is it going to happen again?" Sami asked.

"I don't know. I'd like to see her again."

"She has never been with another man," said Sami pulling a thick file from his briefcase.

"That's everything there is about her. Case closed." Sami concluded.

"What do you mean?"

"She's a free woman, no more phone tapping, no more surveillance, she's free."

"Why?"

"In case any of my men gets himself involved with her."

"I don't believe this."

"I do, if I say she is fine, and order to be left alone, she would be left alone, well what do you expect? You did it for her."

"It's all still a mystery."

"This woman has been watched day and night, day in day out, telephones, mail, every single move, the cars which come and go, photographs of all the people, including you, if I didn't stop it in time, I did what I did, I always thought there are some good people left in this world, but this woman does more good than bad. Anyway I must go now. I have work to do."

"Thanks a million Sami."

"Not at all, you are welcome."

Rami read Julia's file. There were hundreds of pages, complete with photographs, names, telephone conversations, and money transfers to England, everything Julia had done for the past few years. By eight o'clock at night, he realized he had been reading her file for the past four hours. He called the shop. "Nabil, how are things?"

"Very good."

"Do we still have one shop unoccupied?"

"Yes, but there's someone interested in it."

"Can you hold him for a week or so? I've got a friend who might be interested."

"Okay, as what?"

"A hairdressing salon."

"Well that's different. I must go now as I'm on my own here and I've got some customers, see you."

Rami lifted the papers and started reading the report. He felt sad for everything Julia had gone through over the years, the loss of her husband, the child in England, and her brother's death at a young age. He wondered why anyone wanted to condemn her. He turned the pages quickly and found her telephone number so dialled it.

"Hello Julia."

"I'll call her for you."

He waited for few minutes, then he heard her voice, "Yes."

"Hello gorgeous."

"Who is this? Is that you Rami?"

"Yes."

"What do you want?" she asked coldly.

"I missed you. Life is boring without you; the flat is so empty and the bed is so cold. The only way I'll be happy is when you take a taxi and come straight over here."

"You don't give up," she laughed. "Bye, I can't talk to you now."

"So are you coming?"

"Bye sweet heart."

He felt happier; he knew that she was going to come. He felt the need to write something, so he went to his study, pulled the pack of papers in front of him, and let his pen flow from one line to another. When he finished, he looked at his watch and realized that his hopes of Julia coming were fading. He wondered whether to stay at the flat, or go back to the house that he treated as a hotel, and he wondered why his father had kept a blind eye to all the time he spent sleeping away from the house.

Suddenly the door bell rang. He looked at his watch, it was past eleven o'clock. He opened the door. "Julia."

"I hope I didn't wake you up?"

Rami pulled her towards him and kissed her. "Wait, give me a chance. I'm out of breath carrying all these."

"I can smell food."

"You are very clever, anyone can smell food from miles. I've been cooking for you, that's why I'm late."

"For me?"

"Yes, you need the energy, after last night."

They set the table, lit a few candles and sat facing each other.

"You forgot the wine; I left it in the kitchen, in the bag."

"I'll get it."

She heard him shouting from the kitchen, "1959 Vintage!"

"I like my Wine."

"So do I and my father too."

"This is the first time you have mentioned any of your family."

"And the last time…" He sat down and poured the wine. "You cooked for me, and you weren't going to come today or forever and ever?"

"Well just eat and enjoy it, I felt like cooking for a man, and you are more than that."

Not another word was said between them. They ate, drank and looked at each other. Words were not needed, as their body language said it all.

"Eat some more, there is plenty of food left."

"I am really full thank you. You cooked for ten people."

She laughed.

"What are you laughing about?" Rami asked.

"Just a thought crossed my mind."

"What?"

"I thought I slept with ten people last night, you bring the worst out of me. I have never been so open with anyone like this before. I wouldn't let anyone take you away from me. God I enjoyed that."

"I have a surprise for you," Rami said finally, when they had finished eating.

He went to his study and returned with her file. He put it in front of her on the table.

Her smile disappeared as she opened the first page. She turned the next page and read a few lines, then another and another. He cleared the table, watching her puzzled face. Her hands shook and her eyes watered. She had told him a lot about her past, yet seeing it in black and white with photographs it was beyond her self control.

"Where did you get these from?"

"Your case is closed. No more surveillance, no more telephone tapping and no more police. You're free."

"What are you?" she asked with fear in her voice. She tried to hide her feelings. She stood up and went to the sofa, hoping it would give her more support for her shaking body. "What are you?" She screamed.

"A man who likes you very much."

"Who are you?"

"What you see is what you get."

"No, what I see is a young man who I fell for, a young man who is so powerful beyond my imagination, and I am left here puzzled. It says top secret and you tell me my case is closed just because you slept with me! Why should I believe you? Yet why shouldn't I?" She took a deep breath. "I'd better go."

"But why? I thought you were going to make this a night to remember."

"You certainly made mine one, thank you."

She felt very weak and she pushed herself up with her hands.

"Please sit down," Rami demanded. "Don't ask me any questions. Accept the fact that you're a free person again. This file is for you to do whatever you wish with it. It's yours and there is no other copy."

"I don't understand."

"You're free to do what you like."

"How? Why?" She was completely puzzled.

"You're a good person, that's why. I managed to get your freedom , and don't ask me how. I have connections."

"What's the price? How much do you want? Or is it more than that?"

"One kiss, and one night."

"In other words you bought my freedom, you own me now, is that it? And when you've had enough of me you'll give me back to them."

"No, you don't understand."

"I understand very well. I wish I'd never laid an eye on you. I wish I'd treated you like all other men. I wish I'd ignored you. I stood there cooking for you and thinking, why not? I'll give it a go. I meant it last night when I said I love you. I really did feel love for the first time in many years and I was a fool."

"Listen to me."

"No, I don't want to hear any God damn rubbish from you. I want to go."

"You're going nowhere until you hear me."

As she tried to stand up, Rami stood quickly and pushed her back to the sofa. He shouted, as he lost control. "Look here you silly woman, I've just about had enough of your stupidity. Just stay there and keep that big mouth of yours shut, ok?"

"Are you going to beat me now?"

"I might do, listen..."

"If you lay another finger on me I'll kill you. I mean it Rami. I didn't come here to be man-handled."

"Please just shut up and see who I am." Rami put his hand in his pocket and took out one of his identification cards.

"Look at this."

"I'm not interested."

"Look at it you stupid woman."

She shot him a daring look and snatched it out of his hand. "Army intelligence! I might have guessed."

"I have more power and authority in this country than many others."

"Big deal! What does that prove? Do you want me to kiss your feet for you?"

"You don't understand."

"What's the price Rami? Your type don't do anything for nothing. What are you after?"

"Nothing, you can walk out of here any time you want. I only wanted to make you happy, that's all."

"Bullshit, what's the price?"

"Your friendship."

"Who are you trying to convince...yourself or me?"

"You need sixty years in prison until you'll understand."

"I bet you can fix that as well."

"Yes very easily, one phone call."

"Do it then, if you are man enough."

"I don't have to do anything, or prove anything. If you don't believe me that is your heartache."

"You're false Rami."

He lit two cigarettes and handed one to her. He stood by the window watching the cars passing by. She looked at the cigarette in her hand amazed at the simplicity of his movement. He told her yesterday he'd never done that for anyone else before, only for her. She watched him standing there, looking outside. How could she mistake him for being false? He could not be false and love her the way he did, although he'd never told her that he loved her, he said he liked her, but is he a man of action, and no words? She asked herself.

"I bet you still have steady hands?"

"Yes ... I always do."

"Did you order the halt on me?"

"No, my boss did."

"Are you really not after anything?"

He stayed still and silent, feeling hurt for being mistrusted.

"Are you going to screw me tonight?"

"No ... I don't feel like it, you can go if you like," he said finally.

"I'd rather stay if you want me to."

Rami watched the street below.

"I am sorry. I thought it will make you happy, I thought its one way to show you what you mean to me."

"I'm so confused," said Julia. "I always depended on myself to doing every, but you appeared yesterday, and everything changed. Did you know how much you have changed me?"

Rami did not want to listen to her anymore.

"I was strong, hard on myself and everyone around, I survived. I was afraid inside, but I was ready to put up a fight then along you came, I want to be laid there and made love to. I want to sit on this sofa and be talked to as a woman, are you listening to me? I cannot face life alone any more. I'm not capable of deciding for myself anymore, so please Rami, help me to stop what I'm doing now. Who cares about tomorrow?"

"You mean no more abortions?"

She nodded and moved into his open arms. They held each other close.

"I am a frightened baby." She whispered.

"I feel so much for you."

"Rami help me by trusting and supporting me. I want to do it my way. I need you with me."

"I do trust you in a way."

"What is it? Tell me."

"I remember you told me you like hairdressing," said Rami. "I have a large empty shop, so you could do it there."

"And how am I going to fund it?" Julia said. "All my money is outside of the country and I can't get it back. How am I going to pay the rent or buy the lease or anything?"

"I can fix that."

"I don't know any landlord who will accept that?"

"You're looking at him."

"No!" She couldn't believe what she was hearing.

"And I can help you with some money."

"No..."

"Okay move here, and sell the house."

"Rami, slow down! Don't arrange my life for me, I'll think about it."

"Say yes."

"Let's do it again."

"Do what? Go out for a dance?"

"Okay I give up, I'm moving here and selling the house. Now come to the bedroom, and see what you can do for me."

"It will be my pleasure."

"Bastard..."

- - - - - - - - -

Rami's dream was short lived, as in the morning she changed her mind yet again.

"You can't make an honest woman out of a whore, and you can't straighten a bent tree," she said as she walked out.

"I guess not!"

The days passed very slowly for Rami, no flickering lights, and no sparkling wine. He needed a woman around to bring a smile back to his face. He needed a woman to hold him tight when he felt low, and who let him free when he rode high. He needed May badly, but he could not walk back into her life after such a long time. He needed a whole woman, not part of one. He wished Farrah was there, as she understood him better, he wished that he had listened to her, but he enjoyed what he had got himself involved in, and loved what he had to deal with so far.

He felt as if he was descending down a ladder fast. He lost his hunger for success, to be number one, and stay at the top. He found his grief for Leila helped to release some of the anxiety inside, but not all of it. He thought about her all the time. He couldn't forget her.

"Rami snap out of it, come on." Ahmad said.

"I am alright; there is nothing wrong with me."

"You could've fooled me, you are lonely, or really you think you are."

"I am..."

"Well don't shut us out, you have many friends."

"I want a woman. Can you fix that for me?" Then both of them laughed.

"What probably is wrong with you is that you had everything in such a short time, you are fulfilled."

231

"Money, cars, women, do you really think that is all what life is about?"

"Wife and few babies…?"

"Probably…!"

"Oh leave it out, you haven't suffered, sorry yes you have, but you never went hungry for days, you never walked because you haven't got the money to get on a bus, or wear the same clothes all the time, or spending weeks eating only bread, and having doors close in your face, every time you knock on them, or people laughing at you, when you ask them for a job."

"So you had it tough? You never told me about your past."

"The past is buried. It's the future which matters for me, and you."

"I know."

"Well go and find yourself a woman."

"Tell me about your past."

"Both parents died when I was seven. My uncle took me in, and every bit of money that my father had left. Soon he opened a shop. I went to school at night, as he wanted me to work at the shop during the day. He didn't pay me anything, while his sons and daughters went to the best schools in the city. I finished my schooling with the help of one of my cousins. He bought me books, and gave me pocket money, behind his father's back, and he made me go to University. When I was eighteen, I asked my uncle for the money that my father had left for me. He said what do you think you were eating for the past eleven years? At the end he gave me five hundred Dinars, and I was asked to leave the house, and I did. I was in my first year university, so I had to work at night to support myself, also my cousin helped . The Government sent me to Egypt to do my M.A. in Arabic. When I came back after a year, I took my uncle to court I won thanks to my cousin."

"How much did you get?"

"My cousin found some papers, what my father had left me was tens of thousands, but I got six thousand."

"A joke…"

"Yes."

"I've got a secret to tell you. The day I was released, I told the men not to go to sleep, because I was going to get everyone of them, well I got their addresses, but not the ones high above, the ones who gave the orders."

Ahmad did not say anything.

"Well what do you say?"

"That was three years ago. Why can't you let things be?"

"Did you?"

"I suppose you are right in a way."

Rami did not tell him, that he had ordered their removal out of Baghdad and transferred them to different parts of the country.

CHAPTER TWENTY EIGHT

RAMI finished his first term examinations just after the New Year and started a three week holiday. He asked his father if he could travel to Lebanon to see his aunt who he had never met before.

"Why now?"

"I've got three weeks holiday, and I haven't met my aunt yet."

"No...What's the point of going now? You have the whole of the summer to do what you like."

"But I don't want to go in the summer, I love the summer here, it's the only time that I look forward for."

"And how do you expect to pay for this holiday?" his father asked.

"I've saved some money."

Rami noticed a great anger in his father's voice, he looked at his mother for some support, but she left the room, and did not want to intervene.

"I suppose you bought the car from your savings as well?"

"Yes dad!"

"Yes that expensive car parked at the top of the street. How much did that cost you? Ten thousand? Twenty? Thirty? "

"It's not...."

"How did you get money like that?"

"What do you want from me? I have the best marks in college, and I work very hard at the factory, what more do you want?" Rami raised his voice.

The rest of the family sat in the living room listening to their father shouting in the study.

"The truth...I want to hear the truth from you, but you aren't capable of that either."

"I told you."

"You're under age! Have you got a driving licence?"

"Yes, a special one."

"And what about the flat? What about the newspaper? "

"So you had me watched? Your own son watched, as if I was a criminal."

"I want the truth Rami."

"I do write in the newspaper, as..."

"As Rami A....?"

"Yes...the best writer in the country, and have you ever said well done son?

No...because you are a control freak. I remember when you showed me up in front of all our visitors, when May and Samir visited us the first time. You always knocked me down, even at work, I sit and drink tea and eat with the workers, they love me for it, and I can ask for the impossible from them, and I get it. Is it such a crime to be popular? Is it too much for you to say well done, and I'm proud of you."

"What about the flat?"

"You are mean and strict. You don't let anyone breathe outside this house. I make more money than any writer in the country yet you pay me peanuts when

I work for you. My brother and sisters get the same pocket money and they do nothing for it. They don't even help mum around the house. I do it to help you out, and you don't stop and think for one minute that now and then I need to be told well done son, you're doing a good job. Is it so hard for you to praise me? Is it?" Rami shook as he spoke. The whole of his body felt numb and his bottom lip trembled.

"I'm glad you're making so much money, because from now on you won't get anything out of me."

"That's because you're so mean, I don't need your money. I have a car more expensive than yours, I have expensive clothes and you didn't buy me any of them, and they are tailor-made, I have everything I need." He took a deep breath, "What I get from you in a year, I make it in less than a week. I give the beggars in the street more than what you give me."

"If that's your attitude then what the hell are you doing in my house?"

"That's exactly how I feel. I'm not going to sit here for the rest of my life, waiting for your approval on everything. You suffocate everyone in this house and you're not going to do it to me too."

"Get out of my house. I don't want to see you anymore. You have no respect for anyone. I have only one son."

"At last you said it. You admitted that you only have one son. I will leave right now. You can have my brother, as he can do no wrong whatsoever."

"And don't come back until you learn how to respect my wishes."

"That'll be the day. I have learnt not to bow to anybody, including you."

Rami left the room and apart from a few books he left all his belongings behind. His mother followed him upstairs to his bedroom, begging him to stay.

"Son, just say sorry to your dad please do it for me."

"I love you mother, but that means I've got to give up everything for him, I worked hard, very hard for what I have."

"I know son…I know."

"Don't worry about me I am a big boy now."

"You are still my baby."

"Mum I make more money than him. I can look after myself, okay? I've got a cleaner, and I won't go hungry, I love my food."

"Bring your dirty clothes I'll wash them for you."

"I will do that, I love you mother, even though I have a washing machine." He managed a smile.

"I love you son, remember that."

He felt that part of him had died. He had been born in this house and loved it, even though he was hardly ever there. He was amazed how his father had found out, but it had to happen one day, and he had to get out, otherwise that would be the end of his freedom.

He decided to call to see May on the way back to his flat. He needed a woman's comfort. May opened the door to find him standing there laughing. He tried hard to stop and explain but he couldn't. She dragged him inside and shut the door behind him.

"What's so funny?" She was laughing at him.

"My dad kicked me out of the house and I ended up here, instead of the flat."

"What's so funny about that?"

"I don't know! Beats me...it is though, like a small child coming to have a sob."

"Not funny."

"You were laughing."

"I was laughing at you."

"Oh God...!"

"You need to be moved to a secure unit at the hospital, you are dangerous!" She commented.

"Where's your husband?"

"He's at the hospital, on night duty."

"One kicks me out, and one wants me in a mental hospital. I can see how much I am loved."

It was such a small statement, yet tears ran down Rami's face.

"What's the matter this time?"

"I either do what he wants, or I am out. He found out about everything."

"How...? Did he have you followed? I thought you were joking at first."

"That's exactly what I thought, he had me followed. It's not that he knows; it's like a thief has gone through all my private affairs. Like someone stealing the most valuable thing in my life, someone intruding into my personal possessions. I am so angry, yet I have nothing to be ashamed of."

It had been a long time since they were on their own. She looked at him, he was a man, but he still cried and wiped the tears on the back of his hand.

"What brought all this about?"

"I just asked him if I could go to Lebanon for two weeks, as I have three weeks off."

"And he said no?"

"Yes, he found out about the car, the flat, the paper, everything. I'm so sad as I love that house."

"What difference does it make? You're hardly there anyway. You treated the house as a hotel. I haven't seen you since the day you came to invite us to the engagement party. Sorry I shouldn't mention that, and really for the past year and a half, I only saw you..."

"Do you want me to leave as well?"

"No...this is your home, and you know that."

"I am sorry, it seems that I always hurt the nearest, and dearest people to me."

"Do you want to stay here tonight?"

"No...I don't want to use you."

"I want you to stay."

"What about Samir?"

"He won't be here until after nine."

"Okay."

"Come to the kitchen with me and I'll fix you something to eat."

Rami sat on a stool in the kitchen. "I feel something is dead inside."

"You belong to that family, but it's your own doing in a way, you did everything behind his back, and all of us went along with you."

"But I haven't done anything wrong."

"To him you have, you went out of the family circle."

"Anyway I don't need him."

"But you need the family."

"You have nothing to be sad about, you have me."

"I don't want to die alone."

She laughed, "Give me a ring and let me know, so I can be with you, stupid fool. Why don't you go to Lebanon?" said May, "Nothing is stopping you now."

"That's a good idea. Can I use the phone please?"

"Sure, go ahead."

Rami called Ahmad, Khalid and Nabil to tell them the news. Finally he called Sami, and asked whether he could have a passport urgently to go to Lebanon.

- - - - - - - - -

The following day, at six at night, Rami rang the door bell of his aunt's apartment not far from Hamra Street.

"Who is it?"

"Me..."

"Me...?"

"Your beautiful nephew, aunt Magi. The most gorgeous relative you have on the face of the earth."

She opened the door and examined him. "No one told me you were coming. Give your aunt a kiss."

"I decided to come at the last minute."

"I could've come to the airport, and picked you up."

"I like surprises."

They sat and talked for a while, until her daughters came back from music class with their father.

Rami talked all through his supper, he felt as if he had known this family for a long time. He told them everything about himself. He needed family support in a way, even though they were living in a different country.

"Rami, your father is a very old fashioned man," his aunt remarked.

"Narrow minded more like it."

"Well let's forget all this. What would you like to do?"

"Hit the city. I came to see you first then everything else that's worth seeing."

"You can take your aunt with you, I've got work tomorrow."

An hour later, he and aunt Magi were walking together along Hamra Street, the main street in the Capital.

"I am so happy that you are here."

"I am too, first time out of Iraq,"

"That husband of mine, doesn't like doing anything, except work, and walk. He can walk for miles, and never gives up."

"Shall we go from one place to another? I want to see everything."

"Whatever you like my nephew, I love dancing though."

Aunt Magi was in her mid-thirties. She was tall with long fair hair, and very attractive. She did not look her age at all. Rami felt as if she wanted to talk about something, which was bothering her.

"You can talk to me if you like, what's on your mind?"

"I am just glad that I got out of that house, thanks to you."

They went to a few nightclubs and bars and had great fun. She found him amazingly friendly with everyone, and fun to be with.

"I'm taking you to the Lovers Nest," said his aunt. "It's on the sea front."

"What do I want to go there for?"

"Experience..."

"For me or you...?"

"Come on I've never been there before."

They walked towards the nightclub.

"Oh how I love the sea! I can smell it, I really can. I've written about it so many times, but I've never seen it before."

"You are crazy.....come back here."

"This is wonderful, who wants to go to a club when the sea is here?"

Rami ran towards the water, jumping and screaming. She could not believe how happy he was. He was like a child in a man's body. His voice shattered the stillness of the night.

"I am not dreaming, this is it, black, horrible and ugly but I love it."

Magi walked towards Rami and kissed him on his cheek. "We'll come back tomorrow in the day time."

"No, tonight is mine." He sounded as if he did not want to be awoken from his dream.

"I am cold." She moaned.

He took off his Jacket and handed it to her, "Put this on you, I just want to stay a bit longer please."

"Don't you wish that you were with someone else?"

"No...This is my moment, for years I wanted to do this, see the sea, and smell it, the only power that I fear. I want to fight it."

"Show me..."

He took his clothes off and handed them to her then he ran towards the water, completely naked.

"Are you crazy?"

He stopped for a second or two as the waves hit his feet, sending shivers up his spine.

He laughed as he continued deeper into the water.

She saw him through the few lights reflected from the ships anchored in the distance. She wanted to join him, she wanted to live again, even if it was for few seconds, but her courage failed her.

"Haven't you had enough you crazy Arab?" she shouted, "You crazy Iraqi."

He did not answer, she heard him slapping the waves, and laughing, "Come on, it's nearly two in the morning."

It was a scene she would remember for a long time. He was totally free, and she was jealous, she did not really want to go anywhere, just stand there watching him making love to the sea. She did not want to go back to her house, or her workaholic husband.

At last he emerged from the water, feeling like the happiest person in the world."Aren't you cold?"

"Not a bit .... Did you see that beautiful sea?"

"Put these on...before you catch a cold."

"No let me dry up a bit first, the wind will dry me up a bit."

"You have a beautiful body."

"Keep your hands to yourself, you randy aunt." But her hand just moved to brush away the trickles of water.

"Come on let's go, before your husband thinks that you are having an affair."

"I am."

Rami looked at her wickedly, "Should you be telling me this? I could blackmail you."

"You are so naughty, terrible."

"I am sorry. I am a very shy boy usually." He teased her.

"You haven't got an ounce of shyness or shame in you my dear."

He giggled.

"Here you'd better put your clothes on before you freeze and your bits will fall off."

"Don't worry they are attached very well."

"Come on let's go."

- - - - - - - - -

The next morning Rami was awoken up by his aunt. He was still feeling slightly fragile from the night before

"It's beautiful outside," said Magi. "Come on get up."

"What are my plans for today?" Rami asked.

"To go and see Elaine."

"No, what's in the past stays in the past."

"But Rami, she needs someone like you."

"How do you know her?"

"We met through Ahmad when your mum sent us some presents with him and Jean, and we became friends. I go and see her now and then. Please go and see her."

"Oh please not today."

"Life isn't easy with a dying man."

"What?"

"Oh, I thought you knew. Her husband has cancer and supposedly he's been dying for the past five years."

"Nobody told me, even Ahmad, oh no, poor woman."

"He's in hospital now, he might die at any minute, God only knows what he had put Elaine through the past five years, or to be exact, since they got married, he was born to punish her."

"I honestly did not know."

"They had to sell their house, the furniture, everything they owned, so they could pay for his treatment. She even got herself a part-time job to help pay for the bills-. Her two daughters are in Syria with their aunt because Elaine hasn't got the money to feed them."

"What about Ahmad? Why couldn't he help with all the money he is making?"

"She won't accept charity from anybody. I went once to visit her and she hadn't eaten for four days. She had enough money to feed him only and she wouldn't take any money from me."

"But why...?"

"Self respect... call it what you like."

"I'll go and see her now, I'll take a shower and go, I'll take a taxi."

"She will be at home around twelve." She looked long in his face, "Be gentle with her please, she loves you a lot, and you can be boyish with your behaviour at times."

Elaine had a ground floor flat in one of the poorest areas of the city. The streets were dirty and the houses were old and falling apart.

"All these houses need demolishing and new houses built," said the taxi driver as they drove into the area. "But who cares about the poor, even if they die in their own filth?"

"What about the government?" Rami asked.

"What government? They're all a bunch of thieves and a bunch of gangsters. All what they care about is filling their own pockets."

"Well I don't understand politics in this country. I'm from Iraq."

"At least you have a government there."

"That's what many people think, although it is a big shamble."

Rami knocked on the door. After a few seconds which felt like eternity, Elaine opened it. Rami's mouth opened in disbelief as she tried to tidy herself up, including the many strands of grey hair which ran through her once blonde hair. She tried avoiding eye contact with Rami. She forgot how to invite people into her place, she forgot to say 'Hello' she forgot what life used to be like. She looked at herself, and felt like closing the door behind her, and starting all over again.

"I hope I didn't stop you from....."

"I wasn't expecting anyone," she said.

"Well now I am here, are you going to ask me in?"

"Sure."

She nodded, she was confused, she did not know what to do or say. She had loved that person once upon a time, she had loved him from all her heart, and he had grown up to be a real man, But at that moment, she wished that she had never laid an eye on him.

"Am I intruding on you?"

"No... I am just surprised."

She was numb; she couldn't define how she felt. Although she was so happy to see him again, she wasn't sure if she wanted him there. Maybe, if she met him somewhere else, somewhere in the city or on her terms, or even when her husband had gone. She was trapped, and she didn't want to be trapped even more.

Rami walked inside and examined the room as she left to go to the kitchen. It was a dark damp room with a round table and two chairs occupying the corner to his left. A few hand painted pictures hung on the wall. The room was clean, and there weren't many articles to make it look untidy. It didn't feel homely at all.

Elaine walked in again, wearing an old dress she wore when she was in Baghdad.

"Do I get a kiss?"

She took few steps towards him. He held her face with both hands, and kissed her. , "I'm sorry darling," said Rami. "I didn't know until this morning."

"I know, please sit down , how is Ahmad and Jean?"

"Fine ... they're both good, happy as anything."

"Family okay…?"

"Okay I suppose."

"What are you doing here?"

"I'm on holiday, and it's an excuse to see you too. Also came to buy a few things for the shops."

"Good, I hope you are staying a few more days."

"I am, I only came yesterday, and I want you to help me."

"It'll be my pleasure, but I don't know where to go if you need anything special."

"I need someone to take me to the right address, instead of stopping everyone in the street, and asking them for directions."

"I'll go and make us some coffee."

Rami followed her into the kitchen. There was no refrigerator, no cooker and only one table where a type of paraffin burner sat.

"What are you doing the rest of the day?" Rami asked.

"Nothing, why?"

"Let's go out."

"No, I can't, just in case the hospital rings. Also, I don't want to be seen with another man."

"You have been waiting for years for something to happen, haven't you waited long enough? Come on show me the city, like I did with you when you came to Baghdad."

"No Rami."

"What happened to the Arab hospitality?" Rami smiled.

"Rami please..."

"What…? What happened to you, my sweetheart? Why are you doing this to yourself? Are you punishing yourself for some unknown reason? "

"Please...!" She begged.

"I still love you and care for you. I am no stranger. We shared many things together, or maybe what we had in the past did not mean a thing to you? "

"Okay...but."

"Remember how close we were, remember?"

"Rami, don't."

"I'm only staying for another two weeks and I want to enjoy myself with you around."

She put the cup of coffee on the table in front of him and sat facing him.

"My husband is dying. He has got cancer and they have given up on him."

"I know, my aunt told me, but why and how did you get yourself into this situation?"

"When I first met him, I thought the world of him, but he tricked me and I fell into his trap. I went to the church for a divorce, but they told me no way and to go and confess my sins. My whole family were against the marriage, but thank God I have my sisters to lean on for a good cry every now and then, and for looking after my girls in Syria."

"Why wasn't I told?"

"What is the point in telling you? I made my bed and I had to lay on it."

"Why did you refuse Ahmad's help?"

"Your aunt's got a big mouth, bless her. I do love her a lot."

She looked away with tears running down her face. He put his hand on hers and gave her a few minutes to compose herself.

"How do you expect me to pay Ahmad back? I can't work full time because someone has to care for him. Oh, if only you knew how hard it is trying to pay for medicine. I went to the nuns as I was so ashamed of asking for charity and they gave me a few bits of bread."

"And who said Ahmad wants to be paid back. He wouldn't take it back, I know him better than anyone."

"I just couldn't do it. Soon he will be gone then I can get a full time job and have my girls back."

"Well I am not buying it, as simple as that."

"I am not selling it. I thought you wanted to go to the city."

After a long conversation they took a taxi to the centre of the city. Rami was amazed how lively the city was.

"I haven't been here for months."

"It's fantastic, come on, I want to treat you to something."

She gave him a questioning look, but she gave in as she knew him well enough he wasn't going to take a 'no thank you' for an answer."A hairdo would make me feel very happy."

"Okay you got it."

"I can never say no to you, you will throw a tantrum like a small child."

"I am glad you've got your memory back." He laughed, and she joined him.

"Here's a hairdresser, right here." Rami quickly paid the taxi driver, and dragged her behind him.

"That's the most expensive one in the whole of the Lebanon," she said, pulled her hand from his, stopping in the middle of the pavement.

He took her hand again. "Come on my beautiful queen."

"You can't just go in there, you have to book first."Rami went into the salon alone, while Elaine waited outside. She watched him shaking the manager's hand and talking for few minutes to him, then they came out and the manager shook her hand and showed her in. She looked in amazement at Rami. While he sat her down, in front of a mirror, Rami smiled, "I only told him who I am."

"I'll kill you one of these days."

"Thank God you are back to your usual self."

"Get out of here and let me have my hair done in quiet. Go on give me some space."

"You're having the lot done, from the top of your head to the little toe nails on your beautiful feet."

She shot him a questioning look.

"It's my treat."

"I hate you."

"I am crazy about you."

The manager spent a few minutes talking with Elaine about what colour she would like her hair and how she wanted it styled. Then he turned to Rami. "You might go if you wish Mr. Rami, madam will be here for at least two and a half hours."

"Ok, I'll see you later darling."

Rami went back to his aunt's house. "I want to get a nice flat for Elaine," he said. "How do we go about it, I can't let her stay in that place for one more day."

"If you have the money, nothing is impossible in this country."

"How much do I need?"

"That all depends on the area and whether you want to rent or buy."

"Ok, let's go to some estate agents and see."

They were very lucky to find many flats available at that time of the year. Rami left his aunt with the estate agent while he went to the Iraqi Embassy. He phoned Sami and asked him to transfer funds. Although it was forbidden in those days to take money outside the country, it was not a problem for Sami to do so.

Three quarters of an hour later, he was back with his aunt at the estate agent. He handed her the money and left her there to finish the deal while he returned to pick up Elaine from the hairdressers.

"Wow, you look stunning."

"Thank you, you are late."

"I got lost."

"Can I have the pleasure of escorting you to somewhere as beautiful as you tonight?"

"Have I got a choice?"

"No ... only for picking the place."

He paid the manager and they walked out to a road full of shops.

"I am amazed at the quality of the shops here."

"Oh yes...Arabs of all nationalities come here to shop."

"I wish we had something like this back home."

"Treat yourself to some clothes" She suggested.

They walked into a shoe shop, somehow he managed to turn everything round, she came out carrying three pairs of shoes for herself, and he came out with nothing,

"Rami stop buying me things, I didn't know where to hide my face when the woman handed me those. I thought that I was just trying them on."

"They looked just right on your feet, I couldn't resist."

"Thank you but no more."

"It makes me happy."

"No...I said no...Read my lips....no."

"I'd rather eat your lips than look at them."

"God you are so stubborn."

"Like an ass, come on, let's spend some money, and you can look even more beautiful when we go out tonight?"

"As you wish, but let me pick the things I want and nothing too expensive, you hear me?"

They both got carried away, from one shop to the other. It was a distraction for her, from all her problems, she felt on top of the world. She'd got a man to spend money on her, a man who made her feel like a woman again, made her feel alive again, and she had not done so since the day she had married. He abused her for years, hitting her and beating her, he then punished her with his illness. She accepted all that for reasons not known even to her.Rami talked for the entire time about his writing, the shops, his parents and even Ahmad with his funny ears when he got angry. She laughed like she hadn't laughed in years. She listened to him, touched his face with her hand and planted kisses on it every now and then.

When they couldn't carry any more clothes, they took a taxi to his aunt's house.

Magi opened the front door. "My God, here let me help you."

"You'd better, we are out of breath."

"Did you rob the shops?"

"Yes ..."

"Oh Elaine, you look beautiful."

"Thank you, it's all down to this nephew of yours."

"The miracle man...!"

The two women went into the bedroom, so Elaine could show Magi what Rami had bought her. While she changed her clothes Magi left the room and gave Rami the keys for the apartment.

"All done, she's just got to sign these papers and take them back to the Estate Agent."

"Fantastic, I liked the furniture and at least it saved us time trying to buy everything.""I loved it myself. I also phoned Ahmad and Jean."

"Great thanks. Do you think that she will accept it?" Rami asked.

"After all this today, yes I do, you changed that woman in a matter of seconds."

"I'd better go and have a word with her."

Rami entered the bedroom. Elaine was sitting on the bed looking into the mirror.

"Can I talk to you please?"

"Yes sure."

She looked at him, and for the first time that day she saw the puzzled look in his face, "Hey, sit here and tell me, is there something wrong?"

"Elaine, tell me, I don't know how to put this to you. What's the most important thing in your life?"

"My two girls."

"And why aren't they here?"

"I told you, I haven't got the money to look after them." She was quiet for a minute or two. She put her hand on his, "With the money you spent on me today, I could've had my kids for a year, plus where I live isn't that healthy to bring kids up."

"Well I have a little surprise for you."

"What have you done?"

He took the keys out of his pocket and put them in her palm.

"What are these?"

"These are for your new apartment. It's four blocks away from here."

Her eyes filled up quickly. "No Rami, I can't afford anything with…"

"Everything has been seen to, so you don't have to worry about anything. Here is the contract for you to sign."

"No, no."

"What is more important to you; your pride or the children?"

She looked into his eyes, then at the keys in her hands and the contract in the other hand. She wondered how anyone could be as loving as him.

"The rent is paid for the whole year and any bills you might have."

"I know you mean well but."

"You don't want to hear buts."

"Rami, I don't know where to start. I'm lost for words. I could make love to you right this minute."

"Save it for tonight, as tomorrow is your day when you are going to get your kids back."

"Oh my god…"

She knelt on the floor and tried to kiss his hands, but he pulled her up and sat her next to him.

"I'll be a servant for you for the rest of my life," she said hugging him and crying from her heart.

"Why are you crying now?"

"Because I am so happy you silly man."

Magi walked in. "Are you eating here or are you going out?"

"I dare say I'm not hungry today," Elaine said laughing. "Did you know that this one went and got me a flat?"

"Yes, I know."

"So you had a hand in it as well. Thanks Magi, you're a true friend."

"Tomorrow you can phone Syria, and get your kids back."

"No, I'll leave it until Rami goes home. I want to spend every minute with him."

He objected, but she did not accept.

"Once my aunt's husband comes back, I am going to open an expense account for you in his bank."

"No ... thanks, you have done enough damage in one day."

"Elaine you have no choice, but looking the way you are today, you can get a job anywhere you want."

"I know, I can feel that my life is changing at last, especially now, they are keeping him in hospital until he passes away."

"Well then, that's settled then."

"I love you, and Magi is my witness."

The two women went into the kitchen, while Rami sat with a glass of beer in his hand, watching the sky of Beirut, through the balcony door.

"He's something else," said Elaine.

"You're a lucky woman to have him," Magi said.

"But he doesn't belong to me."

"He does in one way or another."

"I don't know how he made me accept all this, when for years I've refused everyone else who tried."

"Hopefully this is the start of your happiness."

"I hope so, thank you Magi."

CHAPTER TWENTY NINE

WHEN Rami returned to Baghdad he felt more confident than ever before, probably because of the experience of travelling on his own, and taking charge of someone in need, or even living on his own, and being independent of all ties with his family. He was at last trying to achieve what his father regarded as waste of time, and childish.

His daily life was quiet but fulfilled. He had time to read, study, and write and he visited the newspaper every day.

Six weeks later he returned to Lebanon to see Elaine again. Her husband had died three days after he had last seen her. This time she had her two girls with her and she had found a full time job at a ladies fashion shop. In her spare time she was studying shorthand and typing.

Rami encouraged her to go out and meet people and to be positive about life. He told her that he loved her, but not enough to spend his life with her. She agreed. They had loved each other in the past, but life had changed for the both of them.

Her letters arrived regularly. She had changed her job and enrolled her two daughters into a private school. He looked forward to reading her letters, she made him laugh at times, giggle at others, but she was always positive, he even felt jealous at times.

'Dear Rami,

I can never thank you enough for everything you have done for me and I don't know how to repay you. I did as you advised me, I went out and met people and I enjoyed myself. I met a man who is two years older than me and he has his own export and import business. He is wealthy and from a very big family. I haven't told you about him earlier because I didn't know where we were heading.

We get on very well with each other and all of his family. His first wife was American, and ran away back to her country with another man. He loves me and my two daughters very much, and he never stops buying us gifts and taking us out to different places. We have never been to bed together. As you know, there are only two men that I ever slept with, you and my husband.

He asked me to marry him, but I said I'll think about it. He wants me to tour Europe with him and the kids as well. What do you say? I told him about you and he accepted what you had done to me as very noble. He said that you are my guardian angel and you are.

Darling I am going in circles, tell me what to do.

Rami please tell me fast, before I go mad. I love you.

Elaine.'

He read the letter again then left his flat and went to the post office. He wrote a telegram, and sent it away. "Go for it, I wish you all the best, all my love."

As he left the post office, he felt total emptiness. But on the other hand he felt happy for her. At that minute he remembered Farrah. Why had he never listened to her advice? It was too late to do anything about it, it was history.

For days afterward he did nothing but eat. He did not go to university, or anywhere else except for restaurants, as if he was passing the time waiting for something to happen. But, nothing did, except the realization that he was killing himself with all that self inflicted eating and drinking.

He drove to the Centre one evening to try and find something to do, to occupy his mind, but he felt like an outsider.

"Car Eleven…to Control…"

"Go ahead Car Eleven."

"Anything need doing? I am bored."

"Sorry Eleven, nothing, it's been very quiet the last few days."

"Any paperwork or filing needs doing?"

"I will tell Sami to find you something." The voice chuckled laughing, "Probably you can do the cleaning and the washing up…!" They both laughed.

He felt as if he had entered into a bottle neck and could not get himself out. He drove to the house, but his father's car was there, so he continued driving. He tried to see Ahmad, but no one was home. Then he rang the bell to Julia's house. A young woman opened the door.

"Is Julia in please?"

"No she isn't."

"When will she be home?"

"I don't know." She tried to close the door, but he put his foot in the way to stop her.

"Where's the old lady?"

"Get your foot out of the way or I'll call the police."

"Call them why don't you?"

Rami lost his self control and he pushed the door as hard as he could, sending the girl flying. "Sorry I didn't mean to hurt you."

He looked in the adjacent room, but nobody was there, so he ran inside the house looking in every room. He heard music coming from a room upstairs, he opened the door and walked in. Julia was sitting in the corner, with a low round table in front of her. A half full bottle of wine stood in the middle of the table while an empty bottle lay on the floor next to her slippers. The whole room was filled with cushions and pillows, but no other furniture. The walls were covered by a fantastic selection of paintings collected from all over the world. Candles lit the room.

"Rami, is that you?"

"Yes."

She raised her hand and waved in his direction for him to come in. She appeared to be drunk, or on her way there.

"Get another bottle from that cabinet and come and sit beside me. I can see you're really bored."

"But this bottle is half full."

"This is mine, and that's yours if you want a drink."

"No thanks, I think I had enough to sink a ship for the past few weeks."

"Sit where you like, why are you here?" Her hand dramatically brushed the air in front of her.

"I came to see you."

"Great...I can very well see that." She sipped her wine. "That's really great, I am thrilled." She raised her eyes to meet his. "You've changed a lot Rami."

"I missed you. I don't know why we ever stopped seeing each other!"

"Because you were trying to run my life for me and I wouldn't have it."

"You didn't tell me not to. I thought I was offering you a helping hand."

"No you didn't...you only...oh shit what difference does it make?" She raised the glass to her lips again, and drank more wine.

"You have nobody else, is that it Rami?"

"Yes...you are right."

"Get yourself a drink; you need it more than me."

"Why not...? I'll join your state of relaxation."

As she looked at him, her heart pounded, she thought how long could she keep up her act. Only then she truly realized how much she had missed him, only then she understood what the words being alive meant, she knew that if she would let him enter her life, it would be for good, for keeps, forever.

"What's wrong?" she asked.

"Nothing," said Rami quietly. He felt a lump growing in his throat and he tried hard to control his feeling and emotions, but his strength failed him, his fighting power had collapsed before he had put a foot inside her house. He tried to speak but a choking sound escaped his throat instead.

She moved and sat next to him, she had never seen him in such a state before; the might of that person had disappeared suddenly, leaving behind hopeless fragments of a man. "Rami that's enough, tell me."

She held his head close to her chest. It was more comfort to her than him. She wanted to cry for a long time, although she had no reason to do so. But, her man was hurt, he was in pain, she felt helpless watching him, and she could not do anything about it, like watching a baby in pain. She cried, and she did not think at that moment that it was a sign of weakness, and she knew that Rami was not weak.

"I feel lost."

"How...?"

He felt somehow bewildered by her question and he couldn't answer her.

"No women, no excitement, and nothing to do," she added.

He felt stupid and worse than before. He wondered what on earth he was doing there, with someone who hardly understood what he was going through.

"I know what crossed your mind Rami, what the hell are you doing here, am I right?" He looked at her in amazement.

"Yes..."

"Come on tell me."

"There's nothing to tell."

"You're lost...is that it?"

"Yes!"

They looked at each other and burst out laughing. "Is that it? Is that all that's eating you up? Good god man...you gave me a heart attack. You even made me cry with you."

"Can we be together?" he asked.

"For what? Love…you must be joking, or a bit of sex? Or excitement, and the thrill of going out with a woman older than you, just to boost your image, and to show every bastard in the land that what's between your legs can satisfy any age, especially me, your brain is twisted in the wrong direction honey."

"I think you are right, I'm going now, I hope to see you one day Julia." He stood up and headed towards the door.

"Hey you!" He turned around and she opened her house robe, exposing her naked body. "Are you going without a fight?"

"I haven't got the energy to put up a fight today. Bye now."

"Come back here," she ordered.

"What for?"

She put a brave angry face, "So you only came here to display your weakness... fantastic!!...Well done...I believe you are weak, and this body of mine doesn't interest you...close that damn door, I don't want everyone in the house to hear me shouting." She was silent for few seconds, "Where was I?"

Rami smiled, "Talking about your beautiful body!"

"Yes... and..." She exploded laughing, there was no use shouting at him, or pretending any more. She was as weak for him as he was for her.

"Come here and hold me tight."

He did, then he told her about Elaine, about his father asking him to leave the family house and about his life since the day he could remember.He was insecure, and needed someone to reassure him. He wanted someone to lean on, someone to take all his worries, hurt, and emotions away. But, maybe he was knocking on the wrong door.

"Well is that all?" She said laughingly, trying to cheer him up. She wasn't in the right state of mind to think of how to deal with the situation.

"Yes."

"You are a very emotional person, always seeking love and attention. Your affairs seem to be highly charged up, deep feelings, and it gets out of control at times, and if anything had to happen, you went to pieces." She felt good about her comments, in fact she believed everything she said.

"You deserve a medal, very clever aren't you dear?"

"Oh shut up clever ass, so what do you expect from me?"

"Friendship…"

"You got it."

After they made love that night, Julia realized she was falling in love with him. She tried to fight her emotions, but in the end she gave in. She moved to the flat to live with him. She cooked, washed his clothes, waited for him to come back from university and sat listening to him at the end of each day as he gave her full details of his daily activities.

She loved looking after him and he treated her extremely well, often showering her with presents and gifts. They went out dining and dancing as often as they could. She loved all the attention she was getting, she shared everything with him. She took charge of all the small matters, like paying the bills and getting the shopping, so he could concentrate more on his interests.

She enjoyed dressing up for him before he got back every day, and she loved the look in his eyes when he examined her. She adored those moments when he held her tight to him, and told her how beautiful she looked, or how much he loved her. She tried to look younger for him, in the way she dressed up, and styled her hair.

He didn't like the political changes at his university, with the Baath Party taking charge of the student union. He saw how little those students attended their classes, even the weekly or monthly exams, yet they all passed with flying colours. There was no pride left to be successful, to be the best in his class. After all, it was only a degree that he knew he wouldn't use in the future.

He looked for any excuse to stay away from college, and use that time to write articles and interview celebrities. He began to widen his readership to other magazines and newspapers to the dislike of Farruk, yet he kept supplying him with the best materials.

Nabil and Khalid saw the change in him. He began to interfere in matters that had never bothered him in the past. He hoped to find ways of increasing the turnover of their businesses, as well as the returns. Any extra income went towards paying the loan on the property. His partners couldn't object, because they believed in everything he said, even though they were aware this aggression might lead them to disaster.

Two weeks before the end of the year examinations, the telephone rang at the flat and Julia picked it up. "Hello, is that Rami's mother?" said the voice on the other end.

Julia did not know how to answer. "Who is it please?"

"Sorry to bother you Madam, I'm Rami's tutor. Is he there?"

"No, he's in college."

"Errrm, I don't know how to say this, but he has hardly attended college for the past few weeks. He has missed many lectures and I wanted to find out if he's ok. I'm sorry if I have caused you to worry."

"I don't know what to say," said Julia. "He leaves here early in the morning to go to college and he comes back in the afternoon, or early evening."

"He's a very clever student, but I believe he has some problems, which need discussing. He's a brilliant writer, who all the lecturers and students love very much. If it was someone else I wouldn't have bothered."

"Thank you for contacting me," said Julia. "I will have a word with him when he comes back."

"I hate to see him wasting his studies and the whole year, and if you need any help or advice I am always here."

Anger wasn't the word to describe how she felt at that moment. Julia sat on the sofa and waited for Rami to come home.

A few hours later he walked in. "Darling I'm home. What's there to eat?"

"Nothing," said Julia.

"Good, I fancy going out."

"No you don't, sit down."

"Are we going to have an argument?" he asked laughingly.

"Sit down Rami" He sat down and looked in her direction. "How's college?"

"Good today, a bit on the boring side, but one of the lectures was very interesting."

"How do you know? You weren't there!"

"Yes I was, from nine in the morning until one."

"Your tutor phoned looking for you and he thought I was your mother."

The smile left his face and he felt angry at being found out, but the battle wasn't lost just yet.

"How are you getting on in college?"

"Not bad, he probably didn't see me today."

"Not bad....not good is the word."

"I know, but I made up for it by making good money."

"When was the last time you went to college?" Julia screamed. "You lied to me all this time. How do you expect me to trust you from now on? You're out of order and what if you fail your exams? You'll be taken straight into the army and what good is that to me? I hate liars."

"I'll pass all the exams," said Rami. "I have never failed an exam in my life."

"I lost my husband in the army. I can't take it anymore. You've got a golden chance in your hand and you're out there wasting your time. You can always make money, but you'll only have one chance to put a degree in your pocket."

He felt sad, the last thing that he wanted was to make her angry and distrust him, he had never lied before, and he did not know why he had to then, he did not know what had urged him to do so. He knew that he did it for her, he probably had enough money to buy a house then, especially after Elaine's new man paid him back all the money that he had spent on her. He felt trapped, and she tried not to make him feel that way.

"This is our last day together," said Julia.

"What do you mean?"

"Until you finish your exams I don't want to see you, hear from you, or even be near you. If you come to tell me that you've passed your exams, then we'll talk about the future."

"But the results don't come out for at least a week after the exams finish."

"I don't care, you lied to me Rami, and you are paying for it now."

"But I will pass, I just want you with me."

"I don't trust you anymore. I want to see those results in your hand and that's final."

"Fine!" he said in an angry tone of voice.

"Now you're acting like a child."

"I am acting my age."

"There is no need to take that attitude."

"I do what I want to do; nobody tells me how to behave."

"Rami, have it your way. I was going to stay the night, but I'm leaving now."

"Good, you go," he shouted. "

"You said it! You still have more years to grow up yet."

"And take all your belongings. You said once that you can't make a lady out of a whore and it seems you're right. I spent all that time trying for you, making money so I could give you what no one else ever gave you, but I knew you couldn't stay away from the filth for long."

"Child, I didn't ask you to do anything for me, whatever you want to do, you went ahead and did it, it doesn't matter to me anymore."

"Yes... you go and leave me, just like my parents."

"That's it, I've heard enough."

"I am sorry…I didn't mean what I have just said."

She did not say another word. She went to the bedroom, pulled out her suitcase and began filling it with her belongings. He followed and watched her for a while.

"I'm sorry…I didn't mean any of what I just said. Please stay, I'll do anything for you. Please Julia."

"No ... you made it very easy for me, I thought it would be much harder."

"I am really sorry Julia, I love you, and I'll do whatever you say."

"No, what you said was very hurtful."

"I didn't mean what I said."

"Okay you didn't, I forgive you."

"Thank you, would you stay now?"

"I meant what I said, I am going. I'll move back here when you show me that you've passed your exams."

"I love you."

"I love you too. You've only got two weeks to study, eight days to do the exams and another week for the results, so it's not the end of the world. I want you to be successful that's all."

"Oh no .... I hate this."

She gave him a questioning look, "You are acting like a child now."

"So what…? Nobody ever gave me chance to be one; everyone wanted me to grow up very quickly, oh what's the use?"

"If you love me, you'll do it for me, then yourself. I love you, and I want to be proud of you."

"Can I see you for half an hour every day?"

"You haven't got half an hour to waste."

He helped her put all her belongings in a taxi and she left. He felt a terrible loss and he didn't know what to do with himself. He walked around the flat from one room to the other, avoiding the study. In the end he gave up. He sat behind his desk, looking at the shelves full of all his college books and notebooks. He cleared his table of everything and piled his college work on top.

He flicked through the first book, then the second and the third, and he felt incredibly lost. He did not know where to start with revising as there were so many notes missing from the days he had missed at college.

He left his flat and went to see one of his classmates to borrow their notes and copy them at the newspaper.

He started reading. Every page he finished he felt more relaxed, every chapter he understood he felt more relieved, and his confidence began to grow. He trusted himself to be the best in class again. He was doing it for Julia and he realised how much she meant to him. She was not the sex object he had once thought of her as, but a complete woman, with a mind and a personality. For two weeks he hardly slept, hardly ate and forgot to shave or bathe. He lived on cigarettes and coffee and it did not bother him. He hardly spoke to anyone who visited him, as he made it clear that he wanted to study, and if they wished to stay in the flat, they could do as long as they stayed out of his way.

On the first day of the examinations, he awoke early, had a large breakfast, then shaved and showered. He prayed as he drove to the university and when he arrived he kept away from his classmates, as he didn't wish to enter into any discussion which might interfere with his preparations.

He retained the same attitude throughout all the examination days and when the last day finished, he walked towards the car park and sat in his car. It was a hot summer's day. He knew he'd done very well and achieved something spectacular, and it was all for her. It was midday and he felt tired and exhausted, and wished he could go to sleep for a whole week. He felt like a good cry to release all the pent-up tension inside him.

He put his head on the steering wheel then his hand moved to the ignition to start the car. He drove to Julia's house, he was not prepared to wait any longer and he thought she would change her mind once she saw him.

He rang her door bell, but there was no answer. He rang again and waited for a few minutes, but he could not hear any movement inside. He looked through the window, but to his surprise there were no curtains or furniture inside.

"Julia, please open the door."

The next door neighbour came out when she heard him, "She left two week ago and sold the house," said the lady. "She has moved to a different country."

"What do you mean?"

"She sold the house, someone has bought it, and she left the country, and you better go young man." And she walked in back into her house.

Rami turned around and his legs stiffened up. His car seemed so far away and he could not breathe. "She said she would wait for me. She said she can't live without me. Why am I crying? I can't think straight." He fell to the ground, his legs refused to carry him any further. He stretched his arms out and crawled towards his car, feeling faint and exhausted. "There's something wrong. What's the matter with me?" He tried to reach the door handle and after a struggle he managed to open the door then he slid back to the ground. "Please help me."

The street was empty, not many people would wander around in that heat. He managed to hoist himself into his car and he pressed the button so the radio transmitter came down. He struggled for the handle, but he could not reach it at first. He pushed hard with the other hand and laid half way inside the car.

"Car eleven."

"Go ahead car eleven."

He tried to press the button again, but he could not. Somehow his hand failed to respond.

"Go ahead car eleven."

"Help!"

"Go on Car Eleven."

He managed to press the button again, "Please, help me!"

"Car eleven where are you?"But the handle was not in his hand anymore, "Car Eleven where are you?"

"Car Eleven can you hear me?" The voice repeated.

Rami could hear them, yet the voice seemed miles away. He reached for the red button under the steering wheel and tried to press it, but he felt faint and weak and he did not have any energy, he wanted to sleep.

At the back of his mind he recognised Sami's voice taking charge.

"All cars, we have a code one in progress."

He could hear people talking, people shouting, others reporting, but he felt as if he was sinking deep, his hand was still trying to press that red button.

Sami's voice sounded again. "Rami, press the red button under the steering wheel. Rami can you hear me? "

"We're looking for you, press the red button."

But Rami continued lying there, with half of his body stretched outside the car. He heard sounds and voices coming from a distance.

"Control, car four, his car isn't next to his flat."

"Control, car nine, he isn't near his shops."

"Control, car seven, he isn't in the university car park."

"Control, this is Ahmad, can you give me Julia's address?"

"Yes, hold on a second, we have an SOS alert. Car eleven is in the Saadoon area."

"Send an ambulance."

Five minutes later, Rami was held close to Ahmad's chest. "Rami open your eyes please."

He was carried to the ambulance and the police helped by clearing all the streets leading to the hospital. A team of doctors awaited his arrival.

"Ahmad, how is he?" asked Sami.

"He seems to be in a coma. I'll phone you back from the hospital."

- - - - - - - - -

Two days later Rami woke up to the sight of his mother sitting next to him. He blinked his eyes few times, trying to clear the blurred vision, but he only saw a few shadows.

"Is that you mum?"

She bent down and planted a kiss on his forehead. "Welcome back son," she said smiling.

"Where am I?"

"In hospital…"

"What happened?"

"You collapsed from exhaustion."

"I can't remember."

"The doctor said that it was the combination of studying too hard and the lack of rest or sleep, lack of good food, and lack of rest."

He looked at the bottle hanging upside down, with a tube leading to his arm and he managed a smile.

"I hope there's some whisky in that."

"That's your breakfast."

"Tell the nurse to take it away and to bring proper food. I'm hungry."

Rami fell asleep again. An hour later he awoke and his mother was still sitting there.

"Hi Mum, give me a kiss."

So she did, she held him close to her, then pulled slightly away, and looked in his face, "Your father is outside," she said. "He wants to see you. He has been here all the time you have been out, for two days."

"Two days...? Was that how long I have been out?"

"Two days."

"I can't even remember."

"Your father wants to see you."

"I'm not stopping him from coming in."

"He was just worried that you might not let him, or want him to."

"I'm not like that."

"I love you."

"I love you too, Call dad in."

She opened the door and his father walked in. The two of them looked long at each other, waiting to see who would make the first move.

"Hi dad," said Rami and he opened his arms.

His father rushed to him with tears in his eyes. "Hello son."

"I'm okay, dad, will you stop crying please? I can't take much of this drama." Rami said laughingly with tears running down his face.

"You're coming home with us, son, we all missed you, I'm sorry for whatever happened between us. We all worried about you so much."

"I've got my own life now I want you to understand, that I live the way I want, and I haven't done anything that you would be ashamed of."

"Son all the relatives and the neighbours are talking."

"Let them Dad, they have nothing to occupy their little brains."

"Rami come home, and you can do what you like, I'd rather have a disobedient Son, than a dead one. Well just think about it. You're always welcome, it's your home."

"I will, I promise."

"Ahmad phoned us, and told us what happened. He is the best thing that ever happened to us, as a family."

"Yes Dad, he is, just a damn good friend."

"He was crying on the phone when he told us, poor man, he thought he had lost you."

"Please take mum home and have a rest."

"I will ."

They left the room as Ahmad walked in, followed by Leila's father.

"You do like drama Rami, you thrive on it." Ahmad laughed and gave Rami a hug, so did Leila's father.

"It's alright for you to laugh now." Ahmad said, "When I saw you there with half your body inside the car, and the other half twisted out on the ground, I thought you were dead, I was shaking with fear at that minute."

"And all that I wanted to do was to go to sleep."

"Oh really…?" Leila's father commented, "And from what I heard, a woman is involved in all this."

"I am sorry, I studied so hard, so I would pass my exams, otherwise it was goodbye for us, that's what she said, and when I finished the exams, all what I wanted to do was to go to sleep. Never mind now, I am sorry for all the worry I have caused."

"Never mind, it'll be forgotten shortly."

"And there won't be another woman in my life ever again."

"I believe you."

"So do I." Ahmad laughed, "Yeah I can just see that."

CHAPTER THIRTY

PUSHING a pram, Farrah walked into the Iraqi Embassy in London one Monday morning. A man sitting behind a desk examined her, then spoke. "What can I do for you?"

"I want to add my son's name to my passport."

"Your son..?"

"Yes..."

"Go to the first door to your left."

She sat in the waiting room, in two minds whether to put the child on her passport and take him to Iraq to meet his uncles, aunts and her parents, or stay in England and forget her past life ever existed. Her child was entitled to British Citizenship, as he had been born in England.

She entered the room at last and gave her name to the man sitting behind the desk. She took an instant dislike to him, with his thick moustache, indicating that he was a member of the Baath party. He looked at a list next to him, "Yes, take a seat."

She looked at the list, after watching him leave the room. Her name was on it and the page was headed as 'addresses unknown.' She began to worry as she recognised some of the names on the list as well-known leaders who opposed the Iraqi regime. After few minutes he returned. "This is for you," he said and handed her an envelope, before beginning to fill in a form.

"Your son's name?"

"Rami."

"The father's name?"

"No father."

He examined her with a dirty smirk. "No father! Is that why you came to England, to hide your sins?"

Her face filled with raging anger. "No, his father was killed in the war. He was a hero, so what have you got to say for yourself? I'm not hiding from anyone. Thank you for your help, but I don't need to put his name on my passport. He was born here and he shall have a British passport. Thanks again."

"I'm sorry."

But Farrah had already left the room. He followed her out. "I need your address."

"You can't have it."

Farrah had been working very hard as a freelancer to a range of Arab magazines, as well as holding down a permanent job as a reporter with an Egyptian based magazine. On top of that, she had been making some useful contacts with alternative outlets in England and Europe.

Her writings, articles and comments were growing in popularity and she had begun to establish herself as a leading Arab journalist. Little Rami was growing up to be an exact image of his father which used to make her laugh at times.

"Son...out of all features, you had to inherit your dad's big nose."

When she got home that day, after visiting the Iraqi Embassy, she tried to calm herself down. She had never been so insulted before in her whole life. "If only Rami was here, he would've killed them. Oh Rami I wish…" And she burst out crying.

It wasn't easy being a single working mother, neither was living in a strange country with different cultures and values. She had reached breaking point many times, but somehow and for whatever reason she proved that she could survive.

After feeding the baby and putting him to bed, she took the letter from her handbag, examined it and decided to open it and read it.

There were a few letters inside the envelope and she recognised the handwriting as Ahmad's. She read all the letters, but the last one disturbed her. *"Rami is now out of hospital, after a whole week there. I thought we had lost him. He had stopped caring about himself, stopped eating, drinking, and living. Farrah he needs you terribly, please reconsider. I think he should know about your baby, please write back to me. Rami won't last for long, he loves you and he would never find anyone to take your place in his life.*

Rami would do anything to have you back, he has spoken about it a few times and I believe that you two belong to each other. He is on holiday in Greece at the moment, recovering from his bad ordeal on an island called Crete. He saw the photos of the place and fell in love with it.

Please think again and I'll support you in any decision you make.

Love, Ahmad."

She threw the letter away and stood up to have a look at little Rami asleep.

"I love you son and there's no way I'm going to let you near that crazy father of yours, not now but one day. I do love him very much, and he loves me." She planted a kiss on the baby's forehead. "Maybe we should go back soon. You have the right to see your grandparents, aunties and uncles. However, our society will never forgive and forget. You're my son, my life, my whole world and as long as I have a breath in me, I won't let any harm come to you."

CHAPTER THIRTY ONE

RAMI returned home to a staggering number of cases for him and Ahmad to solve. There were many cases of serious abuse on individuals , killings and torturing of innocent people, attacks on a number of Holy men, and worst of all, no one knew who was committing these crimes and why.

It was somehow welcoming work, as since they had joined the CIC there hadn't been much for them to do, apart from visiting nightclubs and restaurants to investigate who had used his membership in the Baath party to gain entry or not paying for their meals and drinks.

The government, on the other hand, began to control the masses through the brutality of its elite members. They had no fear, even to the extent of killing opposition leaders in public, without sending them to prison or to face a court.

Rami returned from his holiday happy and cheerful, but all his close friends were keeping an eye on him, in case his behaviour took a turn. For almost two months afterwards he buried himself in his work for the CIC and at the flat, reading and writing. On occasions he visited Leila's family. He was in a way contented with his life.

Ahmad spoke to him one day, about general issues mainly.

"I feel as if I'm slowing down," said Rami suddenly.

"Good, for the last few years you've been running too fast and too far, well it's a good thing."

"To me it feels like a slow-moving dream. I do know that I'm fully awake now, but I like it this way."

"Do you regret anything?" Jean Asked.

"Yes." He looked into the distance with a sad look on his face. She remembered him laughing and joking all the time, his carefree behaviour, but he had changed, the last few years had no mercy on him. She stretched and held his hand, Ahmad smiled to her proudly, she shared the feeling to their best friend.

"Not the things I did, but the things that happened to me."

"Tell us, get it out in the open," said Ahmed.

"It's Leila...I'll never recover from her. I loved her deeply and I still do. At times I wake up in the morning and wonder what to wear so she'll find me sexy, or when I go to see her parents, I can see her coming out of the front door acting silly, then she would hug me and kiss me. I miss her terribly and I'll never forget her face when she went down. I knew Elaine wasn't for me – sometimes I make the mistake of not knowing the difference between love and lust; maybe I will never know."

"What about Nadia?"

"She was there when no one else was. She was a good friend and lover at that time."

"And Julia?" Ahmad asked, knowing that he hasn't spoken about her at all, as if she didn't exist.

"Oh Julia, Julia." He shook his head left to right. "A real woman who I respected very much, we set each other's feelings on fire. She knew we couldn't be together forever. Neither of us wanted to make the first move to end it peacefully, then she found the excuse. I lied to her and she didn't like that. My fault, probably I wanted her to find out; I wanted her to know that I was doing everything for her; oh I don't understand it myself. I loved her, yet now I'm not sorry that she has gone. She was wonderful in every way and I do hope she's happy now. It was such an intense relationship; we never did anything in half measures."

"And you've not mentioned Farrah."

"She is my only love. I wish I knew where she has gone. She was and still is the only person for me. I'd give my two eyes away to have her back. I just wish I knew where to look for her. I've written to all the newspapers and magazines she writes for, but no one would give me her address."

"You might get together one day," said Ahmed.

"No, I know her better than I know myself. I used her terribly when she was around. Let's talk about something else."

"Ok, are you going to write another book?" Jean asked.

"Didn't I tell you that I'm working on another one?"

"No!"

"Give me a few more months and I'll have another best seller."

"Good, but what else do you want to do?"

"What's the matter with you? You've been asking me questions all night! I'd like to travel the world and see every country possible."

"Do it, you only have one chance in life."

"I can't go on spending money. We're opening more businesses and we might need that money."

"What on earth for?" Ahmad asked.

"Money...!"

"This is stupid; the three of you are killing yourselves."

"Well Khalid and Nabil are determined to make a million each before the five years is up since we opened the first shop."

"And they will do it."

- - - - - - - - -

Khalid finished writing out a few bills to send to some of their contracts. "This needs your signature," he said to Nabil. "And also these few cheques, Rami will sign them tomorrow when he's here."

"He said he's coming here tomorrow."

"Well I'm going to see him later, so I can take these papers with me," said Khalid.

"Can't you find him something to occupy his brain?"

"He'll come round."

Khalid wasn't sure. He didn't feel happy about the way Rami looked recently, even though he wasn't the closest person to Rami, but he liked him very much. "Listen Nabil, the couple of hours he spends here isn't helping him at all. He doesn't talk unless you talk to him first and this has been going on for months. He hardly smiles or jokes anymore, come on Nabil, we've got to do something."

"Okay, we'll find him something to do and keep him here for as late as possible; afterwards we'll force him into coming to a party with us."

"Yes, good idea."

"He just doesn't want to involve himself in anything he isn't sure about. Look at him in the Sodality meetings, he just sits there listening, he doesn't talk or say anything…I do feel sorry for him. No I don't feel sorry for him, but I am worried sick about him."

"I am as well."

The next day Rami found himself surrounded by people who worked in their three shops constantly asking him for help. He ploughed on without even noticing the time.

That night, he was forced to go out with Khalid and Nabil. He was hungry and thirsty, and all he wanted was a quiet night, a big meal, and a cold beer. But he found himself surrounded by nearly forty of their friends from the centre and others they had made over the years. He smiled at Khalid and Nabil, realizing what they were trying to do.

"Thanks, I was looking forward for a quiet night, the three of us together."

"Sorry, do you want to go somewhere else?"

The nightclub was called 'Hammurabi.' It possessed some truly magnificent gardens by the side of the water, adding beauty to the majestic atmosphere. The nightclub was spacious and it could cater for hundreds of people at the same time without giving the impression of being crowded. It had a large dance floor and the band which played there succeeded in making everyone get up and dance.

Soon Rami managed a smile and started talking to whoever sat at the table next to him.

After a while he decided to go for a walk and Nabil followed him. "Where are you going?"

"I just fancied looking at the grounds and the flower beds."

"I never took you to be interested in flowers."

"I got it from Leila's dad, although my father is very keen, but since Leila, I spend many hours in the garden with her dad. It's very relaxing. It's being close to nature."

They walked around the gardens and Nabil respected Rami's quietness. Rami spoke first. "It's my first time here, what an incredible place. They must have spent some money on this garden and the rest."

"It was a government grant, but they put in several thousand themselves."

"Wow, let's sit there."

There was a table with two chairs, where Rami and Nabil sat down.

"Do you want a drink?" Nabil asked.

"Yes please, why not?"

They talked about different subjects, but Rami's eyes focused on the table behind Nabil, where five girls sat. Four men approached them and asked them to dance, but one refused and sat on her own.

"What's the matter Rami?"

"That girl, don't look just yet."

Nabil waited for few seconds then turned and looked at her. "She is how I feel."

"She is nice." But Nabil realized what Rami wanted to say. "How do you feel?" He asked.

Rami did not answer at first. His eyes never left that girl's face.

"She's very beautiful, very sad, and she feels that she doesn't belong here."

Nabil kept quiet, as this was the first time that Rami had talked so deeply for a long time. "I loved Crete, but I hated being on my own. I hated looking at couples walking on the beach hand in hand, or sitting in a taverna sipping ouzo or wine, looking at each other lovingly. I felt so lonely...so out of place."

"I know the feeling."

"Whenever I sat down to eat I got the impression that everyone was looking at me. I went to a club to cheer myself up, but seeing all the men and women together, loving and kissing, laughing and dancing, I started to wonder what was wrong with me."

"Do you like her for the way you are looking at her?"

Rami stood up and walked over to the girl and Nabil smirked and walked back to his crowd.

"Would you like to dance?" Rami asked softly.

"No thank you, I hate dancing."

"Oh, I'm sorry to have bothered you," he said feeling awkward and disappointed.

Rami turned to leave. His bottom lip shivered. He felt so lonely and he wished that the ground would open up so he could sink inside it. He never had been refused a dance before.

"Please don't go, sit with me."

"What about your friends?"

"Until they come, anyway they won't be back for another hour, once they start dancing, that's it for the night. They warned me before we came here." She smiled.

"Your glass is empty, would you like another drink?"

Before she had a chance to answer, Rami had already asked the waiter to the table, "A large whisky for me, and..."

"Coke for me if I may...? Thank you."

He looked at her. "You don't like dancing? Or is it the music?"

She looked into his eyes for a few seconds. "The truth is, I don't know how to dance, as this is my first time out."

"Never mind, you'll learn one day. I'm Rami."

"I'm Saher."

"What do you do? Do you work or study?"

"I'm a nanny, I work for a German family, looking after their two kids."

"You aren't from Baghdad, are you?"

"No, I'm from up north. I'm staying with my aunt. What do you do?"

"I'm studying science in the university."

"Very clever."

"I had no option, it was either that or the army."

They sat chatting for about an hour until Saher's friends came back. Rami went back to join his friends.

A smile crossed his face as he sat next to Nabil, then suddenly he leapt out of his seat and hurried back to where Saher had been, but all the chairs were empty; the five girls had gone.

"What's the matter?" Nabil asked.

"I forgot to ask for her address or phone number."

"You idiot," Nabil laughed. "Wait until I tell Khalid."

"No doubt he will say something worse than that." Rami joined in the laughter, "I don't know what I was thinking about."

"Exactly what were you thinking about?"

Rami slapped him at the back of his head, "So called friends!"

- - - - - - - - -

A few days later, Rami spoke with a neighbour. Although they were the same age, he didn't have much in common with him, but they conversed every now and then as a symbol of respect.

"Is college going well?" The neighbour asked. He was joined then by his elder brother.

"Fine no problem there, how were your exams?"

"I passed, but my average is low, so I might go to the technology college, not what I wanted."

"Any gossip?" Rami asked.

The neighbour told Rami a few pieces of uninteresting information. "No not really, our dad retired from his work, he's been there twenty five years. He decided to open a convenience store on Fifty Two Street." The elder brother answered.

They talked for few minutes, then the neighbour had a question. "Have you seen the new nanny working for the German family?"

"No." But a bell rang in his head.

"That's her walking down the street…the one pushing the buggy."

"She's gorgeous, but she doesn't talk to anyone and she doesn't smile. The second brother added."I'll bet you twenty dinars if you can say hello to her and she answers you."

"I'll accept the bet," Rami answered, smiling.

"You have a week."

"No problem, I'll even go a step further and walk the length of this street with her."

"You'll be lucky if she even looks in your direction!"

Rami took a sudden disliking to his neighbour. "Well I'd better start right now...why waste time?"

He walked towards her. "Hi Saher..."

"Oh, I didn't recognise you, hi Rami, how are you?"

"I'm good thanks. I went back to where you were sitting the other night, but you'd gone. I forgot to take your phone number!"

She smiled. "Why would you want my phone number?"

"I wanted to see you again. Do you want to walk to the top of the street?"

"Yes fine. What are you doing here?"

"Just passing by and I stopped to talk to those clowns."

"Oh, I hate them. Every time I pass by, they and their friends say something rude, or make a nasty remark. "

"Just ignore them; although they come from a good family, they haven't been brought up right. They are from the street and to the street they return." He laughed and she joined him.

"It's a small world how we have met twice in a matter of four days." She said.

"People will start talking," he giggled. "Do you fancy coming to see a movie at the centre on Thursday?"

"That all depends on my work."

As they returned, they said goodbye in front of her workplace. The neighbour approached them and handed Rami the twenty Dinars.

Rami didn't know where to hide his face, "Well done. I never thought you had it in you."

"What's going on?" said Saher.

"We had a bet that he'd walk with you to the top of the street and back. And he did."

She shot Rami an angry look and walked hurriedly into the house.

"Why did you have to do this?" Rami said, feeling embarrassed and ashamed.

"Well she deserves it, she's a stuck up cow."

"She isn't actually, she happens to be a very lovely person," said Rami and he left without even saying goodbye.

He felt very upset and angry about what had happened. How could he accept such a childish bet, especially from that idiot? He was going round in circles not knowing how to rectify the situation. He waited in his car for days to see if he could catch her taking the children for a walk, but after three days baking in the sun, he decided it was an impossible task in the heat.

"Send her a nice bunch of flowers." Jean advised him.

"Are you sure?"

"All women love flowers."

He tried sending flowers but she refused to accept them. He sent her letters apologising, and asking her to telephone him, but she never did. It almost became an obsession; he simply wanted her to tell him that she'd forgiven him, but she wouldn't give him the satisfaction.

"What do I do now?" He asked Jean.

"You can't force people to talk to you, if she doesn't want to than she doesn't want to, and you've got to accept that, whether you like it or not."

"I hate hurting people, especially someone as beautiful as she is."

Ahmad walked in with a tray filled with a variety of knickknacks for them to eat.

He had an envelope in his hand, "I've got news for you both."

"What news?"

"We are invited to a wedding in six weeks time."

"Elaine's…?"

"Yes…"

"Wow great…brilliant."

"And she wants Rami and me to give her away."

- - - - - - - - -

One day as Rami drove home, he was called by the CIC to pick Ahmad up. He left the receiver on as he drove as fast as he could to Ahmad's house.

"All cars, this is code one." The calm voice of Sami echoed straight away.

"Car Eleven reporting, you said it's a quiet night."

He enjoyed these moments of action and there had not been many in the past few weeks.

"All cars, this is Sami. Head to zone eleven."

"What's going on?" Ahmad asked as he stepped into the car.

"I don't know, but we're in charge, as it's in our zone."

"All cars, search for a white Mercedes, 1965 Model, be careful, the two men in the car are armed, they have fired their guns twice in front of the Italian Embassy." Sami's voice came back.

"This is serious." Ahmad commented.

"How many cars like these are there in our area? A white Mercedes."

"Exactly…!"

"Car Eleven to control, can you send us a list of how many cars are there of this model in our area."

"Working on it…hang on!"

They drove in silence for a few minutes, then Ahmad spoke. "What have you been hiding from me all this time? I know you too well, Rami."

"I was sort of going out with another girl; a long story."

"Who is she? Do I know her?"

"It's a long story." Rami felt frustrated with the questioning, but nevertheless, "I am only trying to pass time; we will never find the damn car."

He told Ahmad the full story about Saher. "But there's something odd about her, as she reminds me of other girls I've been out with.

"You are getting weirder by the day." Ahmad scoffed.

"You are a snob Mister Ahmad."

Ahmad laughed at the remark.

"Everything about her reminds me of something in the past. I like her very much, I believe that she comes from a very poor family, but I never asked her, never talked to each other about anything serious, it's all been one big joke, I feel sorry now for what I've done."

"What does she do for a living?"

"She is a nanny. She looks after two children; she works for someone from a foreign Embassy."

"Oh my God Rami, how old is she?"

'My age I think.'

"Look...I was poor, but I had education, what has she got?"

"I don't know."

"Nanny is only a servant that's all, oh come on wake up how much does she earn?"

"I don't know."

"And what type of a job is that? In Europe and America a nanny is very important, but in our country it is no more than being a servant. What's wrong with you? From going out with an abortionist to begging to go out with a servant, yet girls from high class families would give their right arm to be in your company."

"Leave it out please. I'll go out with who I want."

"Don't you agree with me about that girl?"

"No ... she is beautiful Ahmad, smart, and I like her very much and I hope I get the chance to say sorry."

"You did say sorry, and she didn't accept your apology. So just leave her be.""God...! You never stop, like an old Armenian woman."

Ahmad laughed and laughed, "Have you met one yet?"

"No...never had the pleasure, but I am sitting next to one.'"

"Look there's that car. Stop here."

Ahmad ran towards the car, which was parked inside a garage, with the outside gate left open. He put his hand on the car, and returned to their car.

"Car Eleven to control."

"Go ahead Car Eleven."

Ahmad gave them the address of the house, while Rami took a gun out from the side door, and checked it.

"Don't do anything...wait until all the cars are there. Remember that you are in charge."

A few minutes later, all the other fifteen cars had turned up. Rami and Ahmad gave the orders to surround the house, while the regular police surrounded the whole area.

Ahmad knocked on the door, as the others hid behind the wall with their guns pointing in his direction. A woman's voice came from behind the door. "Who is it?"

"Police, open the door."

She opened the door slightly, but they all rushed in quickly, pushing her out of the way, with a gun pointing at her.

"You open your mouth and you'll be dead."

She nodded her head. The rest of men ran inside the house and a few minutes later they appeared holding a man, who looked very drunk.

"There are three children asleep upstairs."

"Is there anyone with them?" Rami asked

"Yes sir."

Ahmad examined the man in front of him. He looked absolutely pathetic and he wore a sorry look on his face as he stood in front of the crying woman. Ahmad nodded to the man standing by her side to let her sit.

"Name?" Rami asked.

"I give you nothing," said the man. "I have Political Amnesties."

"What's your name?" Ahmad demanded.

"You can do what you like, but you'll get nothing out of me."

"That's fine by me. It's been a long time since we killed someone." Ahmad bluffed. Rami went to his car and radioed Sami. "The man says he's got Political Amnesties."

"You must be joking. Search the house." Sami ordered.

"You're the boss."

Rami ordered his colleagues to search the house, and the car outside. A few minutes later they handed him a few passports. He examined them and looked at the man.

"You are in deep trouble here. You have an Israeli passport, a Jordanian passport, an Iraqi passport, a British passport, and many more. Now tell me, what are you?" Rami asked.

"Which country do you belong to?" Ahmad questioned him too.

"I have nothing to say," the man shouted. "Especially to a child, like you."

Rami's facial expression changed to one of anger and hatred, but he stopped one of his colleagues from hitting the man.

"How old are you Son? Does your mother know that you are here? I bet you will get a smack on your bottom when you get back." He tried to belittle Rami, but after a while, he realised that he was talking to the wrong person. Rami grew ten feet taller when he managed to control his reaction to all the insults as well as being backed by his fellow CIC members, showing him the respect that he deserved for being in charge.

Ahmad retreated to a corner, to let his friend handle the investigation. Rami loved acting, and he was good at it.

Two of the men returned to the room carrying a box filled with guns, rifles, and hand grenades.

"What have we got here?"

The man smiled. Rami turned to the woman. "I feel sorry for you madam, I shall bring your children down here."

"Leave my children alone, you bastard," the man shouted.

"Please," the woman begged.

"You can be shot for calling me a bastard," said Rami. "I can simply kill you for honour. In fact, I'm going to kill you right now."

"I'd be happy to do it for you sir," Ahmad bluffed.

"Your children must be heavy sleepers, madam, with all this noise going on? Never mind, we'll just have to wake them."

The man tried to stand up to hit Rami, but he was pushed back into his place quickly.

"If anyone puts just a hand on them, I swear to God I'll kill them with my hands."

"Take the woman to her children for a while and don't harm any of them."

"Yes sir," one of his colleagues answered with a smile.

The man tried to stand up again, but he was again pushed harder than the previous time back to his seat.

"Who do you work for?"

"I won't answer any of your questions. I have a higher ranking than any of you. Do you understand? I want to see your boss, you idiots."

One of Rami's colleagues spoke, "Sir shall I show this bit of a man, how you should be spoken to?"

Before Rami had the chance to say another word, a few policemen walked in, holding a young man, in his mid-twenties.

"Sir, I think this one belongs here, he was trying to escape out of the area."

"Thank you officer, well done. Make sure no one leaves the area without a complete search," Ahmad ordered.

The policeman walked towards Rami and whispered in his ear. "Sir, they are Palestinians I think."

"I gathered that, thank you."

Rami looked long at the younger man. "What's your name?"

"Abu ...." But he stopped talking when he saw the older man's face.

Ahmad burst out laughing, "These are jokers, real jokers."

"What are you? Secret police? Army intelligence, or what?" The older man asked. No one answered him. They paid him no attention as they decided to play around with his younger mate.

"What's your name?"

"I'm not answering, so get that into your head."

Rami took out his identification card and placed it in front of the man's face.

"What do you think this is?"

The man looked at it in horror. He'd heard of their organisation and their power, but he had never come across any of them before.

"Name...?"

"Abu Saad."

"What is your rank?"

"Captain."

"PLO...?"

"Yes Sir, Fattah"

"Did you use your gun tonight?"

"Yes sir, I was drunk."

"You're charged with trying to kill the Italian Ambassador tonight. If you have anything to say, you can keep it until you're in the station."

"Wait, I have to be out of the country in two days."

"I really don't care where you want to be in two days time. You might like to be a cowboy everywhere else in the world, but we have worked very hard to make our country something to be proud of, but people like you take advantage of our hospitality."

"You're going to kill me aren't you?" Abu Saad asked.

"No, I wouldn't dirty my hands. You know that you're not permitted to carry or own guns inside Iraq, but you think you're above the law."

"Yes I know but…"

"The law doesn't allow you to have buts…"

"I'm sorry, very sorry."

Ahmad put his hands on Rami's shoulder and took him to the room next door.

"He's pathetic, and I don't think you'll get much out of him."

"I really don't want to arrest him either. I just want to give him a bit of hard time. The man's got family."

"Ok, I'll leave it to you."

The man was crying. "What about my children?"

"Your wife must find them another father."

"Oh God no. I'll tell you everything you want to know."

"Like what? Tell me now and if it is useful information, we might consider letting you live to fight another day."

"We bought those weapons from a dealer in Al-Thawra district. There are four houses connected underground with massive cellars and tunnels. They get all the weapons from Iran and other organisations. They also manufacture and produce spare parts for most weapons."

Ahmad went out of the room and contacted Sami immediately to tell him what was said inside the house.

A quarter of an hour later Sami arrived, and went straight in. He recognised the Palestinian man, although it wasn't the case the other way round.

"How many people are we talking about here?"

"I only dealt with two." Answering Sami's question, "But, I am sure every house in the street is well armed, and well trained."

"If you cooperate with us, we'll forget the attempted murder on the Italian ambassador," Sami told the man.

"I'll do anything."

"You are under house arrest until further notice."

"Thank you sir," he said and he hurriedly kissed Sami's hand.

- - - - - - - - -

Al-Thawra city was built by General Abdul Karim Kassim, the Prime Minister of Iraq between 1958 - 63, after he had led a revolution against the young King Faisal. Kassim's idea was first to clear the city of mud houses, and if Iran was ever to invade Iraq, and especially Baghdad, they would have to pass through this small city first.

The majority of the people who lived there were Shiite Muslims, a very tribal setup, who were well integrated between themselves. An attack on a house could result in civil unrest, which would go on for several years.

Sami asked his team to come outside for a small conference. "I am in two minds," he said. "Either we go now with the help of Army Intelligence people, or we leave everything to them to sort out."

"And by that time someone will breathe to those people, and all the arms will be shipped to another location. I think we should go now, the sooner the better," one of the men suggested.

"I agree that's why we trained to deal with anything."

Everyone was ready to go. Rami and Ahmad were reluctant to agree. They believed that it will be a bloodbath.

"I think dropping a bomb on top of these houses will sort out the problem," Rami added casually. "That'll save us getting shot at and killed."

"You have a point there; every house in that street could be well armed." Sami commented.

"Every house in the city is well armed, not just the street," Ahmad added.

"If we go we must use civilian cars and we've got to be extra fast, as once they wake up and we are still trying to get in, we might as well put a gun to our heads and do it ourselves." Rami said.

"So what are we going to do?" Sami wanted action, not a debate.

"Rami and I will go now and bluff our way in," said Ahmed. "We'll use this idiot as if he sent us to buy weapons."

"Good, let's do it."

Ahmad and Rami bluffed their way into the house and arrested two men, followed by a further sixteen, all from the same neighbourhood. Not only were they selling arms, but manufacturing them by the hundreds. It took more than a dozen army personnel carriers to empty the warehouse underneath four of the houses.

The arrest of these men led to more arrests of a number of high ranking army personnel who were trying to overthrow the government, who were buying arms in large quantities from the this factory.

The whole operation lasted for an entire week and hardly any of the men involved had any rest or sleep, except for a quick shower, shave, and a change of clothes. They conducted the operation wisely and efficiently and they saved the country from a bloodbath.

Sami ordered everyone to return to headquarters. When they walked in they were faced with a large table covered with a delicious spread of food and drinks.

"Quiet everyone," Sami, shouted. "This is a thank you from someone high in the government, on a job well done, thank you team."

"Rami fill your plate and follow me. I want to have a word with you."

"What's the matter boss?"

Rami followed Sami into the room.

"Sit down please," said Sami.

"I feel shattered."

"So does everyone else."

"What's wrong?" Rami asked.

"You asked the girl in the office to look for information for you."

"Oh yes, I forgot about that."

"Good, because you aren't getting it."

"Why not?"

"There's nothing for you to investigate at that address, am I right?"

Rami read behind the words. "Why? What's wrong with that house?"

"Nothing, there are many things wrong with you. You need your head to be examined. You, my boy, want to live it up with a servant."

Rami remained silent. He didn't like the way he had been spoken to and he tried to stand up, but Sami stood up pointing at the chair.

"Sit down"

"Fine what do you want from me? That is my private life."

"What's the matter with you? You want to go out with a servant? Is that what your father wants for a daughter in law? He can get hundreds of them in a flick of a finger."

"What has this got to do with anyone?"

"Where's your self respect? How can you expect people to look up to you?" Sami paused, took a deep breath and continued. "Now listen to me. She comes from somewhere up north, a small village in the middle of nowhere."

"I know that."

"Great, and do you know she only earns twenty Dinars a month? You wouldn't even wake up for that amount of money. Tell me how much you are worth a month?"

"Quite a bit, more than many people!"

"She lives in the house where she works."

"No, she lives with her aunt."

"Her aunt and her aunt's husband have one room in a house, which they share with five families. They sleep in it, eat in it, and probably shit in it. Do you understand?"

"So…?"

"She might be beautiful in your eyes, but she is uneducated. She left school at the age of thirteen, so she could work as a cleaner and earn some money, because her father is a lazy drunk."

"It's honest work."

"We all do honest work. Can you imagine both happy parents visiting each other? Your mum and her mum are of the same social standard and education."

"Do we all do honest work? Do we?" Rami asked sarcastically.

"Come on Rami, think. None of your friends will have any respect for you, and what about your family? Can you see your sisters sitting next to someone like her? Wouldn't it hurt you if your mother kissed her, and said thank you to her for looking after her son? I know you're not on good terms with your family, but family in our society runs like thick blood. Please Rami, leave her alone, turn your head to the other side, there are hundreds of girls out there waiting for you."

"Why the sudden interest Sami? You never objected about Julia?"

271

"Julia was much older than you and I knew it wouldn't last long. She was good for you at that time, but this girl is trouble Rami, and once you get involved you won't be able to get out of it."

"What if I don't want to get out of any relationship with her?"

"You are crazy."

"What if she stops working there and I supported her?"

"Will that seriously change what she is? I doubt it very much."

"Well it's my life."

"Have it your own way, I've said my piece."

"Thank you for warning me." Rami concluded sarcastically.

Sami shook his head in disbelief. He never expected that his words would not change Rami's mind.

Rami left the room and joined the others for a short period. "Ahmad, I'm leaving now. Do you want me to wait for you?"

"Yes I need a lift home."

"I'll wait for you in the car," said Rami then he walked out.

"I'll just finish my food and come."

Sami threw his hands in the air, as his eyes met Ahmad's.

"What's the matter with him?" Ahmad asked Sami.

"I told him off."

"But he did a very good job."

"I know, it's nothing to do with that." Sami told Ahmad everything that went on in that room between him and Rami. Ahmad defended Rami.

"What will happen if he gets involved with her? What's wrong with you too?"

"Nothing is wrong with me, but I think if he gets involved with her, he'll have a very good time," Ahmad said laughing. He always defended Rami, whether he was right or wrong, no one was allowed to talk about his friend, no matter what. He always had said, 'I can call my own family and friends what I like, but nobody else can.'

"Thanks for your concern, but Rami is eighteen, and he knows what he's doing."

"Does he? Oh come on."

"I agree with you, she's a different class, education, and the rest, but he could make that girl drip with gold and no one would know any better. It's up to him really."

Ahmad was furious when he sat in the car. He looked long at Rami. He felt like hitting him. It might just do the trick and wake him up. He was shaking with rage but somehow he managed to control it.

Both men were quiet, but Rami spoke first. "Do you believe in the class system in our society and all that rubbish?" But before Ahmad had the chance to open his mouth and answer, Rami answered himself. "What a stupid question! After all these years of knowing you, I should know the answer to that. You're the one who taught me about classes and how important they are to our backward society."

"What are you trying to say?"

"What class do I belong to?"

Ahmad laughed, trying to think fast. "Well I should think a high to middle class."

"And what did you base that on?"

"Rami, you know more about sociology than anyone else I know. What are you trying to justify?"

"Oh thanks, so you believe that I'm capable of bringing someone from low to middle?"

"No, the answer is no, you cannot do that, it would take generations and generations. If you're using this excuse to go out with a servant, then it's not good enough. Your family will disown you and your friends will walk away."

"What about you?"

Ahmad didn't answer; if Rami knew him well after all those years, then he should understand how he felt.

Rami didn't need excuses to do what he always wanted to do, but this time he needed to satisfy himself, he didn't want to put a foot wrong. What people think of him mattered to him, and he didn't want to let anyone down.

CHAPTER THIRTY TWO

IT was ten days later when he spotted Saher in Al-Karada Street; a busy shopping area in Baghdad. He parked his car and decided to follow her.

She visited almost every shop, but bought nothing. Many young men tried to talk to her, but she ignored all of them. There was something about her that attracted so much attention from everyone, women and men alike. He followed her for almost half an hour until she noticed him walking behind her through the reflection of a shop window.

"Will you leave me alone?" she said in a loud voice as she turned to face him.

"We need to talk."

"There's nothing to talk about, absolutely nothing."

"Please just listen to me."

"If you don't go away I'll scream."

Her ultimatum unsettled him. He hadn't been brought up to have a street confrontation with anyone. He'd never experienced that before and he didn't even know how to conduct himself.

"Please, just give me ten minutes of your time."

"No, leave me alone! Go away!" she screamed at the top of her voice. A few passersby stopped to watch.

"Is he bothering you young lady?" a stranger asked, hoping to win her attention.

"Well Rami? Are you going to leave me alone, or shall I have you beaten up?"

He turned to walk away, but a police car stopped suddenly and he found himself surrounded. Everyone in the crowd pointed their fingers at him.

"What's going on?"

"This man was harassing this lady."

"Come with us now," said one of the policemen.

"Captain, my identification card is in my back pocket. Have a look at it." Rami asked but there was an order tone in his appeal.

"Put your hands in the air." the captain ordered and a policeman searched for the identification.

The captain looked at it before he decided to put Rami in the police car, and drive him away from the embarrassing situation.

"I'm sorry sir, I didn't know who you were."

"Thanks captain, I'll put your name and number in my next report. I'm parked just over there."

"Anything else you require?"

"Thanks a million." Rami took some money out of his wallet to give it to them, but they refused to take it. Rami insisted that it was for their children.

His body shook violently with shame and sheer anger. Never in his life had he felt so belittled or challenged by an uneducated mob. He was not far from being beaten up and for no reason. Yet he wasn't angry with her at all, it only made him even more determined to talk to her.

Back in his apartment he poured himself a large whisky and sat on the balcony watching the world pass by. Before long, he found himself writing another short story. As the sun went down, he moved to his study, put some classical music on and sat thinking. He felt he did not need any of his friends to tell him what to do and how to do it.

What difference did it really make? It was he who mattered, no one else, he was number one.

"I want her," he said loudly to himself.

He stopped writing and gazed into the distance through the window. He thought of her beautiful body that he had fallen in love with! He loved the cheap dress she wore. His mind wandered to all the women who he had been out with and how much they meant to him.

He was in love, he confessed, even though he hardly knew her. He went into the spare bedroom, which he had avoided for a long time. The room was bare from all the clutter Farrah used to create. He opened one wardrobe, then another, but they were all empty. He felt sad and sat on the bed. "Oh Farrah, I do miss you."

He felt her presence stronger than ever before. This was her domain, and at that moment he noticed the spare keys to the flat on the sideboard and he realised that his dream of her returning had ended. He raised his glass in the air. "Here's to you my love, wherever you are, for your eyes only."

Sitting behind his desk his imagination took him to a different world, away from people, real people, away from life. He felt that life held his hands and feet tight down and stopped him from stretching out as far as he wanted. He wrote for hours, without realising how long he had sat there for, or how much of the bottle of whisky he had drunk, and how many cigarettes he had smoked, until the morning sun lit his room. He went to his bedroom, closed the curtains, and fell asleep, totally fulfilled.

Later that afternoon, he went to the newspaper, where Iman was busy typing.

"Is the boss in?" he said.

"Rami," said Iman."Come here and give your aunt a kiss.

She hugged him, "Good to see you Son, where have you been?"

"Busy...How are you?"

"I am fine, what have you been doing with yourself?"

"Going crazy I suppose."

"You look sad my love, what's the matter?"

She smiled with that comforting look on her face. "Life doesn't get easier. I've got all your stories, which you put in the mail box."

"Good, how is he in there?"

"Now go and cheer Farruk up, he has been in a bad way lately."

He walked into Farruk's room.

"What's the matter with you?" Rami asked. "Everyone is complaining."

"Hello you, sit there, let me finish this first then I'll talk to you."

Instead, he walked behind Farruk and began to read what he was writing.

"This doesn't make any sense."

"Who asked for your opinion?"

"Well read it yourself."

Farruk did, "Yes you are right, oh hell, I can't put my mind into it today."

"Why?"

"My eldest daughter is about to have a baby any time now. It's her first."

"Blame it on her, poor woman, give me this, I'll do something about it."

"What do you know about politics?"

Rami sat in Farruk's chair, after pushing him out of it. He changed a few lines and a few paragraphs around, and added some words here and there.

"Here...what do you think now?"

Farruk read it, "Thanks...very good. But not as good as mine when I am in full swing." He laughed.

"Charming…!"

"Where the hell have you been? And how are you? You should have told us you were coming, I would have put the red carpet out for you."

"It's good to feel missed, and feel free putting the red carpet out now."

"What has been going on? How's life? Tell me, as I've finished work for the day."

"I don't know Farruk. Society, that's the question! Classes."

"What's on your mind?"

"Say a high class person decides to marry someone from a low class, will it work"

"Not unless the high class side accepts going down, as there's no way the low class side can jump so high to meet the other side.

"Good."

"Why?"

"Because I fancy a girl who's very low class, poor, and she's hardly had any education."

"No Rami, don't do the impossible, or else you'll regret everything one day."

He quickly changed the subject and talked about different matters. Half an hour later, he returned to his flat.

He sat on the balcony thinking again. All what he wanted was to be happy in life and for someone to need him and want him for who and what he was. It had been a long time since he had been with anyone. He was crying for love and attention, and all his friends and their ideas could go to hell. What had they ever done for him? Apart from patting him on the back when he had achieved something, or when they had tried to wake him up! They did not know him. They did not realise how lonely he was. They all had partners and security. They didn't care what happened to him, and if he disappeared somewhere, all they might say is, *'We did know him.'* They didn't need him, they never did, and he didn't need them either. In all honesty he only spoke to them because he had no one else to speak to, but he knew deep down inside that it was not the truth.

He wished he had taken that report from Sami and found Saher's telephone number. But it had been a week or more since he had last seen her and he thought it was probably too late.

He telephoned control and managed to get the telephone number he wanted. He gathered his courage and called the number. "Can I speak to Saher please?"

"No, she's too busy, phone back in the morning."

The woman put the phone down even before Rami could say another word. "You silly bitch..." He shouted loudly, "Nobody puts the phone down on me like that, bastard who the hell..."

In anger, he stormed out of his flat, got into his car and drove away. He passed the house a few times, trying to catch a glimpse of Saher, but he was unsuccessful. Finally he stopped his car not far from the house and sat there watching it. After a while he fell asleep, only to be awakened by a man knocking at his window. "Get out of the car," the man ordered.

Rami looked around and saw another two men standing around his car with their hands in their jacket pockets. "Come on, step out of the car and keep your hands where we can see them."

Rami smiled coldly in the man's face, and stepped out of his car.

"What are you doing here?" the man asked.

"I felt tired so decided to go to sleep as you can see." Rami felt as if he was in control of the situation.

"Don't be funny with me."

"Who are you anyway?"

The man showed him his ID.

"Ah special branch!" Rami muttered. "And I'm not allowed to sleep in the car?"

"Not in this street, you'd better come with us to the station."

"Why? What are the charges?"

"It's a restricted area."

"There's nothing to say it's a restricted area! Don't you want to see my ID?"

The man in charge looked at the other two men. "Put him in the car," he ordered.

By the time Rami tried to move, one of the men had jumped on him and twisted his arm behind his back.

"Get your hands off of me. You're making a big mistake."

"Get him in the car."

"Wait!" Rami shouted. "Look in my back pocket and check my ID."

"We'll have a look at it in the station."

"Let go of my arm. I'm ordering you to look at my ID first, or I'm going to throw you in jail myself."

"Check his ID," one of the other two men said.

"Okay," He freed Rami's arm. He in turn took out his Identification Card out, and walked towards the man who was giving the orders, "What do you think this is?" he said. The man looked at it in a state of disbelief that the young man was from the CIC.

"Sorry Sir."

"Now do you believe me?"

"Sorry sir, it won't happen again."

"Give me your name and address."

"Please sir," he begged. "I have a wife and two kids at home."

"What are you doing here?"

"We're watching this house."

"Why?" Rami asked.

"A new family moved in a few days ago. He's a military personnel from the German Embassy."

"Well then you can do me a favour. I want that Iraqi girl who works there out, with all her belongings. You can charge her with whatever you like and I'll meet you down the road."

"But we can't do that sir, it's against the regulations. We can't enter someone's house if they work in an Embassy."

"Follow me."

Rami rang the bell and waited. After a while the door was opened and a man who appeared foreign spoke.

"Can I help you?"

Rami produced his identification card from the secret police. "Sir, we're looking for a girl called Saher. We believe she has stolen some goods from a shop and we would like her to come with us for questioning."

"But-"

"Sorry sir, but she is unworthy of being in your household. It's not the first time she has done something like that."

The man felt surprised at Rami's good level of English. "Have you got a warrant for her arrest?"

"She isn't under arrest, we're sending her back to her home in the north, but if you wish, I could get one in twenty minutes. I do know how things are done in your country."

The man examined Rami's honest face; he thought it was a terrible waste for someone like him to be involved with secret police, and in such a country.

"Well young man, I do believe you, I myself thought she was a very quiet person and I don't like quiet people much. I always think they're hiding something. I'll go and tell her to pack her bags."

"I'll leave my man here to collect her, if that's alright with you sir?"

"Sure not a problem." And he went back inside the house.

Rami left the scene and went to talk to the other two men waiting by the car.

"When the girl comes out, take her to where the Strand restaurant is and leave her there. Don't harm her, or say a word to her, understood?"

"Yes sir."

"Good work mates."

"Thank you Sir."

He drove away, but a sudden thought crossed his mind. "What if that man were to phone the police station?" He felt childish and irresponsible.

"Car eleven to control."

"Go ahead car eleven."

"Is Sami there?"

"No."

He told her everything that he had done, then added."But I had to do something. I pay more for my cleaner in the flat and she only comes twice a week."

"What you did was terrible. I'll do my best to cover up for you, but if Sami finds out then we're both in trouble. I'll contact the police myself now, just in case, but don't go doing silly things like that again."

They didn't realise that Sami was listening to their conversation at his house. He smiled to himself and said, "I'll help you son."

Rami waited in his car and before long he saw the unmarked police car stop across the road from the Strand. They let Saher out and handed her the suitcase.

He watched her sitting on her suitcase, looking into the distance, and she burst out crying. She put her head between her palms and leant forward in pain, her body shaking as she cried.

He got out of the car and crossed the street.

"Saher!"

She stood up as she saw him walking towards her.

"Saher hi."

She swung her arm back and slapped him as hard as she could. "Thank you very much you...you..." And she burst out crying again. "So you had a hand in this, you fucking bastard. I hate you."

"What?"

She kicked him on the shin. "You lost me my job and for what? I haven't done anything to hurt you, so tell me, why did you do it?"

"I wanted to see you."

"I said I'm not interested. So now you've seen me, why don't you just get lost?"

"Saher, please listen."

"Go away, just go to hell."

"I like you very much."

"Well you have a funny way of showing it."

She sat on her suitcase again and started crying. None of them was bothered about people looking, and the attention.

"What am I going to do now? Where am I going to find another job?"

"I've got another job lined up for you and it pays three times as much as you were getting before."

"Oh yeah! Where?"

"Let's go for a meal and we'll talk about it."

"No, I don't want to be with you, just tell me now." She replied.

"I'm hungry."

"Please let me be...I need nothing from you, or your jobs." She was quiet for a while avoiding his eyes, "Where do you want to go?" She asked suddenly.

"Right here in that restaurant." He pointed in the direction of the Strand.

"I'm not dressed up for anything like that."

"You must have something in your bag; just go to the ladies and change."

"Okay," she said reluctantly.

He was surprised by her sudden change of heart. By the time she joined him, he'd already ordered the drinks and the meal.

"Well talk now," she said.

"Well getting straight to the point, I want you to come and live with me."

"But…"

"Let me finish. I'll give you as much money as you want to send back to your family, also I don't want you to work anymore, but to go to school and educate yourself."

"That's a bit too much! Do you think I can't speak or write? And what right have you got to organise my life?"

"I like you, do you like me?"

She didn't answer him, she felt like killing him at that moment.

Rami smiled. "And you still do."

"No, I hate you."

"I see, well why don't you get out of here then?"

She looked into his face. By then, the waiter was serving them. When he had finished, she decided to answer him. "The food looks good it seems you're out to impress me."

"And?"

"Stop acting like a child. You have another twenty years of growing up to do."

"Ok, have you finished now?"

"I suppose you could give me five Dinars so I can take a taxi to my aunt's house."

Rami put his hand into his pocket and pulled out a bundle of ten Dinar notes. "Here, you might need all of that."

"Very funny, you think everything is a joke, I could kill you, and I really could."

"Well then what's stopping you? Perhaps you still like me just a bit?" he teased.

Their eyes met for the first time that night. She was full of anger and remorse, but the longer she looked into his eyes, the calmer she felt.

She tried to avoid his eyes and look in a different direction, but suddenly she found herself drawn again to them.

"Sorry Mr. Rami, is everything okay?" the waiter interrupted.

"Yes thank you, excellent as usual."

She forgot that she wasn't hungry and ate her food quietly, watching every move he made. Not a word was spoken, she accepted the fact that whatever happened had to happen. She felt safe by his strong presence; to her he was a giant of a man, powerful and a gentleman, even after what he had done to her. She smiled at last.

"What are you smiling about darling?"

"Nothing."

"Come on, tell me."

"Just the way I slapped your face and kicked you."

"You really hurt me."

"I'm sure I did, I wanted to kill you." She stared into his eyes. "That's the end of fighting. I don't want to argue with you anymore"

"It's a deal."

"How much do you know about me?"

"Not enough." He answered.

"Why did you do all this?"

"I like you."

"Tell me the truth."

"I want you to look after me, talk to me, and be with me wherever I go. I just want to sit and talk to you day and night and share my thoughts, my dreams with you. That night we met you touched something deep inside me and I couldn't let you go. You're in my veins, my thoughts, and for the past two weeks I couldn't do anything without your face on my mind. I saw you everywhere I went."

"Thank you, I believe you."

"I come from a respectable family, but I left the family house to be on my own and have my own life. I do get on with my family now and you just happened to come into my life, but I can't get you out of my brain and I feel I could achieve so much with you on my side, except for the fact that we come from different backgrounds."

"You're right."

"Also education."

"But I had no choice, I had to go out to work Rami."

"To support your family, I know. I want you to start reading, and learning. You can take all the exams as a private student if you like, you don't have to go to school. I can help you."

"That has always been my dream."

"Good."

"What can I say? You're the most wonderful man I've ever met. And, what about my aunt and my family?"

"Tell them that you're working for a writer."

"Yes ... okay. What about my family?"

" I'll give you some money to send to them and we'll tackle each problem, one at a time."

She thought about what he'd been saying all night. She felt worried about one thing, but she didn't know how to put it to him.

"Rami, I don't know how to put this, but are you with the police?"

"No, they were friends of mine."

"I see."

"Tomorrow I want two photographs of you and your birth certificate."

"Why?"

"Do as I say, it's a surprise."

"I haven't said yes yet."

She felt trapped, but she always been trapped since the day she was born. But, this time she felt different. Rami wasn't being aggressive or nasty, but on the opposite, he was generous and wanted to give her what she hadn't had.

They left the restaurant. It was funny to her to see someone else carrying her suitcase, usually it was the opposite. They drove to Rami's flat. He opened the front door, put the light on, and announced, "This is home."

"Wow, this is fabulous."

"You like it?"

"I love it. It's beautiful."

"Come, I'll show you your room."

She was somehow surprised that they didn't share a bedroom, yet very glad in another way.

"What do you think?"

"This is so simple, so spacious, and so perfect."

"I am glad you like it. Come and I'll show you the rest."

"This is beautiful. What do you want me to do Rami?"

"Nothing, just be here and look after me. I'm not the easiest person on earth, but I know I have a good heart."

"You carried my suitcase up, and now you're making me a cup of tea, it's after midnight, and I'm totally puzzled and confused, as if I'm on cloud nine."

"Come on, sit down."

"Here we go, I ask, you answer, and I want truthful answers."

"You got yourself a deal." He patted her hand.

"Are you going to use me for prostitution?" She couldn't help laughing when she saw him bursting out himself. It took him a while before he could answer, but even then he was struggling to get his words out.

"No...! I come from a very good family. I hate prostitution because I think its degrading."

"Thank god for that. Do you want to use me until you get fed up with me?"

"No...I will let you use me. You are free to do whatever you like, whenever you like."

"Do you want me to cook for you?"

"Yes...but I am very fussy, I also like everything done properly, and I love cooking myself too."

"Not my favourite thing to do, but I need your help here."

"Fine." He paused, and continued, "I have Um Ali who comes and cleans for me twice a week, and she treats me like a son. I also tidy up here and there myself."

"I am frightened, I am shaking, and if it's alright with you I'd like to lock myself in the room when I am asleep."

"I have no problem with that."

"Why are you so pleasant to me?"

"I think it's bed time."

"Yes, and I am exhausted physically and mentally."

It was a sleepless night for both of them. Rami had long given up on planning for the future and ended up in his study writing, or trying to write, but his mind was pre-occupied with hundreds of different thoughts. Saher turned from one side of the bed onto the other, she just couldn't get comfortable.

It was not the arrangement she had planned on to be living with a man, it might be accepted in other countries, but not in Iraq, and not even the modern civilised Baghdad. She knew well she will be called all the names under the sun for her action by family and friends.

"I can't sleep." She said as she joined him in his study.

"Nor can I." He raised his head then handed her a book.

"Read this, it's a lovely story."

She sat on the couch with her feet tucked in underneath reading. Over an hour later, she was asleep on the couch, while he put his head on his desk and fell asleep too.

- - - - - - - - -

Three days later, they flew to Beirut and booked into a hotel by the Roshah. Saher had never been near the sea before. They stood on the balcony together watching the sunset. The sky was a mixture of oranges and purples sending her heart racing. She wished Rami would put his arms around her at that minute, but he never did.

"It's so beautiful Rami...Oh God thank you for bringing me here."

"Let's go out," said Rami. "We have lots of shopping to do. Beirut never sleeps, but some of the shops do!"

"Ok."

During the shopping expedition Rami never questioned a price or make. If he liked it he simply bought it. He insisted that Saher spend some money on herself.

Before long they were struggling out of a taxi in front of their hotel. Even the doorman laughed. "Have you bought the city sir?"

"I think I have, not finished yet."

"Leave it here and I'll get the boy to bring it to your room."

"Thank you," Rami said as he tipped the doorman generously.

"How much did you give him?" Saher .

"Why?"

"I'm just asking, you seem very generous with your money. I was told never to pay the price advertised in the shops, but you did. And now, you've just given that man twenty Liras."

"In the shops I pay what I want to pay by the tills, and for the doorman, well you'll see how we'll be looked after for the next few days."

"So you never paid the full amount for the clothes."

"No I didn't, but I won't stand there knocking him by half, and settle on three quarters of the price. That is so common in my opinion, although some people might enjoy it. I am starving...!" He announced as he opened the door to their two bedroom apartment.

"So am I."

"Get dressed please, and we'll go out, I'll just get in the shower."

"Can't we stay here in the hotel and have something to eat."

"Yes, we'll do that."

That evening Rami sat proudly in the hotel restaurant admiring Saher in her new dress. She wore little makeup, but she attracted everyone's attention as they entered.

He ordered Arak for himself, while she had a glass of white wine. The hotel was famous for the variety of Mazza brought to the table, in all they had forty-four small plates with an incredible selection of delicious foods.

"Beirut is fascinating," said Rami. "It's like a woman traditionally dressed, fully covered from head to toe, but when she takes it off, she's wearing a mini skirt."

"What a comparison!"

"You see Baghdad combines old and modern. They're so different."

The conversation continued. Rami had the gift of keeping her amused; make her laugh, and making her feel important. He never looked elsewhere while he was with her; he gave her his full attention. Yet, for the few days that they had been together he never kissed her, slept with her, or made any suggestions and they slept in separate rooms, even when they were away from home. She felt that Rami was living in a different world to anyone else, she felt so close to him yet so far away. She was surprised to find out that he had businesses, and had so much to occupy his mind, but he had never for once failed in pleasing her, and he was always there for her.

Rami took her to visit many different parts of Beirut, including museums and historic places, as he had such a vast knowledge of it all. He introduced her to different varieties of food, and showed her the proper way to hold her knife and fork, and she did exactly as he had told her. She thrilled him, as being a fast learner. In a way she was frightened of him although he never for once had lost control, or even looked at her in anger, but still she was afraid to cross his path. He gave her the impression that he was very interested in her, she was jolly when he tried to show her how to do certain things, she realized that he was only doing it for her own good.

On the second day he took her to the world famous Lebanon Casino, with a non-stop musical show. Never in a million years would she thought of seeing anything like this.

For the short period that they were in Lebanon, Saher was overwhelmed by the respect the people had shown towards him. Wherever they went, they welcomed him with open arms. , and they went out of their way to please him. She felt like she was always in his shadow. Since then, she had started to watch every move that he made, when to smile, and how to smile, when to talk, and when to keep quiet and laugh. She was sure that he was not taught all those things, but the way he was brought up in his high class society. He made all the decisions, she let him do it, and enjoyed it, and not once had she felt that he had made the wrong one, his word was a law not to be broken, after all, wasn't that what attracted her to him.

As the days went by and as she got to know him better, she felt like she was falling in love with him, but at times she questioned what she was doing there in a strange place, lying in strange bed, next door to a strange man? Who never stopped talking, but never talked about the subjects that she wanted to know.

She wouldn't dare question him, even when it concerned her: she was happy to let him take charge of her destiny.

The day they returned to their flat, she decided to stamp her authority. She realised that she must set rules that suited her.

She wrote out a shopping list and asked him to go and buy the things for her. She felt powerful and superior when he got back, and she told him to leave her alone, because she didn't like being watched while she was cooking. She told him to go and write, as he needed the money after the way he had been spending it. He left the kitchen and she smiled to herself feeling that she belonged to that place for the first time, but soon she felt sad again, as the thought of not owning anything around her crossed her mind.

"Dinner is ready Rami," she shouted.

"Coming."

They sat next to each other at the small table he loved in his kitchen that he had shared so many times with others.

"You're a good cook," Rami said, rather impressed with her presentation.

"Thank you."

She thought, 'He only wants a servant, and a cook, that's why he's got me here.'

"What's wrong? Why aren't you eating?"

"I just don't feel hungry."

Rami put his knife and fork down and pushed the plate away from him. They both stared at the wasted effort in front of them.

"What's bothering you?"

Saher played with her knife, pushing pieces of food around her plate. Her mind worked hard to try to find the exact words to tell him how confused she felt. She didn't want her words to sound harsh; she wanted to be diplomatic like him and say the right words, in the right context. She was grateful for all he had done for her.

"I feel like a very cheap whore! I feel trapped, as if I'm an object. You tell me to buy and I buy, you ask me to walk and I do, you say we go to Lebanon, and we do, you say laugh, and I laugh, you ask me to enjoy myself, and I enjoy myself. What else do you want me to do? I don't know whether I am going or coming, it's like an adult game played by children. Not once have you held my hand, in the street or in private, unless we're crossing the street. Mind you, you did hold my hand that first week that I met you. Not once have you got up from your seat and held me close to you, or reassured me, or thanked me for being with you. Not once have you showed me that I'm a beautiful woman, who's in love with you. Rami, I'm trying hard to please you, but I feel like I'm failing you each time. Do you understand, or is my way of talking too low class, so high class people don't understand? I don't know how I got myself mixed up with all this. Who are you? They say that money doesn't grow on trees, but the way you have spent it since the day I met you is beyond imagination. I don't know what the hell I'm saying! I'll pack my bag and go. I doubt you want to see me again after everything I've just said."

Rami smiled, pulled the plate back towards him and started eating.

"Well?" she said, looking at him with amazement.

"You have a mouth, and you can actually talk."

"Don't laugh at me please." Her eyes filled up.

"I'm not, but that was a fantastic speech."

"I give up with you."

"Why don't you join me and eat?"

She lifted the fork to her mouth and chewed her food slowly. "I feel like saying no to you, but I'm hungry."

She wondered what was wrong with him! How could he sit there and pretend as if nothing had been said. If she hit him hard on his face would he respond to her, or just carry on eating.

"This food is the best I've had for a long time," said Rami.

"Thank you but-"

"You have the hands of an angel to cook a meal like this."

"But...?"

"Eat first and we'll talk later."

"No, now."

"There is no need to shout."

Rami was trying hard to find an answer, but should there be an answer? Or an explanation? Why couldn't she accept the changes in her life?

"Is that all you could say? We'll talk later."

"No, we'll talk now, as you wanted."

"If I'm going to live here, I want to know what I'm getting myself involved with. I don't want to get myself in trouble. I come from a small village and a small family, from a biggish tribe. If they find out that I'm living here with you, they'll kill me for honour, even if they were my sixth cousins. Please tell me everything."

"Ask me and I'll answer you."

"What do you do?"

"I'm a student, writer, and I have a little business. Happy now?"

"Not yet. Are you with the police?"

"No, but special type and that's top secret, understand? Not a word about this to a living soul."

"Okay I won't talk. Are you in the Baath Party?"

"No."

"Good, tell me more."

"I'm mad about you. I want to see you happy."

"And-"

"I love watching you; you have this simple undeveloped attitude to life. You're clever and you play at it, but I found it fascinating and I still do. You're still naive about lots of things and that's not an insult, but it's in your makeup as a woman. To me you have just been born, untouched and unspoiled. You're something else and I'm trying the best I can to introduce you to this new life, just in case you face some unpleasant experiences one day, and you might find yourself in an unanswerable situation. It's hard to explain."

"Try! I don't understand a thing you've just said."

"Being with me, you'll meet different types of people, for example writers, publishers, businessmen, all classes of people. Our society, my dear, is very materialistic, and very critical about education. Without it you are nothing. My goal is different to anyone else's and I want someone like you to share everything with me."

"I know you're trying to explain everything to me, but I can't concentrate. I don't understand."

"All I'm trying to say is that I like you, and I want you to have more education to protect you against our changing surroundings."

"Okay."

"Are you happy now?"

"I think so." But she was still unconvinced.

Rami finished his meal and left the kitchen.

"Rami..!" Saher shouted.

"Yes."

"I love you."

"I'm going to bed, I feel really tired," he said.

"Ok, I'll stay up for few minutes, good night."

"God bless."

She sat on the sofa thinking again. He'd never asked her to sleep with him and she respected him for it, but she felt as if this was abnormal. That only made her want him more, but she wasn't going to jump into sexual activity. She knew what her family was like. She had to be a virgin on the night she got married, so her mother could show that small piece of white cloth to her relatives and friends with her blood on it. She wondered if Rami's family were the same. She herself did not believe in all that, but why should she go against the family traditions and anger them?

She hated schooling when she was a little girl, but at that moment, she felt determined to study as hard as possible so Rami felt proud of her. She realised there was a big gap between the two of them and she was determined to close it. She had to come up in life in order for him to be able to introduce her to his family and she couldn't wait for that day to come. With that thought she got up and went to her bedroom.

CHAPTER THIRTY THREE

OIL was found in Iraq around the nineteen hundreds. During the First World War, in 1917, control of Iraqi oil reserves was considered a priority to most oil companies, especially British. In 1925 the Iraqi government was forced to sign an agreement granting a concession to explore oil until 2000. It decreed that the company would remain British and its chairman would remain British. The fact was that Iraqis were going to receive royalties for their own oil. A single number percentage was given to the government, until it was increased to twelve per cent under General Qassim.

In 1972 the Iraqi government decided to nationalise the oil industry, giving the country full control. The eyes of the world focused on Iraq and the wealth it was going to generate for its people. Companies from the Soviet Union, America, Europe, Japan and many other countries fought for contracts for building and developing. Factories, roads, bridges, processing plants, agriculture and leisure compounds were given to foreign companies. Labour was imported from various Arab countries, especially Egypt and the Far East.

This created an incredible shortage in the housing market, sending the price of land and houses to a new high. Luckily, the three partners, Rami, Nabil and Khalid saw the potential early and decided to buy a large plot of land not far from where the shops were. They hoped to develop it into either luxury houses or apartments. And when the government advertised that they would be selling more land for houses seven kilometres in the south of Baghdad, near the military base, they bought a plot each.

They stretched themselves financially, which created a bad atmosphere between the three of them. Although the three businesses were doing extremely well and all the shops and the apartments were rented out, they were struggling to pay back their loans.

They sat in their office talking about their future plans and for the first time they felt that they might lose everything. They were in serious trouble.

"I hardly spent any of my money. You can have it all and pay me later," Said Rami.

"That isn't a solution Rami and you know it." Nabil said.

"I have enough to keep us afloat for the next few months and I also have savings and money in Lebanon from the book. You can have that by all means, and I will go and get it. I need an excuse to get out of the country."

"You amaze me," said Nabil. "You throw your money around as if it means nothing to you. Don't you think this will put us in an awkward position? We're partners; we're not leeches depending on you."

"How long have we known each other?"

"For years and years," Khalid answered.

"And do we trust each other? I already know what the answer is, so let's get on with it."

"Rami, we have a massive plot of land which we need to develop. If we don't the government will take it away, as that's the conditions set on this plot. We can't even afford to pay the architect."

"Damn I didn't realise, sorry."

"Don't say sorry."

"I'd hoped to build houses, playgrounds, shops or a little complex. There isn't one like it in the country."

"This is Baghdad, Rami, not any European city. We need to educate our people first. If we give them a playground, they'll still play in the street dodging cars. There's no fun in anything else."

"How long have we got?"

"Two years and it'll cost us thousands, which we haven't got, plus we need a quick return on our investment. We can't afford to wait for maybe another two years until all the building is finished. Most contractors want some type of money in advance."

"That's a huge project and will cost us everything," Khalid said.

"Rami, what's the matter with you?"

"Think of a way. We can't wait for two years, then another two or three until we make our money."

They looked into each other's faces, wanting to get out of their commitment towards the project, but none of them had the courage to speak up.

"How much do you think this building is worth?" Rami asked.

"You can't sell that; it's our baby."

"I know, but what if we sell that land with the planning permission, get the money and then do what we like with it?"

"I agree," Khalid said without giving the idea a second thought.

"Me too," said Nabil. "I was afraid we were gambling with our future and everything we'd worked for. Adding to that, the whole country is in short supply of building materials. Do you know how much we can get for the land now?"

"No, but more than we paid for it," said Rami. "I'll phone Leila's father, and ask him."

"Do that please, he knows the game better than anyone else."

Rami spoke to Leila's father on the telephone for a few minutes, then he came back.

"Will you take that stupid smile off your face and tell us what he said?" Khalid demanded.

"If the land was a small plot, below fifteen-hundred square meters, we could sell it tomorrow, but as it's much bigger, it'll take longer."

"Is that all he said? How much can we get for it?"

"Oh, you want to know if we'll make any money out of it?"

"Yes!" Khalid screamed. Nabil laughed. He hadn't seen Rami enjoying torturing Khalid for a long time. It was like heavy weight had been lifted off his shoulders.

"He said we can get at least four times as much, and he might know someone, but he'll take one per cent off the deal."

"That's fantastic," said Nabil. "We could pay off what we owe on this building, and still have some money to play with."

"Yeah and we can start minting money again, buy houses, do them up nicely and sell them," said Khalid.

"What about cars? All the people we know who work in different Embassies, only use their cars for few months then they get rid of them. We could buy them, do them up and sell them straight away. We'd make a few thousand on each car." Khalid suggested.

"At last you've started thinking again," said Rami.

"Cheeky bastard…"

"I am going to tell my dad you called me that."

"Funny man."

"I'll go to Lebanon this week to get my money," said Rami. "At least by the time the plot is sold, we're safe."

- - - - - - - - -

Rami went back to his flat that afternoon, "Saher, where are you?"

"Here, in the bedroom."

"What are you doing?"

"Cleaning."

"Didn't Um Ali come today?"

"Yes, but I felt like cleaning your bedroom, and she isn't a young lady any more. I can't see her doing this job for much longer; she can hardly straighten her back."

"Poor woman, I'll see if I can get my friend, doctor Samir, to take a look at her. Anyway, I'm going to Lebanon, do you want to come?"

"No, I'd rather stay here."

"I am flying instead of taking the car."

"I've got too much studying to do."

"Well I'm only going for three days. I'm flying on the ten o'clock flight tomorrow morning."

Rami did intend to only stay in Lebanon for three days, but once he was there he decided that he needed more time. He spent a lot of time with his publishers, as they were trying to translate his book into different languages, and he was also waiting for new music releases to arrive into the country.

Saher could not motivate herself to do anything. She felt lost without him. Even though when he was around he spent most of his time away from her, but she knew then that he was there, she still felt safe and secure. But after three days had passed, and there was no sign of him, she began to worry. For a period she welcomed the high fence that they built between them, but at that moment she wished he was there next to her. She had hundreds of thoughts floated around her mind, driving her into panic that something had happened to him.

She went round the flat in circles thinking of what to do. She tried to open his desk in the study, but stopped herself, 'What if he had left me?' She thought, 'How am I supposed to stay here? I just have to pack my bags and go.' By the time she walked into her bedroom, 'No he wouldn't do that to me he's not that type of person.'

She looked at the piece of paper in her hand. He had left her an address for her to contact him in case of an emergency. On the morning of the fifth day that he was away, she seriously thought there was something bad going on. She decided to send him a telegram.

When she walked into the post office, she felt more confused than ever before, and hesitant about whether she was doing the right thing. She sat on a wooden chair at the post office totally baffled as she ripped yet another piece of paper. She felt out of place, unsecured, lonely and foolish. She tried to stop herself shaking, but couldn't, and she wouldn't dare move from her spot where she sat, in case her legs wouldn't carry her.

"Can I help you my dear?" A woman asked her. Saher turned around and stared straight at the woman "Can I help?" she asked again.

"Thank you, I am..." Saher could not say another word. The woman sat next to her. Saher felt like crying, but stopped herself.

"My husband..." The words rang in her ears. "My husband left the country five days ago on a business trip and he was supposed to return two days ago, but he didn't. I have his address here, but I don't know what to write in the telegram, I don't want to worry him over nothing."

"Men! I know the feeling dear, they're all the same. Why don't you write 'miss you very much' or something like that."

"Yes, I think I will, thank you."

Saher left the post office, feeling more relaxed than before. She decided to go shopping. She thought Rami would come home soon, and she wanted to cook him something special, she looked in her handbag, and saw that bundle of money that he had left for her, how thoughtful he was, she thought, 'Oh Rami, if only you know how much I miss you.' She cried inside.

She spent the morning wandering around the shops, buying different selections of food and looking at other things she needed for the apartment. That afternoon, she prepared the meal and phoned the airport to find out what time the flights were due back from Lebanon. She looked at her watch and realised that there were only six hours to go until she would see Rami again.

She cleaned the whole flat again, which did not need cleaning, but she wanted to kill some time by keeping herself busy.

She looked at her watch again, noting that there were still another three hours to wait at least. She looked around, but nothing else needed doing, so she set the dining table, and took a bath.

She sat in front of the mirror in Rami's bedroom. She liked using his dressing table as his room was much lighter than hers. She styled her hair, and decided to do it differently than usual. When she finished, she stood up and looked at herself in the full size mirror. She let the towel wrapped around her drop to the floor, and studied her body in the mirror. She ran her hands down the side of her breasts, and down to her thigh. She smiled to herself with satisfaction. Never before had the thought of a man touching her crossed her mind, never before had she stood in front a mirror examining herself, but this time was different, she knew deep down that Rami was for keeps.

She walked back to her room, feeling free with no clothes on. She felt as if she actually owned the flat. She looked in her mirror and decided to put some make-up on. Rami had told her that he liked a bit here and there. Then she dressed up, went to the living room and sat there watching the television.

Time passed by, and she woke up after the television programmes had finished. It was now gone midnight, so she switched the television off and went to her bedroom. A feeling of loneliness overcame her, the flat seemed to be ghostly quiet, and big. She took her clothes off, but shivers went up her spine, as she looked at her bed. She felt as if everything around her was out of place and unfamiliar. She went into Rami's bedroom, pulled the bed covers back and laid on the bed. She wanted to cry, but the smell of the bed gave her that little security that she was missing. She pulled the covers on top of her.

"I love you Rami," She said and on that note she fell asleep.

At just after two in the morning, Rami walked into the flat and smiled as he noticed the dining table. He was hungry, but also very tired from travelling, so he went to his bedroom and saw Saher was asleep in his bed. He was overwhelmed; he felt so much love for her sleeping so peacefully in his bed.

"I miss you too darling," he whispered.

She moved and slowly opened her eyes. She couldn't believe it when she saw him sitting on the edge of the bed. At first she thought she was dreaming, but then she grabbed him and hugged him as hard as she possibly could, "Oh Rami, I missed you so much. Don't ever leave me."

Before he could say a word, she planted a kiss on his lips; their first. Tears were running down her face and she didn't want to let go of him. She pressed herself even nearer to him. He gently pushed her away. "What's the matter Saher?"

She put her hands around his face and stared into his tired eyes. "I missed you, I."

"Hush, I'm here, don't say another word."

Their lips touched again and she put her hands around him once more. She knew then that he was hers, as he pulled her even closer to him.

"Do you want anything to eat?" She asked him, after a while.

"No...I don't think that I have the energy for that."

He took his clothes off and got into the bed beside her. She moved closer to him and he noticed that she was completely naked as well. He put his arm under her head and she laid her head on his shoulder, her arm across his body, with her leg on top of his legs. Everything fell into place, and everything felt natural, as if they had been sleeping in that position for years.

"Thank God I'm home."

"You're late. I was really worried. I phoned all the airways to check the arrivals of the planes from Lebanon."

"I came back by car."

"But you didn't take the car with you!"

"I bought another car. I had so much stuff with me, it was impossible to bring it all back on a plane, that's why I had to stay for couple of extra days. I was delayed by customs for over two hours to fill in hundreds of forms, in the end I lost my temper and showed them my ID and I got through. You should have seen their faces when they saw it. I had an officer with me to drive back to Baghdad and I went to the shop first to empty the car, then I came straight here."

"Did you get my telegram?"

"Yes, as I was leaving."

"I missed you."

"I missed you more."

They held each other tight as they felt relieved at last. They could not carry on sleeping in different rooms any more.

"From now on I am sleeping in here," Saher announced.

"Good, you have such a warm comforting body."

"Oh no, I forgot to put anything on," She said, suddenly realising that she was naked. They both laughed.

"I like it this way!"

She giggled and moved her head to his chest. Her fingers wandered around the triangle of spiky hair. "Did you behave yourself Rami?"

"Yes, I didn't go out with any woman."

"Do you usually?"

"Yes."

"I don't mind so long as you tell me."

He smiled. "I don't need another woman."

"As long as I know that you're coming back to me at the end of the day."

They were quiet for a minute or two. They wanted each other so badly, but neither of them was prepared to make the first move.

"Rami, do you want to sleep?"

"Not really, I just want to talk. It has been all work, work, work for the past five days. Thank God I have a day off tomorrow, so I can have a lie in."

He ran his hand over her body, smooth like marble, and warm. Never in his life had he wanted anyone so much. He cupped her breast, it was firm and round, and her nipple was erect. She did not object. Instead she planted a few small kisses under his chin.

"Have you had many girls?"

"Yes, and sex?"

He did not speak, but she already knew the answer. She did not feel jealous, in fact she was proud to be with an experienced man.

"I never thought that holding a man's little boy would be so comforting."

"And I never thought you would come out with a statement like that." He laughed as she rolled on top of him.

She took a deep breath. "I love you so much." She laughed and planted a kiss on his chest. "I like being naked. Today, after I had my shower, I walked naked from one room to the other and I loved it so much. I could never do that before. I dressed in front of the mirror, watching my body, moving and I

293

felt as if I had been born again. I was brought up to think that it's a big sin to feel our bodies. When I had my monthly period, my mother used to tell me to walk on the other side of the road if we came across man, in case he smelt me and chased after me, would you believe that? And if a man shook my hand I had to go and wash it straight away because my mother used to say that we didn't know where his hand had been. That's the way I was brought up and I'm not ashamed at all."

"And now?"

"Since I came to Baghdad a year ago, I've changed a hell of a lot, and since I came here last month, I've changed even more. I've started to know myself better and I've learnt many things by watching you. I'd love to be naked if you allow me, as for it's the first step to being honest with myself. I hate clothes, but I have to wear them outside. Do you think that I've gone crazy?"

"No, not at all, you have created a revolution in your life."

"I touched myself today for the first time in my life and I enjoyed it. It was fantastic and I can't see that there's anything wrong with it."

"You are so innocent, like a baby discovering new things. And I hate clothes too. I like to be naked whenever I can, let my body breathe."

Rami thought of Farrah. Saher reminded him of her so much. But, he did not want to be reminded by anyone else at that moment.

"You have so much flair about you, you do put on an impressive performance when you are with a woman, is that why you had so many? Tell me the truth."

Rami pulled her close and kissed her mouth.

"One day, my man, you'll teach me everything."

"Let's go to sleep. I have a lot of surprises for you in the morning."

"Good night."

"God bless."

"Sweet dreams."

"Yes…With your body next to mine, but of course."

She fell asleep, but he stayed awake, staring at the ceiling. He had been looking at that ceiling for four years, and had never once thought about changing it, but he decided to do so in the morning. He thought that all the coloured lights were not meant for a man who wanted to settle into a relation with someone like Saher. He turned round and looked at her and felt happy to be there.

The next morning he was awoken by the sound of the shower so he went into the bathroom. Saher was in the cubical and he knocked on the door.

"If I close my eyes can I join you?"

"Yes," she said laughing and she opened the door and pulled him inside. "Now turn your back."

She picked the shampoo bottle, and poured it over his head. "Lower yourself, I can't reach." She was still laughing.

"What have you done? You emptied the whole bottle on me."

"Stop acting like a child, and shut up."

"Saher, careful, I've got shampoo in my eyes."

"Turn around and let me see." She washed his face.

He opened his eyes with a big smile on his face. She hit him happily on his shoulder, "You are a cheat."

Rami looked at her face then down to her body. "You're beautiful."

"And you're not bad yourself." Their bodies touched and they kissed each other for a long time, as his hand touched every part of her. In the end she had to forcefully pull away from him.

"Come on Rami, let me wash you, and stop getting excited."

"God I can eat you all over."

"Turn around please my precious one." She teased him, "I'll wash your back for you."

She surprised herself on how well she handled the situation, she did not feel shy, and she enjoyed their intimacy, he was hers, and why should she feel shy?

"Turn around now." She looked long in his face, "You are a beautiful man." She hugged him close to her. It was a moment of complete fulfilment, and she was afraid to let go of him.

"Thank you."

"Do you want me?"

"Terribly..."

"You'll have to wait."

After the shower they sat together on the sofa.

"When are you going to Lebanon again?" Saher asked.

"Three weeks time, why?"

"I'm coming with you."

"I am going to fly there, and back the following day."

"So? Are you taking me?"

"Yes ...fine."

"I can't go on the pill yet because doctors here don't give it to unmarried women, so I've got to go to Lebanon."

While she prepared breakfast, Rami went to the car and struggled back with three large suitcases. "Saher, please help."

"Oh my God, what have you been doing?"

"Take them to the bedroom."

Rami laid two of the suitcases on the bed. "Close your eyes." She did. "Now open." By this time he had opened the two suitcases. "And this is all for you my love."

"No Rami." She sat on the bed looking first at the suitcases then at him, her eyes filling with tears. "Why do you have to do things like that?"

"I like my woman to look the best in the whole country."

"But I can't buy you anything in return."

"Don't worry about me I have bought a lot for myself too."

She took out one piece at a time. He had bought her everything, from underwear, to dresses, skirts, shirts and lots of pairs of shoes. The tears trickled down her face.

"I've never had so much in my whole life."

"What's the matter darling? Why do you look so sad?"

"It's just my family. I often think of how poor all seven of them are. The money you have spent here would feed them for a year." She dried her eyes then hurried towards him and kissed him.

"I would love to meet your family." Rami said to her surprise.

"Thank you Rami."

She returned to the bed to take more clothes out of the suitcase. At the bottom there was a small black box, she looked at him, trying to question his smiling face but instead he said.

"That's for you too," said Rami. "Come on, open it."

Inside the box a diamond ring shone and her eyes opened and looked at him. "No, no more."

"But it's your engagement ring." He also handed her an envelope. "And this is for you as well."

She opened the envelope and inside there was an air ticket to Mosul, where her parents lived on the outskirts of the city.

"Oh Rami." She put her head down and cried. It had been almost a year and a half since she had last seen her family.

"Well I thought you'd better show your mother the ring."

"Can I go next Monday?"

"Yes, but why Monday?"

"It's my little sister's birthday. It'll be a nice surprise."

"Okay."

"I might stay for a couple of days or longer."

"That's fine with me."

He felt as happy as she did. "Are you going to tell your parents about us?"

"No, nobody should know yet, because of my family's customs and traditions. If they ever find out that we're living together they'd kill both of us. It's the honour of our tribe."

"How about if I go and shoot every one of them first?" He teased her.

"I know that you hate me being from a poor family and so do I. I hate being uneducated, but I want you; not for your money, but for your looks, your soft heart, your thoughtfulness, and because you make me laugh. I want you now more than ever before and more than anyone else in the world. It's like a challenge; a fight I have to win. I need to please you and make you happy."

"You don't have to fight to get me; you have me already, but fight for…"

"I love you, Rami, and nothing in the world will ever change that.""You can have the ring back."

"No, I don't take things back after giving them away. We're still engaged and that's that. If you pass all your exams in two years you'll be in university. Do it for yourself and not for me. I want to show the whole world that you did it. I don't want anything to come in between us; people might talk, others will stare, and the rest will try to stop us, and trap us…that's the way of our society."

"I'm not afraid of anyone, I trust you, and I know you trust me, so come here and give your woman a kiss." She looked into his smiling eyes. "And no more spending money like that, promise me."

"Ok."

While she busied herself again, his mind wandered off. He felt frightened of the unknown. His happiness might not last long as he had learnt that nothing lasts forever, just like Leila, Farrah and Nadia.

'What the hell am I going to do with it?' He walked into the kitchen, and repeated his statement again.

"Do with what? Have you gone crazy?"

"My degree when I get it!"

"Are you feeling alright?"

He hugged her and kissed her, and left her standing there giggling, while he went to his study, and closed the door behind him.

She was aware from the first day she moved in that, when Rami was in his study, he was not to be disturbed; she herself got her books out and started studying. But she found it hard to concentrate, after the memory of the night before, and what Rami had done for her. At last she managed to dismiss all her thoughts, and got on with her work.

A few hours later, Rami walked out from his room. The look on his face said it all, he was pleased with himself.

"I can eat a horse now, I am starving."

"You have to wait five more minutes."

"I've been waiting for a month." He teased her.

She gave him a seductive look, "And you'll have to wait a bit longer for that." That night Saher gave him a fashion show of everything he had bought her. She showed him herself wearing her new dresses, skirts, underwear, shorts, and everything else.

"Thank you, thank you for everything, I feel as I am living in a fantasy world."

"But you are."

Three days later, Saher left Baghdad to go and see her family in the North of the Country. Rami gave her extra money to spend as he knew she wanted to treat her family to a few gifts.

When she was there she realised the huge gap between her family and Rami and she felt like an outsider to both. She no longer belonged to her family, yet she was trying hard to live up to Rami's standards. She felt as if she was lost between two worlds. She knew there was no way of mixing the two sides together. She would never let her family attend the wedding, if there ever be one, as they wouldn't understand and they wouldn't fit in. Rami wouldn't be able to believe his eyes when he saw her father buying bones from the local butcher so he could carve off the little bit of meat and boil the rest for the taste of a meaty meal. She thought the two sides would never understand the social difference between them. She forgot how poor her family was after spending more than a year away from them. She almost forgot what they were like; their habits and customs, and that she once belonged to them. Even if she sent them more money her father would spend it on showing off in front of the neighbours and the men in the village, rather than spending it on the family. She was not rejecting them, but she could not go back to that life. In fact, she could no longer wait to go to Baghdad, to her man, to life.

She was going back more willing to change her life than ever before. She did not stop telling them how to do things differently, how to cook, how to eat, how to wash after every meal. And now, she was going back for peace of mind.

Back in Baghdad she was determined to study hard for her first set of examinations. She influenced Rami to work harder. She was jolly and happy. She watched after him like a hawk, she chose what he should wear every day.

She made him go and see his father at the factory to ask for his job back. Saher saw him as a man full of power, imagination, and determination, and she found a place for herself next to him, and she took it.

She watched him get into bed every night absolutely exhausted, but he never complained, as she always managed to comfort him and relieve his aches and pains.

They never forgot their friends either. They made time every week to visit them. Saher made sure she never let Rami down and everyone liked her, as she knew where she stood, she knew when to speak, when to laugh, and loved showing her love to him in front of others.

Every week she handed him the shopping list. He always gave her extra money. She banked what she had not spent. Rami used to laugh on how mean she was, it tickled him when she switched the lights off behind her, or the television when there was nothing worth watching, just to save electricity. He was living the time of his life, he couldn't wish for better harmony between him and Saher.

CHAPTER THIRTY FOUR

THE day her examinations ended, Rami asked Saher if she would like to go out for a meal to celebrate.

"No, I'm tired, plus it'll cost us a fortune."

"But we haven't been out for a meal for a long time."

She realised apart of the time when they went to Lebanon, the only other time was the night she moved in with him.

"Rami, why can't we stay in here and I'll cook us something nice."

"I insist, we're only young, we need to go out and enjoy life."

"Don't be such a child."

He was disappointed and angry. "Look my lady, I work hard, study hard, and I make more money than many people in this city. I have the right to spend it the way I like, if you don't mind."

"Do what you like and go out where you want. Maybe you'll meet a better woman than me."

"I've had enough of this, you're running my life and I have no say in anything any more." He felt it was time to moan.

"Do you want me to leave? Is that it? You're bored with me and now it's time for a change."

They had few disagreements in the past, but never did she threaten him of leaving or ending their relationship.

"What's wrong Saher?"

"I can't tell you."

"Why?"

"Because I'm ashamed of myself and you'll kill me."

"I'll kill you, but come on out with it."

"No..."

"Don't tell me then."

"I stole money from you."

Rami looked at her in amazement. That morning when he went to the bank, he was shocked to see how much money she'd saved for him in such a short period. He had been praising her in front of Nabil and Khalid about how organised she was, but there was one thing he really hated and that was stealing.

"How? When?"

"Last week."

"Tell me."

"Nabil gave me the envelope with the money in it, as usual, and I took two-hundred Dinars and sent it to my parents for Christmas."

"Is that it?" He laughed.

"Well I had to send them something."

"Come here." He gave her a big hug. "You're a real child sometimes, my money is your money."

"But I've got no right to send them that much in one go. I send them enough every month."

"Hey you actually sent them four-hundred because I sent them another two on your behalf."

"You have no right." And she kissed him, "You are truly a wonderful man, thank you, but why did you do it?"

"How about tonight…?"

"Whatever you say, I can't refuse you anything, can I?"

She was overjoyed and overwhelmed, she rushed to the bedroom. She had a small cry to herself, she was happy, and her man never forgets anything, except her birthday, that particular day, but at least he was taking her out for a meal. She would tell him when they got back, she said to herself.

She took a shower and sat facing the mirror, she did not realize that Rami was standing by the door watching her, "You are one lucky girl." She said loudly to herself. Rami smiled, and went to have his shower.

After his shower Rami laid on the bed with a towel wrapped around him and watched her styling her hair. She had the gift in her hands as a stylist, and applying make-up on her face. The towel that she had wrapped around her fell to the floor, but she did not make any effort to pick it up. Rami watched her naked body, as her breasts moved with each and every movement of her arms, her thighs as she put one over the other, her bare feet, and neatly painted toenails. He imagined what it would be like to make love to that body. He might have felt it with his hands on odd occasions, but he had never made love to her, even though she was willing, he could not find any explanation for it inside him.

"What do you think?" She asked.

"Beautiful, perfect… come here."

"No…You'll spoil my hair."

He jumped out of his bed and stood behind her. "You look something else tonight," he said and he bent down and kissed her shoulders.

"Oh that's nice."

"Do you want more?"

"No because we are going out, and don't try and change your mind now."

He laughed, and got dressed quickly. "How do I look?" It was his turn to ask the question.

"You will do for tonight." She giggled.

He waited for her in the living room, it was nearly eight at night, "Take your time why don't you, there is no need to hurry." He shouted sarcastically.

"I am coming."

Rami was pinned down to the floor as she walked in. His heart beat faster than usual. She was wearing a long dress in midnight blue and as she spun around he noticed it had low-cut back open almost to her waist and the front was studded with small beads.

"How do I look Rami?"

"Stunning."

"Really?"

"Yes really. I've never seen you looking as beautiful as you do tonight. Except, you need something to wear around your neck."

"But I haven't got anything, oh...I'll go and wear something else, I won't be long."

"There is no need."

He took a longish black box out of his pocket and handed it to her.

"Happy birthday!"

"Oh Rami…"

"Come on, no tears or else you'll spoil your make-up. Now open the box."

Her mouth opened at the sight of the necklace. It was made of gold, a fox's tail design and it boasted a flowery design made of sapphire and diamonds.

"Turn around and I'll put it on you," said Rami.

She was lost for words, as she looked in the mirror with flickers of light reflected by the diamonds. She turned round, and planted a long kiss on his lips.

"I do look different," said Saher. "You've changed me completely."

"Yes apart from two things."

"What?"

"Put your back straight, and cover a bit of your breast, I don't want everyone to see what is mine." And he smiled lovingly to her.

She kissed him on the cheek. "I love you. Thank you very much."

"Ok ... let's go."

She adjusted her dress, "How about now?"

"Terrific."

"For your eyes only…" She said softly.

Suddenly Rami felt as if ice water had been poured over him and the smile left his face.

"What's the matter Rami?"

"Nothing, you look fantastic, now come on, let's go."

"Ok, just give me a few seconds to do my make-up."

For the past few weeks none of the past had crossed Rami's mind. He'd managed to keep all his memories tucked into a far corner of his mind. He did not know why Saher reminded him of the past.

They sat quietly in the car then Saher spoke. "Where are you taking me?"

"Thousand Nights."

"Thousand nights and a night, but what about the extra night?"

"I asked the same question when I saw the owner last week, and he said that for the extra night is spent with them, something like that. You started thinking my way."

Soon they were talking, Rami forgot that little incident

"Look, is that the place?"

"Yes, that's it."

"But they don't seem to be open, as there are no lights on."

"But it's Thursday night, so they must be open."

"Probably ran out of food!" She joked.

They parked the car and went to investigate. He allowed her to walk ahead of him and as she opened the door, the lights came on, and two-hundred people screamed, "Surprise! Happy birthday!"

She glanced around and the restaurant was full of their friends.

"Wait until I get you home!" She muttered under her breath.

"Promises…!"

Everyone was shouting and cheering. Rami stood watching her, kissing everyone, thanking them for their presents and cards. Now and then Saher glanced at Rami, with a big smile on her face, waiting for the congratulations to end so she could go to him. The waiter brought another table for her to place all of her presents on.

When Rami saw Sami and his wife with Ahmad and Jean, he went to them and shook their hands. Sami spoke first and placed his hand on Rami's shoulder.

"Is this the same girl we talked about once?"

"Yes Sami."

"Well I take back everything I said about her."

"She has surprised all of us," Ahmad commented.

"Thanks for coming any way."

Saher couldn't wait to get back over to Rami. He stood talking with few of their friends, so she came from behind and planted a kiss on his cheek. "Thank you," she whispered.

"I love you."

"I know you do."

"That was a great surprise Saher." One of the girls said.

"And I thought that he forgot about my birthday at first."

"Come on darling, let's go to our table." He carried two glasses of drink in his hands. "Saher, can you get my cigarettes out of my left pocket please."

She did as he asked and she felt another box in his pocket.

"You."

"Happy birthday…"

"I'll kill you."

"Open it."

"But everyone is watching, oh you're a real swine."

"They're our friends and I love you. He said with a loving smile, "Open the box darling."

Inside there was a bracelet to match her necklace.

"This is the best night of my life, but no more surprises."

"No more."

"You are hiding something."

But before he could answer her, the lights in the restaurant were dimmed and a big birthday cake was wheeled into the middle of the dance floor, with eighteen candles lit.

Once she had blown the candles out, almost everyone took to the dance floor. The party continued until the early hours of the morning and everyone was happy and joyful, especially Rami, who was the proudest person there.

- - - - - - - - -

It was well after four o'clock in the morning when the two of them crawled into bed. They were happily exhausted with all the dancing, singing and simply living their lives to the full.

He put his arm under her shoulders and pulled her towards him.

"I love you so much," said Saher and she kissed him. Her hands moved quickly to his body, teasing it.

"It's my night...let me be," she whispered.

She sat on his chest. She wanted to feel complete, she could hold back no more. Her wild body moved and twisted over his. He gently touched her skin with the tip of his fingers sending shivers down her spine. She was completely uninhibited and panting hard from sheer ecstasy. She slid herself down his body and he watched her face as she closed her eyes expecting great pain. Bending down she held him tight, took a deep breath, and allowed him to penetrate her. She opened her eyes and sat up again to meet his searching look.

"I know now what I've been missing."

"How do you feel darling?"

"I don't know. I've never felt this way before."

He moved with a controlled rhythm. "Oh God Rami, don't stop."

He turned her around and she lay on her back. He eased himself on top and the ritual began again. Although it was January, and the temperature outside was below zero, trickles of sweat ran down their bodies.

"I don't know what's happening, oh...! But don't stop."

Saher's body shivered and she was out of breath, her heart pounding. He pushed himself up to breathe and smiled to her, but he did not say anything. It was a moment of intense emotions, both mentally and physically. The effect was so severe that her body continued to shiver. He tried to ease himself away, but she held on to him, she wanted him to stay.

"I am all yours...Are you happy Rami?"

"Yes..."

"You have a way with words." She teased him.

"I only said yes..."

"Exactly...!" And she burst out laughing.

"Funny girl...!"

"Can I have you again please?" She whispered in his ear, as if she was frightened to be heard.

- - - - - - - - -

Saher amazed all those who knew her. Once she looked like a common servant yet within months she had changed into a completely different person. She had developed into an elegant young lady; she walked with pride and dressed extremely smartly. She enjoyed being looked at by Rami and others. She saw how proud he felt when heads turned in their direction wherever they went. She made a law for herself to dress up before Rami got home every day She knew she excited him If Rami happened to come home early she would scream at him because he caught her unprepared, but soon everything cooled down once Rami made a bit of fuss over her.

She became very popular at the centre and the Sodality, as well as at the record shop, as she helped to serve the customers if she happened to be there with Rami. Everyone admired her bubbly personality, her discussion, and her wit. She always managed to finish whatever she was saying with a joke. She was quick to answer any question put to her. She never tried to take over from him in anything, but found her place next to him as equal. She was the new blood in the Sodality. She was full of ideas and plans, but she held everyone at arm's length. No one knew her, her past, or even her present, and that was just how she wanted it to be.

Weeks passed and she fitted into her new life perfectly. Rami couldn't wait for the summer. He hoped to take Saher to Europe once the end of year examinations were over and the results were out.

She had decided to decorate the flat by herself. She objected to having strange men coming to the flat, also she was saving money. He was spending more time at the shops and everyone was stretched to the limit as it was the peak time for business.

"Funny how people only live for the summer...!" Rami remarked to his partners "The whole population seems to come alive, the parties, the nightclubs are full, the cafes, the little Casinos by the river, everywhere is full. It's funny this city of ours."

"Do you want to go out tonight?" Khalid smiled.

Rami's mind seemed to be vacant. He didn't answer.

"Do you want to go out tonight?" Khalid asked again.

"No...I don't know..." Rami looked in the distance, "Saher seems to be off colour lately and I don't know why," Rami told Nabil and Khalid at the shop one day.

"Tell us..."

"She seemed very happy before, but since the exams have been over, she asked me to leave her alone so she could decorate the flat, but she didn't do anything to it. All she wanted to do is sit holding on to me, nothing else, she hardly talks, or laugh, and I don't know what's wrong with her."

"Have you asked her?" Nabil asked.

"Yes, of course."

"She's probably just worried about the exam results."

"That's what I thought at the start, but then I don't think so. I am very concerned."

"Why don't you go home now and take her out or something."

Rami had noticed so much difference in her attitude; more than he could explain to his friends. She had ignored herself of late; she looked as if she had given up hope. She did not make any effort to dress up before he got home and she did not feel like eating most of the time. Even when he was making love to her, he had to stop, as it felt as if he was in bed with a dead body. He asked her if she would like to go and see her family, but she gave him such an angry look, that it made him retreat to his study.

The following morning Nabil walked into the office at the shop.

"Hey Rami your results are out. I've just seen one of your classmates."

"Oh God! Come with me, you drive, I don't think I can."

He was full of apprehension and it grew as he walked through the corridors of his college. When he asked his classmates about their results, they told him that only thirty per cent had passed. His legs turned to jelly, but when he walked out of the Head of Department's office his face was all lit up.

"Fantastic...I can see it on your face, come tell me." Nabil was jubilant.

"Let me take my breath, first."

"I am so proud."

"I came top of the whole department," Rami said.

"My God, you have worked hard! It's all because of that woman you have with you.""Come on, home James." He couldn't wait to tell Saher.

Nabil drove as fast as he possibly could to Rami's flat.

"Are you coming up?" Rami asked.

"No I wait for you here."

"Oh come on, I want you to see her face when I tell her."

Rami knocked on the door, but there was no answer.

He turned to Nabil. "Have you got the car keys, or did you leave them in the car as usual?"

"I left them in the car."

Rami knocked again and looked through the letter box. He could see a hand on the floor.

"Oh my God..." His face turned to white.

"What is it?" asked Nabil. He looked through the letterbox. "Oh no, I'll go and get the keys." he said and he ran downstairs.

Rami's head was pounding and he was shaking uncontrollably. He found it hard to breathe and hard to concentrate. "Saher...please move...move your arm, please..."

Nabil returned with the keys and handed them to Rami. His hands trembled as he tried to find the right key and the bunch fell to the floor. Nabil quickly picked them up and tried two or three from the bunch until the door opened.

As they dashed into the room, they saw Saher lying on the floor, swimming in a pool of blood.

"Oh my god...! No please god no, not this time" Rami felt his stomach turning. Nabil knelt down and felt her pulse.

"Get an ambulance quick," he shouted.

Rami could not think straight, the only number he could think of was that of CIC head office. "Sam, please help, Saher is dying."

"Pull yourself together, where are you?"

"At the flat."

Within minutes she was carried away in an ambulance and hurried to the hospital. Ahmad turned up at the hospital not long after they arrived, as did Sami.

Rami's face was pale white, he was in a state of shock and he did not know what to do. He did not understand his own feelings. He tried to cry, moan, or scream, but he was very confused about what was expected of him. All the past came flooding back to his thoughts. Almost two years ago he was there and almost two years ago he felt as trapped as he felt that moment. If anything happened to Saher, he would not be able to face the world. But he fought back the tears and he fought hard to stay in control.

His brain was numb as he looked up and saw all the faces staring in his direction, wondering what was going on in his mind.

"Why are you looking at me like that? Do you know something I don't know?" His brain screamed with incredible pain, "Judgement day?" He said to the others, but no one answered him.

Rami saw the doctor coming in his direction and he turned his face away. He did not want to hear a word from him.

"Can I have a word with you?"

"Yes." His lips trembled.

The doctor took Rami into a corner outside the waiting room.

"How is she?"

"She'll be fine, she's resting now. We had to give her blood, but I'm sorry as she lost the baby. We did our best. She needs all the help she can get mentally."

"Baby? What baby?"

"I'm sorry. She was around seven weeks pregnant."

"Can I see her please?"

"She's asleep now, but yes you can, just for five minutes."

He was shocked to learn about the baby, but he thought the doctor must be wrong. How could she be pregnant when she was taking precautions?

"The doctor must have made a mistake," he kept repeating in his mind. Saher was always the careful type of person. She was looking forward to doing her exams the following year and going to university. Having a baby was not part of her future plans.

Saher opened her eyes in the morning see Rami watching over her. She closed her eyes again. She was tired, and the nurse had taken away the drip that she had connected to her arm.

Rami was disturbed by the whole scene. He couldn't believe she would hide something so important from him, but at least she was still alive. The doctors kept her in hospital for a few days and Rami never left her bedside for more than an hour.

- - - - - - - - -

She sat on the sofa in the living room after Rami had driven her back from hospital. "Thank God I'm home again."

"How are you?"

"Okay I suppose."

"I'll get you a cup of hot milk."

When he came back he sat next to her and put his arm around her.

"I'm sorry I should have noticed. I was so involved in my studies and everything else that I forgot you were here."

"Don't be sorry, you have yet to fail me. You are such a sweetheart and you deserve someone better than me."

"Don't ever say that again."

She tried to talk, but she could not. She tried to find the right words to explain what had happened, but instead she pushed herself towards him even more, looking for security.

"The doctor said you will be alright."

"Yes."

"And you will be able to have more children." He did not want to hurt her feelings, but she burst out crying.

"Talk to me darling."

"I love you."

"Why didn't you tell me about the baby?"

"I felt so ashamed that I just couldn't tell you. Oh Rami I felt so cheap, and broken inside, it was my fault as I forgot to take the pill. I prayed so hard when my period was late, but it was no use, the doctor confirmed it. I tried to tell you, but I did not have it in me. I didn't know what to do, I was so confused."

"It's all over now."

"Is it?"

"What are you trying to say? Tell me please."

"I did it for me and you." She burst out crying, she knew she had no choice but to tell him the truth. He was building up with anger and tried hard to calm himself.

"Oh god...! What did you do woman? What did you do?"

"Please don't be angry with me. You have your studies and your future to concentrate on. A baby would be a huge distraction and if my family found out, they'd kill the three of us."

"So you killed my baby so you wouldn't have to tell me? What on earth is the matter with you? Didn't you think of asking me how I felt about a baby? Did you even stop to think about me?"

"Yes, I think about you all the time you stupid man. I love you."

"You love me? My God you are crazy."

Rami left the flat. He drove away as fast as he could, trying to escape from her, trying to escape from the ugliness that he felt. He did not know where to go. He wanted to hide. How could she do that to him?

He drove to May's house and walked in before she had the chance of asking him in. He sat in the kitchen and suddenly Rami started shouting and rambling about Saher, feeling very angry. But May could not understand a word he was saying.

"Do you want a drink?"

"Yes..." He shouted back, and carried on screaming about Saher. May was still no wiser. She could not make out what his anger was all about.

"Keep your eyes on the cooker, I'll send the girl home, I believe it's going to be one hell of a day."

As she walked in the kitchen again, Rami said, 'Thank God Samir was not involved in all this.'

"Tell me all about it."

"I just told you, but you don't listen to me, no one does."

"Calm down and tell me."

"Calm down! I am calm." But he was shouting.

"You are shouting."

"So what...?" His voice was louder than before. She gave him one angry look, and left him with his drink in his hand, "If you need me, I am in my room."

She heard him crying loudly, she had the urge to go back to him, but decided to let him burn his anger out.

After a while, he walked into her bedroom. She was sitting by her dressing table. As she looked at him, she saw that powerful wanting look in his face. How could she resist? How could she say no to him? She never did before. She was his first woman, and he always came back to her. He might have needed her every now and then, but she always needed him. It had been months and months since she had him to herself. She could not sleep with another man, and she wouldn't either. She tried to call him on many occasions, or even talk to him, when he visited her with Saher, just to tell him, to let him know how she felt, and that her and her body ached for him, to tell him that she needed him, she needed his seed inside her, to hold him close to her, and to hear him say that he was still in love with her no matter what, and she would tell him the truth.

She felt his anger when he made love to her. She felt him through the pleasurable pain that he gave her. She thought that if that lovemaking was instead of the crying and shouting, she would rather have it every day, and anytime.

He told her how much he had missed her, and asked her for the first time to leave Samir, and go somewhere else with him, but she refused. She knew he was speaking with anger, and did not mean anything he said.

Rami followed May into her bedroom and they made love for hours. She did not know where he got his energy from, or how had Saher managed to make him so angry.

"Can I come tomorrow?"

"Please do."

She did not want him to go. She enjoyed that day more than ever. She loved his anger, even though he hurt her more than once, but she loved that lovemaking pain.

Rami drove to the city centre and parked his car in a side street. He decided to take a walk in Rashid Street, which was the main street in the Capital, and the oldest street in Baghdad, which combined modernisation with historic buildings. The shops on the two sides of the street stretched for miles. On one side of the street stood old buildings, adjacent to each other, like terraced houses. Somehow they supported each other to keep standing for centuries. Some said that they were as old as Baghdad, but Rami didn't think so. On the other side of the road, modern buildings had been constructed; banks and office buildings.

He thought about his anger and he asked himself hundreds of questions, yet he couldn't find the correct answers, logical answers, or answers that made sense.

What was he doing with his life? Why couldn't he just be another normal teenager?

Faces of people passed him, but he kept on walking with no idea of where he was heading.

He missed being young and he had to behave like a grown-up. He missed his family and seeing them every now and then wasn't enough, but he pretended to be very independent. He tried hard to be independent, and he realised that sometimes it came at a price. He missed that football game he had once played with his brother in the garden. In all those years he had only had one game, yet his brother idolised him. He remembered playing Scrabble with his sisters on maybe two occasions. He knew they loved him. He had been selfish towards his family. He gave so much of himself to others, yet to his family he was a mean person.

What about Saher? Why was he angry with her? She did what she had to do for him! He wasn't there for her, and he wasn't there to listen to her. He was there to be her master, he ordered, and she obeyed. In a way she was his slave.

Why was he angry? He turned round and headed back to his car. He didn't want children just yet running around the apartment anyway. He didn't want stains of food on his clothes when he went to university. He didn't want spilled milk on his papers when he had to submit a story to Iman.

He started almost running back to his car. He had left Saher with all that guilt on her own, and what if she wasn't there when he got back? Or what if she did something stupid to hurt herself? Where would he be without her? How would he function without her laughter and love?

There was no excuse for the way he had behaved, no explanation whatsoever. He started his car and drove back to his flat. Why was he still angry? Was it because he remembered Julia for the first time?

"Saher," he shouted.

He found her in the bedroom. They stood looking at each other then she opened her arms to him.

"I love you and I'm sorry."

"No baby, I'm sorry, I'm really sorry sweetheart." He held her tight.

"I kept jumping on the stairs, four or five steps at a time, so I could lose the baby. I used to hear old people talking in our village when they couldn't feed another mouth in the family. How stupid I was?"

"Yes, but it's done now. I'll make you a cup of tea and you had better rest."

"Thank you, not for the tea but for being here. Don't ever leave me."

"I won't."

CHAPTER THIRTY FIVE

IT was late morning on a Friday when the door bell rang. Rami was in his study putting the last touches to his second book. He was late submitting it, but argued that it was better to be late than having the book filled with mistakes. Saher ran to the door, and opened it.

"Good morning, is my son about?"

Saher wished the ground would open up and swallow her. She was caught unprepared. She had a small pair of shorts and bikini top on, she was barefoot, with no makeup on and she had her hair tied back in a pony tail.

"Oh sorry…Morning…Are you Rami's mum? Oh please come in, please…I'm sorry I'm not dressed, I've just finished the housework."

"It's alright dear, the flat is spotless, better than ever before. No smell of cigarettes either. Is Rami around?"

"He's in his study, I'll call him for you."

"No leave him, I know what he's like when he's writing, but I'd love a coffee with you."

"Ok, I'll put the kettle on and change my clothes."

"Stay as you are, this is your home I suppose, and you do live here?"

"Yes…" She answered shyly as both women sat in the kitchen.

"How long have you been together?"

"Over a year now, how do you like your coffee?'

"As it comes please, and do you both love each other?"

"I worship the ground he walks on. I adore him. I think he feels the same for me, well I hope he does." She smiled shyly.

"Well he's got good taste in women, as you're stunningly beautiful."

The blood rushed to her cheeks, she felt embarrassed and didn't know how to answer her.

"So why didn't he ever bring you home with him, not that he visited us that often."

"I don't know, I am sorry, probably it's my fault for not making him."

"Are you getting married? I am sorry for asking so many questions, but I like know who my son is mixing with."

Saher didn't like that last remark, although Rami's mother didn't mean anything malicious. She was saved by Rami coming to the kitchen. "Mum, what a lovely surprise!" He gave her a hug and a kiss.

"I can see why you hardly come and see us, you have been spoiled. Sorry my dear I forgot to ask you your name."

"Saher…she has been spoiling me."

"I can see that you never looked better."

"What brought you here?"

"First I missed you and second I have some good news as your sister is getting engaged. We're having a big party at the house and we need some music and help."

"No problem, I'll get a nice band for you. Are you having it in the garden?"

"Yes. I've invited Ahmad and Jean too and you can invite your friends, Nabil and Khalid."

"You're a real devil mum."

"Now I must go, as I told the taxi driver to pick me up in half an hour."

"Phone and cancel, I'll take you home, plus I need to buy a present for my sister."

"Take Saher with you, look at this apartment, she has made it so elegant, and don't forget to bring her with you, I am sure the whole family wants to meet her, more than meeting the future son in law." His mother laughed, and kissed both of them and left.

When Rami came back after seeing his mother off, Saher was waiting for him in the lounge, with her hand on her heart.

"God Rami, look at me."

"Stunning as usual!"

"No I'm shaking like a leaf. She's such a sweetie your mum, and very shrewd too. She knows more than she lets on."

"Spot on…"

"She left without saying which of your sisters is getting engaged, without saying which day, or anything."

"I was just thinking that, I'll phone her later, I know she wants to talk about something, and that's why she didn't go into details."

Rami sat quietly for a while staring into space. Saher couldn't wait any longer for a comment from him.

"Well?" Saher asked.

"Well what?"

"What are you thinking about? I feel as your mum meeting me was a problem for you."

"How did you work that one out?"

"She must know my background, because of my accent and my naturally blonde hair."

"Probably but she didn't say anything. I'll phone her in a minute."

"You do that, I'd better put some clothes on. I don't feel like anymore surprises."

"You look fine for me, just relax and don't jump to conclusions."

Ten minutes later he phoned his mother.

"I bet you're thinking how silly I am not telling you which one of your sisters got engaged."

"You got it in one."

"It's your eldest sister."

"When's the party and who is he?"

"Three weeks on Thursday. He's an engineer, he studied in London and he comes from a very good family."

"Good and what's his name?"

"Salim."

"And do you want me to book a band, a good nice Armenian band."

"Your dad, next to me, said why not?"

"Ok will do."

"Make sure you bring Saher, as I really like her."

"Do you really mum?"

"Yes, she's a lovely girl and I noticed the ring on her finger too."

"That isn't an engagement ring. It was just a present."

"And do you know any chefs who could help with the cooking? There will be over two hundred people: our family and his."

"Typical engagement Mosul style, and yes I know lots of chefs."

"If I think of anything else I will let you know, I know I can depend on you. Bye son."

After he hung up the phone he had a smile on his face.

"Well spill, what did she say?" Saher asked.

"She likes you a lot."

"Did she really say that?"

"She said you are a good girl and she liked your engagement ring."

"Oh God, I suppose I've got to go with you then?"

"You suppose right, as she asked me to bring you along."

"I could say my parents are ill and won't go, all your family will be there, and they will be asking questions."

"They will be too busy looking at the happy couple than you and me. I hate those family parties and celebrations."

"Never been to one, we never had money to buy new clothes to go to family weddings or celebrations, we used to sit in the fields watching from quite a distance."

"This time we can afford to buy you a new dress, get your bags ready we are going to Lebanon. I shall go and renew the passports tomorrow."

- - - - - - - - -

Never in a million years would Saher have believed that not only would she travel outside the country, but once they touched down in Beirut, that Rami would apply for Visas to France and England. He told her that it was a trip to buy stock for the shop and also to impress her.

They stayed for a week in both capitals and after they headed back to Baghdad with suitcases full of shopping.

"I've never seen a man who loves shopping like he does," Saher said to Jean on the phone.

"Ahmad hates shopping, I have to drag him to come with me, an effort to do even the food shopping."

"I have so many things to wear I don't know what to do with them all."

"Lucky you!"

"I'm dreading this engagement party, as I don't fit in. And if anyone finds out where I come from, the whole family would put a stop to us. I can't help being born into a very poor family."

Jean couldn't answer; she could see the two sides of the coin.

"Please say something."

"I don't know what to say," said Jean. "Have you spoken to Rami about it?"

"Yes and no. I think he'd rather not go, but if he doesn't show up he'll upset the whole family. It won't look right, especially with over two-hundred people present; they'd start asking questions."

"Just play it by ear, as we'll be there, plus Samir and May and Khalid and Nabil, so just stick with us and stay safe."

- - - - - - - - -

They arrived an hour early to the party. Rami's brother was busy spraying all around the garden with water to cool the atmosphere. His sisters were busy getting dressed, while his mother was busy with the chef and his helper. They were running slightly behind.

Rami wore a light blue coloured suit which he bought in Paris, with a shirt in midnight blue to match. Saher looked like a movie star. She wore a long evening dress in baby pink and her hairdresser had left her hair looking wild.

"Hi auntie, does anything need doing?" Saher asked.

"Can you find out if the band wants anything to drink?"

"Ok."

Saher saw an apron on the side and decided to put it round her.

"Here auntie, leave it to me, you go and get ready."

"No you'll ruin your dress."

"Go and get ready and relax…don't worry about me."

She gave her a hug and a kiss and left her in charge."Right boys what needs doing here?" And she meant business.

Almost an hour later Rami's dad asked who 'that girl' was.

"She's your son's girl. I left her with total chaos and now everything's sorted. She's amazing and very good for him."

"She's stunningly beautiful too."

"And she's got him under the thumb. I'm happy to say that she has made him give up smoking and drinking. The flat is so clean and tidy that you could eat off the floor. They live together, but don't go telling everyone."

"That's not right. I should put a stop to this nonsense."

"Do you think your stubborn son will take notice of what you say? Just accept it, and be happy for them. This is the 1970's after all."

There she comes now."

"Saher, darling, this is Rami's dad."

"Hello uncle, how are you?"

"Hello, I've heard so many things about you."

"All good I hope?"

"Yes they were as a matter of fact, and did my son invite your family to our house or has he been totally thoughtless?"

She was glad to see a visitor walking into the garden. "Here comes your first visitor."

"Grandma and Auntie grin and bear it." Rami's mum commented which made Saher chuckle hiding her giggle.

"How are you keeping mother?"

"I am fine, just a pain in my back." With a flick of her hand she dismissed everyone except for Saher. "And who might you be?"

"She's your favourite grandson's girlfriend." Rami's mother answered.

Saher kissed her hand as a sign of respect. "Come dear, walk me to my chair. I'm no good on my feet these days. You're a pretty thing aren't you?"

"Thank you nana, my name is Saher."

"It's no good telling me that as I'll forget it in two minutes."

Saher looked back at Rami's mum and she in turn winked at her, smiling.

"Can I get you anything to drink?"

"Just a glass of water please, and you can hide the Cinzano , as they don't like me to drink. They said that when I get drunk I show myself up."

She sat the old lady down and went to get her what she wanted. On her way, she whispered in Rami's mum's ear, "She's a sweetheart."

"You can have her and you'd better call Rami, wherever he is. We all slave for her, and somehow according to her, he does more for her than anyone else. He only sees her once in a blue moon."

"Typical...She asked me to hide her drink."

"Oh you are honoured. That is Rami's job, no one is allowed to touch her glass." Explained Rami's mother sarcastically, and Saher laughed and walked away.

More people began to arrive soon after, and the garden filled up. The music played and food was served, with a traditional stuffed whole lamb called "Kuzzie".

Everyone who was close family and friends helped to look after the guests, but Saher was in charge of making sure everyone had drinks or food, directing the waiters to where they were needed, talking to the guests, and most importantly making sure the grandmother had her Cinzano.

"She phoned me to say she wanted to disappear instead of coming here," Jean commented to their friends. "But just look at her now, she's the centre of attention. The girls are all trying to find out where she bought that stunning dress, old women can't stop kissing her and old men are licking their lips at the sight of her."

"She is lovely, so loving." May said.

"And Rami has one eye on her and one eye on the guests," Ahmad added.

"Wouldn't you? She danced with every young man who asked her to dance.""She sure is popular tonight."

"Talk of the devil! There she is." May said.

"Are you going to rest for a change?" Jean asked when Saher approached them.

"Yes I 'm exhausted," she said, "At least everyone has been fed and watered, including grandmother. She's a sweetheart."

"You have a great fan in her."

Rami came and joined them minutes later. "You have both done a great job."

"Thank you, I suppose you want me to get you another drink?" Rami teased Ahmad.

"In fact my dear friend I was going to ask if you would like a drink with us, and I will go and get it for you."

"I'll have a whisky please if you insist."

"Saher…?"

"Anything but Cinzano, I think grandma can out drink anyone here."

"You're only supposed to give her two drinks and dilute the rest with water." Rami explained to everyone's laughter.

"Damn…oh well she will sleep happily all night then."

"When are your results coming out, Saher?" asked Samir.

"They came out today." Everyone stared at her and Rami was shocked.

"You kept that a secret," he protested.

"I passed…I don't know how I did it, but I passed."

Rami couldn't control himself any longer. He gave her a hug and kissed her on her lips. He didn't care about their traditions and customs, he was proud of her, and if he felt like kissing his woman in public, so be it.

People began to drift away shortly after midnight and for the next two hours it was time for the younger generation to enjoy the dancing and the live music.

- - - - - - - - -

Shortly afterwards, Rami bought a plot of land from the advance on his second book. He wanted to build his own house. The land was not far from his shops. Saher objected at first, she loved their apartment and she had it decorated the way she wanted, but she came around when Rami explained to her the benefits of having their own house.

September came and with it came endless arguments between them. No matter what Rami did to please her, it simply was not good enough. After spending endless hours making suggestions to their architect on how they wanted the house she changed her mind to the frustration of Rami. And it didn't stop at the design of the house, but developed to every subject he talked about, everything he wrote and everything he did. Her whole attitude changed and Rami could not break through the barrier she had put up to find out what was wrong. She refused to go out with him, even to the shops to buy food. Whenever Rami tried to get near her, she shouted at him, and ordered him to leave her alone. She found every excuse so she could stay in the house. And if he was late for a few minutes, a whole series of questions were thrown at him.

She stopped cleaning the flat after telling him their cleaner was not going to do it anymore because of her back trouble.

"It's like a prison in here," Saher said.

"You're the one who doesn't want to go out," Rami commented.

"You only take me wherever you want to go."

"Where do you want to go for heaven's sake?"

"That's what you say now, but soon you'll change your mind."

"Do you want to go and see your family?"

"No, I hate them."

"It seems that you hate everybody lately."

"I hate you too. I just can't stand you anymore. You put me in this prison, like you did with so many people."

"Saher stop all this."

"No…You treat me as if I was bought like a slave. Yes that's it, I'm your slave, do this and don't do that. Breathe now, sit down, and stand up…don't forget to smile. Am I your property so I know how to behave?"

"Shut up, I've had enough of this, you're lucky to be here. You don't know what prison is, sometimes I think that you forget the luxury you are living in."

"Yes I know and I'm paying for it every night. That's the only reason that you got me here."

"I think there must be an end to all this very soon, we can't carry on like this anymore."

"Have you got another woman?"

"No I don't…but I wish I did have."

"You don't care about me anymore, you only care about yourself. You never ask me if I need something or not."

"What do you need? What do you want for heaven's sake?" Rami was angry and his voice raised. "I will take you out of this prison, just tell me where the hell you want to go?"

"I don't want to go anywhere. I hate being seen with you, they think I 'm your new whore," she answered quickly.

"I think there's something wrong in your head."

"Who the hell do you think you are talking to me like that?"

"Shut up, just shut up. If you don't like it here, you know what you can do. I've had enough. I've really had enough of arguing with you to last me for years." He shouted.

"I am leaving, I'll do anything to get out of your sight and out of here. I've had enough of you."

He took the ring off his finger, which she had bought him for his birthday. "You can have this back as well." He threw the ring at her.

She stared into his face, turned her head and looked through the window with tears running her face. He left her there and went to his study. He tried to write, but he could not. After a while he stood up and opened the door to get out. Saher was standing facing the door with her back pinned to the wall behind her. She looked very sad and her eyes were dark red from crying.

"When do you want me to leave?" she said looking at the floor.

"Now," Rami said smiling, but she did not see his smile and she turned to head to the bedroom, as if she was obeying an order.

He moved quickly and grabbed her to stop her. "Get your filthy hands off me," she screamed.

"What's the matter darling?"

"I'm not your darling, don't touch me."

"Okay, tell me what's wrong?"

She sat on the bed and looked around. "This fucking round bed, I hate it."

316

Rami sat next to her, he tried to put his arm around her, but she shouted again. "Don't you dare touch me, I'm warning you."

Rami lost control. He forced her to lie back on the bed then he sat on top of her, forcefully took off her small shirt, then pulled her shorts down, turned her round onto her stomach and tried to spank her, but instead he carried her on his shoulder. She screamed, kicked and hit him as hard as she possibly could.

"I'm going to cool you down," said Rami.

"Leave me alone you bastard."

He carried her to the shower, and between her kicking, and punching him, he turned the cold water on and pushed her in.

"It's freezing..."

"Good."

"I hate you...I really hate you." She broke down crying. "Please let me out of here." She begged.

"No." And he pushed her in again.

"Oh please don't hurt me."

"I am not...but you hurt me terribly." Slowly he turned the hot water on.

She cried from all her heart. "Please let me out Rami, I love you."

"I love you too, now have you cooled down?"

"No you bastard." She tried to push her way out, but he was much stronger than her. He held her tight to him and walked into the shower with her, with all his clothes on. "Try again now."

Suddenly they burst out laughing. They both looked at each other in amazement, they had not laughed for a long time.

He let her free and gently she raised her hands to his face and kissed him passionately.

"I'm sorry I was behaving like a bitch."

He nodded. "Yes, you were."

She helped him take his clothes off, in between crying and laughing. She was happy in a way that they were together again. "Make love to me Rami."

He carried her to the bedroom. "Not on the bed darling, you will get everything wet."

"So..." He tried to throw her on the bed, but she clung to his neck, and shouted, "No ... no careful, don't throw me." Her face changed suddenly.

"Tell me."

She tried to escape his searching eyes, and she tried to hide from his questions that he was firing at her.

"Do you love me?"

"Yes."

"Take me now, what are you waiting for?" She laughed and giggled. He knew that there was something she was hiding from him. He knew that there was a mystery behind that laughter. They made love for a long time, then both stretched back exhausted from looking at each other.

"Do you still want me to go?" She asked.

"No this is your home."

"Than make love to me once more, gently slowly like you used to do."

Like a slow waltz, he made love to her. She put her arms around him, pushing down , afraid to let go, as if she did she would lose him forever.

"Will you love me like this after forty years?" She asked.

"I will try if you haven't drained me completely out by then."

Her hand moved to her stomach.

"Are you alright?" he asked.

"Yes."

"Are you sure?"

"Yes..."

"I'll take you to the doctors tomorrow"

"Please no...no doctors."

They were quiet for a while then he broke the silence. "How many shall we have?" he asked as he looked at the ceiling.

She turned round and put her head on his chest. "What?"

"Children!"

She examined his face. "How many do you want?"

"A football team..."

"Very funny..."

"One now and the rest later, after I finish university."

"Ok..." Saher replied. He turned his head towards her and smiled.

"Hi...mum."

"You bastard, what do you want, a boy or a girl?"

"Boys make too much noise I'd rather have a girl."

"Girls are a pain to dress up, and make them look pretty, and when they grow up, I'll be worried sick who they are going out with."

Rami laughed at that thought, "We'll have a boy first, so he can look after his sisters."

"Make love to me."

"Don't you ever get enough?"

"Make love to me....gently."

"What's all this gentle business today?"

"It's the baby silly."

"What baby?" He teased. He knew what she was hiding from him.

"Ours, I'm pregnant, I thought you knew, oh damn...when you started talking about babies, I thought...Oh Rami...No...I'm sorry. Don't look at me like that... leave me alone and take that smirk off your face."

Rami found it fascinating watching her as she hid her face under the pillow. He felt proud of her and he freed her hand, which was holding tight to the covers, and kissed it.

"I love you. Will you forgive me for being so ignorant darling?"

She removed her head from under the pillow. "I love you too."

"How many months has it been?"

"Two I think."

He pulled the covers away so he could have a good look at her, but he could not see any difference. "I've never been with a pregnant woman before," he said.

318

She could not make out what his thoughts were. "Tell me how you feel."

"I'm very happy and I should keep an eye on you from now on." He thought briefly about what he'd just started to say then he continued. "No heavy lifting, fewer long walks, a healthy diet, no drinks, no smoking in the flat anymore and no sex."

"Get lost! No sex?"

"That's fantastic," he said. "You only objected on one thing."

"It was an accident, I was more careful this time after the last incident."

"Never mind, I still love you."

The next two months passed very slowly. For most of the time Saher wasn't feeling very good, and she needed all the attention and help that Rami could give her.

Rami wrote less and less as there was so much on his mind. His shop visits became less frequent too, and he had a handful of excuses to give to his partners, not that they needed him there, but for not visiting them either. He even told Sami that his studies were taking most of his time, and if it was possible that he was given less assignments to deal with.

He could not tell anybody about Saher's pregnancy as he felt afraid that they might think less of her, or that someone might interfere in their lives. He always found an excuse not to take her with him when he visited his mother. He created a small world for them to be in, to feel safe and secure. They avoided all types of gatherings, from Sodality meetings, to parties. People asked questions, but he always had an answer ready.

Saher went along with whatever he suggested and accepted the fact that no one should know, no one should be near them, and when the time was right, Rami planned to take her to Lebanon to have the baby. He even suggested that they should live there for a while until the dust settled.

- - - - - - - - -

The doorbell rang one late afternoon at the flat and Rami went to answer it.

"Hello stranger."

"May! What are you...?"

"I never thought that you are going to be surprised to see me? Are you asking me in?""Hmm….."

"Are you saying 'yes' come in?" She was determined to find out what was wrong as he and Saher had been avoiding her invitations for months. Also, she had found out from Ahmad that she wasn't the only one who they had avoided. May pushed him out of the way gently and walked in.

"I've been studying very hard." Rami said, but she did not believe a word.

"I see."

Saher came out of the bedroom.

"Who was it Rami?" She did not realize that they had a visitor.

May stood up and examined her, then turned back to Rami, who was looking down at the floor. She covered her face with her two hands and shook her head from side to side. She held her hand out to Saher, brought her back to the sofa and sat between them.

"Saher is seven months pregnant;" he said, feeling terribly guilty.

"I can see that," said May. She put her arms around the both of them and hugged them. In a way they were relieved that someone else was there to share their agony and despair.

"Why didn't you tell us? Why did you want to keep all this away from all of us?"

"Don't ask because I don't know. I didn't want anyone to look down on Saher."

"Tell me what's on your mind?"

"We look like a bunch of irresponsible, immature kids, I can't...Oh May...We love this baby."

"And how are you going to hide the baby?"

"We'll cross that bridge when we come to it."

"Where are you going to have the baby?"

"At first we thought in Lebanon, but after all the thinking, we've decided to have it here at home. I've been reading about it and I've bought all the necessary equipment."

"I have heard enough for one day, are you crazy? Have you gone out of your mind?"

"Do you want a cup of coffee?" He asked.

"I'd rather have something stronger." She said angrily.

Rami left the two women talking, while he went to make some coffee.

Saher spoke first. "He has been fantastic. I had a bad time and he was quite capable."

"I know him, after all I was his first woman."

"I knew that, he told me."

"Good...Now I am phoning my husband."

"Please don't." Saher begged.

"You need to be examined," said May. "I bet you haven't even been to the doctor?"

"Wait until...." She stopped in middle of the sentence when he walked in with the coffee.

"I thought you would have more sense than this," May said to Rami in anger.

"He knows what's best for the two of us," Saher said in defence.

"You mean the three of you?"

"Do you really think all of your friends will think differently of you? No, you stupid fools! The only people who you'll probably have to avoid are your parents. Now Rami get out of here, go somewhere else and leave us two women alone. We have a lot to talk about. Go and don't come back for another two hours. Move it, I can't see what the hell you are doing here, when I am here? Samir will be hungry when he comes, how about getting us some dinner?"

"Yes, ok." At last there was a relieved look on his face, he smiled and left.

Rami went to see his parents. He felt happy as he shared a drink with his father; they came to terms with each other. They talked about the factory, the university and his writings, which his father admitted that he liked very much.

Two hours later, he drove back to the flat. He opened the door and to his surprise all his friends were gathered there.

"What the hell is going on?"

"Congratulations!"

"And whose idea was this?" he said laughing.

"Mine," Samir said.

"I thought it was the big mouth that you have married."

Rami looked at Saher and she seemed more herself than she had looked for a while. He walked towards her and put his arm around her.

"Thank God for all of you."

The apartment soon filled up with friends, including Nabil, Khalid, Ahmad and Jean, then the bell rang again and it was Farruk and his wife, Sami arrived with his wife. The atmosphere was a happy one.

"I feel like crying," Nabil said as he drunk his champagne.

"I didn't realise that my cousin is such a big softy," Khalid remarked.

"And you had better learn how to change babies, being the uncle." Said Nabil.

"No way, that turns my stomach."

"What if we need a babysitter?" Saher asked.

"Get a gorgeous girl and I will be babysitting with her."

- - - - - - - - -

The following two months passed quickly, but they were very hectic, as if someone had called for action stations. All their friends helped the young couple. May turned up as soon as Rami left in the morning to go to university. Ahmad and Jean came almost every day, while Nabil and Khalid took charge of all the shopping for them and decorated the baby's bedroom, as well as supplying all the new jokes which they had heard in the shop.

Saher insisted on having the baby in the apartment and everyone accepted her wishes. It was a happy time, and nothing was going to go wrong. Samir arranged for a midwife to help him with the delivery, as well as having alerted the hospital in case of any complications.

By the end of April, Rami was attending a university lecture when Nabil excused himself to the Lecturer and asked him if he'd allow Rami to leave, due to an emergency.

Rami drove as fast he possibly could and Nabil followed trying his best to catch up with him. As Rami ran to the flat, Samir was already there with the midwife. Khalid and Jean were sitting in the living room.

"How is she? Is she alright?"

May came out from the room as she heard his voice. She hugged him lovingly. "Just go and see her."

"What do I say?"

"Hello!"

By five in the afternoon the living room was full of people. Ahmad came in as soon as he'd read Jean's note on the kitchen table. Farruk and his wife were there, as well as Sami and his wife. Rami was pushed out of the room, as he was not needed any longer. He sat with the others waiting and making little conversation. The coffee pot was filled up and emptied every few minutes. Suddenly a baby's cry broke the silence. Rami stood up, not knowing what to do next.

"Just sit there till you're told what to do," Farruk ordered him.

"The baby is alive. Hey Ahmad, I'm a father!" The tears ran down his face.

Everyone's eyes watered. They all waited for someone to come out from the bedroom, but no one did.

"What's keeping them?" Rami asked.

"It has only been few minutes," Nabil laughed.

Samir came out at last. "Wow that was a long labour."

"Well tell me," Rami cried out.

"It's only a baby boy!"

Rami looked into everyone's face in disbelief then suddenly he hugged Samir. "Thank you…thank you."

Everyone shook hands, wiped away the tears, laughed and cried at the same time, it was a moment of deep mixed emotions. They felt as if they all had a hand in making this baby.

"This boy is going to be one hell of a spoilt brat, with all the uncles and aunts around," Farruk said.

"Come on Rami, come and see your son."

Samir took him by the shoulder and walked him into the room. As they walked in, the midwife put the baby next to Saher. She smiled at the baby and looked up at Rami. "He's as beautiful as you my love." she said.

"Oh darling, I love you more than ever before, I'm so proud of you two, thank you." He held her hand and kissed it then he kissed the baby's head.

"Thank you Rami for being you," said Saher.

"Come on you two, stop all that or else I'm going to burst out crying myself," said May. "Take the baby and show him to the others and let Saher rest."

Rami did not know how to hold the baby, he looked so small next to his hands, but the midwife came to the rescue.

As Rami left the room, Saher called him and Rami turned round. "Yes darling."

"I love you."

"And I love you too."

CHAPTER THIRTY SIX

OCTOBER came and Syria and Egypt decided to attack Israel and recapture the territories they lost in the 1967 six days war. The Egyptian army managed to cross the Suez Canal, while the Syrian army recaptured part of the Golan Heights, but after the initial advances, they began to retreat. The Iraqis sat on the border for six days before they were allowed into Syria, after assurances that they wouldn't topple the Syrian Government. They went in and found the Israelis knocking on the doors of Damascus. Successfully they pushed them back.

With all what was going on, nothing was more important than little Anthony. It felt like their apartment was never empty of visitors. Friends found any excuse to buy little toys, or clothes, for baby Anthony; any excuse to come and see him, and any excuse to grab a quick cuddle and a kiss. He was the most spoiled child on the face of the earth, according to his dad.

With the baby came maturity and a responsibility, and Rami knew exactly what his role was; to provide for two people. He wanted to build an empire, a new business that wasn't a short-term adventure, but a business built on solid ground, a business that had the potential to grow bigger with time.

"Does anyone have a trigger to know where, and when to stop? I've done enough is a big sentence." He said to his friends. Everyone around him tried to slow him down, including Khalid and Nabil, but at the end they had no choice but to join in with him.

At night, when he arrived home, he felt totally exhausted. He used to sit and eat his supper with half his body functioning and one eye to the bedroom door. Saher knew he was doing it all for her and the baby. and she was happy to think of the word 'Them'.

Anthony proved to be a blessing, a beautiful, happy child. He never woke up during the night and one look at his gorgeous smiling face was enough to make his parents forget any problems they had.

But soon Saher started to hint to Rami that he wasn't spending enough time with her. She was very diplomatic about it. After all, it had been months since they had the apartment to themselves, it had been months since they made love, which Rami had forgotten about and it had been months since he held her close to him and kissed her.

"When are you going to take some days off my darling?"

"Soon very, soon."

He came out of the shower and looked at her, "What is it?"

"I miss you."

A smile crossed his face and he put his arms around her and kissed her.

"Come on let's go to bed."

"Yes please." She smiled wickedly, but that was the last thing on his mind. He realised he was neglecting her, but in a way he was frightened as he did not want another child.

"It's safe. I know what you are thinking about."

"I wasn't thinking about that."

"Liar ... what is it then?"

"I forgot how beautiful you became since Anthony was born."

They made love and afterwards they sat talking, reflecting on the past, how they had met and argued at times. They laughed and giggled as they discussed their child. They felt as if they were finally back together again after a long separation. They were a happy family after all and they loved sharing their happiness with all their friends.

- - - - - - - - -

Life revolved around Anthony. If Anthony cried, everyone jumped up to see to him. If Anthony laughed, then everyone jumped up to watch the little boy laughing, as they took photographs.

Anthony was baptised at the Catholic Kaldanian Church in the Karada district. A small party followed, as a way for Rami and Saher to say thank you to their friends for sticking by them through all those months, and for the love they showed to the little brat.

Ahmad held Anthony on his lap, after all he was his godfather.

"This really suits you my love," Jean commented.

"Thank you."

"Soon you'll be changing nappies on a regular basis."

"Fine," he said casually, but suddenly he realised what Jean was hinting at. "Oh my god darling, are you sure?"

"Very sure."

"I'm going to be a dad everyone."

Everyone was genuinely happy for them. This strong bond between friends started ten years previously when Rami decided to impress his Arabic teacher. And now, two more little souls have been added to this group. They sat reminiscing about the good old days for hours afterwards.

- - - - - - - - -

Rami tried to see the world from Anthony's eyes. He wrote children's books with great success. He took many days off work to concentrate on writing them and he spent hours talking to his son, playing with him and watching him sleep.

At the beginning of April, Rami had to go to Lebanon. It was going to be his last trip before his final examinations. His children's books were completed and he had arranged with his publishers to meet them that particular week.

Three days after he had left Baghdad, a telegram arrived at his aunt's house. Rami read it and smiled, "She misses me again. Rami come back soon."

"Give her a phone call, and find out."

"I'll be going back once I have heard from the publisher."

His negotiations with his publishers about the new books went on for more three days. They were to be published in many Arab countries and translated into different languages, if they proved to be successful. He was the highest paid writer the publisher had on his books. Rami was also approached about publishing all the short stories that he'd published in the newspaper, but as he didn't know the legal aspects of it, he told them to wait until he had asked the Editor of the newspaper..

Rami flew back to Baghdad after spending a whole week in Lebanon and it proved to be a successful trip.

He left the airport and took a taxi back to his apartment. He wished he had contacted one of his friends to pick him up. He filled a whole suitcase with clothes and toys for the baby. He opened the door to the apartment quietly, in case Anthony was asleep.

"I'm home," He whispered, but he heard nothing. He went from one bedroom to the other, but he couldn't see Saher or Anthony. Everything had been left clean and tidy. He poured himself a whisky and sat down reading his mail.

"Enough is enough, where are they?" He said loudly.

Then he poured himself another whisky, picked up the telephone and called Ahmad. "Hello…it's me."

"Hello Rami." His voice was shaky and dry.

"I hope I didn't wake you up?"

"No you didn't."

"I just came back and no one is here. I thought Saher might be with you."

"She's at May's house."

"Thanks, I'll give them a call there, bye for now."

Rami thought there was something wrong with Ahmad, as he telephoned May. "Hi, it's me, back safe and sound."

"Hello Rami, Saher will be with you in few minutes."

"I'll come and pick her up."

"There's no need, see you later."

Ten minutes later the front door opened and Saher walked in. She was wearing a black dress, black shoes and she had no makeup on. He looked at her then at the sad faces of May and Samir behind her. Rami stood up quickly and Saher stood there quietly looking at him.

"What is it darling?"

No one moved as they saw his face change colour quickly.

"Where's Anthony? Where's my son? No…No…" he screamed.

Saher broke down crying. "Where's my son?" he shouted again. His legs couldn't carry him any longer. He tried to reach to something or someone and he fell to his knees.

"Anthony passed away four days ago and we buried him the day before yesterday. We waited for you, but when we didn't hear anything we went ahead with all the plans," Samir said.

"Oh my darling baby." Rami heard a scream escape from deep inside. "Oh God no…Not my child…No…Why God? We loved him completely, everybody did, and he did no harm to anyone. Why did you have to pick on us? He was a child of love, a child who had everything. I worked hard for him and for all of us and his mother carried him for nine months with pain, we suffered. Are you listening? Are you really there? You have no right to do this to us, you have no right, pick on someone your own size, not a year old baby. I hate you God wherever you are, I hate you. I fought all my life to be happy, but you ..." He cried loud, "God no more, please I beg you no more, I love you God, oh Saher, forgive me, everybody forgive me, I was building a future for my son, and I neglected all of you."

"Rami please, that's enough."

"Oh the pain, the pain, oh the pain, it hurts so much."

His body went numb all of a sudden. He could cry no more. May handed him another whisky, and helped him to the sofa. Saher could take no more of what had happened. Samir took her to the bedroom and gave her few tablets to help her go to sleep. May asked her husband to go home and leave her there. He gave her a long hug, kissed her forehead, and left.

She poured him another drink and it seemed to her that it had no effect . He looked at her with dry tears in his eyes and he tried to speak, but he could not. He felt as if he had lost the ability to produce noise. He opened all the windows in the living room and walked from one room to the other. May cried for him. She understood what he was going through and knew how he felt. She handed him Anthony's photograph. Rami looked at it for a long time, then he smiled and touched the frame.

"My son...I was waiting for you to call me 'daddy'. I got you a lot of clothes for the summer."

She put her hand on his. "I'm here for you my darling."

"What happened?"

"He had a temperature. Saher phoned me, but Samir was working away that day, so she took him to another doctor. He told her not to worry and gave the little angel an injection. He asked her to bring him in two days time. By the afternoon, Anthony looked worse, she phoned the doctor again, and he refused to come out. He said that Saher was over-reacting, and to bring the baby in two days as he told her earlier. By the time I got here, Anthony was gone."

Rami did not move. He sat there looking in the distance. After a long period, he asked May for the name of the doctor.

"Dr. Jalal Al-Aziz." she said with a low voice. "We tried to find you and we tried to phone your aunt, but we couldn't get through. We sent you a telegram too, but you didn't acknowledge it. Oh Rami it was horrible."

"I'll get him."

"Don't do anything stupid."

His face was stern. She tried to get a reaction from him, but he failed to respond to her that night.

"Why don't you go home May' You have a husband who needs you."

"Are you going to bed?"

"Yes."

"Ok, I'll see you tomorrow then."

"Thanks May, you're a good woman."

"Go to bed and I'll phone Samir to pick me up."

He stayed awake all through the night. By the morning he changed his clothes, walked into Anthony's bedroom, looked around the room and sat on the chair beside the bed. He passed his hand over the pillow where that little smiling face had slept. He picked up a few of Anthony's toys and held them close to his chest. "I wish I saw him before he died," he said loudly. Two tears ran down his face as he walked out of the front door.

"Car eleven to Control."

"Go ahead car eleven," said a shaky voice.

"Give me the address for Dr. Jalal Al-Aziz," he said. He had never given an order before and his voice sounded firm. After a while she gave him the address.

"What time does he open?"

"Half past eight."

"Thank you."

"I'm sorry about what happened. My deepest sympathy to you."

"Thank you." Rami looked at his watch. It was twenty minutes past eight. He drove to the address he had been given and waited in the car for a few minutes before entering.

At first the receptionist smiled to him, but her face changed as she saw the fire in his eyes when he walked past her.

"Sir wait, you can't go in."

On the door next to the waiting room, he saw the name of the doctor. He opened the door and walked in.

"Madam please take your child to another doctor," he ordered the woman in the doctor's room.

"Who the hell are you?" the doctor shouted.

"I said get out woman." Rami felt the gun in his hand. His grip tightened on it, as he tried to take it out of his pocket, but the presence of the woman's baby stopped him. "Get out please lady." She left, hugging her baby.

"What do you want? Get out of here," the doctor shouted. He tried to pick up the telephone, but Rami hit his hand and pushed him as hard as he could back to his seat. The doctor tried to move again, but Rami slapped the doctor around the face and ordered him to stay in his place.

"What medicine did you use on my son?" Rami shouted.

"What son? I've never seen you before."

"My son is the one who you killed, Anthony... Remember?"

The doctor's face changed, he saw the death wish in Rami's eyes, and he saw revenge that the child's father came looking for.

"What are you going to do, kill me?" He shouted, maybe someone outside would hear him. "Are you going to kill me?"

Rami did not say a word as he put his hand in his pocket again. His eyes never left the doctor's face.

"Which needle did you use?" Rami asked.

"Will someone phone the police?" the doctor shouted.

"I am the police," Rami said calmly. "Which needle?"

"I don't know."

"You're a liar," said Rami and he took his gun out of his pocket.

The doctor at last decided to give in to his fate, believing he was going to die any moment. "Look, I'll pay you as much money as you want."

Rami's anger grew, as the doctor spoke of money, "What money have you got to replace my son? Now tell me."

"Which needle?"

"Please don't hurt me, it was something like this."

Rami took the needle from his hand, examined it, and stabbed the doctor's stomach repeatedly. The doctor shouted with pain. Rami put the gun in his pocket and used his free hand to push the doctor back into his seat as he continued to stab him. He heard footsteps behind him and a few policemen rushed in, pointing their guns at him. The doctor shouted as he saw them. "He's got a gun."

One of the policemen searched Rami and took the gun out of his pocket.

"You should see my ID card," said Rami.

"Should I?"

Rami put his hand in his back pocket and pulled out his identification card quickly, showing it to the officer in charge. The captain of police stood to attention. The other two policemen followed suit, and handed the gun back to Rami.

"Sorry Sir, I didn't know."

"Arrest this man for killing my son. I want all his files to be examined by the Medical Board and get his stomach seen to."

"Yes sir."

Rami sat in his car for a while, and decided to contact Sami to tell him about what he had done.

"I'm sorry son," said Sami. "Go home. Saher needs you. I'll deal with everything from here. I promise you that this doctor will never practice medicine again for the rest of his life."

"I came here to kill him. I had the gun in my hand, but I could not do it, I couldn't pull the trigger."

"You're not a killer. You've never been one as otherwise you would not be a member of my team."

Rami's mother was in the kitchen preparing lunch when he walked in. She took one look at his face and opened her arms for him. He cried and cried. She walked him to the front room and sat him next to her. "Tell me what's hurting you my son?"

"Oh mum it's so painful, my baby Anthony died, your grandson."

"Jesus in heaven...oh you poor soul, what have you and Saher been through? Oh lord, tell me."

He took the photograph of his son out of his pocket and handed it to his mother.

"He had your hazel eyes and curly blonde hair."

"I can see that. God loves him."

"He wasn't even a year old yet."

They cried silently together. "I'm coming home with you," said Rami's mother. "I want to see Saher; she needs our support."

"Thanks mum."

"I'll phone your dad and tell him his lunch is in the oven."

Rami drove back to his flat where many of his friends had gathered. Rami hugged his best friend Ahmed. "Anthony has gone," he howled.

Rami's mum looked at all the faces one by one. Her lips shivered as Saher hurried towards her. "Auntie…I'm sorry, so very sorry."

"Oh my child, I'm the one who is sorry, I missed you and missed my only grandson. You should have told me, I would have understood."

"Rami was going to come and tell you once he was back from Lebanon, as he knew he couldn't keep hiding it from you."

"I knew there was something he wasn't telling me. I thought it'd all come out in good time."

"Oh auntie, I love you so much. Come with me and I'll show you Anthony's room."

Rami's mum couldn't believe where the strength to walk came from. This was a child's room, and in a way, he was an alien to her, but she had deep love and affection for the little one. She sat on the chair next to the bed and looked at Saher with tears running down her face, "God loves him."

She picked his pillow to her nose, and she could smell his scent.

"The same smell like his dad when he was a baby." Rami's mother commented, "Oh Lord, take good care of my baby."

Everyone's grief began again the minute Rami walked back through the door. Saher, who was comforted by May, cried for her loss and for Rami. Jean sat watching the whole sad drama, and felt helpless. She did not know who to comfort. She was Anthony's godmother and she adored that child so much that at times she dreamt that her own baby would be just like Anthony. Now three months pregnant, she held her stomach and walked out of the flat.

The two men sat crying together. Rami felt guilty for what Saher had gone through without him. He cried for the hopeless situation that he was in, and he did not know what to do. He cried for his child who died without being able to defend himself.

"What is left for me, Ahmad?"

"Your whole future!"

"What future?" Rami cried. "Everything I've ever felt and touched has turned sour. There's nothing to smile about and nothing left for Saher and me to talk about. Why us?"

Why did everything go wrong? Whose fault was it? Death is a disease; it takes everything and leaves nothing behind, except for emptiness."

Rami's mum heard him as she walked back to the living room so she went to sit by his side.

"There's something I never talked to you about," she said. "Between you and your sister there are almost seven years and I lost two children before you were born."

"Oh mum…This brought all the memories back."

"Son, you can always have more. Both of you are still young and if the whole world stopped at the death of one person, then none of us would ever be here."

"Listen to your mother," Ahmad advised quietly.

"I'm sorry."

"There's nothing to be sorry for. You have a duty towards Saher. She needs you now, she needs comforting, and she has been through a lot."

"She thought that you would blame her, she couldn't grieve peacefully because of that, and she wanted to hide from you. My friend, you don't know what the poor girl had gone through." Ahmad said.

"I don't blame her at all she was a good mother, a perfect one indeed."

"Tell her that you still care for her and still love her."

"But I don't love her. There's no love left inside me."

He felt dead inside, like black clouds which did not want to move away. Rami walked out of the flat and continued for miles with no particular direction in mind, trying to find answers for everything that had happened to him.

When he returned to the flat he felt as if he could still hear Anthony's voice, his laughs, and his giggles. He wondered if everything was just a dream or some bad lie.

The apartment was swimming in silence. May stood by the kitchen door watching him sitting in the dark smoking again, it was late at night but time did not matter any more. A few street lights flickered on the wall behind her. The picture was magnificent, but the time and the place were wrong.

"I started smoking again." Rami said.

"I know."

"Where is Saher?"

"She has just gone to sleep. I gave her some sleeping tablets. Do you want something to eat?"

Rami did not say a word. May sat next to him and held his face in her two hands, but he looked into the distance.

"Darling, there is nothing in the world that I can think of to say to you, but just think of what you might say to me, if I were in your situation."

She saw the tears running down his face. She kissed his eyes, his face and pulled his head gently down to her lap, and he at last went to sleep.

May stayed awake that night watching over him. She was afraid to move in case she woke him up.

"Why does it have to be death to break a man like him? To destroy him....He could have fire in the shops, a car accident and break a leg or an arm, but God why did death have to be the only living truth in his life?" She whispered and planted a kiss on his forehead.

She looked at him again, "I know you love me Rami, but I hope you will die before me, because you've just had enough sadness." She said it loud enough for him to hear, but he was in deep restless sleep.

CHAPTER THIRTY SEVEN

RAMI lost interest in life. His behaviour became the worry and concern of all people around him. Five weeks to go until his final examinations and he had not even started to revise. Nothing seemed to matter to him anymore. He even refused to visit his son's grave, and found so many excuses not to.

He put up a wall between him and Saher, and she helped in making the wall even higher. They hardly spoke to each other and they never made any eye contact, for they were afraid to show their pain. Their conversation consisted of very few words.

"Hungry?"

"Yes…" and sometimes he had no answer at all.

He drank heavily all the time, and she never let his glass to be empty, she was afraid of his anger. He was never drunk, although he drank day and night, and even when he was at college, which made Ahmad and Sami go and see the Head of Department, in case of expulsion if he was caught drinking. Life had stopped for him.

Saher was having a terrible time with him. She felt frustrated, angry and completely neglected. Ahmad decided to send Saher to her parents after she approached them for help. Nabil supplied the money and paid for all her expenses, but Rami did not even notice. They gave him extra work, and Sami tried him on different cases to solve, he did them all, but he was not there. He did what he had to do, but mentally, no one knew where he was, he was completely absent minded.

Ahmad, with Sami's help, arranged with the Head of Department for Rami to take his examinations in a separate room away from the other students. Many lecturers helped him to answer a few questions, as they all knew about his tragedy.

He received a letter from Saher and it was then that he realised she had left.

'Dearest,

I feel like a stranger here. My mum and dad, brothers and sisters, are all strangers. Mum had another baby. She said she didn't know she was pregnant until the last few weeks.

The village hasn't changed at all, it hasn't changed since I was a child, but I enjoy my little walks up the hill, and the meadows, and I find it peaceful. Sometimes I go by the stream and sit there for hours absorbing this beauty.

It has been hard being on my own and I do miss you very much. Life is simple here, but very difficult. I did bring money with me, Nabil gave me enough to last me a long time, and I hope you didn't mind.

My love, I am sorry about what happened to our child, I am very sorry, I can't help but blame myself at times. I do need your support and assurances, and I am here ready to come back whenever you will have me back.'

This letter brought him back to reality and for the first time in weeks he sat in his study reading a book, without a cigarette in his hand, or a full glass of whisky. Hours later he took a walk to his favourite restaurant The Strand and had a meal.

Another letter arrived the following day from Saher.

'My darling, nothing in the world will replace Anthony in my heart, but I am sure he is with us and hates to see us sad like this. We laughed all the time when he was alive, so why not now? Let us celebrate his short life.

We can build our strength together, and from each other. We can fight together my love, and overcome any obstacles, please let me show you my love. Rami darling, if you are ready, let me know. I miss you. Let me come back soon, I miss your arms around me.

PS ... Have a wild night out with the boys, it might help.'

Rami smiled at her letter.

He called Ahmed. "Are you free tonight?"

"Yes, what's the matter? Are you alright?"

"I'm fine, thanks. I phoned to see whether you fancy a wild night out?"

"That'd be great."

"Sure...hold on I'll ask the boss." Ahmad said, and Rami waited for a minute or two, "Jean nodded her head, and that means yes."

"It's only me and you."

"I gathered that."

"Okay, I'll pick you up at about seven."

"Look forward to that."

Rami looked at his reflection in the mirror. He had not shaved for weeks and his hair was long.

"Let's have an extra special treat Mr. Rami." He said loudly.

Just before seven he was ready to go out. He went to his usual barber where he had a haircut and a shave, followed by a steam towels massage. He felt alive again.

He had one more look at himself in the mirror, 'Saher eat your heart out, I look beautiful tonight.' He laughed.

On his way to pick up Ahmad the red light flashed in his car.

"Control this is car eleven, what the hell do you want?"

"Good to hear your voice, it's only a small job."

"Oh shit! Can't you give it to someone else? I'm on my way to get drunk, please find someone else." He stopped the car and Ahmad got in.

"Car eleven this is control." Rami heard the official voice, it was no joke this time. There was no way out of it. She gave them an address to go to and check three cars parked near it, she also gave them the cars' number plates.

"Park your car around the corner from the road and let me know when you get there."

Ahmad laughed, "I think we are dressed perfectly for this especially you."

"They found the best time for checking cars."

"There is the road, just park here."

"Ok."

When they did so control came back on.

"Take your sub machine guns with you."

They looked at each other, never before had they been asked to carry guns with them, unless it was code one or two. Rami stepped out of the car and threw the keys at Ahmad. "Lock the car."

"You lazy bastard who the hell do you think you are?" Ahmad giggled.

"Your best friend...!" He laughed. He was very cheerful. Ahmad locked the car, and threw the keys back at him.

Rami pulled the lever on his machine gun and put it at the back of his belt. "Oh damn." Ahmad shouted. "The dam lever is jammed. I can't get it to move.""Hit it on the side of the pavement." He laughed.

They were both about thirty yards inside the road, when Ahmad managed to pull the lever, "Job done."

"Not yet, you have to carry me home when I am totally drunk."

Suddenly shots were fired in their direction. Rami and Ahmad dived to the ground and fired back at the house.

"Rami give me your gun and go to the car. Get help."

"No, you need me here."

"I said go, I'll give you cover."

Rami ran to his car avoiding all the bullets, which were fired at him. He had never felt so frightened before in his life. He was shaking as he opened the car door and managed to press the red button, setting up the automatic SOS signal. He picked two heavy machine guns from underneath the front seats and ran back.

The firing started once more, so he fired back, as he ran towards Ahmad.

"Oh no, God no." Ahmad's head was facing the ground, swimming in a pool of blood. Rami lost control and with the two machine guns in his hands, he fired at every window in the house. Somehow he managed to load up the guns and fire again. Someone jumped him to the ground and laid heavily on top of him. "Stay down Rami for goodness sake."

He closed his eyes and covered his ears as bullets flew in all directions, followed by a few massive explosions. He lifted his head and saw tens of men rushing towards the house. Sami pulled him up and put his arms around him. "Don't look."

"Have you seen Ahmad?" he screamed. "Ahmad is there, there, did you? Oh God no..." He screamed.

"Calm down son...Calm down...Get hold of yourself."

"Is he dead?"

Rami unfolded Sami's arms and went to see Ahmad. The blood was still pumping out of his head. Rami lifted Ahmad's head and hugged him. He looked at his face and with his left hand cleaned it from all the dirt on it.

"You bastard, wake up, don't you dare, wake up Ahmad. You have a son coming soon. You left me once before, don't leave me again...Say something, what am I going to say to Jean? Well, tell me you bastard."

Rami raised his face and looked at all his friends from the CIC. He looked back at Ahmad's face and noticed a shadow of a smile cross it. Rami bent down, and planted a kiss on his forehead.

"Carry him gently please."

Silently they helped. "Do you want me to drive you anywhere?" Sami asked.

"No---I am alright."

"Are you sure?"

"Yes…"

"We'll take care of everything," said Sami.

"Thank you."

"I'll be in touch."

Rami looked at the empty seat next to him in his car then he drove to see Jean.

Before he managed to so much as knock on the door, Jean stood there examining him, with Ahmad's blood on his clothes. Her hand flew to her mouth to stop a scream from escaping. Her eyes flooded quickly, but she did not move, and did not say anything. Thousands of questions were stopped by the hand on her mouth.

"He isn't with us any more… I'm sorry. It should have been me."

Jean took one step backwards and closed the door, shutting the darkness of the night away.

- - - - - - - - -

Ahmad was buried two days later and his photograph covered the front pages of the national papers. Farruk wrote a long editorial about the life of Ahmad. His death was announced as a tragic accident. Thousands of people turned up to the funeral, friends, writers, ex-students, publishers, high Government officials and hundreds of fans. They came from everywhere. He was given full military honours and awarded the highest medal in the country, which was presented to his wife.

Rami, Farruk, Sami, and Samir carried the coffin. Prayers were said in churches and mosques, and as he was laid into the ground, Rami read some poems from Ahmad's last book.

Jean left the country after a few days. Sami had arranged all the necessary matters to get her to Lebanon. He promised her that everything would be dealt with back in Baghdad. Her wish was to have the baby in Lebanon and afterwards she would decide where she wanted to live.

"Rami I want you to have this." Jean handed him a small box. "It's Ahmad's pen. I know he wanted you to have it."

"Part of me has died, Jean."

"I know sweetheart. At least you were with him."

"Please keep in touch."

At the airport they hugged each other for a long time, they were afraid to let go, afraid that they would not see each other again.

"This is my flight announcement," said Jean. , "Please look after yourself."

"I will do."

"I hope you come and see me."

"I will, I promise. I love you, and I loved Ahmad, he was everything to me. Jean if you ever need anything, anything at all, just phone or write."

"I will, I promise. You have been part of us, part of our lives. We laughed together, and we cried together."

"Yes … those were the days."

"I never asked you this, did he suffer?"

"No, he had a smile on his face."

"Rami get out of that thing, I can't bear losing you too, let me know that you'll decide to do that, I might come back then, and you are the best friend anyone can have."

"I'll try and talk to Sami."

"I hope so." She put the palm of her hand on the side of his face.

"You'd better go. I love you, and look after yourself."

They hugged each other again, "Come and see me Rami, I need you with me."

"I will ... promise."

"Ahmad will be happy if he knows that you are looking after me, don't forget, bring Saher with you, she loves you, and she needs you as well."

"I'll send for her soon ... when I am ready."

They parted with tears in their eyes. Rami stood watching the airplane disappear into the distance.

- - - - - - - - -

Rami walked into Farruk's office a few days later. Farruk moved out from behind his desk and sat on the sofa next to him.

For a moment Farruk didn't recognise him. He looked incredibly thin and his eyes were red with bags. He simply looked awful, and Farruk was concerned about him..

"Iman, get us some tea and sandwiches please."

Rami pulled a pen out of his pocket and handed it to Farruk. Farruk had seen that pen so many times in Rami's hand. In fact he had never ever seen him use another pen.

"This was given to me by Ahmad when I was twelve. I wrote everything with it. I came to realise that I wrote only for Ahmad and no one else. I wrote for his approval and for his praise. You helped me more than anyone else to win that, and I have written for you for nearly eight years now. You are a great friend and more like a father to me than my own. I'd like you to have it."

Farruk was in no position to refuse or argue. Rami had put down his pen and he was not going to write any more.

He stood up and left without saying another word. He looked at Iman holding the tray of tea and sandwiches, his lips shivered to say something, but no sound came out of him. Farruk thought that it could be the last time he would see him.

"That boy needs help...serious help Farruk." Iman said.

At Sami's office, Rami put all the identification cards on the table. Sami understood the pain the young man was in, who looked twenty years older.

"I want out, I can't do it anymore. I'm completely burnt out."

"I understand," said Sami. "

Rami and Ahmad became close friends not only to him but his family too. They shared so many nights out, so many laughs, and so much respect.

"Stay here please, I'll be back in two minutes." He picked up the phone and dialled a number.

"Get me a passport for Rami now and try and get me a Visa for England, move on the double." Then he telephoned, "It's Sami, Dr. Samir."

"Yes good morning, how can I help you?"

"It's Rami that I am worried about, I want to send him to England, he needs a change of surroundings, probably some medical help. I think the death of Ahmad just surfaced in him."

"I know I do understand, I'd better have a word with his parents, I can't see what else we can do for him."

The two men talked for a while, then Sami then went back to his office. "Why don't you come to lunch with me?"

Rami raised his eyes to Sami, he just asked him to release him from his duties, and instead the man was asking him out for lunch.

"Okay."

After lunch Rami returned to his apartment. There was a letter from Saher waiting for him. He held it in his hands before he decided to open it.

'My dear,

I decided to write to you straight away. From the day we met, I knew deep down inside me that we will never be together. As much as we loved each other, we were born continents apart. We tried, we gave it all our effort, and we did work hard at it.

You were the perfect partner, the perfect lover, my best friend, and a super dad. We did share the most beautiful person in the world, and that is our Anthony.

I will always love you, until the day I die. Rami, I have met someone else from my village, just out of national service after finishing his university in Mosul, and I told him about everything, and he asked me to marry him, and I said yes. I know he will be kind to me, and maybe in time, I will love him.

Thank you for everything, and now you have no one to worry about but yourself. Good luck.'

He read the letter several times before it registered in his mind. But, he had no feelings in response to it. He was completely unattached as Ahmad's death had only just started to sink in, the memory of Ahmad lying in a pool of blood, the way he was carried in a coffin, himself reading few poems that Ahmad had written, they all seemed like something out of a horror movie, or a very bad dream.

Sami received a phone call back from Samir "I've got in touch with a top doctor in London and he 's ready to see Rami straight away.""Do you think it will help?"

"They are far more advanced than us, and I also contacted his parents, and I am about to pick them up and go and see him in the flat."

"When Anthony died, he had the help of Ahmad, Ahmad was his life, but now I asked him out for lunch after I had phoned you today, and he followed me like a machine, he ate like one, I can't describe it, everything seemed like it didn't matter, like filling a car with petrol, well even that matters."

"He is depressed, and about to have a major nervous breakdown. I think he's suffering from belated shock."

"I'll make the travelling arrangements."

Within the hour, his parents turned up at the flat, with Samir and May. It was his father's first visit there.

"I need help," he confessed. "I need some peace too."

Two days later, May took Rami to the airport. He had not said a word to her throughout all the time she'd spent packing his clothes. There were times when she understood his needs, but at that moment, she felt hopelessly useless.

"Life could be one big deception," he said, as he kissed May. "God made it, for man to believe otherwise."

He arrived in London after a five and a half hour flight. At the airport he was met by someone from the Iraqi Embassy, which Sami had arranged in advance. He was taken to an apartment which was already rented for him.

He went to see a doctor on the second day, but he found it very hard to communicate with him. He tried hard time and time again, but in the end he gave up because of the language barrier. He found it very hard to explain himself, to explain his feelings, to explain his relationship with Ahmad, and to explain his feelings about Anthony. Not only that, he lost Saher for good, and he missed the friendship of Jean.

He felt he could never replace the past, and no doctor would understand. He was not looking for any treatment, but to be peaceful within himself.

He gave up and he felt lonely in a big city where he did not know anyone. He was just one between millions. He hated everything around him, the people, the cars, the noise, the underground, and the rain. He lost himself somewhere between all those effects, and could not find the way out. He disliked the little flat he had been put in and, he disliked himself. He hated himself for being there, what did he do to deserve all that? But he did nothing to change anything around him. Sometimes he had the urge to do something, but soon enough, all the doors were closed again in his face.

He spent days just walking the streets, avoiding people in his path. He felt weak, and he forgot to eat most of the time. He did not change his dirty clothes, so everything around him felt damp, and smelled damp. He saw people eyeing him and walking yards away from him and he laughed inside. "The best way to keep them away." But soon, the tears ran down his face.

"Ahmad, Anthony…Jesus how much I miss them both?"

One day he woke up in hospital. The nurses told him that he had collapsed in the street. He was bathed, shaved and given new clothes to wear by a charity for the homeless. They also fed him, but the following day, he discharged himself. He lost track of time, and place.

He lost a considerable amount of weight, and some of his neighbours felt sorry for him, but they could do nothing to help him. He was hospitalised again, and lived in a daze most of the time, but a week later he walked out. He did not want to be looked after, he did not accept being a vegetable, watered and fed. His freedom was not to get outside of four walls, but to get out of himself, and it was not negotiable.

As he was walking in an underground station one day, pulling and dragging his tired legs behind him, a voice came to him, which at first sounded like a whisper.

"Rami."

Then the voice shouted again. "Rami."

He did not look back, as he didn't want to be recognised. His legs moved faster, the steps that he took were much quicker than those that he was used to recently. He did not want anyone to know him and he did not want to know anyone. He wished they would leave him alone.

"What on earth do they want from him?" He asked himself. "I want to be left alone, I don't want company, and I don't want anyone company." But, he was the only one who heard the plea. His mouth was dry.

"Rami wait, please wait."

He tried to run, but he tripped and fell. He got up and ran again, with people screaming, shouting and swearing at him.

"Bloody tramp, watch where you're going."

He tried to run up the stairs, but someone pushed him back angrily and he fell down. He was in pain and he felt humiliated knowing that people were staring at him. He wanted to cry.

He opened his eyes after a while, to see many people staring down at him. "Another drunk...go get a job," someone from the crowd shouted.

He examined the faces and through the many of them he saw a familiar one holding a child by the hand. His dried lips moved after a long struggle.

"Farrah!"

She looked at the boy who was holding her hand with his eyes focused on the man laying on the ground.

"Son. Meet your father," she said with a loving smile.

The End

ABOUT THE AUTHOR

Bob Zablok was born in Baghdad in 1953 to a loving family, but he had a very strict upbringing. He was educated in various private schools then he attended Science College in University, leaving Iraq in 1974 to further his education in Great Britain.

Bob began writing from an early age and published many short stories, poems and articles under different pen names, in a number of magazines and newspapers.

Returning to his beloved Baghdad in 2001 after so many years was not a vacation, but an experience. He was inspired to write about the good old days and spent many years researching.

While recovering from a major surgery on his spine, Bob wrote this book. There are three children stories and a second novel in the pipeline.

Lightning Source UK Ltd.
Milton Keynes UK
UKOW020955170712

196089UK00001B/4/P